P9-AGH-463

Come Back to Erin

BY THE SAME AUTHOR

Novels

Bird Alone

A Nest of Simple Folk

Biography

King of the Beggars: Daniel O'Connell, the Irish Liberator

Short Stories

A Purse of Coppers

Midsummer Night Madness

Anthology

The Silver Branch: A Collection of the Best Old Irish Lyrics

Come Back to Erin

A NOVEL BY SEÁN O'FAOLÁIN (JOHN WHELAN)

NEW YORK THE VIKING PRESS MCMXL

198416

COPYRIGHT 1940 BY THE VIKING PRESS, INC.

PRINTED IN U. S. A.

FIRST PUBLISHED IN AUGUST 1940

PUBLISHED ON THE SAME DAY IN THE DOMINION OF CANADA

BY THE MACMILLAN COMPANY OF CANADA LIMITED.

Il n'y a que le dernier amour d'une femme
qui satisfasse le premier d'un homme.

BALZAC: *La Duchesse de Langeais*

PART ONE

In Ireland

"Excuse me, sir, for interrupting your meditations," said the beggar in a muted and curiously refined voice. "But would you by any chance be interested in the Chinese missions?"

Very gradually the spy in front had begun to look about him—so casually that he might well have not been looking for anyone in particular. He always broke the arc of his head-movement by a sudden natural droop, as if he were sighing deeply over his prayers; but the head always lifted at the same point and the sweeping arc went on its way.

"What missions?" whispered Hannafey crossly.

"The missions! The Chinese missions," gabbled the old man. In his eagerness his index finger feverishly scratched his beard as if there were a louse in it. "Beautiful work, sir, they're doing down at Cahircon in the County Clare, where they have the seminary. It's a beautiful place—my own brother is there. The Vandeleur family used to live there once. It's on the banks of the Shannon. Thank God"—he bobbed his head to the high altar—"all that old crowd is gone out of the country—not that there aren't some fine people among them. Lord Monteagle at Foynes, and the Knight of Glin has a grand spot on the road to Tarbert. I need hardly say I know them all, some personally. In fact, I'm indirectly related to many of these families. You see, sir," he went babbling away at his monstrous lies, "my brother is the junior dean, and will soon be director of the mission. I'm poor because I've given up everything for the mission. Given away every penny. I'm an accredited collector. Excuse me, sir, for interrupting your pious meditations! Would you be pleased to look at this?"

Again he began fumbling madly inside his old coat; now it was as if the mouse had gone racing helter-skelter over him. He produced a soiled envelope. Up overhead in the organ loft the wind suddenly began to groan, and then a long moaning cry came from the tuner.

"Very awkward time for the tuner," apologized the beggar. "He was at it all this morning, too!"

The spy was still sweeping the foremost benches and examining the rows of penitents waiting in guilty silence before the boxes. Distastefully, but with curiosity, Hannafey took the envelope and drew out the letter, dust-creased as an ancient manuscript. The printed heading was genuine; it showed an old engraving of a mansion among trees, with a crucifix on the pediment; young priests in birettas and soutanes walked about; and two motor-cars stood by the door. The typewriting seemed genuine, and the signature was free and bold. Possibly the old scoundrel had found it—or was he off his head?—and was making a living out of that lucky chance. The organ did a sudden run up the scale and held a long-drawn-out top-note. The tuner seemed to like it and held it for half a minute. When he stopped they could distinctly hear voices from the organ loft.

"Oh, a beautiful place," went on the whisper. "All for the honour and glory of God. My brother, the director, is a most able man, of course—he has seventy-five acres of wheat set this year—a beautiful crop—I helped him, myself, to plan the whole scheme—he was ten years in Fu Chow. I'm thinking of going to Fu Chow myself, as a lay assistant of course."

The spy had made a clever move—one which would not attract attention to himself but would give him a chance to see where his quarry was. He had begun to do the Stations of the Cross, starting where he now stood beside his bench, at the fifth station. In that way he would naturally circle back around under the gallery for the sixth, seventh, and eighth stations. Hannafey shoved back the letter.

"Go away," he whispered. "Go away. You're telling me lies."

"Sir?" protested the beard.

"Run away," muttered Hannafey, fumbling for his hat, his eye on the detective.

"Aren't you interested, sir, at all in God's holy work in the foreign fields of the Faith?" protested the beard, slewing his face about under Hannafey's, and baring his tawny teeth.

"Missions my backside! Get out of my way, you fool!"

The old man stared, astonished at such irreverence in a church. His defeated eye sank and saw the Maupassant on the bench. Glittering, he pushed with his forefinger at the gaudy purple-backed, gold-plastered volume.

"Are you a Catholic?" he asked.

The spy moved nearer. The tuner ran up and down the keys with abandon. Up and down. Trip, tap, trip, tap, trip, tap, and an "Oh! Yes, indeed!" said the top-note—a whistling, wind-whirling, skirling, screaming, ear-splitting "Oh!"—gone broken, stuttering, finger-testing, to a piping "Yes, indeed!—Yes, indeed!—Yes, indeed!"

The clerk was furious. He ground his teeth and snarled, "Go away. I'm not a Catholic. I'm an atheist!"

Beard scratched again with his forefinger; leering, he again nudged the Maupassant, with a wink to his victim.

"I have a great admiration for the French authors," he divulged in a purl of hot breath. "There ought," he whispered, with the most lewd secretiveness, glancing about him at the sighing images of penance who were stacked up against the curtained confessionals, "be a Maupassant in this little city of ours."

There was a husky liquor of suggestiveness in his voice as he spat out the name *Maupassant*. Hannafey, in astonishment, looked down at him. The bearded skull of a face had gone hollow and horrible. The circles under the eyes had fallen forward in pouched bags as if a liquid had suddenly been released into them. The old lips clapped together and parted with suction. "There should be fifty Maupassants. I could tell you stories . . ."

Hannafey looked up. From a near-by confessional a penitent came out with the faint swirl of curtain that, with the occasional sighing murmur from the priest, is the only sound ever heard from these crowded boxes—the tribute of silence to a mystery and a sacrament. The spy moved to station number seven. As he did so he looked back into the odorous cavern under the loft where the two men sat clutched together; where the poor are herded on Sundays; where their fetor sticks in the airlessness of that unventilated vault for the rest of the week. As Hannafey and the old man leaned over one another in the dusk of this part of the church, the mad skirling of the tuner overhead ran round and round, and replicated itself by the forced union of its imprisonment.

". . . stories," lucubrated the old sinner, "that'd make the hair of your head stand on pins!"

Hannafey looked behind him. He remembered the back entrance for the poor, wondered if it were open. He did not know why they were following him. He was accustomed to police attentions—that was the price of having a family like his. He gripped the old tout, who gripped him back just as tightly.

"Come out this way," he commanded. "And be quiet."

The spy had stopped contemplating the station and had knelt. The two behind shuffled out, followed by the gambolling of the tuner's fingers; ushered through the great, greasy, domed, red-resined door into the damp hallway by another "Oh, yes, indeed!—Yes, indeed!—Yes, indeed! . . ." The pair dipped their fingers (from habit, or from mutual distrust) in the furrowed limestone font. The usual agglomeration of dark mortuary cards and Lenten notices was missing here—as if the very poor could not be expected to read. There was here nothing but the four clammy walls, and the flagged floor, and in a corner a strange pile of wooden standards with tasselled dark-red cloth shields dangling inside hollow shapes of brass, the face of the red cloth itself all cluttered with more brass insignia—the crown of thorns, the crossed spears of Longinus, the sponge of gall. In the cold of this passageway the clerk halted the beggar, and listened. The beggar gaped up at him. They could hear only the skirl of the organ, the sound of children's voices at play, and the faint hum of the city.

"Is somebody after you?" asked Beard, curiously.

"Nonsense," said the clerk, as the cleaner air of the city began to cool him, and its sounds give him sanity. The old man had put on his hard hat, and was already whining professionally about hunger, hospitals, homelessness, and how he was soon to be evicted from his one half-room. . . .

Pleased at having dodged the spy, Hannafey laughed; he was further titillated by seeing a poster across the laneway—

SEARCH FOR MURDERERS OF GENERAL

"What's wrong with you," he condescended to the bowed wretch beside him, "is that you want a drink and won't say so. Isn't that the truth?"

"Oh, sir, 'tis food, 'tis food my poor stomach wants this blessed and holy minute . . ."

"Drink," bullied Hannafey. "That or nothing. Will you take a pint?"

"Oh, sir, I suppose there might be some sustenance in it," temporized the wretch.

"Come on, then!"

The sideward step, long practised, took the clerk from the

pavement before the old beggar could observe what was happening. He followed timidly, and the two were at the back of a sawdusted bar from whose dimness the still-bright pavement outside and even the brown wooden tar-blocks of the street were pale as morning. After the mad noise in the church and the excitement of his escape Michael Hannafey relaxed.

"The chapel"—he nodded to the wall at his poll—"is behind there. Wouldn't it be grand," he teased, "if the pubs were open on Sunday morning? Sure we could sit here with a pint and be as near the altar as the boys who get no nearer to it than the entrance-hall or the edge of the pavement."

The beggar squirmed, then smiled a toadying smile, then shook his head deprecatingly. He did not know whether to say, "Ah, now, now, that's not right!" or, "Ah, you're a terrible man!" His eyes shifted right and left, and he licked his lips. Hannafey would have tortured him some more if he had not needed a drink himself just as badly. When the great yellow-frothed pints stood before them he drank deep and, leaning back, cross-examined. Beard took off his hat from his bare skull and, brushing it reverently with his clutched cuff, laid it aside.

"Where did you ever hear of Maupassant?"

"I got a very good education when I was a young man," confided the beggar. "I studied for the bar. My people are very highly connected, you know!" He saw the cynical look in the clerk's eye. "No, I won't try to deceive you. You're a man of the world—I can see that. I made a fool of myself. The old story. Drink and women."

"Not here in Cork?" said Michael Hannafey.

"In it and out of it. London. I once had a nook in the Temple. Believe it or not, as Dan Leno used to say."

His voice was doubly refined; his gestures elegant; he handled his great pint as if it were a liqueur; the poise of his shattered, hunched body was that of a clubman in his club.

"And . . . I can still see my name on the board at the doorway—the white lettering on the black ground. . . . And above my name was the name of the man now known as Sir Patrick Hastings, and underneath it was the name of the Pandit Nehru, now Gandhi's right-hand man. Believe it or not. I tell fibs." His hand threw a fib into the air as if it were coin. "I tell . . . lies." His other hand cast down a lie as if it were a crawling insect. "Thank you, sir, much obliged" (as the clerk gave him a cigarette). "But that is the truth. I ruined my life. My people got tired of me."

The drink seemed to sink him lower in his misery. It was as if necessity kept his courage up, and he sank as soon as there was no longer any need for it.

"Why wouldn't I know Maupassant?" he almost snarled. "Tshah!" In infinite arrogance, self-hate, anger with self and world. "I could *teach* Maupassant! I know the world as nobody, I suppose, in this dirty little town knows it. Except, of course"—remembering his host—"the few educated people you get in every town. I have a great affection for Maupassant, really," he piped as he drank another slug from his pint. He put it down emphatically. "But, if you'll excuse me, sir, for saying so, Maupassant didn't know these women. Not as I know them! The man didn't understand them. *I* can tell you what ruins them. It's what ruins all humanity. What is it? It is that they are vain. Vain!" He snarled the word. "I know it"—tapping his chest—"because I've run my race. I've been through it." Hate poisoned his tongue. His eyes dripped with venom. They had murder in them, as he said, "The world is run by the flattery of fools."

If there ever was a man who hated (not merely men, or a

few men, or a man or two, but life—all life) it was he. He would have killed Life if he could have met it in a dark lane. His face worked devilishly. Agony at his own impotence shot through it. The lips curled down, and the eyebrows raced. He was trembling as he slugged down his pint to the very end. He panted as he put down the glass.

"Vanity. That's the world. It makes people and it breaks them."

"I don't know," murmured Michael Hannafey. Interested, he began slowly to search his own heart, gazing at the wreck before him as at a prophetic mirror. There was no vanity in himself, he felt; God knows his conscience was free of that. Too much humility was what was wrong with him; letting his chances go by; letting the world ride him; his family, for instance, the fellows in the Post Office; giving in to other people all along the line. It embittered him to think of it; and they were mostly fools; that was true at least, fellows he could teach if he was put to it. He ordered two more pints.

"Excuse me, sir," said the beggar, "but I feel I am right. I know it. Look at Maupassant himself. He killed himself through vanity. Ruined himself. Keeping up grand living in Paris when he couldn't afford it. Mixing with the cheapest kind of women. Died of disease. But search his stories, and what will you see? Not one single vain character. Not one vain man. I've tried to find them. I search every book I read for that. But take Dickens—full of vain people, full of them. Oh, a great man, Dickens. The greatest of them all!"

"It sounds," mocked the clerk, "as if you spent your life examining your conscience."

The beggar shook his head.

"Too late," he bassoed into his glass. "Too late."

The two sipped. The bar was crowding up now that closing time approached. They retreated into the farthest corner.

"Maupassant is very cruel," said the clerk, thinking of the brutal story he was reading.

"He never appreciated the beauty of life," said the beggar.

"I wonder why?" quizzed the clerk.

"No humility," said the beggar. "That's why. And that, if you don't mind my saying so—excuse me for saying it if you are a great admirer—that is why he is a second-rate writer. Oh! A third-rate writer. No! . . . No?" He weighed his judgment and delivered it. "No! I say a *fourth-rate* writer."

"That's severe," said the clerk. "I think third-rate is more just."

The old beggar raised his dirty palm.

"A fourth-rater. Definitely a fourth-rater."

The pints sank in their glasses, the wrack of each gulp marking as on a barometer their decreasing thirst.

"Look at the famous story," whispered the old man. "What do you call it? God help me, my memory is going! About the little . . . Excuse me for not saying unpleasant words."

The clerk grinned at the change of tune, and wondered what this return to propriety portended.

" '*Boule de Suif*'? About the fat prostitute?"

"Yes! What's wrong with that story? I'll tell you. The woman is all humility! It's impossible! Humility in one of *them!* It's fantastic! I know!" The voice dropped, and his face softened, and his eye-bags became squashy again. He pulled Hannafey's sleeve and whispered with his wet mouth and moustaches. The susurrus of his breath suggested the drip of malt. It was hideous. "I know," he conspired, "because I happen even at this very moment to live next door to a . . . excuse me . . . to a bad house."

"Rubbish!" cried the other. "There's no such thing in Ireland. You mean a brothel?" Because of the other drinkers they had to lean together so as not to be overheard. "Oh, no! There might be one in Dublin! But not in Cork. Even in Dublin it would be unofficial. Definitely you're inventing now. The priests would know about it in a shot. No! No!"

The old mouth cackled and drew still closer.

"They would. They do. It won't last long. What will happen then? It will just go away and start somewhere else. I am not deceiving you, sir. I am *not.* On my honour. It's always country girls in these places. In London? Dublin girls and women from the provinces. In New York? London women and women from the other states. I'm told"—leaning so close the other was clammed against the wall—"the east coast of Africa is *hell!* The leavings of the world!"

He was shaking and the clerk was shaking.

The clerk was thinking, "What an extraordinary find, what an old ruffian!" The old fellow was clearly feeling physical relief in being able to talk to another man as to an equal.

"And," said the clerk, "where is this—this—this so-called brothel? Just," he added hastily, "for the sake of curiosity."

The bartender had begun to cry, in a cheerful voice, "Time, gentlemen, *please!*" The other drinkers were presenting to him that hard wall of deafness with which the last few moments are always defended against the law. The two rims of the bowler hats in the corner rubbed one another. The pimp glinted at the two hot eyes of the clerk. The barman removed the glasses with a disapprovingly inquisitive look. The clock struck ten, the fast clock of the pub: it was really only five to ten.

They parted in the street, the clerk condescending, the pimp cringing, now that his round of labour was begun again. He was explaining that he must return to the church; he smiled, and deprecated, and shrugged.

Away from him, along the soft tar-blocks beside the church, into the hum of the Saturday night streets, Michael Hannafey walked with purblind eyes, compressed into himself by his own vacuum. He may be followed if there is anything to be gathered from that slouched back that drags a leg along the shadowy lane; although one thing he does is a kind thing—he steps from the pavement where two little girls are playing hop-scotch. He does not seem to hear, through the leaded windows high up, the busy testing finger of the tuner in his loft, troubling to have the organ ready for Sunday. He lights with his stealthy hand a cigarette, and inhales it with a breath that trembles as it runs in and out of his lungs. In the English Market, through the closed gates, he sees, by the greenish light of the gas, a butcher's boy scrub the blocks, and a butcher sharpen his knife, and the flesh-cool halls vanish into their own perspective as the clock overhead tolls the hour. Then, blue-serge-suited, bowler-hatted, head-dreaming, he sinks down into the crowds of the main shopping street, and is drowned. As if to run after him and tell him so, the tuner raced up the scale like a madman and let the top-note wave its sword of fire. The sky was dark.

10 p.m.

With relief, Josephine Hogan got out of the bus at the terminus, two hundred yards from the English Market, and, with her little papier-mâché attaché-case in her hand, made for the Hannafey house on Morrison's Island. She walks faster than usual. Being a country girl she knows that the sky is not dark with night so much as with impending rain.

When she reached the island houses they glowed because they faced south, but as she looked across the river at the corresponding houses, almost black against the sky, every window went flash as if a lighthouse had lit them. In the sky, in the region of the answering roll of thunder, the cold rim of moon rolled over and over like a blown-out cinder. The air began to gasp the dust of the quay into wavelets. She looked up at the twenty shut-mouthed faces of Carlton Terrace, all greys and dull pinks, rising flush with the pavement, rounding with the round of the quay like a windmill. There was nothing alive here but the coming storm and the smells of the island—low-tide smell, soap-smell, paint-smell, basement-smell, dust-smell, the animalculæ of all the island-smells that ever were, endlessly parturient and ending up in something like a smell of liquorice. As she looked along the grey-into-pink fronts she breathed as if she would choke. Had her soul for these few moments gone into her nose, that one miserable sense would have found life just as unfathomable, as when (so often) at home she sat by her cottage fire and lost herself in contemplating worlds decipherable by no sense at all. Miserably she rang the bell in the Hannafey door, and rubbed the worn holes at the corners of a brass plate that had swallowed its inscription. As she did so the flash in the sky and the answering glimmer in the windows ran, for the second time, down the quays to the sweet-factory, around the nose of the promontory of the island to the Capuchin Friary and the humped bridge that ended the quays. She could not see its entire course. She could only imagine how it lit the candelabra of the Friary pinnacles, until their aerial lacework was white against a purple north. Far away she could see the humped hill-up, hill-down of the clustered roofs of Irishtown cowering from the rains.

Suddenly, in her loneliness, she thought with pleasure of the sweets called "Liquorice All Sorts" that she sometimes used to buy as a child in Fermoy on fair-days. When the door opened and Eolie Hannafey peered out in surprise at her and then shrieked, "Josephine Hogan!" she said, "It's me. Listen, do I smell liquorice?"

"Oh, God!" groaned Eolie, in despair. "This island is dug out of a smell. It's the sweet-factory. Or maybe the pickle-factory. Or they do be tarring nets by the Friary. Come in. Where did you come from? I'm delighted to see you. How are you? How's Manus?"

Then she closed the great door with its eleven panels (the favourite design of the eighteenth century) and in the huge musky hall she kissed Jo, and whispered, "Have you any news? Are they raiding for him?"

"I came for news," said Josephine.

"Oh!" groaned Eolie. And then, "Come up!"

She was led up the too wide, too ample stairs (impossible for middle-class people to keep as it should be kept) to the sitting-room facing the river, and was there asked to wait for a minute. The far, mournful whistle of a train hurled her back to her own view of the Galtee mountains and to hours when the same whistle, more far and faint, curdled her wonder inside her until she could almost spit it out. Already she was wishing she was at home. Falling drops of rain covered the river as with a dust.

Eolie came back, drew the blind, lit the gas, and took Jo's hat and coat, talking all the time. By the gas she showed herself not much younger than her brother, Michael. She was beaten thin by a hammer of work; her fair-greenish hair had the same look of thin-drawn wire; in her body and face there was no lusciousness; even the eyelashes were sparse, and the under lids had no lashes at all; her mouth was kind but it was being sucked in by the years. Only her eyes were full of fun, and life, and kindness, and patience. There was a masculine cut about her.

"We have a visitor here," she was saying. "An important one. St. John. Yes, the American brother! First time home in, I think, thirty-two, or is it thirty-three years? Imagine it. And his wife and son are coming to Cove tonight. Imagine it. On top of all this trouble about Frankie. And Mother is ill again. Imagine it." She rushed over to Jo and looked her up and down, holding her at arm's length—at her lovely slim figure, her folded black hair, her enormous brown eyes. "You're lovely," she said without envy. "You're not keeping anything back from me? You *have* no news? Honest to God?"

Jo shook her head. Eolie sighed and believed.

"Sit down. I'll get you a cup of tea. Put a match to the fire. It's turning to rain. Imagine it!"

Jo took the box of matches and looped herself before the paper and sticks. She knew the economies of this kind of house, but she also knew its pride of hospitality, so she did not demur. She was a little happier as the paper ran with flame and the sticks began to crackle, though it oppressed her to sit and look at the photographs—the room as full of them as a photographer's salon—the framed diplomas, Claude's drawings from the antique. Then Natalie came in, and they disliked each other at the very first glance; it was their first meeting. She was dark as Josephine; her face was as smooth as a holy statue; she was only divided by a blade's breadth from being beautiful; she was stout and almost tubby. In her presence Josephine became so polite she almost got a crick in her neck.

"I am very pleased to meet you," said Natalie. "You are Josephine Hogan. Our brother Frankie has often spoken of you. I was away the time you called a couple of years ago."

Jo smiled politely.

"Please do sit down," said Natalie, with deliberate eagerness. "Wasn't it a lovely day?" she asked, begging for agreement. Jo nodded, but did not agree with enough enthusiasm to make a success of it; so, to retrieve her losses, she said, passionately:

"For May, too!"

"Yes," said Natalie, and added, "You must have a grand dressmaker down in Fermoy."

Eolie with the tea and a biscuitaire interrupted that friendly approach; it did not end it. With her two little fingers stuck out like snail's horns Josephine sipped her tea; she was dying for a cigarette but wondered if these girls smoked. Natalie was asking about the reveres in the skirt, fingering curiously.

"I made it myself," said Josephine at last.

"Oh, but it's lovely," said Natalie. "It's painted on you. It fits you like a glove. Stand up."

"Let the girl drink her tea, yerrah!" stormed Eolie. She patted Jo's knee. "That one"—glaring at Natalie—"has no gumption."

"Oh, law, I'm sorry!" cried Natalie. She laughed down the scale a gay little trill of joy at her own folly. "I forgot all about your tea. Finish it up."

"And don't do that, either!" cried Eolie from her knees before the fire, where she was blowing hard under the grate. She was red and out of breath, which suited her. "That one is always thinking of clothes. Take your time, Josephine."

"I'm an awful ass," groaned Natalie. "And, by the way, Eolie girl, why don't you use the bellows?"

Puffing, Eolie grunted, "Ornament," and puffed again. Natalie shrugged to Josephine and said, confidingly, " 'Tis a terrible house. . . . But, of course, 'tis easy to fit clothes to you. You have a beautiful figure."

She gave a gusty smile of admiration, which Josephine weighed for a second, accepted tentatively with an answering smile, and then quenched like a cigarette stub.

"I don't think I have such a good figure. How could I? Always stamping about in the dirt and mud. We're rough country people." But then she veered like the wind. She was evidently not inclined to be too humble, either. She put down the cup smartly on the mantelpiece and standing out on the floor gave herself a quick twirl. The brown tweed moulded her slim waist like a uniform on a man. Her shoulders were unusually wide. The skirt hung from her thighs. She held her chin an inch higher than normal.

"The brown suits you," said Natalie, subdued.

"That's why I got it," agreed Jo complacently.

"You're as tall as myself," said Eolie, and put herself back to back with her cousin. Pleased, Josephine began to cheat, stealing up on her toes. The other was also cheating. They whirled and wrestled with each other, laughing.

"God help me," moaned Natalie, in an armchair. "I'm a perfect barrel."

"All the Hogans were tall," mocked Eolie. "You're a Hannafey, so you must put up with it. Look at her"—pointing jeeringly to her half-sister in the chair—"a dumpling. And Claude is a fairy. And Frankie's no giant."

"He's tall enough," declared Josephine and blushed. It was the first blunder she had made; and she knew she had made it by the way they began to clear away her cup and poke the fire. She looked, in confusion, from one to the other. The silence was awkward. At last, defiantly, she threw out her two hands and cried, "Well, I came to talk about him!"

They stopped fidgeting and looked at her.

"Well?" she concluded.

They said nothing.

"He must be got away. He isn't strong enough for another winter on the hills. If he's arrested . . ."

Natalie intervened, looking hard at her sister. "I think it much better not to discuss it, don't you, Eolie?"

Josephine lowered head and eyelids; she felt she was being pushed into the position of a stranger.

"I'm not interfering," she murmured.

"We know that," said Natalie, kindness and understanding, too much of it, in every tone of her voice and every muscle of her face.

"After all," protested Josephine, "he's been with us a lot. And he's a kind of relation."

"I don't think so," considered Natalie calmly. "Your father and Eolie's father were brothers. So you two are cousins. You are Michael's cousin, too, and St. John's, and Father Leonard's, and Sister Eulalie's. But when Mother married again, she married somebody who was no relative of your father. So neither am I, nor Frankie, nor Claude really related to you at all."

Josephine looked from one to the other and at the windows. The rain was blowing freely about the terrace. She thought of the way it would be lashing down the Ballyhouras, up from the great plain of Limerick, across from the Shannon estuary. She could not possibly return tonight. The last bus left at eleven, and that would take her only to Fermoy.

"I came specially to talk about him," she said firmly.

She turned to Eolie, but Eolie was unable to look her in the face. Natalie quickly intervened:

"You see, we've found that there isn't anything to gain by talking over Frankie's doings. He's a law to himself. Have you ever seen these photos of him when he was a kid?"

She took out the old family album.

"I wonder what's keeping Michael," muttered Eolie. "I know he'd like to meet you. When did you come?"

"I've just arrived. I'm not going back tonight."

Eolie gave a look at Natalie, but Natalie had opened the album and was not receiving her looks.

"If you don't mind sleeping on the sofa?" said Eolie. "On

account of Mother and St. John. Not that there can be much sleep tonight. The American boat is due at Cove about five in the morning, or something. Imagine it! I'm sure St. John will want to drive to meet it. He has his own car."

Eolie rubbed her thin hair all awry, and looked for help to her half-sister. Natalie stubbornly kept her eyes fixed on the first photo in the album.

"I'll be all right," said Josephine. "I'll go to a hotel." (But to be asked by relatives to go to a hotel!) She searched Eolie's face. Eolie knelt forward to her from the smoky fire and clasped her thighs.

"Jo, is he in danger?"

"Eolie!" chided Natalie, with patience written all over her —patience and something more than exasperation.

"I know there's no use in talking!" groaned her half-sister.

"Do look at that picture of Mamma in her first wedding-dress!" bustled Natalie. "And your father, Eolie. (Your uncle, Josephine.) That"—turning the heavy page an eighth of an inch thick, with faded sprays of flowers on each board, and the arched cut-outs like vaults for the dead mottled daguerreotypes—"that was his shop. There's the name, 'John Hogan and Sons.'"

Natalie admired the shop and held it up for Josephine to admire. Josephine gazed through it, furious.

"'And sons,'" sighed Eolie. "Sons! God help us! St. John ran away to America. Michael in the Post Office. Leonard a priest." She looked at the creeping fire and bit her nail.

"There's St. John, the eldest," prattled Natalie. "That was thirty-five years ago. It must be extraordinary seeing him after such a long time. I mean for Mother, and Mick and Eolie. Of course I wasn't born when he ran away, nor Frankie, nor Claude." She turned the heavy boards. "This is Mick. He's changed a lot. Look, there's Mummy in her second wedding-dress. The way the fashions change!"

Her merry laugh trilled downwards.

"That's coming in again," said Eolie idly. "The fashions are gone back thirty years." She looked at Josephine longingly, made a move to speak, and stopped.

The boards turned to a small boy in a sailor suit, and lace collar, and velvet jacket. He was sitting on the lap of a man with dashingly wide moustaches. Natalie did not speak. Josephine leaned eagerly to look. The boards turned again, for the same man in a different setting.

"That's my daddy," said Natalie, "as President of the Chamber of Commerce."

The years fell heavily sidelong, and the boy in the sailor suit looked up at them in the uniform of an Irish Volunteer, cocked sombrero, belt tight, arms crossed, proud and young and fearless. Josephine took out a battered package of Players and lit a cigarette with a silver lighter. Natalie stared at the cigarette and at the lighter and buttoned up her face. Jo spread her long knees wide and stared at the flames.

"That's a nice lighter," probed Natalie, holding a poised page.

"Frankie gave it to me," said Jo, too proud to deceive even by silence.

"What are you thinking of, Jo?" asked Eolie in her frank way, while Natalie looked back in puzzled irritation at the President of the Chamber of Commerce, as much as to say, "Sorry, Daddy!"

"Jakus," said Josephine. "I was thinking if I had only forty or fifty quid."

"What would you do with it?" said Eolie.

("There," said Natalie to nobody, "is Frankie again in his Volunteer rig." Josephine glanced at it.)

"I'd give it to that bloody fool. I'd get him out of the country right away. I suppose there's no use asking you if you know where he is?"

She caught the hot looks that passed between the sisters, and felt that she had shocked them again by her language. She shrugged. This photograph of Frankie showed him with his jaw more stiff and his look more arrogant; his chest was out; his arms were locked behind his back; his fair hair fell on his forehead and his flat nose gave the whole pose of the body a final bluntness.

"Swank!" taunted Josephine, fondly and crossly, and then she let her head down on her fist and began to cry. Eolie put a hand on her shoulder. Natalie said, "Oh, Josephine!" The girl stuck up her jaw and glared at the two of them through her handsome wet eyes. "I was thinking of Patsy."

"Who is Patsy, girl?" asked Eolie.

"Who is Patsy?" mocked Josephine. "That's all anybody knows or cares now. He was my brother. The Black and Tans took him out of a house near Kilworth one night and he was found with his hands tied behind his back like that, in a deep pool in a quarry. He was adjutant of the Ninth Brigade."

She half rose and looked about her to see how she could escape from their eyes and their pity. Natalie, apologetically, obligingly, held out an ashtray. She sat back.

"Frankie always reminds me of my brother. They were two idiots. The two of them started one of the first hunger-strikes and it nearly killed them."

Her eyes deepened into the memory of those thirteen years; her brother's murder would have been her first horror, the first time death came home to her.

"What rubbish you're talking!" scolded Eolie. "Sure, didn't the two of them sit up in bed in hospital and, the first day out, eat a pound of plum-cake between them! The doctor said they must have the digestions of ostriches."

Josephine smiled weepily and drew down her lip to control it.

"It took a lot out of them, all the same. Some day Frankie will show the signs of it." She jumped up. "Look here, I didn't come here all the way to Cork to look at photographs and talk old stories. If that boy ever goes to jail again, he swears he will —you know that, don't you?—and you mustn't let him . . ."

"What?"—from the two girls.

"Go on hunger-strike again."

"No!" protested Eolie, going red.

"Don't you know anything about your own brother? If he does, it will finish him. It's not like old times. People don't care any longer about boys dying in jail. When Patsy died there were thousands at his funeral, and the flag over his coffin, and they fired over his grave. But now the country is so lousy they wouldn't . . ."

"Jo!" appealed Eolie.

"What kind of talk you're going on with!" upbraided Natalie. "Of course I always say there's no use in talk."

Josephine blazed.

"Then can you *do* something? You must get the boy out of the country."

"But," begged Eolie, "nobody believes he shot General Blennerhasset."

"Then," taunted Jo, "why did they raid us today looking for him?"

"You never told me that!" protested Eolie.

"I didn't want to bother you. Have they been here?"

Eolie looked at Natalie, who said, promptly:

"No."

"You're lying!" cried Josephine. "Eolie, did they come here? Don't dodge me. I'll easily find out."

"They called to the door. Mother wasn't well, so they didn't . . ."

"You're fooling yourselves," warned Josephine. "I am telling you that boy is stuck. He's afraid of nothing, God nor man; but he's afraid of one thing. He's afraid to desert his friends. You must persuade him to go. There's only a handful of them. I tell you the people are gone rotten. They'd let Frankie and every other Frankie rot in some Dublin jail and not lift a finger to help them. Money, money, money! That's all the people care about now. It makes me mad to hear people like Frankie going about at this hour of the day, with his gun on his back, talking about the Irish Republic to people who couldn't spell it—and every fellow he ever knew getting fat in big jobs or piling up the money. . . ."

"You're being disloyal!" cried Natalie.

"To what? Whom?"

"The cause!"

Josephine nearly sobbed.

"The cause. God, I thought you were going to say the Army. The one-man army. It makes me laugh. With all the 'tecs and G-men and Civic Guards in the country after his tail as if he was a trick-o'-the-loop man!"

She flung away from Natalie's restraining finger and turned and rent her:

"Since I was that high I've heard about the cause. Night and day—Mother of God!—for the last *twenty* years men have been coming in and out of our house—there's been nights when we had a dozen men there, and I've sat up all night long making bread for them and they snoring in chairs in corners of the kitchen. And I don't begrudge it. I'd do it again. I'd do it till the flesh went off my bones—if there was any good in it.

I've fed men and watched them from the door go sloping across the hills, and come back into the kitchen and sat down to a cup of well-water and the crusts they left behind because there wasn't as much as an egg-cup of flour in the bin to eat after them. For twenty years! And I'd do it tomorrow if there was any good in it. But when it comes down . . ."

She wrung her fingers. She kept on through a hateful face of tears and anger:

". . . to one man . . . wandering around the mountains . . . from north to south . . . like a lost sheep . . ."

She fell gasping in a chair, her consumptive's cough racking her, clogging her nose and mouth.

"After all," soothed Natalie, "hasn't that always been the way? Somebody has to . . ."

"To what? Who hears him? Who heeds him? Who minds him? Who cares if he lives or dies? Who'll remember him two months after he's dead?"

"It isn't for that he's doing it," insisted Natalie. Eolie sat on the floor by the fire, gripping her bony hands, staring at the red coals. Jo sobbed:

"He's doing it for obstinacy, and for courage, and for the folly of man. For what sense is there to it if nobody hears or heeds him? It's only vanity. Half of it is vanity and nothing but vanity, but can I tell him that? It's like Patsy. I met two men in Fermoy last week—men I'd fed and given up my bed for them to sleep in it—men Patsy spent the night out on the roads watching for, for fear they'd get caught by the Tans. And who watched for Patsy when his time came? Did *they?* Did *they?* They didn't even know me from Adam."

Natalie no longer concealed her disapproval; her lovely little dark face was gone cold and hard.

"You should have spoken to them," she pointed out. "Anybody might, in a crowd, not observe. . . ."

"I did speak to them." Her voice fell. "They had forgotten Patsy. They mixed him up with Manus."

"Anybody might forget," defended Natalie. "It's thirteen or fourteen years since those days."

Jo looked at the fire.

"They were prosperous," she murmured. "They had a Chrysler car. They laughed and joked as they drove away. They were happy. I don't blame them. God send it to them. But it will be the same with Frankie. He'll squander his substance and vanish and leave nothing behind him, no more than the froth of the river."

Her voice was now as soft as the murmuring fire. Her snivel resounded in the room.

"It all feeds into the one thing," said Natalie.

"God," scorned Josephine, "you'd think it was a cow we were talking about!"

Natalie left the room haughtily. Her sturdy legs, slightly flat, made the little tut-tut of a schoolmistress across the carpet. Josephine felt she must soon go. And yet she had accomplished nothing.

"Is Mrs. Hogan-Hannafey sick?" she asked of Eolie, using the double-barrelled name for greater formality.

Eolie scrambled up, tall and thin; if she were a man and it was fifty years ago, one would say she was a ramrod. Whatever one said, with her red hands, her worn face, and nothing but her straightness salvaged from her youth, one could not help thinking of something serviceable.

"For goodness' sake, Josephine," she begged wearily, "don't *you* start being polite now. If you can talk straight about one thing you can talk straight about another. Yes, my ma is sick. She's rambling again. You know as well as I do that she's off her rocker. All Cork knows it—what are we pretending about?" In one swoop she was beside the girl. "What will we do about Frankie?"

"Get him out of the country," replied the girl, as promptly as if it were a password.

"How? Even supposing he'd go. He couldn't go. The ports are watched. Since the shooting of this general down in Waterford they're looking for him and all the rest of his crowd like bloodhounds."

She went to the window and carefully peeped out. "No. He's gone. Or I don't see him. He was there all the morning talking to the men in that yawl that's loading coal from Sutton's."

Josephine did not ask, "Who?" She said, "Have you any money? Ten pounds?"

For one brief moment Eolie let herself go. She dragged up her skirt to show her stocking darned and redarned on her narrow shank. Her little flame died out. She looked away, shamefaced.

"The American brother?" asked Josephine without emotion.

Eolie was making a face that said, "How do I know?" when Natalie came back. She was worried.

"It's eleven o'clock and Michael isn't in."

"I must go," said Josephine.

"Wait for Michael," said Eolie. "And St. John! Imagine it—I almost forgot him!"

She waited until nearly midnight and neither Michael nor the American brother had come in. Eolie would not, after all, let her go to a hotel. They slept in the same bed. The rain had stopped, but the moon still rolled over and over in the sky. In bed Eolie told her the truth. At about a quarter to twelve they heard Michael steal to his room.

Midnight

The long cream Lincoln drawn up by the edge of the deserted quay—the river-water at low ebb, not a light or sound on that side of the island—had the air of a photograph that somebody had forgotten to take, a pose for an elegant advertisement for fine coachwork. First the dusk and then damp night had sunk on the cold side of the car; the crapulous buildings overhanging the river had become dark; the girl with the borzoi had wandered home. What had intended to be picturesque had become macabre. A Civic Guard in his black domed helmet came silently along under the silent houses of Carlton Terrace—all as hollow as a row of old bottles. He made no sound on his rubber heels and soles. Halting, he looked at the car, and when the moon faintly glinted the windows of the terrace they also seemed to look over his shoulders at it. They looked at the black ringed buoy sagging in the middle of the river, which breathed back its fog. Across the river the other quay was unbroken in all its empty length except for a hand-winch crane which both commented on the general emptiness and implied, by its own rusty age, the reason for it.

At last the Guard walked over to the car, and saw St. John Hannafey sagging under the steering-wheel, breathing heavily through his nose. He shook him lightly. St. John shivered, sat up slowly, and looked about him.

"I reckon I've fallen asleep."

Reassured by the American voice, the Guard leaned his elbows on the edge of the door.

"What are yeh doin' here at this hour of the night?"

"Sleeping," said St. John happily, stretched his arms to the skies, yawned, slapped his paunch, and settled down again to rest.

"You have no lights," said the Guard, more to explain his intrusion than because it could matter to anybody.

"What do I want lights for?" laughed St. John. "I'm in Ireland now, thank God."

He switched on the headlights for a second, and they shot along the quay into the fog over the river; as he switched them off they cut a prowling cat in two. He drew a bottle from the wide pocket in the door and offered it, with an almost excessive friendliness.

"Sit in and drink it in peace. It's good stuff. I've got plenty of it."

The Guard (a long night before him) sat in, clicked the door, took the bottle, raised it on his head, and handed it back with a grunt.

"Cigar?" offered St. John, and the Guard took one and lit it from St. John's gold lighter. He puffed, at his ease.

"I suppose"—he puffed, after a while—"that 'tis the way"—puff—"you're on a class of a holiday?"

"I am, brother," agreed St. John warmly. They both looked at a startled seagull where it fluttered with a little squawk out from beneath the wharf-piles and then settled down again whitely on the ebb. "I've had a full day, too, brother. And a great day. I've been here a week, and, gee, what a country this is! Oh, it's a grand and glorious country. Ireland is a great country, sergeant. We Irish should never forget that."

"Ach! It's not a bad ould hole."

"It's a *great* country. Do you know how long it took me to realize that? Let me tell you. Do you know just exactly how long I've been out of Ireland?"

"Oh, so 'tis the way you were born here?" probed the Guard.

"Yes, sir. I left Ireland—I left Cork city, in the year nineteen hundred and two. You weren't even thought of then. Friday night, May the second—this very month—thirty-four years ago, I left Cork. The angelus was ringing. From that day to this week, I've never once been back."

"Yerrah, why so?"

St. John drew back impatiently.

"I had reasons of my own. I'm a busy man. I suppose you never heard of H. H. Shoes? Well, I'm the man who makes H. H. Shoes. Coast to coast in the United States there isn't a town where you can't buy Hogan-Hannafey Shoes. That's my work. Thirty-four years I've spent building up that business, and believe me it has taken up all my time."

"I'm sure," said the Guard with the indifferent interest of the man whose interest is not easily roused in what lies outside his experience.

"But I'm sure glad to be back at last!"

They rested on that.

"I went down, yesterday, to see where my people came from. Myself and the old mother. We drove down to Kilavullen, on the Blackwater. Know it?"

The Guard took his cigar from his mouth and laughed with pleasure.

"Didn't I poach every foot of the river between Castle Hyde and Kilavullen? I did so, and"—confidentially, lest the houses hear—"I'd do it again. Do I know Kilavullen? That's a good one! What name did you say you were? Hannafey?"

The Guard looked up at the blind face of the house opposite them; the dark-green door was masked by the shadows of its jambs; only the hollowed footsteps, before it, shone.

"Yeah! Hogan-Hannafey I call myself. I'm really a Hogan,

but my mother married again. And I believe they're all beginning to call themselves Hannafey now."

"Oh?" said the Guard.

Hannafey was looking down at the dark river. He took out a little notebook and wrote down in pencil: *It's the emptiness.*

"Hogan-Hannafey?" mused the Guard.

"Kilavullen," grunted the other.

As he was putting away his book he saw the folded and rough-edged road-map in the little shelf of the dashboard; he saw how it browned deeper and deeper up out of the city with contour lines that had narrowed with every mile the Lincoln had spun on that journey to Kilavullen. It had climbed up out of this pocket of hill-city until the whole plateau of the county spread itself beyond the nose of the car; a roll of hills to the west, the high lumps of the Galtees to the north-east. Before them the fields were grouped in patches, light or dark according as the clouds blessed them with sun or shade. Deliberately he had photographed them in his mind so that when he was back in New York he would be able to close his eyes and see it all again—the cloud that was "like Queen Mary's hat," the mountain that was "like Abraham Lincoln," the sky that was "full of ice-cream cones on plates" (he felt proud of that, and had said it again as he gazed into the sky-ocean with those unstirring clouds). But he did not get very far with his mental photography because his old mother beside him had begun to sob, and when he looked at her slightly lunatic eyes he began to laugh. "If you didn't think you'd ever see them all again," he teased, "what about me?" Ten minutes later she had to tell him that if he didn't go slower she would go out of her mind. Secretly, as he slowed down, he chuckled at that too. It was good from an old lady who had been more or less out of her mind for the past twenty years.

The ravines had grown steeper. When they came to the

hamlet where her father (his grandfather) once taught in the local school, and where she learned her first lessons, she did not recognize a stone of the place. She despised it for not having stayed as it was in her time. They did not halt long; they climbed up another of the little blue nerves of river, into the blueness of the sky, went down again until they saw another and final pine-glen, cool and dark, swinging its hammock of river just below the road. A turn of the switch-key brought them the shrill whistle of an unseen lark. When the bird swooped, the glen put its finger to its lips. They could not even hear the soft rain. Another mile and they were in the village where she was born.

How ladylike she was, then! Chuckling over old names, old stories. It was, "Look at Leonard's. Glory be to God there's not a change in it. And isn't Roche's gone very shabby? Wisha, for goodness' sake, wouldn't they at least give a rub to the window!" He teased her that they had not known she was coming. "I wonder is that old boozer Matty Nagle alive yet? And look at that shop there! And *that* one! Goodness, and I used to think 'twas such a grand little town. Tututut, the whole place is gone downhill. . . ."

So it was—thatch fallen in, shutters off many windows, the base of the woodwork rotted away, one of Ireland's new Deserted Villages, the mark of the modern rush for the large towns and cities. It pleased her, however, because it had not built up a new life since her time; she would take her youthful world with her to the grave. It saddened him. Ireland should never change.

They drove down to the burial-ground. He did not ask her if she knew where the grave was. Instead he took out another of his mind-photographs—the private asylum where his brother and sisters had put her when her second husband died; he had seen it in one of his drives about the city. As she stumbled over the mounds through the wet grass she was interested in other people's monuments, and, as she stooped, her eyes closed to peer and her white hair fell out under her hat. She smiled with delight—in friendship—at a familiar name, and gave it a pity that from one so old was itself pitiful, the condescension of a merely nominal life. They found their own last bed, and he read out from the still-white limestone:

Philip Hannafey
Died June 3rd
1915
On his soul, Sweet Jesus
have Mercy

Among the docks and the wild heliotropes she knelt and prayed; he, who had not prayed for years and years, knelt beside her. Her husband. A man he had seen only once. A stepfather—frightening words. The silence of spring was thickened by the sinking haze.

"How much did ye pay for the stone?" she asked brightly as she stumbled up, and when he said he believed he had sent home a draft for two hundred dollars, she said those funeral people were all robbers and she could have got it for ten pounds any day of the week. Then with the excitement and the closeness of the day she grew faint and he had to lay her out under the wild fuchsia hedge—its drops of blood scattered drops of water on her face—and race back to Leonard's pub for brandy. The village people were kind and garrulous, and warmed to him, and he to them at once—but, then, all Ireland had been nothing but kind and warm since he landed a week ago at Cove.

By the time he reached the city, taking the quickest road, she was gabbling nonsense into his ear. Near the city the rain had stopped—such as it was—a mere sprinkle. The cool May evening, the little yellow lights on the estuary of the Lee, the brimming tide, milk-smooth after the slight rain, deep with the deeps of the sky, the twinkling houses across the lochs of the river, the chugging of an outgoing steamer, the laughter of young cyclists passing them down—all stabbed at him, every one with its gentle warning of life that itself becomes fogged, fades away, and passes out to sea.

"Ahadee," she was cackling as she leaned on his shoulder in the car, clawing him fondly, "and ahadee, again and again, hard I reared ye and hard I bred ye, and the cake is baking, my love and my dove, the cake is baking and the children home from school, and all the day gone on me, with my two poor hands full but what can I do, my love and my dove, I tell you it's all I can do to make ends meet, and I'd slave to make a home for my children, why did you leave me, my love and my dove, you never stinted me, but the way I am now, not like the old days. Oh, the fool I was!"

With his mouth clamped, he drove, her white hair blowing on his face and her hat all askew as if she were drunk. The evening bells of the city's churches rang quietly for devotions as he drove up the narrowing river. The city glowed into the sky as he entered it. The sun was gone but the streets were bright. Children played their last games.

"And I have a son," she was babbling now, "in America, St. John, a good boy, a good lad, he's gone from me, but I should be the proud woman with sons like him, and a daughter is a nun, and a son a priest, and a boy in the Post Office—hard I reared them all, clever children. God be good to them, and to the kind father who reared them. Oh, Johnny, my love and my dove, the fool that I was!"

He closed his hard American eyes to it. He tried not to notice that she did not speak of her second husband, whose grave she had just seen. He noticed too, with curiosity, that she often mentioned one particular name: Frankie, the brother he had never seen. They had told him he was in the country; that he would be back "in a few days."

The squawking gull fluttered out and settled its breast into the dark tide.

"What disturbs that bird?"

"Rats," said the Guard. "Carlton Place," he said with sudden briskness, "is a queer name. I do be interested in names," he explained. "That was a Lord Lieutenant in the old days. Did you know that?"

The American glanced idly at the terrace that rose plump off the path. One or two houses had steps, and two had twisted iron hand-rails. When he was a kid he had played tag around those steps and rails. One house, a doctor's, used to have jalousie shutters, in dark green, on the lower front windows; they were gone now.

"And that's another queer name," mused the Guard. "Charlotte Quay. Who do you think she was, now?"

"Dunno," said the American.

"Nobody knows"—positively—"nobody. Because there was two of 'em. There was a Queen Charlotte and there was a Princess Charlotte. I talked it all over one night last winter with a German off the Shannon Scheme. 'You're drunk,' says I. 'I'm not,' says he. 'Read that sign,' says I—'twas a moon like daylight. 'Charlotte,' says he, 'and what's more,' says he, 'I can say Mecklenburg-Strelitz. That's who *she* was,' says he. You couldn't arrest a man," explained the Guard, with a quiet challenge in his voice, "who could say Mecklenburg-Strelitz."

"Mecklenburg-Strelitz," said St. John wearily, and the Guard laughed.

"Ah," he went on, "it's a bloody queer country! There's a Brunswick Street in Cork, too. And a George the Fourth bridge. Ireland had a great regard for George the Fourth.

Though damn the bit anyone knew about him—or, that is, anyone but Dan O'Connell, and he knew everything."

"A great man," said the American. "And a great country!"

"Aye! But there's no interest in history in Ireland."

"I don't agree!" protested the American warmly.

"Well," challenged the Guard, sitting up, "how well nobody but me knows that *she* was Mecklenburg-Strelitz?"

"It doesn't matter," said St. John. "All these are the names of our conquerors and they should be wiped out. We Irish in America can't understand why you haven't wiped them out long ago."

"Ah," growled the Guard, "if you put up Tara Terrace there, people wouldn't know if Tara was in Donegal or Connemara!" He went on growling. "It's a queer place. A queer dead and alive place. Dead and alive! Tshah!"—and he spat disgustedly.

"I never see it like that," muttered St. John. "Only—how quiet it is. How quiet!" he sighed happily. "Quiet . . ."

"How's Frankie Hannafey these days?" asked the Guard casually.

Very carefully St. John took out his cigar-case, slowly chose and cut a cigar, and lit it. Then he said, basso, not lifting his jowls from his collar, or his eyes from the river, that he had never seen his brother Francis in his life, and that he had only been in that house a week; at which they both lifted their eyes in time to see a faint light pass across a blind high under the roof. They smoked in silence, and then Hannafey drank and passed the bottle across. He clicked on the dashboard light and saw that the clock glowed half-past twelve. The river stank. A little wind blew. The whole city was like an empty porter-bottle. The feminine chimes of the new city hall beat out the half-hour.

"I gather," said Hannafey, after a while, "that he's been in trouble with the law?"

"I needn't tell yeh," said the Guard in a kindly voice, "that it's none of my business. I wasn't trying to pump yeh."

"I believe that, Guard," said Hannafey warmly.

Far away another bell (the English Market clock) rang the half-hour in a flat, cracked chime—very quickly, as if it had woken up to do it. The gull now rose and made off down the river, taking their eyes to the saw-toothed gables that grouped another little knot of sleep against the sky. The Guard shook his head a few times as if to shake up a few ideas, and the American sank lower in the seat, and let his soft grey hat tip over his eyes. For being shadowed his face seemed older.

"Aye!" said the Guard. "History is wonderful."

It was not age or weariness that was puckering the tremulous lines about the eyes of the American; it was the old familiar who had tormented him for years with thoughts of home teasing him, now, with a revelation of a place where the clock was stopped, a place where he might have been young for ever.

"Wonderful!" repeated the other. "But there's an awful lot of it to remember."

In those thirty-four years of exile the mind had been whirling in top gear, the heart had hung like a Lazarus in a cold sleep. Childhood had become as simple as a toy, its images sweet as honey—no more than the coloured bits of transparency that delight children: a cottage lit up at night, or a church all brightly coloured glass. More actual things had tormented him recently, and with the frequency of heart-attacks: a gate to a yard, a square meadow holding a heart of cold well-water, these steps to his door. Being, after the manner of all men in love, superstitious and fearful, he took these visitations for symbols, and got drunk whenever they tormented him. He could not know he was suffering from revenge of the heart.

"I knew a man, do yeh know," said the Guard, "who never smoked anything but cigars all his life long. And he once told me that he sometimes smoked two cigars together, at one and the same time, one out of each side of his mouth. What do you make of that, now?"

"Strange!"

" 'Tis! And *damn* strange!"

Not one of his images had betrayed him. May—so soft, so sleepy, unbusy; season of the first throaty cuckoos vibrating their contralto as from the centre of all sound; life in every drying ditch; green tips through cracking mud. That very first re-sight of the old house on the island, with its worn step, its brass plate polished into holes at the corners, with his two sisters, and two brothers, and the old mother at the tea-table, and the angelus ringing—it was just as if he had not run away that May night in 1902, but stayed his steps down to the quays and come back as usual to tea. It was all as cosy as a hot coin in the pocket. When the bell rang they had stopped their chatter, and it seemed to him that the whole city stopped its sparrow-chaffering, to pray. That was an item he had forgotten to recall in New York. It was then, less than one hour after he landed in Ireland, at that faint pulsation of the evening bell, that Lazarus lifted his eyes and saw. That night, in his bedroom, he had written down in his notebook the one word: *Bells*.

"What would be the name of this car, now?" asked the Guard.

"Lincoln," said St. John, smiling. (He felt he loved this childlike Irish policeman.)

"Ah! Abraham Lincoln. Look at that, now! There's history in everything."

From that first night on he had geared down in one long, quick slide like a sleep. The family was almost too good to be true; heard of hitherto in letters only, visualized only from photographs—Natalie when she took her teacher's certificate, fawn-eyed, life-untouched as a nun; Michael, his eldest brother, the only one he really remembered, bearing the corner of the canopy in a public procession through the streets, with the old bishop beneath it grasping the sunburst monstrance and little boys in scarlet velvet capes scattering roses before it at his feet. Of Eolie he had a merry "snap" taken when she went to the seaside at Youghal after an illness. He had no photograph of Claude. They did not more than mention Frankie. Until that trip yesterday to Kilavullen his holiday had been without flaw.

"There's always some trouble," comforted the Guard. St. John forgot that they had been talking of political trouble until he added, squeezing out the cheerful juice of youth, "But it'll all come out in the wash. Frankie will be all right. Are you sure," he probed, "you're not waiting for someone?"

"No," said St. John. "It's just that the old lady is sick, and I have to go to Cove to meet my wife. I don't feel like bed. The mother got a stroke of some kind yesterday."

"That's bad," comforted the Guard. "But God is good. My own mother was sick there four months ago with the bronchitis. 'Twas terrible the way she was coughing. Put you in mind of a cow on a wet night. We thought she'd pass out—oh, we were sure she'd be whipped. 'Tis the heart goes first. Cardiac failure," he defined, and he sucked the words (learned, probably, in the police court), "cardiac failure. But she overed it. Is that the way *she* is?"—nodding to the dark house.

Hannafey fluttered his fingers to his forehead.

"*Now*," said the young man, "I know you. Sure I often see

her about the island. She do be toddling along by herself at a great rate, with her nose out before her. Not doing a bit of harm to anyone, the poor soul."

"Guard," said Hannafey, suddenly turning to him, "this is a great country, and we're a great people. That poor woman has been a trouble and a cross to everyone connected with her for the last twenty years. Yet they wouldn't put her away. And they didn't until she was picked out of the river one night! And only then because she was a danger to herself!"

"Was that last month? We were watching from the barrack-window, and listening to the roaring."

"No, sir. Twenty years ago this happened. They brought her home after four or five years. Since then they're always watching her, for they never know when she'll go off again. But do you think, Guard, that anyone else in any other country would put up with her for so long? No, sir! They'd have popped her into the bughouse in a brace of shakes and left her there for keeps. Ah, this is a *grand* country! A *grand* people! They're so warm, so natural."

Again the little glow of light centred the high window-blind, and again both of them looked up at it. The Guard threw away his cigar and turned abruptly to the American. He shoved out his neck. The pose of his body was taut and sharp.

"Is that where the old lady is sleeping?"

Hannafey was taken by surprise. He stuttered that he didn't know. "No . . . I don't think . . ."

"How long are yeh in this city, did you say?" demanded the Guard.

"A week. What's biting you?"

"Nothing." He relaxed. He tightened again. "Who lives on the top floor?"

They were both alert now, face to face.

"Why do you ask?"

"There never was a light there before." His eyelids almost met. He jumped out and slammed the door, and at the same time looked up expectantly. The faint light came, and stayed, and vanished. It was as if a curtain had stirred behind the blind. The sound echoed over the water.

"What the hell are you making the noise for?" cried St. John. "Didn't I tell you there was an old woman sick in the house?"

The Guard leaned in sarcastically and said: "Did you never hear of a man named General Blennerhasset?"

Having said that and explained it with a glare, the Guard moved off under the shade of the tall houses. He made no more noise than a night-cat.

Leaning out, St. John called: "Hi!"

He watched him until he had rounded the terrace. Then he leaned back and considered for a few minutes. He looked up towards the roof, got out, and was himself lost in the maw of his doorway. His latch-key clicked. The city hall sent out one single chime.

1 a.m.

In the sick-room St. John could barely see the old woman's face. It was buttoned in a tormented sleep and the little oil-lamp before the home-made altar made a cavern of her mouth. The shadows rising and falling on the ceiling might have been her dreams. He looked about the room and listened, and heard the cracked chime of the English Market strike once, briefly, as if out of breath. Natalie lay asleep on a couch, her face as calm as a morning lake. One of her long dark plaits of hair touched the carpet with its paw; beside her a book had fallen, or been laid open on the floor. He picked it up but could not read it. She had been at her studies. It was a book of French poetry.

Not until he had looked in and found Claude also asleep, the moon throwing the shadow of his calliper nose and chin on the pillow and lighting the pale sheet of thin-drawn design on his drawing-board; and in his room, also sleeping, his eldest brother Michael, his face inexplicably ravaged by some worm of melancholy, did he return and touch Natalie on the forehead. (He did not go near Eolie; he knew she had been at work all day—the family housekeeper.) Natalie woke with the smoothness of a rising diver, and smiled. She went across and looked at her mother's face and looked back at him questioningly. He beckoned her after him to his own room, where the black slack on the fire lit up under his poker and the flames shone cosily on his white bed with its brass knobs. She sat and drew her dressing-gown about her and took his cigarette.

"Will I make you a cup of tea, Cursor? Or what about a glass of hot milk?"

They called him the Precursor, because of his name St. John, and then shortened it to Cursor for a pun, to make a joke of their mother's love for airy names.

"What a fine family you all are, Nat!" he said, leaning forward on his knees on the edge of the basket chair.

"Huh!" she grunted, surprised, and then, grinning, "Cheese it, big boy."

"It's true, just the same. I've been thinking of it all day. I've been thinking it ever since I came home. But listen! Who's upstairs—I mean under the roof?"

"Why? Nobody."

"I saw a light."

"No."

"Yes, I did."

"Nonsense."

"I saw it more than once," he insisted.

"Motor-cars down the stable-lanes behind often shine through the back-windows," but she flicked her ash unnecessarily and said, rising, "I'll make some tea."

Because she had fobbed him off, all the strangeness of his thirty-four-years' absence, and the strangeness that came from their having had different fathers, and from their never having seen one another until this week of their lives, hardened between them. He said brutally:

"There's a Guard outside wanting to know about it." Then flung at her frightened eyes: "Who's General Blennerhasset?"

For all the softness and smoothness of her face, an innocence that might be expected to raise a dam between mind and body, she walked with decision to the electric switch, blacked out the room, and then looked with a firm caution through the curtains down at the car. A hundred times St. John had met Irish girls in New York just like her, just as soft-eyed, the smell of the peat still in their hair, the distances of the country in their eyes, and they had braved the New World with the same expressionless animal courage. He looked out from the other window. The same Guard was examining the inside of the car; a man in plain clothes was leaning on the door.

"How much petrol have you?" she whispered.

"Plenty. I have to go to Cove to meet the liner. I filled up this evening at Blarney."

"Sit down, Cursor, and wait a bit, will you?"—and she trotted out of the room. He did not sit down. He saw the plain-clothes man note down the number of the car, examine the dashboard, probably for the mileage, and even root about in the side-pockets. Although unaccustomed to the methods of the Irish police, he guessed that they were behaving with unusual boldness, and by the way the man glanced once back up at the house he knew that they knew it. He got a thrill of something very like fear when the Guard stooped down and shone a torch on the tire and the other fellow took down the name, or make, or measurements. When he turned round, Natalie had come back with his brother Michael.

His brother's hair stood up about his head, so that the balding whorl at the crown showed clearly. He had the ugly grin of a man who has just taken medicine. He wore his trousers over his pyjamas. When he had looked out he said:

"It may mean nothing at all. Go and . . ."—he jerked his head to the door, sat by the fire, asked for a cigarette without looking at St. John, and began to smoke it. He kept blinking the sleep out of his eyes. He was prematurely old but it struck St. John that he actually had the body of an old man; and thinking how he had reared the family, denied himself marriage to help the children, especially the three of the second marriage, he began to see him as a kind of patriarch, the final authority in this widowed house, and forbore to question. He merely said:

"They're pretty saucy, eh?"

"I was dreaming I was in Paris," said Michael absently, rubbing cobwebs off his face and mind. They were sitting opposite one another, the American looking on with an affection mixed with puzzlement.

"Huh!" he smiled. "And I in New York have been, off and on for thirty-four years, dreaming of this little town."

"I dreamt a couple of times I was in New York," said Michael.

"It's no dream, Mick."

"I'd give a lot to see it."

"Well, come back with me. I'll pay your fare and you can live with us."

For a second Michael's face sweetened; it shone; then the light faded.

"I only get two weeks' holidays. In September. You'll be gone then, anyway, I suppose."

"Oh, *I* gotta get on with the job," droned St. John sadly. He said "jawb." "I go back next month at the latest. My factories are in the middle of manufacturing the winter stocks just now. I have a conference with my salesmen on July 1. My wife stays on much later—she goes to Paris from here and then on to Salzburg. My daughter Beulah is studying there all winter. That's the big musical place in Germany."

"Austria," corrected Michael. "Anyway, I couldn't leave Mother when she's like this. Besides, I've no money. Ach, it doesn't matter."

"You've always been sacrificed to the family, Mick. It's not fair. But that's Ireland all over. You're all too generous."

Mick rubbed his face again and tousled his hair and glared at the fire.

"If it wasn't for Mother!" he cried, and then stopped dead. He sighed, "Ah, well!" Then shaking it all off he said, almost peevishly, "How much petrol have you got?"

"Full up."

"Blast him!" cried Michael suddenly.

"Who?"

"Frankie."

"It's him they're after? Some political business? This general chap—he's been bumped off?" A succession of tired nods said "Yes" to each question. "Why the hell doesn't he clear out of the country? Why don't you send him word?"

"He's upstairs"—in a wearied-out groan.

"When did he come?"

"He's been there for the past week."

St. John stared.

"You mean, all the time I've been . . ."

He recalled that first evening again—the supper-table, the six of them around the table—Mother, Eolie, Natalie, Claude, Mick, and himself—with the angelus ringing and peace flowing into his heart. Mick was looking around him.

"Things, sometimes, get too blasted much for you . . . I . . ."

His eyes kept moving without rest. When he spoke it was more to himself than to his brother. St. John got up and laid his palm fondly on the tousled head.

"Mickey, old man?" he begged.

"Oh, go to hell!" snapped Michael and flung off the hand.

Natalie came in with Eolie.

"Michael, you were very late!" Eolie chided gently. "How's Mother?" she asked Natalie.

"Sleeping nicely."

Eolie went across the firelit room to the window and peeped.

"That's Caffrey. He's a devil. I'd love to kick his backside for him. With his specs and his buck-teeth." She turned to Michael and with Natalie they began to confer. A strange girl came in—dark, a greyhound figure, tall, with flushed cheeks and burning brown eyes, a beauty; she had the gentle, downy voice, without vibration, of the typical consumptive. Nobody introduced her to St. John. In their private worry they ignored him. He heard places mentioned that his mother had mentioned. He gathered that the girl's name was Josephine. There was no light in the room but the fire.

"Cursor," said Eolie then, "when does the liner arrive at Cove?"

"Some God-awful hour like half-four or five in the morning."

"It fits in grand," said Josephine eagerly.

St. John admired that girl; she was so full of fire and she was bossing them all. She wanted Frankie taken out of the city to somewhere or other, and he was to drive him there on his way to the liner. He peered out over the dim quay.

"You'll have to go with them, Mick," Josephine was saying and Michael was objecting.

"I won't go," he said. "There's no need for me to go. I will *not* go. He can look after himself."

"Go and get dressed," Eolie ordered him.

"No. No. No."

St. John looked back from one to another: from Natalie's gentle-dark, apple-rosy features to Eolie, beaked so hard, yet so kindly; from Josephine, lovely as a tulip, to Michael's face that was old, and cranky and tortured. He came forward.

"Don't you all think it's about time I was told what this is about?" He lifted his hand. "I don't want to know a lot. I gather my brother has got into some kind of trouble. I gather he's been hiding upstairs in this house all the time I've been here. That's all right with me. All I want to know is what you want me to do now. Remember, I may do it. But also I may not do it."

Josephine forestalled the rest of them.

"We want you to give a man a lift down the country when you're driving to Cove this morning. That's all."

"And that man is?"

"You'd better not know who he is. Isn't that the best way?"

Quietly admiring her quickness, he asked:

"I may know him when I see him?"

"I don't think you've ever met him in your life before."

"And this place I might give this man a lift to?"

"It's called Quit Rent."

"My mother mentioned that place, but I don't know how to get there."

"Mick will show you," she finished, turning to Michael, who waved his hands at her and said:

"But I don't want to go! Why should I? Let somebody else go." He jumped up and slipped one brace over his shoulder, and then the other. "I won't go!" he shouted, and Natalie said, "Sssh!" For that second it was so quiet they could hear the sudden squawk of a seagull.

"Mickey!" pleaded Eolie.

The door opened and in came the sharp nose of Claude, the youngest. He glared at them all and cried furiously.

"I heard all the talk," he complained. "Why can't people be allowed to sleep? I was working late, and I have a competition on Monday."

"Be quiet," warned Natalie. "You'll waken Mummy."

A little shamefaced, he stuttered back:

"You're all more likely to do it," and was about to go when Michael threw a wrist in his direction.

"Let him go."

"Where?" protested Claude, and then he came back, as if on an afterthought. "What's all this about, anyway?"

"Go to bed, Claude," hushed Eolie, but he came back into the room, peering sleepily about over his hooked nose. She drew a deep groan of exasperation. "We have no time to waste," she burst out at her brother. "Will you do as we ask you?"

At once Michael (while they stared at him), standing there in the middle of the room, put his two hands tight by his sides as if standing to attention, the cuffs loose, and, vibrating with the force of his voice, shouted out such an unbelievable run of obscenity that the girls gave little choked screams and stepped away from him. Even St. John was horrified. "Damn yeh, damn yeh, damn yeh!" he yelled at the end of it. He was panting and sweating when he stopped—still rigid.

"That's nice talk!" complained Claude, and at once he went staggering against the wall with a crack of his brother's palm. That took the rage out of Michael; he sank down and began to weep. They might all have been looking at a man they had never seen before. Claude, clawing the wall with one hand and holding his jaw with the other, made little whimpering noises that were echoes of Michael's whining—the moans of a man with a toothache.

Just then the girls heard their mother groaning and ran from the room.

St. John sent Claude to bed. Only Josephine remained with the two men.

"Maybe I'd better go with you?" she said to St. John. "You *will* go?"

He nodded, and she went out swiftly—up, he guessed, to tell Frankie, and he was left alone with his brother in the fluttering dark.

He looked at him for a long while. Then he sat down opposite him and gave him another cigarette. They smoked in silence. Then St. John got a brain-wave, and from his cabin-trunk took out one of six bottles of champagne he had bought in town a few days before, opened it, filled a tumbler, and handed it to Mick. As he did so, he said in a rough voice as many as he could remember of the obscene words his brother had used.

"Mick, you're a —— fool, just a ——, —— fool. I know the way they've treated you. A man's a man. Christ, don't I know it." He leaned and whispered, "The girls don't understand. That kid Claude's too young. But you're a bloody fool, for all that. You're taking it too seriously. You'll smash up everything if you go on like this. You want to get away. We take all these things for granted out in the world." He laughed aloud. "Ha, ha, ha! 'Out in the world'—you'd think this was a monastery! And it is! People here are all bottled up. All old-fashioned. But what do you want to be letting yourself go opposite the girls for? Jesus, you're a ——, ——, —— fool, and nothing but a ——, ——, —— fool! And I know what I'm saying!"

But all the time he was miserable because of what he had just seen and heard, and, as he obscened, it was as if he were vomiting and could smell his own vomit.

"Mickey"—and again he risked laying a palm on Mickey's head. "Forget it. Drink up. I keep this in here for myself. The bloody girls think I'm a bloody saint! Ha!" He filled both their glasses again. "Me a saint!" Then he did not know what else to say, so he said, "The hell with it!" and drank back the gently powerful liquor. Mick looked at him as if he would say something, but he only shook his head. They smoked—silent again until Natalie pattered back to say that his mother was asking for him. He held her in his arms, led her outside the door, and calmed her there.

"It's nothing, Nat. Don't heed Mick. It's just nerves. Think how he's worked all these years for you all. Gee, I haven't done my bit at all. Listen. There's a home in New York, I'm told, for priests, and I'm told by priests myself that the things sometimes these poor men say—it's their nerves, you know—they learn it all in their moral theology, and in confession—and it comes out of them—holy men, the holiest men—well, if Mickey hadn't been so gentle, he wouldn't be . . . you understand . . . ?"

She nodded but he could feel her heart thumping, and when she looked at him he felt that Life had at last touched her eyes with its finger-nails. She went away and, leaving Michael alone to get over his fit, he went off to his mother, where he had to comfort Eolie in the same way and flatter and joke his mother, who was now almost normal, calmed by her long sleep. The three of them talked of life in that old island forty years ago. The old woman smiled weakly up at him and touched her abbreviated pigtail of white hair with a mouse-finger. They talked of the old shopkeepers near the island where he and Mickey and Eolie used to buy sweets from Mother Carey, and Bovaniser, and Ma Canty, and the Two Dwarfs, and Moll Sull, who married a Yank who drank her out of house and home, and the only one of them all who was still alive—the widow they called Handsuphersleeves.

"I went around there," he laughed, "the very first night I landed in Cork, and—jiminy!—there she was, not a change in her after thirty-four years. I wanted to go into the old shop, down the two steps, and have a glass of milk and a ha'penny cake with the boys and girls inside the red curtains, just as I did long ago."

"Cakes are a penny now," his mother smiled, her eyes swaying up and sinking down.

"It's great, the way nothing changes here." But he paused on that.

"Your poor father was so proud of you," she sighed, and closed her eyes.

Eolie stole away. He kept on at the round of the city; their world, his egg. He roved the South and West that he knew so well—the docks, the timber-yards, the granaries, the old race-course, now taken over by Henry Ford for a factory, the old Macroom Railway yards, now turned into a bus-garage; the North and East that he knew less well. She stopped him suddenly with a gasp and a rush of quick breaths.

"I was dozing," she said, and he got up from the bed to leave her, but she held his hand in her sweaty fingers. "Where's Frankie? I am dreaming about him."

He said nothing. He realized that he knew very little of the ways of this house; such as, how much she knew or should be told. He was pulled down from the air, where, for a while, the pull of the world had been attenuated. Under the light—the old-fashioned white shade, like a bell with fluted edges—he looked, as for inspiration, at the bedroom chair with its seat of punched holes, at the row of medicine bottles on the mantelpiece, at the picture of the Sacred Heart.

"Isn't Frankie away?" he asked.

"Yes," she said. "He's in the country. That's right. He's in the country."

He looked at his watch, and put it back, and took it out again and saw the time. He would soon have to be thinking about meeting his wife and son. What would they think of Cork? Of Ireland? She was whispering now—gone off the rails again—about "my love and my dove . . ." and "Johnny! Oh, Johnny!" Never the second husband; never Philip Hannafey, the stock-broker; always his father who had kept the provision shop across the quays—"John Hogan and Sons." The flimsy patch of life on the pillow was alive only in her lips and memories. She was murmuring about a boat.

It could be his boat that he ran away to catch—that wet May night when the angelus was ringing, its swing-swong broken when the wind stole away a beat or two. How often had he pulled that rope as an altar-boy, that dark rope vanishing up through its sleeve in the loft! You took it and you swung out of it, and all the power and weight of the great tower was in your mind. No sound came until you had got the great bell to swing freely. Then your mind shuddered when you sent the first bang out over the city. Or it might be the boat his wife was coming in to visit her. Or the boat he had come in to meet her after all those years. She was wavering in a kind of wintry keyhole tremor. She said, "Frankie?" and fell silent. He waited for a moment and then whispered, "Mother?"

She was asleep. He stole out. Josephine flitted past him. "Be ready in half an hour," she whispered, and vanished around the bend of the stairs. The landing-window shook a little in the soughing wind. He went back to Michael, who was now fully dressed, drinking the champagne and smoking, and trying to keep his eyes from roving from a book to the fire.

"Say, Mick! You remember the night I ran away?" Michael looked up through the haze of the champagne and whatever magic he had again drunk in from his book of French tales.

"Yes. No. I mean . . . yes, I do! A nice rumpus you made! My mother was getting married in a week and the police looking for you high and low."

"I suppose that was why I ran away. I hated the idea of a step-father."

"We all did." Pause. "You wanted me to go with you. I wish I had. But why do you want to go into all that?"

He tried to return to his book. They both drank some more, and then St. John said, moodily:

"And Clara went into a convent. And Leonard became a priest. Does he ever come home?"

"Twice since he went to New York." Irritably: "You ought to know. Don't you meet him there?"

"Yes, yes," St. John said quickly, and Mick, who knew that meant "No, no," shrugged and said nothing except:

"Mother missed *him*, too."

"She had you!" St. John defended passionately. "She had Eolie, and Nat, and Claude, and the rest . . . Frankie."

"Not much Frankie"–to the book. "From 1916 wandering about the country as homeless as a . . . as a bloody Indian sellin' rugs." Turning his shoulder to his brother, he added, "Or if he wasn't there, he was in jail."

St. John started up. From the window he saw that the

Guard was now sitting on the running-board of the car. Farther up, the little yawl was showing a streak of wet down its mast. The little city was locked in sleep. So it would go on for ever, night following night, as it had gone for all its lifetime; so it would for all its life to come, deep in its indifference to any form of life outside its own. He turned, and cried:

"How much does she know about Frankie?"

"Everything"—to the book.

"But, God above, she told me he was down in the country. She told me so just now!"

"She was telling you lies. She'd tell anybody lies about him. She's terrified for him, body and soul. She's terrified the police will talk to her when her mind is wandering, and find out about him. It's what has her half driven off her nut. That and other things. It's what drives everybody off their nut. People only thinking of themselves!"

"Ssh!" Then St. John pleaded, "You mean I'm selfish, too?" The only answer was the turned shoulder, the hand trembling on the book. "You were implying it?" No answer. "You think I have a grand time, I suppose? Away over there, never seeing my own people for thirty-four years. . . ." He stopped; he could never get Michael to understand what exile meant. He sat down firmly and got out his notebook and his silver pencil. "Let's get this straight. I'm willing to admit I should have gone into all this before. I'm glad we're having this little chat. First of all, when the step-father died, what exactly did he leave her to live on?"

A shudder of pain ran through the grey-headed man at the fire; he waved his hand beseechingly.

"I gotta go into this, Mickey. I've suddenly realized a lot of things. I'm going to get it all cold now."

Another dry sob went through his brother; he looked sadly at his Maupassant.

"Ask Eolie! Ask Natalie! Only leave *me* alone!"

"I won't keep you two minutes, Mickey," pleaded St. John. "Now"—cold and crisp again—"let's be businesslike. Stepfather had house property, hadn't he?"

"Yes." Wearily but quickly, "He left Mother three houses, this and the two next door. She sold the other two. They brought in about three thousand pounds. Most of that went to make Leonard a priest and Clara a nun. What's left is in First National Loan. It brings in about seventy-five or eighty pounds a year."

"Is that all he left?"

"He had some Great Southern Railway shares, too."

"Ordinary or preference?" asked St. John eagerly.

"Preference."

"How much?"

"Two thousand."

"Fine! That's bully. How much do they bring in?"

"Nothing."

"What!"

"No dividends have been payable on preference or ordinary stocks for years and years. They pay four per cent on the guaranteed preference stock only."

St. John rose to his height, blazing with his own power.

"By golly, but that's absolutely disgraceful! Not a cent? Do you mean to say not one cent on preference shares in Irish rails?"

Michael sighed. He was thinking of the hours, the days he spent arguing with brokers over that unfortunate stock. It was by now a family joke. Part of their mother's feebleness was firmly rooted in the idea that Irish railways were deliberately robbing her of the income of that stock. She had pestered every lawyer in town about it, until their clerks got to know her and now tactfully headed her off. Michael looked at St. John's heavy jowls, his wiry hair that stood up in a little sausage roll across his left forehead, his lined face, his eyes set close together, and he decided that his brother was probably a bit unbalanced by nature and had for years been wearing his nerves raw in New York.

"Look! Don't bother about it, St. John, old man," he said gently. "This is your holiday. Enjoy yourself and forget all about us."

"No, sir!" insisted St. John, striding up and down, his powerful shoulders braced. "I *am* going to bother about it. But why haven't *you* done something about it?"

"For the last ten years"—wearily as yawning—"people have been trying to do something about it. The government. Everybody. Oh!" he cried suddenly. "Look! St. John"—hands out, pleading—"all I ask you to do is please not to bother about us. We're all right."

"That's all right, Mickey. You must keep cool, you know. Mustn't excite yourself. By the way, did you ever take bromide? It's great stuff when you're worked up. It really is. Now, what else has she got?"

"Guinness," moaned Michael. "The stock brings her in about fifty pounds a year."

St. John wrote the items down rapidly in his little looseleaf notebook. His brother sank back softly and contentedly to his book. The fire on his champagne made it light up like an electric bulb.

"But," said St. John, looking up in amazement, "there must be more than that. You can't run a house like this on one hundred and thirty pounds a year? Six hundred and fifty dollars! It's impossible!"

With an alert patience—anybody but St. John might have felt the restraint in that slow, precise voice:

"My salary is three hundred a year. Natalie gets one hundred and thirty. She pays her own fees for evening courses at the Technical School out of that, clothes, holidays, and so on. Claude is earning nothing yet. But he has won a scholarship or two. He brings home extra work. It keeps him in cigarettes. Eolie does the housekeeping, so that saves us a maid. That is the sum total income of this house. Now please go away and work it out for yourself. I must say I don't see what interest it is of yours." He could not stop there. "It hasn't bothered you much for years! What's happened to your conscience all of a sudden?"

He returned firmly to his Maupassant.

"Why do you make it harder for me?" smiled St. John. "If I feel a generous impulse, why make it out to be just conscience? I came home just for this. America sucked me dry, so I came home *just for this!* To see you all—and Ireland—and become a Corkman all over again! I'm not really as selfish as you think, Mickey. I gotta help you. Besides"—glancing at his book—"five hundred and sixty pounds isn't an awful lot to keep six people."

In a low voice that was a summary of years of that scraping and scratching that kills the spirit, Mick said:

"It was much less once, and kept eight of us."

"So be it," insisted his brother, frowning and in a loud voice. "I'm going to do something about it. And"—soothingly, dropping his voice—"by the way, Mickey, you're a bit run down. You don't take enough exercise. Now, I take physical jerks every morning for four minutes by the clock. You ought to try them. I'll teach you some tomorrow. Now, I'm going to see about that drive to Cove, and maybe have a solid little talk with Eolie while I'm waiting."

He found himself alone on the landing, with a rattling window and a little pool of rain-water dripping softly on the floor from the sill. His head was humming with the excitement of the drink (mixed champagne and whisky) and the steam was oozing out of him. He stole to the next door, looked in, and saw his mother asleep and Natalie dozing again on the sofa. He came back to the loose window. He saw the light from the gas-lamp around the corner leap and fall on the pink gable across the laneway. Under his breath he murmured, to himself, "My God!"

Eolie came running up the stairs.

"Tea, Cursor. And then you ought to be going. Call Mickey and Natalie."

Opening the door, he beckoned to Michael. Michael refused, lifting the glass with a wry smile. He went in and opened him another bottle. "Do you good, old boy!" He came down the stairs with his arm on Natalie's shoulder. Below in the kitchen, cosy and bright, the coal-range glowing, the gas lightening the cheerful pale green of the walls (specially distempered for his home-coming), he had tea with the three girls. Because of Josephine—their guest—they talked and joked as gaily as if there were nothing but merriment before them; besides, St. John would be bringing back his wife and son; it was "an occasion." St. John told them some of his favourite after-dinner stories, and they had the greatest fun over the one about the patient who woke up after an operation and saw the raging flames of a burning factory across the road. "Crikey," howled the patient, "the operation has failed!" They had fun over it because Eolie could not see the joke, and when she did see it she laughed loud and long, and then said, in a very superior tone, "Silly! There's no point to that joke!" Then the city hall rang two, and Josephine broke up the little party. She said: "You must leave the quay, outside, at exactly ten minutes past two—to the second."

2 a.m.

A whole flock of gulls rose into the sky when the car's engine began to race. The turning headlights swept the scummy surface of the tide, and they read, "Butter Butter Butter" on a far facia-board. The sky was white and blue, bright with the remaining lights of the city. The Guard was not there, and the plain-clothes man made no demur about their going away to Cove. He merely smiled and observed Josephine with interest. It was exactly ten minutes after two as they drove into the wide Mall, turned left, turned back left again, doubling on their tracks, and slowed down in a narrow street that must have been somewhere to the rear of the island. There a man slipped out of a doorway, jumped to the car, clambered in, and Josephine gave the order to drive on, right, right again, fast, left, down the other branch of the river, across it, through a city as empty as a box, and out finally, down beside the open river estuary into the country. The air was not warm, but it was not cold, either. The touch of spring was kind to their cheeks.

"Is that Frankie?" asked St. John over his shoulder.

"Don't talk," said Frankie. "We're not safe until we're off the main road. Step on it."

Gradually the screen became flecked with night-flies, and St. John became so mesmerized by rolling hedges and swivelling patches of green field, headlamp-lit, that he gradually became fieldness and hedgeness. Night-scents blew into them. Once in a little village, where not one light showed, a reek of turf-tang gave his bowels a dissolving peristalsis; then, once more, the cold freshness of the fields, and the occasional glint of the sinking moon. They were travelling fast now on side-roads which the strange voice behind seemed to know as well as the palm of his hand. The hedges, sometimes, were so close together that their overhanging wisps flicked the pillars of the windshield. Once they pulled up with the brakes squeaking when they saw a moving ray in the sky ahead of them, and as they put out their own lights and switched off the engine they could not hear a sound but the crinkling of the exhaust pipe contracting as it cooled and the distant bark-bark of a dog howling at the moon. It was all exciting and mysterious in that late hour and dark land. They watched the line of the mountain range come out clear when the moon glanced at them. The raying light vanished—some late car on another road, miles away. There Frankie got out, and said:

"I'll take the wheel. Switch on the lights, first."

He put two enormous long-nosed revolvers into St. John's lap ("Mind them. They're loaded"), and going to the headlights spat into the glass of each and wiped them clean. St. John saw his face for the first time. His face was handsome but heavy; the jaw stuck out a bit; the nose had flat, wide nostrils; he wore no headgear, and his fair, wiry hair blew up from his sloped forehead in the wind like a halo. His light-blue, almost grey eyes stared into the headlights without blinking. Grinning, he looked back at them, swaggered around, and shook St. John's hand.

"Glad to meet you, St. John. I'm Frankie."

"Huh!" said St. John dryly. "Have a drink." He fished out a bottle of whisky from the back of the car and the two of them took a warmer apiece. "And now"—as his new brother slipped in the gears, and the car swished forward—"let me explain those gears. I'm fond of this car, you know."

"O.K." He memorized the gear-shift. He was lightning-quick. A dozen times he felt for the brakes and the position of the clutch until he had them printed on his mind. "Got it," he said after about a mile.

"Why do the police think you shot this general?"

"They don't. They just want to get me into jail. They're rounding us all up. They think I'm Chief of Staff of the Army."

"What army?"

"The Republican Army."

"I thought that was all over and done with years ago?"

Behind, Josephine snorted.

"Why should it be?" snapped Frankie, curtly.

"Well," considered the American, "I don't know . . ."

"Then, if you don't know what are you talking about?"

"Don't you try to bully me," snapped St. John back at him. "I'm asking you."

They dipped, and curved, and dropped gradually down to a lower level of river-valley. Between fury and disgust, Frankie drove faster and faster as he talked. He drove so recklessly that St. John had to jam his hat down on his head and grip the door. He turned to Josephine and yelled:

"Say, Jo! You're about the only sane person in this gol-darned racket. Is this fellow to be trusted with my car?"

"As long as he's in it!" she yelled, and laughed—she was enjoying the excitement.

"God! What a country!" yelled St. John, and turned back to his brother. "Go on. Tell me!"

He was told. . . .

In America St. John had seen the Irish revolution as a tight-packed design—a blackness like this night with black shapes rolling past. Like tonight, too, something was holding down a gentler, sweeter, more familiar life as with a curtain of sleep. He had read about it as we read about any foreign war. There is, perhaps, a siege that goes on for weeks, months, like the siege of the Alcazar; we hear of it at intervals when some new excitement floodlights it. But the slow attrition, the wearing of the spirit, the despair of the heart, the stripping of the nerves—that we never realize; not even the casualties come home to us—and that is such a good word for what happens so casually that it is never made personal for anybody but one or two unheard-of relatives. As he listened to Frankie's loud voice, he realized for the first time how these things always must come down in the end to the personal drama. As he listened, it all suddenly came down to one man hiding in a house, with an old woman babbling in her bed, and two or three girls forgetting everything else in order to protect him. The realization gave him a twitch of the nerves—the sort of jab that makes a limb jump when we are asleep. It hurt him to think back to that island house, away down in the pocket of Cork; to Natalie who was no more than a black kitten; Eolie with her sucked-in cheeks, worn body, and good-natured eyes; Claude, least of all affected by anything that went on, asleep in the little return room, surrounded—St. John guessed at a better, and it was the accurate word—"defended" by his books and his drawings, so many fine-drawn, meticulous images of himself. He thought of Michael's life.

That house on the island had so often given him a belly-ache of desire in New York that he had cherished his thought of it as if it were a grail. The very specks of cement floated on the back-yard; the bits of fallen plaster in the lavatory—he had, as a kid, picked them off into shapes of men and countries: the triangle that was India, and then one under it for Africa, and then the two joined for the Americas—the swan-neck drain-pipe under the eave where he hid his first pipe—

all of them, mere bits of clay, mere lumps of iron, black with mud, had the power to cut channels into his heart time and time and time again during the last thirty-four years. He felt Frankie was talking things that had nothing at all to do with what Ireland meant to him, or to anybody. He turned around to have a look at Josephine's face. He shouted:

"What do you think of all this ballyhoo?"

He saw nothing in the dark. He switched on the dashboard light. They were doing fifty. He tried to see Frankie's face. All he saw was a moving lower lip and, to his surprise, a gentle, dreamy eye gazing ahead into the road.

"Revolutions," Frankie was shouting, "are very slow processes. The terrorist never realizes that. It's not his job. You must distinguish between a terrorist and a revolutionary. The terrorist may be employed by the revolutionary. I'm not a terrorist, so I'd never have shot Blennerhasset. What I want is a change in Irish life. And by God we're going to get that change! We fought for it, but we didn't get it. We've got to get it. . . ."

Again St. John looked at that eye before he dismissed it into the dark; and it was Natalie's eye—mild, innocent, beseeching. A mouse trembling in the fist might look like that. Astonished, he gave himself up to the endless swirl of hedge, and the faint pricks of the planets over the rolling line of mountain. Not until they halted finally did St. John see that eye again; and then he saw that it had an enemy. The left eye was all intelligence, abstract, its blueness frozen on the surface.

"Frankie"—suddenly—"if Mother dies, what are you all going to do with the house? Sell it?"

"What are you talking about?"

"The house."

"I don't know anything about the house. I've not been in it, except off and on, for the last ten . . ." He stopped. The car lurched forward into more speed. "Good God, it's nearer fifteen years. Since the Black and Tans."

He fell silent. The accumulation of years might have choked him. The two brothers sat side by side and for miles they said nothing after that. It was as if Time, like sin, having deserted them, came back with redoubled power and was eating them up. How well St. John knew that tyranny! "If you haven't," he used to say to his young executives in New York, "made good by forty you may give up. For, remember this, there's a last date for *beginning*. And it's well before forty. It takes fifteen years for any man—I don't care what he is, whether he's selling hair-combs, or making canary-seed, or painting pictures—to get in the harvest of his youth. Fifteen years. God Almighty"—he would always break off at that point, and the way his face would always cloud over never failed to impress his young men—"what a short life we have! Get out!" he would roar at that. "Get out, and let me work! Let me work!"

No, Frankie was talking through his hat. He didn't understand life. He didn't understand Ireland. Ireland was where you lived, had a home, rooted yourself; or, even if you could not live in it, where you got the sap that you felt rising up in your tiptopoutmost veins when you were feeling down and out. When you were all balled up, Ireland gave meaning to life. That was why you could always trust an Irishman in the long run. No matter how he might swindle, dodge, let you down, you could always dig down to that rich, good thing in him that you could appeal to.

The Lincoln hummed along. They cut across a tree-shaded road. They entered another tree-shaded road, a main road St. John guessed by the width and smoothness of it. They left this abruptly and took another dirt road, and this suddenly petered out into a moorland track, along which, in the headlights, they could see the grass between the wheel-tracks. The mystery of the night spread now on all sides into the sea of darkness about the bog. They had to shift gears—they were climbing. The bog was left behind. A whitewashed cabin, its gable to the road, indicated that farmland was beginning again. They went up and up, and a gale suddenly hit them like a bucket of water or a flat blow by a powerful, invisible hand.

"You're almost in County Limerick," said Frankie. "That wind is from over the gap."

Suddenly, for no apparent reason, they halted, and the lights went dead, and Frankie leaped out.

"We're there," he said, and pocketed the two Webleys to show that he felt safe now. Cold and stiff, St. John clambered out on his side and tried to see what lay around them. They seemed to be in a wide glen, dour with shadow. It had the vacuity of a No! He retrieved the bottle of whisky, took a slug to warm himself, and glanced at the dashboard clock; half-three. Then he followed the girl and his half-brother across a dry ditch into the fields.

By the dim radiance of the stars that came and went, and the upflung light of the occasional moon behind a wall of mountain before them, they crossed three fields. They were poor land, thistle-crackling, tight-cropped bog-fields, otherwise bare except that a giant with a load of rocks might have dropped one here and one there. They came up to a whitewashed cabin with whitewashed outbuildings; the cabin was thatched but the sheds were roofed with black tarred felt. All stood in a little garden behind a slight shelter-belt of larch and a wall of monoliths. A dog was baying at them, hurling himself at one of the outbuilding doors. Frankie went up to the cabin ahead of the others, stood under its thatch that over-hung the door like a porch, and, knocking like a soldier, shouted:

"Manus! This is Frankie."

"What place is this?" asked the American.

"You ought to know it," scorned Frankie. "You were born here. Manus!"

"Here?"

At once the maw of the valley, hitherto cold, empty, negative, resistant, became full of moment. Then it was thrust back into blackness.

"But that's wrong. I was born in Cork city."

"Who told you so?"—as he kicked and shouted. (The dog bayed and the hens woke up and fluttered.) But the house was as silent as the rocks strewn about the field.

"Mother did. Or I think she did."

"Tshah! Part of her finery. Did you ever know the people here have a nickname for Mother? 'Grandy.' That's what they call her. Wouldn't you know it? Eolie, Natalie, Leonard, Clara, St. John, Claude." He mocked each elegant name. "You were born here. My aunt often told me." He kicked savagely. "Manus! . . . Lie down, Griffin. . . . I'll knock down this bloody door. What's wrong, Josephine?"

She had come forward, tall as a queen, and stopped now under the door, and felt for a key.

"It's not there. Light your torch." He did, and by its light she looked into the keyhole. "It's not there, either."

She looked around the valley. St. John was also looking.

"But why wasn't I born in Cork?" he asked eagerly.

"Oh, because your father's people came from here—this hillside. Josephine is your cousin, and so is Manus. Your mother came back here to your father's place to have her first two children, yourself and Mick."

"I have come home," said St. John solemnly, and he took off his hat.

"He must have gone down to Aunt Nell's," said Josephine to the gunman. "We'd better go down before we let the car go, and see if they were raided again."

He said nothing but turned down the field, and Jo led the American after him. He allowed her to lead him as if he were sleepwalking.

"Born here!" he assured her as they went down the path. He kept stopping and looking back.

"You'll turn to a pillar of salt!" she laughed.

"But"—gripping her arm—"I was *born* there. Do you realize I was *born* there? I wish—I'd give ten pounds if it was only light enough to see."

He stuck where he stood. The light wind came up the valley and brought the sound of distant streams. The bog suckled the rain-water. The vast space of the entire county lay below them. The motion of that car was in their bones; the night laid a wet hand on ears that drummed with that dead humming. The marsh-prattling silence of this barely audible and wholly invisible world was a halt to life itself; the background to sleep, itself a sleep.

"Come on," she begged.

He took a few more steps and turned again. Far and wide his senses felt the vacancy of further space beyond this valley, unmapped for him; the great Limerick plain out to the Shannon estuary dilated the void as if the wind blew it up; he felt diminished without knowing what that darkness hid. A little far light in a farmhouse in County Cork was meaningless as a star. Frankie's voice calling them came feebly. Impatiently she dragged him up on a stile. Aerated he climbed, light as a boy, and on top he spread his arms and cried, swaying there in his leather coat and holding out his grey felt hat.

"I feel I could fly! Jo! I *could* fly!"

"Don't be a soft bit of Yankee chewing-gum," she stormed at him. "This is serious for Frankie."

He clambered down heavily, and began explaining to her that she did not understand, she *could* not understand, following her a foot behind, a garrulous, fat old man who had been overdrinking, slopping through pools, bog-slush, falling over outcropping rocks of shale until they came to a lighted window and heard another dog bark. The light was repeated in an outbuilding where they could hear Frankie's voice mingling with other voices.

"Manus is here," she told St. John. "It's Nell's cow. She's in calf."

They went along the causeway to the second light, where they could hear the groans of the cow and through the door of a shed see dim shapes with their twins of shadow. A lantern's light had barely room to steal out between them. There were four people in the shed, too many for the space: an old woman with a goffered white bonnet tied under her chin, a tall, lean man in swallow-tails, Frankie in his mackintosh, and a tubby man who was Manus. Over the grunting and the struggling, the steam of breath, the ruffled straw, the gasps of the woman pulling the calf out of the cow, they heard Frankie shouting:

"Don't let him fall on the floor!"

Manus crawled out and ran past them and was back at once with a sack. He threw it in.

"Chrisht!" He mopped his head. "It's baking in there."

"Have a drink," said St. John and gave him the pint bottle. The tubby man unstoppered it and took a swig. St. John took another swig.

"You're Manus," he said then. "Shake! I'm your cousin."

"You're welcome," said Manus and turned to peer in.

"I'm honoured," said St. John. "You know," he said eagerly, pulling at Manus, "I've just heard I was born up there in your house. I've just heard it!"

"Pull, you divil! Pull!" the long man was roaring at the old woman.

"Here he comes!" cried Frankie.

They looked in at the struggling group. Already two legs had appeared outside the cow. Between two of them the lantern suddenly shone on the head of the calf coming out of the cow's side of fur. The calf seemed to stare at them in astonishment. A third leg was hauled out. With a convulsive rush the last of the body followed and then the sack filled with the wet red calf. There were little cries of satisfaction from the group. Manus turned, and relaxed.

"God bless it," he said.

"And indeed may Gawd bless it," agreed St. John.

Then Manus looked at the American. "You know," he said quietly, "it was not up in my place ye were born. You're St. John?" (He pronounced it Sinjin, with the sweet slender vowels of the Cork countryman.) "No, Mr. Hannafey. I'm the teacher here, and I have the greatest interest in genealogies of all kinds. You were born in *this* house. Your grandmother's house." He halted. He looked along the wall of the outbuilding. He looked up—he was only about four foot nine—at St. John. "Mr. Hannafey, this is the old house, along here. They put up the new house during the war!"

Almost without doing it—as if fearing to offend a stranger—he indicated the interior of what was now a shed and from whose open doorway the rays of the lantern floated out to them with the smell of fodder.

"Mr. Hannafey, if you want to know, you were born in there."

St. John Hogan-Hannafey looked, mouth open, into the

dung-smelling byre. He looked at the cobwebbed walls, the loophole window, the straw of the roof bulging down; an old broken hayfork was stuck into it; one rafter sagged. He looked back over the field. Again the darkness enveloped him. Its mystery reduced him to nothing. It was as if somebody kept pulling the axle out of his wheel, and he kept on flying off into the air.

"It used to be the back-room of the old house, Mr. Hannafey," the little fat teacher was explaining timidly.

"Then Frankie was mistaken in saying I was born up there, in your cottage?"

"Ah! Frankie picks up things wrong. There's no doubt about it. You can ask my aunt Nell."

"Well," said St. John, at last, "we talk, in America, about rising from log-cabin to White House. But here it is—from cowshed to . . . to H. H. Shoes. . . . So this is my paternal origin; the rock from which I was hewn."

"Indeed, it is," agreed Manus, pleased with the metaphor, and relieved that the American had not been offended.

"And my mother's place?"

Manus waved his hand into the dark.

"The Nagles originally came from down there in Kilavullen." He waved up the other way towards the gap from which the wind swirled down. "You have an aunt, too, in Kilfinnane, in the County Limerick."

"I will go there," declared St. John firmly. "But before I leave this spot I'm going to stand right inside in that—in that—I may call it a manger, and I'm going to commune with my ancestors."

"It would be a right thing to do," approved the teacher.

The three inside came out the byre, and to make way on the narrow causeway Josephine directed her brother and her

American cousin to move back to the house. They went along past the brighter light, with its reflection on the causeway, and went into the kitchen. A tall, bony-faced young woman was sitting by the fire, the eldest daughter of the house. It was a family of girls, explained Manus; the others—four of them—were sleeping.

"Frankie," said St. John, "you were wrong. I was born *here*—out there in the old portion of this house."

"Well," grinned Frankie, with the typical cynical Cork humour, "that's neither here nor there. This is my American brother, Nell," he said to the old woman by way of introduction. "Half-brother, if you want to be exact. He's a relation of yours. I'm not."

The old woman welcomed him.

"Now, give us a cup of tea," cried Frankie. "Give me that contraption," he ordered the daughter, and took the handle of the mechanical bellows and began to whirl it until the sparks of the turf flew up the maw of the chimney. He was obviously entirely at home in the house. They had made him one of their own. "Is that kettle near boiling, Mary?"

"It was waiting for you," teased the young woman. "It came all right?" she asked her mother, and the old woman, washing her hands in a basin made ready for her, said:

"It did, God bless it. Jim is without now; he'll make them easy for the night. You'll have to sit up and see she doesn't overlay it. Sit down, sir," she bade the stranger.

"What 'sirring' you have!" upbraided Frankie. "His name is St. John."

"Faith, then," she said, drying her hands, "I'll call you no St. John. That was another of Grandy's notions. I'll call you John, or Jack, but divil the word else. And you can call me your aunt Nell."

"I was born here, ma'am," said St. John solemnly, sitting by the fire, his grey felt hat on his knee.

"Faith you were," the old woman assured him. "Yourself and Mickey. Your father, God rest his soul, poor Johnny, thought there was nothing for children like the country air. It was as well, for your mother couldn't nurse you. She had the best of food, and you had the best of milk, and plenty of us to give her attention. A thing," commented the old woman with dry sarcasm, "that all the Nagles had a great liking for. At that time he had the shop east in Kilavullen. From that he went into Fermoy, and from that—nothing less would please her—she made him come into Cork city. Ah, well!" she sighed. "It killed him. Your mother, I hear, isn't too well. So Jo tells me. She has a hard life of it in the end. But she killed her husband, and that's as sure as I'm talking to you. She had high notions, and poor Johnny paid for them. Nothing would please her but a big house, and finery, and wanting to send her children to the best schools. Huh! She got her wish with that ruffian there"—looking affectionately at Frankie. "Sent him up to the university, if you please. Cock him up with education, if you please. And damn the examination did he ever pass, by the same token."

"Ireland needed me more, Nell." Frankie winked good-humouredly.

"Bring out that drink," ordered the old matriarch, suddenly dismissing the subject of their talk as something that was interfering with hospitality.

"I have some whisky," offered St. John, lifting out his bottle.

"Jim will be glad of it, John," said the old woman. "But we have something special for yourself."

"Nell!" protested Josephine.

"What do I want it for?" said her aunt. " 'Tis all blatherumskite that they can ever cure me. We were arranging the funeral, and we waiting for the calf. Come in, Jim," she bade the elongated farmer, who now appeared in from the byre, stooping under the door. "There's a drop of the hard stuff here for you."

"What funeral are you talking about?" asked Frankie, and St. John saw that he was unusually pale.

"We were talking about it before ye came," said the long man, as he took a glass of St. John's whisky from Mary.

"You don't know Jim Barry?" introduced Nell, and St. John shook hands with the tall man.

"What we were saying," went on Jim Barry, leaning his elbow thoughtfully on his knee and contemplating the whisky, "was it wouldn't be right for Manus to go under the coffin."

"What coffin?" demanded Frankie, and St. John saw that his mouth was freezing hard.

"My own coffin," said Aunt Nell, quietly, as she took a bottle of champagne from her daughter and poured a half-pint glass full for St. John.

"Where did ye get that?" demanded Frankie threateningly.

" 'Tis her medicine," groaned Josephine. "Her throat."

Frankie jumped up. He knew now what they were talking about.

"Nell, were you in with the doctor?" She nodded. "What did he say?"

"Wisha, he told me what I knew. The day before yesterday I went in. They can't cure me, Frankie boy. He told me to be taking that stuff, and to please him I bought a bottle."

"No relatives ever went under a coffin by rights," laid down Jim Barry. "They do be too weak with sorrow to carry't."

"That's right, surely," said Manus. "It is a tradition," he explained to the stranger. (He had taken it on him to be guide for St. John.)

Mary had poured a glass of champagne for Frankie but he brushed it aside in a fury; she handed it to Manus, who accepted it.

"You should thry it, Frankie," chided Jim Barry. "It's comical shtuff the way it do tickle your nose."

"You must go to Cork," urged Frankie, "and see a proper doctor. I'll fix it up for you and it won't cost you a penny. You must go to Dublin to a specialist."

"Now, boy," cautioned the old woman, "don't be upsetting me, and I with my mind settled and fixed on dying."

" 'Tis cancer, all right," said Josephine.

"Look!" cried Jim Barry, holding out his fist, closed. "What have I in my fisht?" He opened. "That's all the doctors can do for you. Nothing."

Manus interposed a ruminative thread of voice:

"Frankie is no relative. If he could be here, he could go under the coffin."

St. John got up. He put the champagne down untasted. He and his step-brother were the only two standing. The others were looking at the fire, or at the old woman, their faces entirely untouched by any expression of emotion. He went and filled himself a jorum of his own whisky.

"Are you all daft?"—from Frankie. "Dozens of people have been cured who thought they had cancer. Are you mad?"

"Ah, wisha," complained the woman, petulantly. "Why do you be upsetting me? You don't understand, Frankie. I'm an old woman now, and at the most my longest is short. My mind is made up. What's put before us by the Man Above is what we have to take, good or bad, soft or hard alike. I have my passage now and all I'm waiting for is the old American trunk to take me home."

"Every single thing is arranged," soothed Barry. "Down to the five pounds will go to the priest. All that is left is who will go under the coffin."

"And," reminded the old woman, "who will wear my clothes the Sunday after the funeral."

St. John swayed over; all he said was, down to Manus: "It's hot."

"My God!" Frankie implored the ceiling. Then he controlled himself. "Nell!" he begged, but Barry waved him back, holding out the champagne St. John had put down untasted.

"Be aisy," he said. "Take a sup of that. Look at the way it jumps!"

"Ye're a mad, bloody lot of savages!" yelled the gunman.

"Frankie!" warned Josephine.

"You're a nurse"—he turned on her—"and ought to support me."

She sighed, and turned away her head, wearily. She knew the country people. Just because she was a nurse she knew how little you can do with them. St. John leaned over Manus and whispered, thickly: "I want to go out, and commune."

The two went out to the godly coolness of the night.

"Don't be long," warned Jo. "You have to drive to Cove, yet."

He waved a hand and staggered along the causeway to the byre. Inside he could hear the cow making wet noises with her tongue; she was licking the newborn calf. The teacher like an acolyte opened the door and invited St. John to go in. St. John, swaying a little, paused as a priest might pause before the entry to the altar.

"My friend," he said, "would you like to get me a lantern? And bring me some of my liquor."

"Yes, to be sure, Mr. Hannafey," agreed the acolyte.

When he went back to the kitchen it was hot with argument. Josephine was between restraining Frankie's anger and trying to persuade her aunt to listen to her as Manus got the lantern and, after filling up Jim Barry's glass, took the whisky bottle. He handed the bottle to St. John and went into the stable to light the oil-lantern. Before he handed it reverently to the American, Manus took his hand.

"I approve, Mr. Hannafey," he assured him, "of your sentiments. You know the Hannafeys were a very famous family at one time."

"Can well b'lieve it," said St. John, leaning on him.

"Yes, Mr. Hannafey. I have a book above that gives the history of all the families of Kerry. The Hannafeys were a great people. They are of the tribe of the O hAinfeain. They are, to my knowledge, of a Nordic type, usually of small stature, and light-coloured in hair. This type"—still holding St. John's hand—"is always of a great intensity of energy, and express themselves in patriotic endeavour, or in business affairs."

"Mosh' interesting," said St. John, contemplating the flaccid body of the calf. "Matter of fact I'm not a Hannafey. I'm a Hogan."

"Oh!" said the teacher. Then, unperturbed, he said: "The Hogans come from the West and Midlands. We find them in Clare, in Longford, in Limerick. They have come into this country across the Galtees and the Ballyhouras. The Hogans are also of small stature, light-coloured in hair, and of great intensity of purpose."

"I feel," said St. John, and began to quote:

"The pressure of an unfelt hand,
The kisses of a lip unseen,
The throb of my dear mother's heart,
My father's smile revived once more.

That's Denis Florence MacCarthy."

The two stood belly to belly, the bottle in St. John's fist, the lantern in Manus's.

"Mr. Hogan, I have the greatest possible regard for all forms of tradition. I have studied local traditions in all their aspects. I record local tales for the Folk Lore Institute. A man came down here from Dublin with a dictaphone to hear me record the memories of the past. Do you know that? A great invention!" he added in a voice that somehow made the invention personal to himself and to his memories.

St. John sat down on an upturned half-tub. He gave the bottle to Manus, watched the bubbles rise in it, and took it back, and drank.

"Tradition," he said, "is the thing we haven't got 'n America. But Ireland? Never changes. I came home for this. I'm happy."

"Tradition," agreed the little fat teacher, as he leaned one hand on the wall, "is a great thing. That, of course, is why Frankie stands for the Republic! Why we all do!"

"He's a great young fellow," said St. John. "But, then, all my family is great. Every one of them. And"—his fist aloft, and his eye roving blindly until it was fixed by the stare of the cow—"look at what we came out of!"

"There you have it!"

"I'm going to commune," decided St. John. "Would you oblige me by leaving me for a few moments?"

"To be sure. It's a proper thing to do."

"Have a drink before you go," said St. John, and they both

drank. Then Manus went out, reverently, closed the door, and going back found the argument fallen into a sullen monologue from Frankie, the others too tired or too courteous to tell him to stop or to hint that they wanted to go to bed; so that, in the end, it was Frankie himself who became aware of the hour. He got up and said a sullen, defeated "Good night to ye!" and went out with Manus and Josephine. They sent Manus home, and stood talking on the causeway, waiting for St. John. Still caught up in the emotion of the scene he had left he put an arm around Jo's shoulder; he was thinking so deeply he let her (unusual passivity in him) fasten his collar tightly about his neck, for her own cough had warned her how cold it must be for him also, after the great heat of the kitchen. The light went out in the window behind them. A faint hint of the end of the night was in the paleness of the stars. The moon had gone.

"It's queer," he said, bitterly, "but if there's one person in the world who put me where I am this minute it's that old woman. I can't *think* of her being snuffed out. The way she talks of the Famine, and Dan O'Connell, and Emancipation, and '98, or the way the landlords ground them to bits—it's all as if she was two hundred. One thing is just as near her as another. These people don't know where their own memory stops and their grandfather's begins. Somehow when she goes everything will go. For me, anyway."

"She knows you since you were a little fellow," she said fondly, and slipped her arm around his waist; and again he permitted it. She was seeing that photograph Natalie showed her of the small boy on the lap of the man with the big moustaches and the merry eyes. All his love for the old woman bound him to her the way an old tree binds tiptop twigs that brush one another at every breeze. The image came naturally to her, but she did not dare say it; he might taunt her with being "soft"—his favourite taunt for many people.

"She and my father," he boasted, "were the only people who ever had any influence over me."

"Yes," she said, hoping he would go on talking. They so rarely talked like this, with the intimacy of lovers. "In his office on the Mall I first met them—coming in to him to know where they would invest their few quid. Coming in to him because of my mother. Keeping up the old connexion they had with the city through the butter-and-egg man."

She knew this was a reference to "John Hogan and Sons," her uncle's shop that died with him.

He squeezed her shoulder.

"Jo," he went on, "if it wasn't for the butter and eggs, I'd never have met you. I'd never—it might easily happen—be a Republican, or never be where I am now."

"I've heard that kind of talk before," she smiled.

"Oh! My determinism? Well, I suppose that's why I'm half a Communist."

"Frankie," she ventured, seizing her opportunity, "wouldn't you think of going out of the country for a month or two?"

"I would if I could." He unloosed his hand and with a sigh she felt it go. "But only for a month or two, mind you!"

"Wouldn't it be a grand thing," she tempted him, "to go to New York and collect some money?"

"I'd love to see America. I'd love it! You know I really would—I've often thought about America. I'd love to meet the New York radicals. Outside of Paris I don't believe there's a finer group anywhere in the world. You know"—warming to it—"America is a country I believe in. It's a capitalist state, I know—a democracy ruled by a bureaucracy for the benefit of the few—but I feel there's *life* there, there's vitality, and there's people who understand what is happening in the world today. Here . . ."

His body dramatized weariness, lassitude; took on an imitative slouch, hostage to a slouching mind. Then it stiffened and became erect, made heroic by the mind, eager, mortal, living.

"Ah! But . . . I'd love to see America," he said in his normal voice, and his normal, human posture.

"Listen, Frankie! It could be managed, surely? In the Troubles it was managed over and over. If you could lie low for a week or two I could manage it for you. If you tell me what to do, whom to see, I'd get some money and do everything you tell me to do."

He looked at her.

"You're a great kid, Jo!"

She put her arms around his shoulders, and said, "You know I'd do more than that for you."

"This bloody country!" he said, exasperatingly, looking over her shoulder, and as he went on she relaxed and drew aside.

She drew aside and drew her coat about her and closed her mouth tight, because she wanted to say, "Oh, Frankie, Frankie, you're off again. You're like a seagull I saw in Cork last night swimming against the tide and not stirring a foot. Frankie, Frankie, for God's sake why don't you give me a kiss and squeeze the guts out of me? Oh, Frankie, I've heard this sort of thing, and I've heard it until I'm sick of it. All my life long I'm sick of keeping my mouth shut while men like you came to our house up there, sat and talked like this, were followed by more men who said the same things—uncaging their rages against priests because they are lazy, and businessmen who are hypocrites and toady to the priests, and politicians who toady to the businessmen, and farmers who trust politicians and can never be stirred out of the old ways—

all caught up in a net of vested interests; that was the password, 'vested interests.' Oh, Frankie, I'm so *tired* of it! I wish you'd make your peace with life, let things settle. Let time do a little work for you. . . ."

She had thought it all so often. She had never said it. She turned and looked at him, where he was railing against what to her was Tom, and Dick, and Jim, and Bill—all the common life that she had lived with so long and so patiently that she had learned how to accept it without being choked by it, and to understand it without hating it. It was like Aunt Nell's throat, and Jim Barry arranging for the funeral.

"Frankie!" she cried suddenly, all her dams down in one rush. And she threw her arms about him and kissed him passionately on the cheek. "Frankie, you *are* going to America, aren't you? For my sake?"

At once she felt her arms taken in his hands and put firmly away. She could almost feel his glare. She shivered with disappointment, realizing that she had done what she always knew she must not do—dared to mingle herself with his decisions. A man, at that point, might have said to him all that she had wanted to say two minutes before; or summed it all up in a "Blast you, you vain little fool!" Being a woman, not experienced, made by nature to hinge on his nature, wounded by his weakness, she knew that she could only again—yet again—keep silent. But of silence she had given all she had; speak she must; and she had only one way of speech left that would not wound him.

"You'll be all right," she said. "I must go home now. It's cold. Say good-bye to St. John for me." She turned and ran—halted to say: "Make St. John hurry. He must be at Cove by five o'clock," and ran away through the haggard and up the fields, bursting into tears as soon as she felt sure that he would not hear her. She found that Manus was in bed; she made a red centre glow in the fire and sat over it, and her crying shook her weak chest, and the tears wrung her until her face was comical in its red ugliness.

For she knew that if he did go away she would not see him for a long time; even if he did not go, such was his wandering life. She thought, then, of the great liner bringing St. John's family to land, and she could image it all lighted in the tranquil harbour out of which she had seen many a boy and girl go—who never returned. Later, when the morning wind came up the glen and ruffled the thatch, she was still shaking a little—like a child recovering from some small misery. There are no words to describe such unhappiness as hers. There is no refuge from it but the refuge she found.

She found one other, and then sleep was kinder to her than her lover had been. The late morning revealed what it was—her rosary-beads, lost down somewhere in the hollow of the feather-bed. She made a funny picture, as she knelt up, poking for them. . . .

5 a.m.

Frankie was driving the Lincoln towards Cove, with a sodden St. John lolling in the back. There had been no other way of getting him to the boat, and as if to make up for his cruelty to Jo he had decided, against all common sense, to chance it. He drove so well that it was only five to five when he halted above the cold expanse of Cork Harbour. Nothing but a naval fleet could have removed the empty look of so much water all in the one place. It was not yet quite dawn, but from somewhere up in the zenith an eye might actually look down at the still-hidden sun, even as to the east, in England, they had already seen it. Here, the forehead of Europe was dark.

In the back of the car St. John woke up and groaned; whereupon Frankie turned and looked at him sourly. He turned away to see if the liner was in the bay and saw it far out beyond the enclosing callipers of the coast that all but met, at the forts of the harbour mouth; it bore a tiny row of lights on its flank; it was a ranked army of jack-o'-lanterns approaching Ireland, a little cargo of the lights that had begun to vanish from the sky. He watched its slow motion for a while—there would be plenty of time yet before it was met by the tender in the bay—and then surveyed the few little yachts, smaller than corks, that floated inshore, their riding-lights still aglow; the street-lamps in the town; one or two night-lit window-squares; patches of life mocked at by the sky and water.

In the surrounding silence of common sleep those odd window-squares in a town seem to break the laws of nature. The mind, night-inflamed, exaggerates its own wonder at them. They grow into images of strange gatherings; of the endless goings and comings, into or out of the world; not merely one birth, or one death, but the ebb and flow of life; and, at last, the abnormal within life that violently asserts or defies it. These few common window-lights made the morning exciting even as that one lighted ship so magically expanded the bay, and the sky, and the land about.

"Where am I?" groaned St. John.

"In Cove," murmured Frankie without turning his head.

So much of Irish life had passed through this small town that Frankie, for whom (no matter what he might think or say) Life and Ireland were still two words for one experience, could not take his eyes from the view before him. He had been interned during the revolution in Spike Island, oblong in the bay; so had the Fenian convicts; so had, for a while,

John Mitchel. The two forts at the mouth of the bay, Camden and Carlisle, something brutal in their very names, and still garrisoned by English soldiers, held the narrow entry in their lions' paws. The roofs of the town itself had sheltered not thousands but hundreds of thousands of emigrants on their eve of exile, each with his wheel-cake for the voyage under his arm, his mattress of ivy-leaves, the ritual knife and fork and spoon and mug, the lemon to suck against seasickness, and a few golden coins sewn up somewhere in his clothes. Ever since the forties the little town had seen them pouring out of Ireland, away from famine, away from brutality, to hope, to life, or, so often, either to a burial at sea—thousands had sunk into the Atlantic during the bad times—or to a new brutality in meeting which they displayed their one and only art.

"Cove?" asked St. John, leaning forward.

Frankie was so moved he could not speak; he stared before him, an image more than a man. Behind him, in answer to some maudlin association, St. John was wailing out the old song "Youghal Harbour":

> "In Youghal harbour, and in your keeping,
> Awake or sleeping, I left heart and mind . . .

"Thash Willie Rooney's song," he said. "He said good-bye down there to Mitchel when they were taking him to Van Diemen's Land."

" 'Twas Ned Walsh," corrected Frankie, "who said good-bye to Mitchel. He taught the convicts on Spike."

"Maybe 'twas, Frankie. I sang that shong every week o' my life in New York.

> " 'Twas not your hair to the breezes blowing
> Or lips red-glowing caused me unrest . . .
> 'Twas some sweet charm beyond expressing . . ."

The cracked, squeaky voice was too painful to listen to. Getting out, Frankie said brutally:

"Your wife is on that liner. She will be here in ten minutes. Are you too drunk to meet her?"

"I'm not drunk. I'm overcome." He got out. He could just stand, and barely walk. He could be helped down the steep hills—so many of them are stepped because of their steepness—but walk down alone he could not.

"I have no wife but Ireland. I love Ireland." He walked to the hedge and, straddling there and still gazing at the sea, he began to make water. He heard the silence of the true dawn spread over the countryside, and when he looked back at the tips of the far mountains they were already fern-red. He heard a cock-crow appeal, a stuttering, wandering croaking, somewhere below them, a Queenstown back-yard calling to the dawn. As he stood there he said again, "I love Ireland."

He did not see Frankie walk away in disgust, because behind the dark and shrivelled sea his bleary eyes had suddenly seen the magical glow. As he looked it was so still all over the wide land and bay that the night might have been spent in arranging for that hour. He almost felt in the air the invisible flutterings of skyey beings putting the last invisible touches to the stage of the world—to every wave and every field. He waited, mouth open, but because his eyes began to wander to the cold green hills in the south-west the final explosion of the sun took him by surprise. There she was, already defying his eyes. She rose up and as she rose she was twin; one sun balanced on another, thrusting up out of her egg; and this second bubble of blood kept rising slowly beneath the first until he wondered was it because of the drink that he was seeing this miracle of a double sun. Steadily balanced on her own mirage, she was delivered whole and circular to the world, and then the under bubble burst. The sun was up.

Straddling and buttoning, he waddled over to his half-brother, but Frankie was also watching the wonder and did not speak. They both looked at it. Nobody else, for all they could see, took any notice of it. The cows munching in the field beside them did not kneel and adore. No birds broke into sudden song; they merely cried their usual indifferent cries; guttural hens and cocks, or the weak sparrow-chirpings of any hour of the day; otherwise there was no new sign or sound, except when away across the bay, in some seaside hamlet, a few cottage windows flashed. At last St. John spoke, blinking twenty green-yellow gold suns from his watery eyes, knowing now that all that his secret soul had craved was necessary for all mortal men.

"If a man," he said, "could do anything as good as that, he'd never stop talking about't. Nature stands and waits. Takes in. Gives out. Everything 'n its own place. That's the way we should all live."

Frankie, sitting on the ditch, was smoking; there was a look of agony in his face.

"Ah," sighed St. John, sitting beside him, caressing his own throbbing head, "this's th' only land where things go on and on. Where people live like that. I want to live in Ireland, Frankie! I *must* live in Ireland."

Frankie got up and went to the car and got out the whisky bottle. He handed it silently to St. John—the "hair of the dog that bit him." The liner was now invisible. It was rounding the point and would soon drop anchor for the tender.

"Can you walk down there?" he said.

"I'll try. I feel better after that." He got up and flung the bottle, with its leavings, over the hedge. "The last drop I drink in Ireland," he said. He looked at his half-brother, and he suddenly seemed to realize how they were situated. "But, Frankie, why'd *you* come here?"

Frankie was watching the unstirring white waves by the distant nose of Weaver's Point. All he said he said in a low monotone, almost spiritless, as if he were confessing to himself, "You and your bloody ancestors."

"Frankie"—taking his arm—"you're suffering for Ireland."

"Shut up. I'm getting fed up with all this. I wish I was on that boat. With its nose turned the other way. I wish to God I was born in the Bronx!" He held up his hand. "Listen to that! That's the tender's siren. That car is a bloody millstone around my neck. What the hell am I going to do?" He looked at St. John, trying to size him up the way he would have sized up a man for some dangerous job during the Troubles. "You can't even drive as far as the pier. St. John, you're a washout!"

"Frankie, I'll drive to the pier, and I'll drive back here, and I'll drive you anywhere in the world you like!"

"I wouldn't trust you. Besides, you'd draw so much attention to yourself that I can just see that nice big car of yours being held up afterwards by a nice small patrol on the road out of the town. A nice, small, polite little patrol! That car, you fathead, has its number hanging up in the dayroom of every barracks in the county. No, the old way is the best way —risk it. I'm going to drive you, blast you, into Cove." Roused as he always was by the excitement of his calling, he became buoyant again. "*Toujours de l'audace*, Mr. Hogan-bloody-well-Hannafey! If you know what that means? Get in!" Humbly, St. John clambered into the car.

The siren was blowing again, up to the sleeping roofs of the town as they drove into it, down through the twisting, narrow streets that followed the contours and went from the higher to the lower with hairpin bends; through the connecting laneways they saw the tender draw away its wake of foam, and the great side of the liner move visibly into the harbour. As they went sliding quietly down to the water-level streets they met nobody but one expectant jarvey and two sleepy-looking baggagemen wheeling their trucks to the deep-water quay. With his eyes roving alertly, Frankie drew up by one of the small wharves, his radiator pointing to the open road out of town and his engine turning over so silently he could hardly hear it himself. The place was so deathly silent and empty, he decided it was safe to get out; with St. John he stood by the water's edge. There they could hear the liner's band playing softly across the water, the old sentimental tune, cheap, almost music-hall level, familiar to every Irishman who has ever emigrated to America, that stupidly cruel, but well-wishing ritual of all departures:

Come back to Erin,
  Mavourneen, mavourneen,
Come back to Erin the land of thy birth.
Come with the shamrock, and springtime,
  Mavourneen . . .

It held them silent. The tender grew smaller. They noticed, down the pier, two elderly people, a man and a woman, who had apparently been too timid to go out on the tender or even say good-bye to it from beside its abandoned gangway. They stood and waved handkerchiefs to somebody leaving Ireland. From the tender, to them, or to others elsewhere, a dim flutter like seagulls answered for a while, and then faded into the foam and the distance. For a little while more they stood and waved, and then the woman began to droop her head, and her seagull of handkerchief fell to her side. They could hear her crying.

"In the old days," said Frankie, "there would be hundreds going."

The Irish-American took his brother's hand in his, and his mouth trembled.

"Draining us," he whispered, and then at the thought that his own life had been drained away, and at other unacknowledged, inexpressible thoughts, his eyes flooded for the departing boat, for the sadness of the music, for himself, for Ireland who was so old and so weak and so poor. Convulsively he clasped and fondled the young hand beside him, and, seeing St. John so wretched—become with all the excitement, lack of sleep, too much drink, an old, tired, worn-out businessman, all the air gone out of his balloon—Frankie led him back to the car and drove him to a hotel. It was not a good hotel. Since emigration had dwindled with the American depression the best hotels had closed (this was becoming another *ville morte*). There were holes in the linoleum, and the night porter was an old man. St. John sat shivering by the electric fire and he insisted on drinking. In pity Frankie let him drink. He drove the car to a hidden side-street for safety.

The hall porter (for all his courtesy he could not hide his surprise at the arrangement) met Mrs. Hannafey and her son at the quay, and brought them with their luggage to the hotel. There she was met by a rubicund St. John at the hall door, the sun striking his face with a morning glow of kindliness. Unhappily, as she approached, he staggered and fell on his hands and knees on the hairy mat. His son, delighted at this, unstrapped his ciné-camera and held back his mother and the handsome American girl who accompanied them.

"Whoa, Pop!" he greeted. "Hold it! You just wait one second, Pop. If that light's good enough I'll take such a nice little film." He focused the thing to his eye and pressed the button. "And when we get you back to New York, you'll just be so ashamed of yourself you'll never touch a drop of booze again."

The girl laughed; his mother sighed, and said, "Oh, Pat!" (Hearing which, from the back-room, where he kept out of sight, Frankie guessed that "Pat" was her pet name for her husband.)

"Welcome!" said St. John to the mat at his nose.

"Oh, St. John!" said his wife, and the change of name was a symptom. "Randall, help Dad, for pity's sake. Mary" —she turned to the girl, who had stopped smiling—"I'm so very sorry. I might have known this would happen immediately I let him out of my sight. Oh, *dear!*"

And she literally wrung her little hands, and her pretty, faded face went old and miserable. The night porter and the man who had just come along with a truckload of suitcases and trunks, in yellow hide and blue morocco, mohair rugs, hat-boxes, all the encumbrances of comfort-loving travellers, combined to lift up St. John and carry him to the dining-room. There they laid him, reverently, possibly enviously, on the horsehair sofa. The baggageman almost kissed St. John; in his solicitude he was as garrulous as a midwife; the nice thing was that he so obviously did it all from sheer motherliness, not because he expected to be tipped.

"Ah, wisha, ma'am," he comforted Mrs. Hannafey, as he tucked a rug about St. John's legs, "wouldn't yer heart melt for him? 'Twas only the way he was so excited at the idea of seeing you arriving. What is it—only a drop of drink? Haven't we all a weakness for a drop, whether 'tis a feast or a funeral?"

Though he was well meaning, his palaver had just that over-touch of blarney that the tourist brings out in even the least disingenuous. Frankie, who had come to the door, found in this Irish "soothering" one more little prick to his discontent, another blow to his pride.

"Look now, Miss," went on the baggageman, turning to the girl, "he'll be so ashamed of himself after this he won't want to touch the hard stuff for weeks to come! And isn't that penance enough for any man?"

Mrs. Hannafey smiled wanly, and looked at Mary, who tried to look appropriately touched, and they both said, "Thank you very much." Then they turned to Randall and both said simultaneously, "What are we going to do now?" and all three looked about the shabby dining-room, with its white cloth permanently on the long table, and the condiments never removed from it. "Are we to stay here for breakfast?" queried Mary in an unmistakable voice, which Randall echoed with, "Here?"

The inevitable embarrassment of the stranger in a strange land had descended on them. They glanced at the porter and the baggageman, who had moved almost imperceptibly closer together and who courteously concentrated on gazing at St. John in the effort to efface themselves. Frankie stood uncompromisingly at the door. The cross-currents of suppressed thoughts tightened the atmosphere.

"I have the car," said Frankie quietly. The Americans turned in surprise to this new character in their little drama. "His idea was that I would show you the car and you would drive. Will you come?"

It had not been part of his scheme to say or do this—in so far as he had any scheme—but he suddenly felt sorry for this little woman with her blue hair, wide, astonished, dissolving eyes, parted lips, and a cheerfulness that was (as it struck him) something between a perpetual gratitude and a childlike eagerness to see the best in everything. There was, especially, a pathos in her eyes that made them shadowed and liquid, as if she smoked too much or read too much; and the lids were tender; he could not see in the dawn-light whether the iris was grey or blue. She was frail, her neck slim, her little gestures incomplete (broken by afterthought), altogether helpless. As an extension of her husband's life she stung him with a suggestion of something in St. John's marriage, like a core of celibacy, loneliness, seclusion, even failure. To that thought the snores from the horsehair sofa seemed to reply with sardonic agreement. But it was all inexpressible, an undefined sensation, a rush of blood; he did not, then or ever, find words for it; he was simply oppressed by whatever it is that we all feel at the first sight of weariness in the face of some man or woman we had always thought happily complete in work or love.

He was looking so intently at her that she turned from him to ask the others with a further puzzlement in those wide-open eyes, poised for some new flight into wonder. She was like somebody looking at a waterfall as she said:

"Did he say he had the car?"

"Yes . . . Oh, yes, I did!"—her wide eyes and shaking head bringing him back to solid earth. "And, by the way, it's not my fault he's been . . . The trouble is he was visiting his old home last night, and he started communing." He drove on, knowing it all sounded crazy. "He was communing with his ancestors. The place where he was born, you know?"

"Oh!" The lips flew apart.

"I'm his half-brother," he finished.

To his annoyance he saw that by explaining so much he had somehow brought the situation not only to earth but to triviality. He suspected that they were forgetting the disgrace of the drunken father and the discomfort of the tawdry hotel, and were living the drama of the thing—something to write home about: a typical lunatic Irish welcome. Sure enough, the young man, whose behaviour with the ciné-camera had shown him so callous, began to laugh.

"Mother!" he cried. "Imagine Dad communing with his ancestors! And getting squiffed with them! And this is his half-brother? Why, then, that means he's my half-uncle! Mary! Ever see a half-uncle before? What's he to you, Mother? Are you"—gaily to Frankie, who glowered at him —"her half-brother-in-law?" He shook with delighted laughter, and nearly sat on St. John's legs, which made him laugh all the more.

"Hell!" thought Frankie. The two women smiled a little. Aloud he said, "We must be going." To the baggageman and the hotel porter, "Get the luggage into the hall. Help him out when the car is ready. You come with me," he ordered Mrs. Hannafey.

Slightly set back by the brusqueness of his manner, she went after him, and they walked down the street. The bay was empty. Already the liner was far out on the Atlantic. The quiet of the little town did to him what the silence of the valley up near Quit Rent had done to St. John—clipped off not alone night but something in life itself. It was one of those sudden breaks that disjoint life as a fault cracks a rock stratum. Her heels tapped quietly. His first impression of her gave way to a second, and that to a third, and that merged into another, much as when we walk slowly around a piece of sculpture. She was not beautiful now, but she had been. Her nose was tipped; her skin was a deep brown; her dark-grey eyes were immense; her teeth were as white, against the dark skin, as snow on a tree. Neck and forehead and fore-arm had the softness and warmth of sea-froth. Later, when he was about to leave her and stood back from her, he saw that she had a figure as dainty and perfect as a statuette. But it was her remote poise, her disconnectedness with his night, his life, his danger, that assaulted him. She was another world. It irritated him and made him envious, and he wanted to tell her into what adventure she had suddenly alighted—a word that hit off exactly his idea of her as a migrating bird that had dropped down to earth and might as suddenly vanish again, leaving behind a sense of discontinuity large as death.

"This is very kind of you," she said and, as with all Americans, she was able to convey ten times the sincerity of feeling the bare words contained. "I hope my husband hasn't been too much of a trial to you all?"

"He's all right," he said coldly.

"You are his brother? You are very young to be my brother-in-law."

"I'm his half-brother. My mother married twice. He was the eldest of the first marriage. I'm the eldest of the second."

"You're Frankie?"

"Yes."

"I'm Bee. That's Beatrice. But everybody calls me Bee."

She had high cheekbones, warmly rouged. Her fur coat thrown over her shoulders was scented. As they walked along the pavement he looked over the bay, already sparkling in the sun. Where was he to go? She would take the car and he would be stranded. Again that bleak effect of a sudden interruption. The sight of the yachts' pricked-out brass, bright and white in the morning sun, gave him an idea. He thought of the man who would help him to get away from that coast and that county and eased out.

"You are coming on to Cork with us, Frankie?"—the familiar name drawing their eyes together.

"No."

"Don't you live in Cork?"

"No." The touch of bravado in him that was part of his driving-power made him say, "I'm on the run."

She lifted her dissolving eyes, interested, solicitous.

"What does that mean?"

He surveyed her calm face, and deliberately tried to assail its calm. "The police are after me."

She was not assailed. She said, with the gentle inquiry of the much-travelled woman, accustomed to adapting herself to strangers' ways:

"Why on earth, Frankie? What have you done?"

The directness of the question, so foreign to his experience of the obliqueness and involution of Irishmen, angered him. He snapped back down to her:

"They say I shot a man."

"Did you?"

Everything about her made her more and more a foreigner, accentuated that notion of her as a lightly poised bird, hardly here because so soon about to be gone. It was so different from the life of his own people, which is that of walking trees.

"If I did," he snapped, "do you think I'd tell you?"

"Well, perhaps not. But since you've told me so much!" she said reasonably, and she smiled whitely up at him. They had turned off to the side-street. It was sound asleep. The sun had not yet penetrated here. The car at the far end of it had the air of having been abandoned. "Oh, there's the good old Lincoln!"

They walked along the middle of the street. The pavement was too narrow for two.

"You're not going to tell me, Frankie?" she smiled, and surveyed him up and down with open curiosity.

"We don't talk about these things to women in Ireland," he said.

Equally astonished, and amused, and piqued by his rudeness, she said, and laughed:

"But you have done, Frankie!"

They were at the car. Something in him resisted the idea of parting there; for one thing, the natural nervosity of his body which had lived for years in constant movement and hated the prospect of a lone walk through the silent country when they would be whirling back into the city; and he was disturbed by her difference, the window she had opened ever so little onto a more normal world. . . .

"I'd better drive you back to the hotel after all," he said. "You might lose your way," he explained. She, accustomed to constant attention from men, took it for granted that he would drive her. "Besides," he added, "I want you to drop me outside the town."

She sat in, and he drove to the hotel. He was more careless this time, indifferent to whether he might be seen or not: the reaction of lassitude to the end of the night. Inside, the boots and the bagman were talking to Randall and the young woman whom Frankie took for St. John's daughter until Bee introduced her; she was Mary Garland, Randall's fiancée. The luggage was brought out and strapped on. Meanwhile Bee chatted about her son and Mary Garland, and their plans for the summer—they had been to London and Paris, and they were going back again for a month to Paris after Ireland; then there would be Salzburg, Vienna, perhaps Tirol. All the while St. John lay stretched asleep before them on the sofa. The bagman kept going and coming.

"He *is* a naughty old man," she said, as he looked down at St. John's sleeping face. Once again, as he looked from her to her husband, Frankie was hurt by the incongruity of their marriage. He realized how much younger she was than he had at first thought—far younger than his step-brother. "You've been awfully kind, Frankie," she said, with such a sad sincerity and so deep a sigh that he softened towards her for the second time that morning. "Especially, when you're in trouble yourself. We will see you again, won't we?"—as the baggageman said they were all ready for the road.

"You're going to see me a bit of the way," smiled Frankie.

"I mean after that?"

He threw out his hands. Randall came in and bade his mother come. Then they were all cluttered in the hall, which was now bright with the fully risen sun, and were about to go out and get into the car when Bee stopped and cried:

"Gracious! I was going without Pat. I'd forgotten my husband!"

"Oh, Mother!" roared Randall, and the girl Mary laughed, and the baggageman to be polite laughed, and she herself had to laugh, so there they were in a bunch in the frowzy hallway doubled up with laughter—all but the hotel man, who was melancholy by nature and sad because they were going away, and Frankie, who went scarlet with embarrassment. She saw it and realized that they were behaving badly.

"I'd forgotten my husband," mimicked Randall. "Oh, Mother! Golly! What a morning!"

"Please," she begged Frankie, "will you help my husband out?"

She went, abashed and haughty, out to the car. As she stood there on the pavement she shrugged at Mary, and made a little *moue* with her painted lips. Her face became so sad and worn again, almost bitter-hard, that it suddenly occurred to Frankie that she would probably be pitiless to St. John when she got him sober again.

The body was removed gently and laid in the back of the

car and made cosy with rugs. The sad hotel man closed the glass doors and peeped out sadly over the frosted portion. The hotel had not even got the price of a breakfast out of them. The town was nothing but a sleeping little seaside Irish town now that the liner was gone, taking the world with it. Waving and smiling to the baggageman, they drove away, past the suburbs yet locked in sleep, between fields that were still grey with dew, past inlets of the sea brooding over their own stillness that the wild crying of gulls made only the more unbroken. Even Randall was silent there.

Bee did not talk much. Frankie was preoccupied with thoughts of the moment when he would get out of the car and standing by the roadside see them drive away to their pleasure. Besides, he was thrown off his balance by that unaccustomed, chance-snatched moment of freedom in Cove, where he had moved about almost like a free man. He had been disturbed, too, by the sight of the departing liner with all its associations and extensions; and when he glanced back to see if St. John was all right and saw Mary Garland leaning happily in Randall's arms, it tumbled him into one of the caves of his own heart. It was all like getting the taste of forbidden fruit. It was conscience. It was a lusting after the amiable, simple, common life whose routine had been going on for all those years behind his back. It so damaged his power of decision that he drove farther than he should have, for he really wanted only to get around to the back of the island on which Cove lies; he drove them on and on, beside the river that flows behind the island and forms it, until they who wished to go west into Cork were soon east of their starting-point. Strangely, he wished she would talk. She would have liked to, but feared more rebuffs.

"I'm going to leave you here," he said at last, but not yet stopping. "You must drive back this road to the bridge and then turn right. The signposts will flag you into Cork."

"You will be all right, Frankie?"

"Yeah!" He grinned at his use of her colloquialism.

"Where will you go? To some friend's house?"

To his own surprise he said:

"I'll probably dodge over to America for a while."

She turned eagerly.

"Yes, yes, you ought to. I know lots of radicals in America who'd help you. I do social work, you see, and meet every kind of person. But couldn't you fight the law? I mean, I don't really believe you ever shot anyone!"

He looked sidewards at her. She added, "Or have you?"

"I've shot plenty, but I've never murdered anybody. I'm a revolutionary, not a terrorist."

"Then why not fight your case? Or is it just that it's all a racket here, too? You know how it is with the law—you sit in the dock, outside the ropes, as you might say, and the lawyers fight it out inside the ring. That's often all right, but it often isn't. You never get a chance to get down to anything. It's not whether you are actually guilty or not, or even whether there was some justification. Take our famous case of Sacco and Vanzetti. It was all just a lousy matter of rules, and procedure, and tricks, and legal dodges, and so on. The French are different. They keep the law human. Or look at the case of Tom Mooney—twenty years in jail, an old man now, and the lawyers fighting for him year in and year out, and now nobody knows whether he threw that bomb or whether he didn't and, what's worse, nobody, not even his friends, care a hang. It's just a lawyers' fight."

Then she laid a hand on his arm.

"I'm sorry for gabbling like this. I'm not being just inquisitive, though I wish I could help."

"That's all right." He drew up and put on the brakes.

Here, too, the water was motionless as a mirror. All along its still far margin another green world, upside down, looked into the lake. A single gull floated on its own reflection.

"I know nothing about the law. If I'm caught I'm caught. I'm standing on my own two feet. But if my friends want to do anything for me when I am caught, it's up to them. Every man must do his own part."

"Oh? So there *are* others?" probed the soft-eyed little woman, solicitously.

"Some!" fended Frankie. (Did she mean that he was trying to rat on his friends?) "But numbers never counted in Ireland. It was always a few men who did everything. Anything can suddenly create a fermentation in the minds of the people. Then all it needs is a few men to keep it on the boil. There's great power in the people here. They seem to be dry and rotten, like old timber withered to a handful of leaves and bracken and twigs, and then, by heavens, you throw in a match and it blazes up and you have a furze fire that would roast all before it!"

She had the gift of excitement; of communicating it, of receiving it, of adding to it.

"Why are we stopping?" asked Randall.

"Frankie's leaving us here. He has to visit some friends," said Bee, and her words pleased him because they made her seem his particular confidante.

"I'll turn the car," said Frankie, and he did so. They both got out. She took the wheel. She held out her gloved hand.

"Good-bye," she said, and gave him a long look. "You *will* look after yourself."

The moment had come.

"Good-bye," he said, and took her hand.

She slipped in the clutch, and smiled at him. The car shot away, and he was left watching it until it was gone around the corner. The last thing he saw was St. John's head lolling over to one side as they took the curve. He filled with pity for them both.

6 a.m.

He sat on a wall facing the tide and lit a cigarette. The silence of the lake had the peace of the moment when a jumble of themes first begins to start a single melody growing out of them like some magic tree; a peace where is also an excruciating pain as if some deep-rooted nerve is being extracted out of the material body of life. It was not broken but deepened when the cathedral bell across the island came pealing out the first stroke of the angelus. It reminded him that it was Sunday morning. He saw the quiet city into which the Americans would soon be driving; he felt the vacuum of that different order of silence, where the Cork streets would never break into busyness, where the shop-windows were blinded, where everybody would soon be streaming to and from mass, and the only loud noise would be of the newsboys crying the Sunday papers; and for every half-hour until noon the churches would replicate this cathedral bell. In the country towns, like those nearest to him, across the water, it would be the same, only more quiet because they were smaller. Farther away, on up through Ireland, it would be everywhere the same Sunday calm, and only he, so it seemed to him, was out of it all.

He felt his two guns inside his coat in their holsters, and took refuge in the dregs of the tumult he had lived through during the past six hours. Men who live at his tempo are always the victims of an appetite endlessly re-created by the food that should appease them. He rose and made for the creek at the east of the island, driven on by the polarity of that calm from which he was outlawed—that normality of which he had tasted, within the last half-hour, more than he had dared for years before it.

Long afterwards, when greater experience brought him a little wisdom, he used to say, "I was like a gangster. And a gangster is a locust. I hid the sun." A great many of the fiercest Irish gunmen became, like him in his adult years, in love with books, and music, and painting, art of every kind: a form of recompense for those early days when they tried to live utterly in the body, devoting it like slaves to the one overmastering idea. Under the lash of their idealism they had become inhuman, as pitiless to themselves as to others, almost brutish. Like beasts they lived for beauty, and died without it, and if death let them go, their thirst for it afterwards was insatiable. It was awesome to meet, in later years, a man whose god had been his revolver, whose body had suffered the sweat of terror, of murder, the itch, lice, filth, sitting devoutly before a Mozart concerto, or lost before "Le Lac des Cygnes." If Frankie Hannafey had only had the wisdom to carry a pocket volume of Keats next to his maps and his bullets, as Napoleon did with Ossian, or Lawrence with Catullus, or Gordon of Khartoum with Newman, he would not, that sunny morning, have had to go driving like a loping wolf across the Sabbath countryside. For what he fled was himself.

The morning was sweet as a buttercup, with pale, primrose distances in the skies—too plumbless for blueness—and this frail beauty was held distant and aerial and tenuous by the rich black and purple distances in the woods backing to the sun beyond the shore of the lake. It was a last smoothening out of the wild motion of the night into the most tender stillness of a spring morning. It was all sun and silence, with

Sunday written even in the sky with its little bows and streamers. As he drove along, twice only was the quiet broken, each time scrawling his nerves. A flock of gulls gathered screaming over an apparently indiscriminate spot in the river-lake. Then they broke up and became white flecks of wings without sound. Later, when he had left the Great Island behind and was climbing to the hills, a bell, from a chapel unexpectedly near at hand cloaked by a copse, banged. After its second beat it became familiar, part of the general peace.

He trudged on all day, driving himself farther and farther away from Cork; not away from danger now but away from the longings whose parched and bloody mouths he was flogging down with the whip of bodily exhaustion. All that he had with which to beat down that thirst was his own thirst: only his own hunger kept that other hunger starved. He drank from streams and a spring-well in a field. He ate nothing. He did not know, or consider, whether it was spirit or lust that was eating him. He knew only that it was something that he had not had to fight before. The day withered. Its eye rolled up under its socket. Light went creeping away over the country to the west. The earth grew heavy. Its trickles and pools of water turned fish-white, tried to catch and hold the last of the light, and at last let it go and died themselves. Man conspired with the night by lighting little cottage windows that contested the supremacy of the day. He saw a school of rabbits white-scutting in and out of hedges and he relieved himself by the folly—a form of pitiful bravado—of letting half a dozen bullets fly at their jumping blobs of brown. The sound of the shots echoed like a blasting quarry. Knowing that in another hour Ireland would disappear, and seeing by his wrist-watch that it was almost nine o'clock, he faced for the main east–west road that divided him from the mountains. He would cross it in dusk, and find the mountain tracks before the last dark fell. He was aiming for the County Limerick, and his aunt's house in Kilfinnane. It was a village, with a police station, but her cottage was at the edge of the village, and she lived alone. Besides, like every hunted beast, he must go to earth somewhere.

10 p.m.

In the city that he had left, the same light waned, and once more its tuning-forks, the bells, began to test the heart. They rang, persistent as grasshoppers, and they greeted back into the pocket of the hills, out of those Ballyhouras, four American tourists. As she dropped into the centre of that grasshoppering hum, so lonely, so beseeching, a lover's cry in the fading day ("My love, my love, my love"), Bee Hannafey also felt the sureness of herself begin to crumble.

"What is the German word we once learned in Austria?" she had asked mournfully of the two young lovers behind in the car.

"*Schnürlregen?*" grunted the boy.

"No. No. Not the laced rain. I know! *Schlamperei.* All old Catholic countries are like that. Happy-go-lucky. I like it!" she had added lightly—condescendingly.

But now, the two young people went away to a cinema, and when she and St. John, after dinner in the hotel, went to the house on the island, they found the old mother was again babbling for her missing son. At once all her solidity became a smoke.

In the lower drawing-room Michael Hannafey was alone, playing over and over again Dvořák's "Humoresque" on a gramophone. She sat with him for a while—St. John gone upstairs to his mother—but it became clear to her as she watched him drink in the pathetic music that it was plucking not at its own strings but at the strings of his mind. She went to the doorstep, where a few lights had sprung up across the river and where she heard a last tired bell still beating. It reminded her of the bullfrogs at home in Kentucky going *cruk-crak* all night long; and at the thought of that a wave of unhappiness filled her heart to bursting.

For a year nobody had seemed to need her. She saw a long, long avenue—it could be an avenue of the mind; and a long sweep of drive, shrouded in trees, and a falling dusk like this dusk gathering this stranger city about her; and she, a young girl, kept looking up that drive. Ashamed to go away, but unable to stir, she stood waiting for the figure that should come—and never came.

As she began to walk back to the hotel, she saw in the very streets that empty avenue of her life, and when she saw, here and there, a boy and girl walking happily together, her own unhappiness became the more profound.

So many people looked after the Yank, the stranger in the fort, that she hurried to the hotel to avoid their eyes. There was nobody in the foyer. She sat in her room, and looked at the old-fashioned furniture, the two mahogany wardrobes, the lace curtains, the carpet that was smooth, the old-fashioned linen blinds. There she confessed to herself, with shame. She was filled with desire for the young man she had seen only for an hour, and who was gone out of her life as lightly as he came. She was ashamed because she was afraid that Mary might have noticed it. She must be nearly ten, at least eight years, older than he was. She had two children. Her husband was . . . but she kept back the word.

From the dark pool of the wardrobe mirror a wavering glimmer of face told her that her beauty was all but gone.

That day she had seen the rough country where her husband was born and where Frankie had spent so many years of his life, and she had seen the young woman Josephine waving them good-bye in a wind that was, no doubt, never at rest. She, too, would be warming similar thoughts over her fire. That place, and the musty island house, were all the background she had for him. It was so foolish that she rose and undressed and went to bed. Then St. John came and she pretended sleep.

By the way he knelt by the bed and said his prayers for an unusual length of time she knew that he was happy with melancholy, rubbing the paunch of a conscience he had bribed with promises. Drowsily she asked for a "Lucky," and as they lay side by side they smoked, and he talked about his people. Since they had parted a week ago his whole interest in life seemed to have centred on a road in North Cork that led him back to the figure of himself, as a boy, waiting at the end of it. She smelled the sweet toasted smell of the tobacco, and listened, while the streets and the hotel hummed with silence, to his recitation of twenty lives. With each name, of each relative, he went from the city, from the island, farther into the country—Rathcormac, Kilavullen, Fermoy, Quit Rent, the farm of Glencam high up on the slopes of the Ballyhouras where his grandfather Michael Hogan had married Elizabeth Roche of Castletown, and bought a few tiny fields in the years of the Famine. On those fields the little fat teacher now lived; and that girl. She saw again the hilly, windy, rocky farm they had visited that day. The view had been magnificent, for from the rocks over it she had looked east to the Galtees and south to Cork, and northward towards the Shannon, a sea of land. His voice went slipping from her to the legion of his people. She stubbed out her cigarette, and let him roam. The last thing she heard him say was:

"I wonder would I get them a kitchen sink . . . it must be wet and windy in the winter . . . or maybe a flush lavatory is what they want?"

Again she smelled the Turkish cigarette-smoke. He had lit up again. Her mind and her body ached. She knew he would be awake for hours. She wished she had, like him, the opium of drink.

In the morning she talked it out with St. John. She could not stand Cork. She had taken the flat in Paris for June; it would probably be ready now. At first he fumed; then when she said that he could stay if he liked, he calmed down and finally shrugged. She patted his cheek and kissed him, and immediately went across the street to Cook's. Paris? As it so happened there would be a boat from Cove to Cherbourg that day: she could be in Paris on Tuesday evening. . . .

The road to Cove, the quiet river-lochs, the tiny quays, the shabby-genteel hotels—it was all poignantly familiar. As St. John waved his hat to the tender, she could imagine that she had not merely seen that little town before, but that she had lived and suffered and been happy in it, in a previous existence.

CHAPTER II

The Brothers

FRANKIE HANNAFEY, in taking refuge in his aunt's house in Kilfinnane, used a certain amount of that cold calculation which had made him, in the fighting days, one of the best guerrillas in the South. He knew well that small villages are a web of gossip; but he knew, too, that their secret life is a labyrinth, and that every new burrow takes some time to reveal itself. He knew the cottage since his childhood days. Though not in the least secluded–it stood on the side of the road, the first cottage seen by anyone entering the village from that end–it was for many reasons the most unobtrusive little house imaginable.

It was long, low, whitewashed, and thatched, with a small annex whose slates were almost hidden by a thicket of ivy. A patch of earth with a wooden railing, sometimes called the garden though only four feet wide, separated the windows from the footpath: the distance was just enough to make the glass opaque. The footpath ended where the cottage ended, so that nobody ever passed nearer than the middle of the road. Long before you came to the end of the village you felt yourself in the fields which invited you, beyond it, and when you came back you abstractedly brought the country road with you into the middle of the main street.

It was a confidential little house. You could have put the windows in your pocket. They barely performed the function of windows. Since the floor inside was lower than the footpath outside, they had whitewashed wooden bars (two to each window, nailed horizontally) to keep the cows on fair-days from pushing their rumps through the glass. Inside they had lace half-curtains, and behind these every window-sill held a row of geraniums, mostly Paul Krampulls, goose-necked from trying to reach the air, which hardly ever did creep in, since it was always troublesome to open windows that lacked pulleys, and the bit of whitewashed stick intended to prop them open was, as often as not, mislaid. The paint about the frame, inside and outside, had over many years invaded the glass for as much as an inch all round. Fine webs of spider-work joined geranium to geranium, and old leaves dangled on threads. Behind the cross-curtains, the paint, and the geraniums, were still more lace curtains, stiff with starch, looped on great yellow ribbons; and behind these in each of the windows of the "room," though not of the kitchen, was a shovel-backed horsehair chair. Beyond all that, to the left of the door there was the kitchen, and the "room" to the right. In the dim vacuum of the room was a cluttered quiet, with mottled and coloured tin daguerreotypes of the dead, a coloured oleograph of Dan O'Connell in his Liberator's cloak—the subject adumbrating memories behind Michael Collins, John Redmond, Parnell, even Isaac Butt; just as the picture balancing it, Leo XIII with his enormous but benevolent fledgeling's mouth, indicated somebody's youth in the happiest doldrums of our times; there were enlarged photographs of relatives more recently dead; there was a lock with weights; there was a dining-table; but there was also a commode, a canopy-bed, and the best harness hung on the wall, while a few grains of meal on the linoleum beside a wooden chest completed the defeat of anybody trying to decide what purpose the room served. In the place of honour, on a doily in the middle of the table, lay an enormous family-album which concentrated what the whole room contained—the slow vibration of a human drama, indeed many such, pulsing yet quiescent, invisibly alive, never to come to life until the trumpet of Judgment, or when, perhaps, some old woman like the old woman sitting by the hearth in the kitchen came in, and turning the heavy pages of the album, began to talk. Such a room, in such a house, becomes, just before it reaches its own end, a form of urn burial for what must be the smallest atom of human society possible to conceive. And it was this, even more than the physical reticence of the little house itself, that made the cottage so unconsidered by the village. Time had smothered and muffled it in familiarity. Everybody knew everything about it. It had become to them as uneventful as a tree.

Even in the kitchen (whose lofty ceiling was the underside of the thatch) there was this sense of a preface to pulverulence. If you searched it for its most significant detail, you might waver between the little hole in the table—a depression under the oilcloth, a pool for crumbs or tea—that, to Frankie's knowledge, nobody had had enough energy in twenty, and most probably in forty, years to fill: or you might, as he did, choose, on the dresser, a row of empty Colman's mustard tins, stripped of their yellow paper wrappers and so often polished that they had a kind of pockmarked silver beauty. Frankie had known these tins since he was a child and played trains with them on the oilcloth of the table. Sitting by the hearth now, he would frequently contemplate them with a sardonic amusement. He would put them up against his own ideas, his whole gospel of life as a revolutionary, and every time they were like iron-clad pillboxes that no assault of his mind could defeat. He read into them an extraordinary number of things about the life of that house: such as frugality without poverty, hours empty but not idle, desires as innocent as a child's and as easily satisfied, an unassailable simplicity of heart, remoteness from all ambition, a blind crypt of what he did not know whether to call inexperience of the world or ignorance of it.

If he went out in the yard he would suffer the same defeat. (It was overlooked by no house, except where, some five hundred yards away, the cement backs of the main street gazed at the white sky.) He would there contemplate the empty sheds that called themselves stables, or look at the dry piggery, or halt before two more mustard tins—two antique cars, one a side-car and the other a covered car, with which his uncle Tom had once earned a living as a hackney-driver. The tires and metal fittings were crusted with rust. The paint was peeled dry. A generation of hens had roosted in them. Yet, old sacks, themselves fraying away, lay on the wheels, and the shafts were propped up with old boxes. Those wrecks would never be sold—more likely smashed up for firewood—until the old woman died. He might amble over to the rain-barrel, empty, echoing profoundly when he put his face into it and shouted; it did not even retain a smell; or thence wander down the lengthy enclosure, protected by twelve-foot walls like a jail, containing only wild grass and stumps of apple trees, these relicts and the memory they evoked alone justifying the vestigial title of orchard. His aunt had cut down every tree because, apparently, little boys used sometimes steal the apples from her. They had, in any case, he guessed, long gone wild, no bigger than crabs. She would not plant new trees because she would not live to see their maturity. He remembered, too, that under the trees there had been a fine kitchen-garden of potatoes and cabbage and, suddenly, on his second day, he looked about him, recalling a little forest of gooseberry bushes. There was nothing but the rank grass. Nothing remained from his childhood memories of that orchard but the four high walls, the sparrows and swallows who nested between the stones, the wreck of a dog-kennel, and, if that belonged to the orchard, and only from the orchard had he long ago remarked it, the intense silence of this periphery of the village which was all the more silent when some childish voice in the distance called out positively but intelligibly and left its echo behind.

He was further delighted when, on his first inspection of the orchard, he met, waddling down the path towards him, two ducks side by side, just like two old gentlemen with their hands in their trousers pockets. At first he thought that these were the sole inhabitants of the orchard. Later he discovered the hen. Its name, he found, was Bobeen, and it laid eggs without shells because his aunt Maggie would not give it proper food. Also, that same silence-humming evening, when the ghosts of the felled trees might have been stirring their invisible tops in the level gold of the sun that made the ivy on the walls transparent, he met a foxy cat. That was Tomeen. As he met no other living thing, he concluded that this was the total livestock on this Crusoe's island.

It should all have exasperated him. He acknowledged that consciously. Without knowing why, or caring why, he felt entirely contented. For hours he would lie against a tree-stump, and if his aunt came to the back-door, far down at the end of the orchard, in the grassy haggard, or if the ducks came sedately by, or if Bobeen broke into an arrogant bugling over her soft egg, he would break the silence with a peal of laughter which, at the memory of what caused it, would repeat itself in sardonic chuckles maybe an hour later. There was nothing to do but lie there. There were no books. The old woman did not even take in the weekly paper. Had a war broken out, she would have heard of it only when some commodity rose in price, and then she would have talked of it much as, hundreds of years ago, men must have talked of the

Crusades. What she thought of Frankie he often tried, in vain, to imagine: he was to her a Public, the word Republican having reached her over the years with a curtailment identical to that process which philologists record in the journeyings and adventures of all human words down the centuries. That was the word with which she had greeted him.

"So you're out with the Publics again?"

"Yes, Maggie," he answered.

"Well, I suppose I have to shelter you."

He was against the Law. That was enough for her, whose whole conception of Irish politics had been formed in the days of the Land League, and never changed.

He could not even smoke, because if his aunt went into a village shop to buy cigarettes his secret would be out at once. He had nothing to do but laze, and think, and, favourite occupation, tease the old lady. This she enjoyed; but it had to be the simplest kind of teasing: her eyes, slightly protuberant from some disease, gave her a false impression of alertness and interest, and even after he had observed this he was still frequently misled into thinking that she was pleased when she was not even so much as trying to convey that she did not understand an iota of what he had said.

Twice in his first four days somebody knocked at the door. He retired quietly to his annex: it was a single room *choc-à-bloc* with lumber and smelling of mice and dust. The first caller was some old woman with a cleft palate. He gathered, through the door, during the two hours that she stayed gossiping, that they talked mainly of his aunt's dead husband, "Honesht Tam." The second caller was the parish priest. They talked only of Honesht Tam. That night, by the fire, his aunt talked of nothing else but Honesht Tam. She described his long illness, month by month, and his death, hour by hour, and she wept all the time. She also attacked the entire village for its roguery, indifference, callousness, trickery, and complete unworthiness, "not like my poor ould Honesht Tam." She attacked even Frankie, and he had to suffer it as if he were again the child who used to come visiting there of summers across the hills in the pony-and-trap from County Cork.

"Ah, then, and, ah, then, and it isn't alike, Frankie," she snivelled down her nose. "Little thought there is of him now he's gone. How often did you come and see him when he was ailin'? Ah, ye have the hard hearts! Many and many's the drive he gave you on the donkey-butt. But did you remember it for him? 'Tis too good for this world he was entirely. Often I said it to him." Here she made it clear that they must have often attacked Honesht Tam himself when he was alive. "I said it to him to his face. 'Tam, ye're a fool. Ye're a soft slob of a fool. They're all making a gom of yeh. Ye're too honesht for 'em.' And so he was, my poor, foolish, innocent Honesht Tam."

Such floods of tears overcame her that she was silent for a long while. It was true that he had never once adverted to her, or to her sorrows. He had heard of the death of his uncle without as much interest as he would have given to his slightest acquaintance. He had had other things to worry about. Now he remembered the old man, with his stooped back (some injury received when a young man) as if he bowed himself in humility to all the kicks of the world. He remembered the heavy-lidded eyes, complete half-globes, whose circles were fully completed by double wrinkles outlining the pouches beneath; and in every wrinkle a benevolence and a patience like the patience of one of his old nags that he used to drive under the cars rusting now outside in the yard.

He did not hear the old woman's words any more. The intense preoccupation of her sorrow shocked him into realizing what their lives had been like—to them. In pain he recollected little details about them that had long passed out of his conscious mind—such as the great red wen on the back of Tom's neck, giving an extra screw to his already bowed head. He recalled that the old man had been for years the oldest member of the Parish Confraternity, and that on the occasion of its jubilee he had received a special medal and been photographed with other old men like him for the Limerick paper. There had been a great to-do about that. A Balaclava veteran could not have been prouder. It hurt to remember how Michael and himself had made fun of it, hurt and shamed. The whole ritual of the man's life was in any one of those days when he would say, "Frankie, come out to the Commons with me, today," and the two would go jolting down the road in the donkey-butt. The grass used to be still dew-wet when they arrived. At some part of the day the dinner of cold tea, from a whisky bottle, cork-tasting, and soda-bread, big as a stone, would be produced and eaten under a hedge. He could remember nothing else, except the jolting journey back in the evening. Childhood had simplified that as vital portion of life as any other, that one typical day, into elements as simple as the commands of the Prophets. And yet while Tom worked in his fields, he must have been doing many enjoyable things, exploring by the lake, building shanties—long, long, heavenly summer hours, now as lost to him as if they had never occurred. It was as if Death works on us by gnawing away the beginning, creeping after us daily, eating away the road over which there is no return, until at the end there is one last day or two left, and then—the pit.

They stayed for hours there talking over the sinking turf-fire. She evoked for him a whole stretch of his boyhood that he had lost. She made him acknowledge to himself that these people in the country keep their lives intact to the very end;

but she so weighted him, too, with her own memories that the little dust of her life, hitherto quiescent, began to sift into his palm and stir there like a living seed, no longer part of her but part of him.

That night as he lay in his bed in the lumber-room, so stuffy and so still, and heard the grave tock-tock of the clock in the "room," and in from the country about no sound but a distant corncrake—as if the sweet, fresh grass of spring had carpeted the whole world for silence—he felt an oppression that was almost a superstitious fear. He recalled reading somewhere that when the first explorers opened the pyramid of Cheops they found a mummy, and in the mummy's hand a seed, and they planted it, and it grew into a strange scarlet flower, and some of them ate the petals of this flower. Her memories had been as withered; and were they as procreant? It was as if, like the animal that smells the knife, he smelled in the dust of the room the quern of Nature that reduces all life to dust. It was the validity and importance of the pattern of their lives to them, and its meaninglessness to him, that oppressed him. They had married into this cottage, lived in it for their space, worked year after year, borne no children, followed no ambition, been "honesht"—their achievement—and were virtually passed out. They would leave behind them not even an orchard. In five years there would not remain of their lives as much as a memory: nothing but a detritus like the dust of flour, meal, and bran formerly stored in this room, whose bursting fullness, once scooped and scattered so lavishly, was now attenuated to a smell of musk. . . .

He was lying, the next morning, in a sombre mood against his tree-stump when he observed her coming up the path on her shaky pins, holding in her hand a green telegram envelope. He leaped up, quick to respond to every hint of danger. She told him that she had made the messenger read it for her, and said that it was all right, and sent him away, but she had not been able to take it in. He read it out. It had been handed in, at Cork, the night before. It said: "COMING TO SEE YOU WITH MOTHER AND MICHAEL CAN MOTHER STAY LOVE ST. JOHN." He explained. It flung her into a torrential rage, astounding in so small and frail a woman.

"And what does that one," she cried, as if his mother were not her sister, "want coming to see me for? I haven't seen her for ten years. What am I saying? 'Tis twelve years. Sure the world knows your mother isn't right in the head. I don't want to see her. Leave her stay away now, since she stayed away so long."

He made no wonder of this lack of natural feeling. To country folk relationship is a usufruct. The sentimental emotions can never be gratuitous among people with whom life's natural care for its own self-preservation is paramount, and who consider that friendship speaks with actions not words. They seem hard only to us who have not merely refined their tough manners but evaded their tough conditions. Of his own concern he said nothing. He just tore the telegram into minute pieces and scattered it, with an obscenity directed against St. John.

They arrived about three o'clock. He sulked in the orchard and refused to meet them. He heard the old forty-times-tarred double-gate creak on its unwonted hinges, and then the stink of the Lincoln's petrol polluted the orchard. A half-hour passed during which he could imagine the greetings, and upbraidings, and the tears of joy between the two sisters. Then he saw Michael and St. John come up the path and knew by the cut of them that they were embarrassed. He gave them a glare under his eyebrows and did not stir while they stood over him, making their apologies. He stared in sullen silence at St. John's black and white shoes, and said:

"Have ye any cigarettes?"

He took a whole packet from Michael and began to smoke. He knew he was behaving like a pup but he could not control himself and he had no pity for them. St. John sank down on his haunches, carefully chucking up his pink-striped flannel trousers as he did so. In that posture his belt cut his fat belly in two.

"Well, Frankie," he asked humbly, "what are we going to do now?"

"Mother can't stay here," he growled. "You ought to know that."

"It was my idea," apologized St. John. "The doctor said she ought to have a change of scene. I thought it would do her the world of good to come and stay in this little place. We had a terrible job to move her. Didn't we, Michael?"

Michael said nothing. He lay down on the ground, drew out a long soft sword of grass from its sheath, and felt the white blade between his fingers.

"Ha?" asked St. John.

"She can't stay, that's all," retorted Frankie.

"Why not?" asked Michael, with a cold gentleness.

"How can she?" he cried back. "She wouldn't enjoy it. She wouldn't get any rest. She would be worrying about me all the time. And I'm not going to move."

"Why not?" repeated Michael, still stroking the blade. St. John stirred uncomfortably on his heels. "I suppose you think we're following your tracks?" asked Michael.

"Aren't you?" challenged Frankie.

"I might as easily say that you're getting in our way?"

"Of course," put in St. John hastily. "Mickey and I can clear out all right. We can sleep anywhere. Limerick city. The old bus would make it in half an hour. We can go every night and come back in the morning. But Mother can't do that. She's tired out now. She's had to lie down. I don't suppose there's a hotel in this little place she could stay in. Anyway, you know she couldn't be left in any hotel. I know she'd love a week here," he pleaded. He stopped and looked to see what effect he had made. He looked about him. "It's a bit . . . I don't know what . . ." His expression was downcast. "It isn't what I expected. It's all changed. But"—he brightened—"the village is grand. It's better than I expected. I never knew it was such a great little place. And the country—oh, my God!—it's lovely. And the weather is like summer."

Frankie bared his lower teeth. He glanced from one of them to the other. They were making him feel the half-outsider—the half-brother—by their collusion. He caught Michael's fretful, resentful eye.

"So you expect me to clear out?" he challenged.

"That's up to you."

"I'm just the family nuisance."

"We've done a lot for you," snapped Michael.

"Not for me. You know well that I don't give a damn for myself. You never did anything for me. I don't want anybody to do anything for me."

The wall of the impersonal idea rose up between them. In the silence they heard the call of the cuckoo, like a cork popping in and out. In and out . . . in and out . . . Somewhere in the village a hen made a great clucking, deep in its belly, a basso qhook-cuck-cuck-cuck.

"A pity they cut down the trees," murmured St. John, his attention wandering. "This used to be such a shady place."

"You know that I'm not much interested in you and your Republic," huffed Michael, tearing a bit of grass to shreds. "I don't know what you're going with this kind of thing for."

"Very well," mocked Frankie. "That's that. And you," looking at St. John, "know nothing about it and care less."

"That isn't true!" cried St. John warmly. "That's wrong. I'm very interested, believe me. I don't understand it, but I see you're after something. And I respect you for it."

"Tshah," sneered Frankie, "you're at the stage when you'd say Judas Iscariot was wronged if you heard his grandmother was Irish. Ye can do whatever ye like. I'm not moving."

Their aunt's piping voice called from the back-door that tea was ready. The two travellers rose.

"Let's not tell her until later on," temporized St. John. "What do you think?"

Frankie dismissed them with a gesture. They walked away. He could see them conspiring against him as they walked down the path.

They did not reveal his presence to his mother until she woke up, late in the afternoon. Then they told her that he would come in at dusk from a house beyond in the bog, to see her, and would be away again when she went to bed. At twilight he came in. She looked long at him, diagonally from her corner of the hearth across to the door, and her grey head lowered to one side like a tree under fruit, and a long sigh of happiness and sorrow and love bowed her back. She seemed to sink down before him as he came over jauntily and took her hands and kissed her, and she smiled up at him with the sad smile of resignation that was now, and had been for years, permanently fixed on her face.

"Are you well, Frankie? You're not getting thin, are you?"

"Me, Mother?" he joked. "I'm getting as fat as a bull. I'll soon be as fat as St. John there. You stay here, now, for a week or two, and you'll be like the pair of us."

They all sat about the hearth, the two sisters, the three brothers. He sat by one corner, facing the door—it was a reflex action for him to sit always with his back to a wall and his face to a door—and she sat opposite him, never taking her eyes from him unless somebody addressed her directly. Michael sat beside him. Aunt Maggie was in the middle. St. John was next his mother, whose hand he patted from time to time or whom he kept asking if she was cold, or too warm, or the like. They all drank punch. It helped to smoothen things to argue with the old women about it, persuading them to take it and joking them that they were getting drunk on it. Three times, Frankie noticed, St. John went out into the yard on the excuse that he wanted to get something from the car, but he had caught his mother's glance each time and knew that he really went out to listen at the old gate. The solicitude annoyed him at first, and then touched him. He made himself merry in order to put his mother at her ease. He teased the aunt. It was he who made Michael laugh with his descriptions of the two ducks and the hen that laid soft eggs and bugled in triumph over her work. The aunt pretended to be furious, but she really liked it because nobody had ever talked of her ducks and her hen before, and it made them more important and more real. Finally his mother asked him to sing—she used to parade him when he was a little boy and had a nice voice —and he sang for her a lullaby. It made her eyes dim with happiness. St. John, by now punch-full, was delighted that everything was going so well, and sang them a tuneless backwoods song in dialect. It ended:

Ducks in the pond and whales in the ocean,
Hi do diddle all the day.
Devil's in the women when they take a notion,
Hi do diddle all the day.

After that the two women shifted close to each other to talk of old times, and the three men were in a bunch, and St. John talked about America.

"It's a royal country for any young fellow who's prepared

to take his coat off. A great country for any lad beginning life. But, mind you, it uses you up. Wears you out. And what have you in the heel of it all?"

That, inevitably, became an argument, in which the other two joined against him.

"But," he kept on saying, "look at me! I've lived there and I know! It wrings you like a dishcloth!"

They kept retorting that that was natural, saying it in a dozen different ways, as men will who are not discussing but persuading (most Irish arguments are that kind of argument, fellows taking out their emotions like watches to show them and putting them back again, and taking them out again with redoubled heat). Only very gradually did they come to the basis of their difference, and there the true discussion began (as so often, again, in Ireland on imponderables). For they discussed now such things as whether it was worth while at all to work as hard as that, the motives of human ambition, the needs of the heart. Frankie pointed to the life of the house in which they sat, bringing up his thoughts of the night before, and saying that that was no life to live, while St. John cried that that was the only life to live and Michael wavered now to one side and now to the other. They were so engrossed that they did not notice the two sisters going to see the yard, and the outbuildings, and the invisible orchard, before the last shred of the afterlight would go completely from earth and sky.

"Everybody who's experienced it agrees with me!" cried St. John. "It's no use talking without experience. Look! Here's a letter I got this very morning from Paris from my wife." He unfolded the letter, commenting before he began to read, "She always writes these queer letters. Of course, Bee's a very intelligent woman. Listen! 'I'm sitting writing this in the Parc Monceau, a day of wayward clouds playing pranks over the roofs, flowing before the wind in fantasies of feathers, plumes, great white plateaux, and magnificent escarpments of the mind. They are all streaming now in procession through the vacancy, in a huge arc, converging to a point over the park trees and the roofs of Les Batignolles . . .' "

Frankie had leaned forward and was listening in amazement. It struck him, at once, that the woman had not written this letter to her husband at all. It was more like a woman talking to herself. Michael had also leaned forward and was drinking it in, fascinated: his dream-life, his dream-city.

" 'The trees are shaking like seaweed in water. There is a dog with the sunlight in his fur chasing a ball. The rumble of Paris is faint. I don't know why I came back here.' "

St. John looked up. He explained:

"When the children were kids she lived with them there for a year." He resumed reading. " 'I've been thinking of those months in '26 and '27.' " He looked up again. "Here's the important bit. 'I feel nobody should ever return to old haunts. The penalty is to know what you have lost. Loneliness. Regret for some loss you can't define. Permanence and change taunting you until you won't be able to say which is which and where is your solid earth. The answer to your "Come Back to Erin" is that it's always too late to mend. Why am I here? Because I'm an exile. Everybody is as he gets older. Only some have somewhere to go back to and I have not. My homeland is wherever I was happy. New York? Not since the children grew up. Paris? Anybody I knew here is gone years ago. The few roots I put down are rooted up. I am more of a stranger than ever. I must stop. The light is fading. Soon the lights down on the Champs-Elysées will burst like flowers and I will walk there looking for what does not exist—a gay restaurant. This faint hum of Paris, all those white clouds over my head, seem to be taking messages all over the world from heart to heart, except from me alone. The honk of taxis. People going places. I will go out past the naked boy who for ever sharpens his scythe, with the copper drip greening his plinth, and remember that Randall asked me ten years ago, "Mummy, why does he wear nothing but a hat?" '" St. John folded the letter. "Some statue or other," he annotated. "See?" he cried triumphantly.

Frankie relaxed slowly. Bits of the letter were exactly what he had been thinking last night: the way your life rots away behind you. It was a strange letter. There was no connexion between it and the person to whom it had been posted. The relationship of marriage had always been a puzzle to him. This made it a weird and somewhat unpleasant mystery. He saw Bee Hannafey as he saw her that early morning at Cove; this husband of hers on the hotel sofa passed out from liquor; the car vanishing around the corner with his head lolling helplessly.

"She always writes like that?" he asked.

"Oho!" laughed St. John. "Sometimes it's just, 'Send me two hundred dollars.' But you see my point? When you've got everything—you've got nothing!"

Then he went on talking about every man wanting to "belong," and that you could never "belong" when you were in exile. Michael, hunched on his straw-bottomed chair, was staring at him, unseeing.

"It must be the loveliest city in the world," he whispered.

"New York?" asked St. John.

Michael did not correct him. He gazed into the pink ashes. Somebody raced a motor-car engine up in the village. It stopped in a backfire and they heard no more. The three brothers were occupied with their thoughts. Suddenly all three spoke simultaneously, stopped, and laughed.

"What were you saying, Mickey?" asked St. John.

"I was just thinking I'd love to . . . Ah, nothing!" He made a gesture of surrender with one long wrist. "Nothing at all."

"No!" said St. John. "This is the kind of place where I'd love to end my days. Grand little place. Clean. Nice and quiet. My own people."

"If I could only get to America for a while," ground out Frankie, avidly, between his teeth.

The women came back and the three men rose, abstractedly. The mother was talking in a toploftical voice about the condition of the orchard, and Aunt Maggie, more pop-eyed than ever, was red to the ears.

"We can't all live in grand city houses," upbraided the country mouse. "We all haven't sons to be sending us fine money from America."

" 'Tis well to have them," the mother agreed with her. "But, wisha," she appealed as if to some weak-willed retainer, "if you even put down a few potatoes?"

Maggie scolded in a voice loud enough to call the cattle home. She barged her sister. She went as scarlet as a turkey-cock.

"Didn't I put in potatoes two years ago, and sure, between the seeds and the labour, ould Pat Mulhern, the idle cripple, it cosht me three pounds five, and I didn't get fourpence a weight for them after. Bad scran to you with your fine advice. Robbers—that's all they are in this town. So then didn't I tell ould Pat Mulhern to put in his lazy cripple of a horse and lave him be eating the grass for me? I thought 'twould keep it from growing wild on me." She paused. "And damn bad he ate it, too."

At this the men roared with laughter, and being good-humoured by nature the scarlet-faced little bargee laughed, doubling down over her blue apron, and showing all her false teeth in delight at her own folly. She lifted her red hands and brought them down in jocose assault on St. John's chest, since he was laughing louder than anybody.

"Wisha, Sinjin, you were always the terror for mocking at me."

They dispersed in great humour after that, first seeing the mother safely in bed in the room. Then the old double-gate, its boils broken by the suns of many summers, creaked open again and the Lincoln purred out with St. John and Michael, who would be sleeping over in Limerick for the night. Maggie waved and grinned after them, and Frankie lurking behind helped to close and bar the gate. The sky was white with stars. A corncrake was wandering in some near-by field. The night air was rich and sweet with growth.

He stole into his back-room and lay down. The cold musk enveloped him. He could hear Maggie flopping about the kitchen at her last tasks. She was restless tonight and she kept coming and going for hours, so that he could not sleep. The corncrake never ceased croaking. He could tell by the sound of his mother's voice that the door between the kitchen and the room was open. He heard, from his aunt, "Aye, they're all gone," and his mother saying something else, to which Maggie said crossly, "Yes, yes. He is."

He had surmounted many temptations. It had been bad for about a year, when he saw old friends getting fat jobs and throwing everything else aside. That year he went home, took to drink, became, and knew that he became, in everybody's eyes, a has-been. Even the police became friendly with him that year, and that was the taunt that sobered him. For a time Josephine had an influence over him. Then the new generation of young fellows seemed to be no good, play-acting, unready to take risks. Then the new government came in and gave pensions all round, and said all the things that he and his party had been saying for years, and what little following they had disintegrated once more. Then raids began. For weeks before this Blennerhasset shooting he had not seen anybody from Dublin. There had not been a headquarters meeting for months. Yet, in some way or another, untidily, in a kind of ragged persistence, he had clung on. Tonight . . . He turned miserably to the whitewashed wall. What rankled most, and had ever since it was said, was Michael's remark, "You think we're following on your tracks. . . . You're just getting in our way." To these people he was a mere nuisance. He suddenly heard his mother's voice saying, "Maggie! Are you sure he's safe?" His aunt, somewhere from near the hearth, said, "Nobody knows but he's a thousand miles away."

That made his lip tremble. Men like him, who spend too much of their lives, more than Nature is expected to bear, confronting trial of body and soul, have a pathetic need for mothering. (How true to human nature, in *War and Peace*, that the brutal Dólokhov, the duellist, the adventurer, the bully, should break down after he had been wounded in a duel because it would pain his mother to hear of it!) He felt that she was the only one who was not trying to edge him out of the house, send him off on his wanderings.

"Maggie! What's keeping you out of bed?" came her querulous voice.

"I always have a sup of hot milk before I goes to shleep."

The corncrake kept on and on. Where could he go? In turn, one by one, St. John had invaded his home in Cork, his hideout on the Ballyhouras, this last and safest of his refuges. It struck him that St. John's desires and his desires were fighting one another. He heard his aunt sweeping the kitchen. The twigs scraped against his door. She always swept the dust into the hole of the hearth, where, surprisingly, for half of it was the friable surface of the cement-earthen floor, it seemed to burn.

He began to hate the house, and he got out his map and examined it to see where he could go. It dropped out of his hands, and he lay back. Presently after a lot of tossing and turning he must have dozed, for he woke up with a start—at half-past twelve by his wrist-watch—to hear a shuffling, secretive noise in the kitchen. He seized his guns and was at the door when he heard his mother's whining voice:

"What on earth are you doing walking around like that in the middle of the night?"

"Ah, 'tis my rheumatics," said the aunt, shuffling around and around.

He went back to bed with an exasperated sigh. Presently his mother said:

"For God's sake, Maggie, will you come back to bed and leave me sleep?"

Maggie apparently did, for everything became quiet again, except for that maddening corncrake wandering through its fawny meadow. But he then heard more little scufflings and a muttered squabble, and the grave tock-tocking of the old clock stopped. He got up again and eased the door an inch. He heard the whispered argument.

"I will not, then," said Maggie.

" 'Tis keeping me awake," said the mother.

" 'Tis company for me," said the aunt, "and I can't shleep without it."

The tock-tocking began again in its slow, grave note. Then he heard his aunt crying and a long monotone began. He caught the words "Honesht Tam" and went back to sit on the side of his bed. He went to the door once more and this time his mother's voice broke in with "My poor Johnnie, my love and my dove." He closed the door and the antiphony died away. For a long time, perhaps three-quarters of an hour, he sat looking out through the latticed window (the only window in the place of its kind). He saw the empty sheds, the starlight on the two old cars, and heard that corncrake that was like a bird driven mad by its own voice. He stole to the door and this time from either, or both, of the old women, there came a contented snoring. He woke towards dawn with a crick in his neck: he was still sitting up by the latticed window, his head on his arm. He straightened himself, stole into the kitchen, and with the bellows blew the seed of fire in the ashes into a flame. He sat there until his aunt Maggie got up.

His mother made no remark at his being there. The two old women were much too bitter with one another to heed anybody else. Each upbraided the other for snoring all night; each declared she had not slept a wink; they talked at one another through him, as if he could judge between them. Suddenly his mother complained that her stomach was weak for want of a cup of tea.

"Ho, then, and indeed," cried the aunt, red with chagrin, "but 'tis fine for you! We can't all have electric light and gas-stoves." He deduced from this remark that much of his mother's threnody of the night before had been a grandiose account of her fine house in the city. "And you may be sick in yourself," went on Maggie, "but you have a fine appetite anyway."

She said this, he knew, not from meanness but from envy and self-pity.

"You're no light eater yourself, faith," retorted his mother. "With your pint of hot milk lying on your stomach all night long. Little wonder for you to be snoring like a throoper."

"What! Snore?" scolded her sister. "Me snore? I that didn't

shut one eye no more than a peeler with your gabbling and gobbling."

So they went on all the morning until they were silent with sourness. By the time the two brothers arrived from Limerick, at half-past ten, the atmosphere had changed completely from the night before. Conspiracy followed. Maggie would take St. John aside and complain. Their mother would lure Michael out to say that she could never put up with her sister's peculiar ways. "She's light in the head," she pointed out. "And she's so rough. The house is a pig-sty. I don't know how she lives in it." When they had thus unburdened themselves, St. John took Michael up the orchard and they debated it between them.

All day the tension flexed and relaxed. Not until the afternoon did one of the real, underlying difficulties of the thing show its face. In accordance with immemorial custom the visitors had brought gifts of tea, sugar, bacon, cakes, eggs, butter. Maggie had scolded furiously when she saw them, refused to accept them, and took speedy possession of them: the whole performance according to well-established ritual. If the mother left now, all these gifts (which she had expected to eat herself) would have to be sacrificed, and her natural frugality could not bear the idea. By evening a second difficulty clarified itself. When Michael was weary of whispering in secret to his mother, "Mother, will we go home?" getting no definite answer; and St. John had asked Maggie several times, "Maggie, ought we take her away?" always to be deflected by some courteous reply, they realized that certain gracious laws of hospitality were involved, on both sides. Furthermore, since Frankie wished they had never come, he was obliged to urge them to stay. While Michael, who had suggested clearly on the previous day that Frankie should leave and that they should stay, felt himself bound now to urge his mother to go.

After a late tea-dinner, about four o'clock, all the meals being upset, Michael and St. John went for a walk in the fields. It had been a blazing day and they came back with their eyes and faces diffused with sun and air. When they rejoined Frankie in the orchard, where he lay full-length with his cap on his face, still trying to make up for the lack of a night's sleep, St. John almost chanted his praise of the countryside.

"Ah,"–he shook his head over it–"the bloom of heat on the hills! Like a grape. We saw a mirage. Think of it. Didn't we, Mickey?"

"Yes. The hot air waving. Like running water."

"We drank from a spring-well, Frankie. It was the iron-well, down on that old farm with the poplars. My God, I can remember drinking there when I was a kid. It had the same old flat taste of iron." He halted. " 'Twas a pity, though; the poplars were gone. I didn't recognize the place." He brightened up again. "We lay down under a hawthorn–the white full out. And do you know, we listened and damn the thing, not a whisper, but a bluebottle or a bee or something up in the blossom."

"Now, now," protested Michael, who had clearly enjoyed it all just as much as his brother. "I heard a hen."

"My God, Frankie, to live here. To end my days here, in a cottage like that one, Mickey, down beyond the river, with a stack of turf against one gable to break the wind, and a donkey and butt all to myself." He gurgled, and threw his head from side to side, almost hysterically. "My God, a donkey and butt all to myself. Imagine me on my own donkey and butt jolting down the road into the village to buy my groceries every week." He clicked his fingers enthusiastically, and laughed like a child for joy. "That's the life. Eh?"

In a tempest of rage Frankie sat up and shouted at him:

"Shut up, for Christ's sake, will you?"

They looked their surprise. He looked around at the four high walls. The birds were darting in and out of its crevices.

"I must get out of here."

"Where?" asked Michael.

"Anywhere. Out of Ireland. It's on my chest like the hot milk on Maggie's belly."

St. John, pouting like a small boy, protested that it was a grand country. Frankie spat at him.

"Is it? Well, I've had enough of it. It's all down on top of you. Like a load of hay. There's no space here. No scope. It's too small. Three million people—you can't do anything with them."

"Five people here," sniggered Michael, "seem to be a crowd."

Frankie squirmed around on his stomach away from their eyes.

"Do you understand him?" St. John asked pathetically of Michael, looking at the broad dusty back on the grass.

"Yes," sighed Michael, and let out an echoing, fainter, "yes. More or less."

There was a long pause and then Frankie muttered:

"You can't move these people. They're like lead. You're only a bit of grit in their eye. A bit of sugar under their boots. You said it yourself"—he flung around to challenge Michael—"I'm just a public nuisance."

After another unhappy silence, St. John said tentatively:

"Just what are you fellows out for?"

Frankie looked long and fixedly at him, and then his glance slowly leaf-spun to the ground.

"I'd have to give you a sermon," he evaded. "Read history." He glanced about him. "Look at it."

"But . . ."

"Yes, I know. Just the same . . . When you have a picture of a country bursting with life. Ach, I'm too tired!"

St. John said, "Ah, dear," and Frankie burst out with, "I don't want to hear about bees and bluebottles. I want the people to fight. To get up on their hind legs. To do things. To fill the country with factories and machines and money and . . . To work like blazes. To get rich. To be strong. To be a bang-up-to-date modern, live, fighting, working country. You and your bluebottles!"

His little spurt died out.

"It sounds rotten to me," complained St. John miserably. "I got all that in America. It's not my idea of Ireland at all. Besides, what's all that got to do with politics?"

"Try and you'll see," snapped Frankie.

"He means," explained Michael, "that Manchester and London run this place. Business and banks. And the Church, too. You know—the Middle Ages. All that kind of thing. A bit of the Empire. It's all mixed up."

After that they did not speak for a very long time. Frankie seemed to go to sleep on his arm. Then Michael said, "Well, what about the old lady? We've got to settle our internal politics."

"Yes," agreed St. John, without attending. "Michael, do you think that cottage would ever be up for sale?"

"Come on! Are we staying or are we going?" insisted Michael, for whom family affairs were never something to be shelved.

The two began to debate the difficult problem all over again. Suddenly they heard Frankie laughing, a cold, sardonic, bitter laugh. They looked at him and he nodded towards the two ducks: they were quarrelling in the long grass, quacking away at one another mightily. The brothers did not see any joke and resumed their serious conversation. Suddenly they leaped up in fright. Frankie had shot one of the ducks with his long-nosed Webley. It turned round and round, ran choking towards them, blood piping out in a neat, thin stream from its neck. It fell at their feet, and was still. They turned to Frankie. He was green-looking, and shaking from head to foot. He had the look of a man who might easily shoot one of them, or shoot himself. He pocketed his gun and strode off down the orchard to the house.

When they went after him he was locked in his room, and Maggie was as white as the wall. He had told her. She went out, up the orchard, with Michael. There was the duck on its back, and its companion stood beside it, saying a feeble "whock-whock." She lifted it, smoothened the warm body, and brought it into the kitchen. The other duck followed them down the path, "whock-whocking" wonderingly. She tied the dead bird's legs with twine and hung it on a big, old, rough nail beside the dresser that contained the rows of empty mustard tins. Then she sat on a sugan chair before the fire, and she cried the way a man cries, with very little noise.

They told her that they were leaving for home.

She tried to make them stay, and her weeping came on afresh when they said that they must go. She said that she would never see her sister again, and that their visit was only a come-and-go: as with all major crises—deaths, births, departures, misfortunes, weddings—where nothing rises but elemental values, the natural emotion of the peasant burst up excessively in her. At last they knocked at Frankie's door to tell him come and say good-bye to his mother. He made no reply. Michael shook the latch angrily and the door opened under his fist. The room was empty and when they searched the orchard there was no sign of him. He had gone.

It was dark as they drove into the city. The brothers passed no comment on what had happened until they had handed their mother back to the care of Eolie and Natalie (to whom she wept that she had wanted to stay with her sister) and had gone out to kill the night with a pub-crawl. Then St. John said, "You know, Mickey, that fellow Frankie . . . he doesn't love this country. He hates it." "Who wouldn't?" said Michael. They began arguing then, and spent the night so, quarrelling fraternally as they wandered from pub to pub.

PART TWO

In New York

I

When Frankie Hannafey walked away from the White Star pier on May 27, he suddenly realized that he knew nobody in New York. There was, indeed, his brother Leonard—Father Leonard Hannafey—a priest in Queens; but he had not seen him, or even written to him, since childhood. At this realization of his loneliness he felt something bounce inside in him—like a ship bouncing upwards in the water when it suddenly releases its ballast: he had seen a dredger do that when it opened its trap-doors underneath. And when he had found a cheap hotel, and begun to walk the streets of the city, so immense as to excite, so untidy as to be comfortable, he almost hugged this sensation of release. Dusk gathered and he was sitting in the park mesmerized by the vast cubes of buildings, recubed by their thousand windows, all now lit and the brighter for the oncoming night. In each building, in each window, he found a picture-in-little of this place where people can be crammed together and yet never meet: every window, every man, an individual pocket of energy; many, near, separate. For an hour he sat, and looked, and revelled. After supper in a noisy, clanging Childs, he came to a halt at the door, dazzled by the sight and height of a noble tower, top floodlit, barbaric in its black skin, its wings of gold on coign and rampart, its light shooting in vapour beyond its pinnacles up into the sky. For on its shadowy cliff-face one window was lighted here and another lit up there, images of power with indifference. Those one or two windows might merely mean a charwoman's finger on the switch. It did not matter. Each lonely light dilated into symbol. He moved on in a daze of rapture at his own like isolation.

For days he lived so; in pure sense, defining nothing. His

phobias slept, and would in time die in their sleep if only sleep persisted long enough. Occasionally they blinked an evil eye; as when he caught himself, a week after he landed, bolting the door of his bedroom; or when he woke up one night at some unusual noise beyond his door, and dived his hand, instinctively, under his pillow, and then found himself taut, staring questioningly at the fire-escape silhouetted outside his window against the neon glow of the city. With a grin like that of a man waking up after an operation and knowing it is all over, he had lain back slowly and gone off into a childlike sleep.

Somewhere downtown there was a hall where he could, and in duty-bound soon ought to, meet some of his comrades of the Revolution. He kept putting off that visit. (He had landed on a Wednesday; the following Sunday he went to mass. In the same way, after that one Sunday he did not go again to mass. The Irish voices, the familiar Irish papers selling at the doors, jarred on him.) It was like meeting a man in Liverpool—he had written about him to St. John—a spy he had tried to "get" in Ireland, away back in '21. He had boasted to St. John that the fellow would be making tracks out of Liverpool before evening. It was really not a boast. It was a wish. His own impersonality had been threatened.

June opened with a gush of heat that baked him. He loved its violence because it added the emphasis of the desert. He astonished a Russian Jew named Mann (originally Markovitch), with whom he had scraped a casual acquaintance in a cafeteria, by declaring that he loved the heat. He visited Mann one evening and found the fat fellow sitting in the basement, working on his designs—a commercial artist—among the coke and dust and lumber of the boiler-room, stuffy but at least cool. Something savage in Frankie was revolted by this flight from the heat, so that he cried that he loved to feel his shirt stick to his back. The Jew just looked at him and told him he was "nuts."

"You wouldn't feel that way if you had to work," said Mann, and licked the perspiration from his fat neck with the tail of his handkerchief. "And look at what I have to work at!" he bleated comically, holding out the damp handkerchief to a rack hung with raccoon coats, fur gloves, skiing outfits, and gazing then at his cartridge-paper, where he was trying to work up a good advertising layout for winter goods. "That's what the buyers are sending in now. Look at the darned things! And last winter I was sitting on the radiator drawing bathing-suits for Miami. And believe me," he screamed after Frankie, "this is only a zephyr. Wait until August! You blasted parasite!"

"I won't be here in August," laughed Frankie down the steps; and he began to wonder if he would.

The days were easily filled. He would spend hours reading (mostly Whitman—in the ideal setting) in a little park down beyond Wall Street where the air seemed thick with motes of heat, and men walked in their shirt-sleeves sucking ice-cream cones, and girls dawdled in the lunch-hour, so lightly clad, stockings rolled below the knee, or barelegged, in frocks of such light material, shantung, commercial silk, that their limbs were moulded clearly. In Jeanette Park or Battery Place, his ears rumbling, his eye dazzled by the million sparkles of sunlight in the harbour, he read with a particular pleasure such lines as:

> When Broadway is entirely given up to foot-passengers,
> And foot-standers; when the mass is densest,
> When the façades of the houses are alive with people,
> When eyes gaze riveted, tens of thousands at a time . . .
> I too arising, answering, descend to the pavements,
> Merge with the crowds and gaze at them . . .

Or, a favourite poem of his, to which he returned over and over again, reading it by day in the heat of the sun, by night in bed, his ears drumming with muffled noise, his eyes and mind still distant with what had blown them out by day, "Crossing Brooklyn Ferry":

Flood-tide below me! I see you face to face!
Clouds of the west—sun this half an hour high—I see you also face to face.
Crowds of men and women attired in the usual costumes, how curious you are to me!

The young man disregarded wholly the old man's insistence on himself; as well as the thought so often hammered home that "time nor place nor distance availed not" to divide them. It was not that he disliked it. As with the spy in Liverpool, he was not interested in that man, or any man. What concerned him and held him was the excitement of the pictures flung before him on paper and in fact. He read these and other such lines in the emotional greed of a man trying to seize one of the rarest things in life—so rare! Does it ever happen?—the joy of simultaneous sensation and awareness; the joy of seeing and feeling with the senses, and of realizing that joy, not ten seconds or one second after, but at the same identical second. It was a boundless greed.

He lived for about fourteen days in this curious state of contented excitement. At an old bookshop he discovered near Charles Street, where he went to live after his first week, he began to buy second-hand books, and he read them as eagerly as if he knew that he was (as indeed he was) making up for lost time. They were always the same two kinds of books, biography and verse. He went to the museums, listened to free lectures. He found endless attraction in the most raucous and dirty parts of the city, either around snuff-coloured Harlem, or the black and grey of the streets that jut off the low- and high-numbered avenues, where the elevated thundered by, the girders gathered dust and dirt in their criss-cross lattice, littered paper strewed the sidewalks or the cobbles, and the mixture of nationalities, all so poor and so struggling, was like a stewpot that curls a hungry stomach with its raw stink.

There was not a single thing about New York that he did not adore. So that when he wrote to St. John and, as the raw immigrant will, gave him his ideas about America, and got back a sarcastic letter in reply, he could not understand it. St. John wrote:

"I'll tell you *my* first impression of that filthy hole where you have landed your little baby self. I walked into an engineer's dream, as it seemed to me, the kind of plan a fellow works out on paper without ever expecting to see it come to life—all so regular. All straight lines. Left turns—right turns. Blocks and blocks. Remember I was a kid at that time. The thing struck me as inhuman. And H-A-R-D. I remember I said to myself, 'You got to be slick here, boy.' And I set out to be clever about finding my way. Somebody explained to me how all the street numbers increase east and west of the central line of Fifth Avenue. That sounded easy. All I had to know was which was East Side and which was West Side and I was well away. Well, I came up one morning out of a subway at Bleecker. I was looking for a job on Prince and I had been told it was below First, so I said to a woman, 'Madam, which is west and which is east?' She didn't even look at me, almost shoved me in the gutter. 'Gee,' I said to myself, 'that poor woman is deaf.' For you know how a Corkman would spend a quarter of an hour directing you—almost take you there by the arm. Then I said to a man, 'Which is east and which is west?' No *sir*, or *please*, or anything else about it, this time. I was learning fast. I wasn't going to be an Irish yob. I was going to be as slick as the slickest Sheeny. The man did what the woman did–shoved me off and walked on. I might have been a ghost. Then I asked a cop–he was Irish–he bawled me out when he found what I really wanted, and said, with a shove, 'Down there, you Rhode Island duck!' And he gave me a dirty once-over as if I was a blasted Wop. I laugh now when I think how I wanted to go right down to H.Q. and report that cop for insolence. I remember telling it, all angry and het up, to my roommate, a Pole called Raskotsky, and how he flapped his hand at me.

"No, baby brother, nobody gives a damn about anything or anybody but himself in New York, nobody believes you if you say you're poor, nobody but thinks you're lazy, and nobody will do a thing to educate the poor immigrants who can only work with their biceps–or so it was when I grew up there, and if it's better now (I don't know, I'm out of the ruck now) it's only because everything else is worse, and *believe me*. So when you go mewling about the 'grand energy' of the place I just– Oh, cut it out! I'm writing this with all the fatheaded cuckoos of Limerick outside the window of my little hotel. They've been at it since five this morning. . . ."

That made Frankie laugh, the June sky, the coffee-coloured meadows, the dusty, wide, dissolving views of Ireland under cloud-shadow, and that typically June cu-cu, cu-cu, just like popping corks. In-out. In-out. He had had his bellyful of that. That kind of thing would be there always. And he said to himself, as he shoved the letter away in his pocket, that St. John must have been a soft boy when he landed in New York, and that he was soft still; though he could sympathize, too, when he thought how the workmen in that packing-store in Prince Street would say, "Sinjin? What's that? Wop name? Oh! *Saint John?*"—with a derisive laugh for poor old "St. John Hogan-Hannafey." It was kind of St. John, too, to enclose a letter for the store-manager of H. H. Shoes, in case a job was what Frankie desired. That enclosure Frankie tore up. How long did St. John think he was going to stay in America?

Suddenly he discovered a new interest, or rather how much an old one meant to him—the theatre. He had long since read most of Shaw and admired him, as he admired everybody who tore up popular ideas. He had read and liked some of the Irish playwrights, such as O'Casey, for the way he faced up to the facts of life in Ireland; and Synge, because he tore the guts out of the priests and made fun of peasant morality. Yeats he respected, without knowing much about him, as a man who founded a national theatre, and had always spoken out for Ireland, and written finely about the men who were executed in the 1916 rising. Now that he was reading more of him he could recognize the lovely imagery. He liked to read him aloud as he lay at night on his bed in his pelt (because of the terrible heat). The younger Irish writers, mostly novelists, he found uncomfortable; they were merely exploiting things he took seriously, making "art" out of them, a despicable business; besides, there was nothing heroic about them, nothing of the sort you could read aloud, or show to people and say, proudly, "That's Ireland." He could not get any real satisfaction out of anything that looked at life coldly, observing and recording without any apparent emotion. He felt towards such writers as he felt towards the rich—a class apart.

But the theatre was not like that. There you were in the thing up to your neck, a living part of the whole, watching men and women talking, doing things, and there was no author obtruding himself with his descriptions and comments. He would go to a play, and then he would go, methodically, to the Public Library, to read all the critiques and compare them with his own opinions—mostly in disagreement—to which he obstinately held. He was thorough about this. He would sometimes go back to his room after a play and write out his own opinion, and then compare it piece by piece with the critics'. After two weeks of this practice he decided that the critics were all corrupt, probably bought, and could not be trusted. Meanwhile he read every dramatist he could find.

Ibsen became one of his heroes; the man who had grown up in a small, puritanical, ineffectually bourgeois society, who was attracted by nationalism and romanticism, for a little while became a Socialist, was always a radical and a hater of politicians, an enemy of sham, a social critic, a bubble-pricker, a lover of the folk-literature and mythology of his people. It is a figure to attract any warm-hearted young man, who will mould it to his heart's desire, as Frankie Hannafey did.

And yet there was so much more than all that in his hero; and although he came to know—or to think he knew—his Ibsen through and through, and read every biography of the man he could find, he could not help passing over those other things simply because they did not concern his life at this time. It is the way all untrained minds work. So, although he read *Brand* at this time, and read about it in books by people such as Koht and Brandes and others, he never really did read the play. The almost maniacal individualism of Ibsen in that fable passed over his head until years afterwards, when he came back to it, and then read it as for the first time and could not understand why he had not read it before. Ibsen in relation to people—that was all he saw now; not Ibsen in relation to himself—that dæmonically egocentric Ibsen who demanded absolutes, the "all or nothing" Ibsen, the Ibsen who created in Brand a figure driven out of the body of the world by a hysterically idealistic insistence on honesty from himself—that honesty which no man can possibly ask of himself, or live with for long, from which all of us spend our lives in flying hither and thither, because life does not tolerate such simplicity, or at least this common life of men and women which is a confusion and a half-truth, and must be if it is to hold together at all. Possibly so young a man as Frankie Hannafey could not have been expected to recognize that honesty, and the tragedy of it. He had not experienced its defeat.

There he either began, in that half-reading, something that would work itself out in time, or he ended something that would become clear to him only when time cleansed his mind of the detritus of that ending. It might never come to anything—the complications of a simple man are more than bewildering. If it were a new thing it might never come to the surface; other desires, other greater needs of his nature might choke it like cockle. Or else some great stress might erupt all his half-experiences, of every kind, in a vomit that would leave him clean of everything he ever ate. Then he would begin again. Like Nora he would end a life and take with him only the echo of his footsteps down the street.

He was thus contentedly bringing June to an end when he got a letter from his brother Leonard, in Queens, the priest he had not met for so many years that the man might have been dead. The letter upbraided him for not making his presence known. Wondering how Leonard had found out where he was living, he decided to see him.

II

That afternoon the clouds were like the underside of ice, and in the dulled light he found the view across Welfare Island a terrifying sight. He had crossed Beekman Place to the waterfront, and stopped dead, as if somebody had shouted, "Halt!"

He was confronted by a wavering sargasso of low buildings—like motionary spiders—fading off into a horizon the colour of dried mud. Slowly, as he looked, colour came out, though all of one tone, sullen as a bored eye. Then a Jacob's ladder of sunlight dropped like a stone on the reiterated gushes of steam that puffed in-out, in-out, from a building that looked like a generating-plant; and at once the whole district became cheerful as a smithy, and the very tugs seemed to rush through their own wake with a devilish, merry energy. Slowly the spotlight from the clouds moved, for about the space of one minute, across the brown terrain of roofs, and for that moment the chimneys came out under their white plumes and their black plumes, and then receded into their general murk. The sunbeam was switched off. The clanging purlieu, at that, smelled like an abattoir.

Frankie, gazing across the river, thinking how people, in their thousands, were going about their business there in thoughtless content, remained looking and looking at Queens for almost half an hour, amazed at the power of such a place to exist and of such people in such a place to be satisfied with life. Then at last he moved on, across Queensboro Bridge, and made his way, with curious eyes, east to Jackson Heights. The close-up of the streets and the people did little to soften his first impression of awe. He guessed that this requisite suburb of New York depended on New York; a reversal of the economic fact that depressed him. He had seen advertisements luring Manhattan to Brooklyn, and even to New Jersey—to some roof-dance on the Heights ("worth the trip for the harbour view"), offering free music at Prospect Park, or in the Museum, the Goldman Band, the Bronx Symphony, the Greenwich Sinfonietta, the New York Civic Orchestra. He had never heard of anybody going for pleasure to Queens. And as he came to his brother's presbytery he was saying to himself, "What a place to exchange for Cork!" and the little town-city at home smelled in his memory like an unfolding flower in rain. He rang, and as he waited he saw Cork, tumbled on its hills, crested by its green fields, threaded by its baby river, girt by spires, rain-washed, sleepy. . . . A man let him in, and showed him to a dampish parlour. The record-book lay on the table, and he read the last entry, *James MacCarthy: 123 47th Road. July 2nd. Viaticum. Non compos. L.J.H.* Some Irish exile wafted, unconscious, by his brother (L.J.H.) into the greater darkness.

Then Leonard came in, and led him upstairs, and to cover the embarrassment of those first moments he said, as they went upstairs:

"Well, Leonard, what kind of a place is Queens?"

"Fine place."

"Has it any life of its own?"

"Queens," said his brother when they were sitting in his private room, taking stock of each other, "is the finest place in New York. The finest people we have live in Queens—decent, hard-working, good-living people—many of them Irish. Ah, I love Queens. A life of its own? Of course we have a life of our own—we never bother about going across the river. We've our own schools, clubs, institutes of every kind, convents, cinemas, fine shops, churches, everything. What do you mean, 'a life of its own'?"

"Oh, I dunno—it looks kind of desperate to me, dirty and . . ."

"Dirty? You don't know what you're talking about. What do you mean—*dirty?* Do you realize the racket of the Street Cleaning Department in New York City? Holy smoke, you only got to look. Do you realize that it was found out, only last year, that not more than one block from the Pennsylvania Railroad terminus, the Cleaning Department"—finger prodding palm—"hadn't collected the garbage for . . ." And so on and on. Frankie was no longer interested. He was looking at his brother with something of the same deflation of spirit with which he had looked across the East River. He had been a lad of nine when his brother was ordained, and he remembered the bitter misery of the day Leonard left Ireland for America. His mother and the others had gone down to Cove to say good-bye, and he had been left alone in the island house. He had gone upstairs to the little room that had, for years, been set apart for "the priest"; there he had found, among the litter of brown paper left over from the packing, a small black rosary-beads belonging to Len. Clutching it, he had knelt by the bed and wept for his lost brother; then he had gone downstairs into the empty parlour, the beads hidden under his red jersey, and looked at the photograph on the mantelpiece. The soft, young face of Leonard, as wide-eyed, as innocent as if he had never read a page of moral or pastoral theology, though faintly chilled by incipient authority and the priestly sense of separateness, had looked over his head. He had taken down the picture and, weeping, kissed it.

Now across the intervening years, he saw how the first chill that so many priests never outgrow—for them, no second spring, no softening love but one and that a discipline—had congealed the mouth until it was as firm as a puppet's that opens and shuts on wires; the voice, until it had become like a thing cut out of brass. Two gold-sheathed eyeteeth gave him a ravenous look; his hair, flattened with oil, heavily greened with age—the grey under the pomade—looked dead and coarse. This middle-aged American priest, talking at him rather than to him, was so little like his young brother that he would not have recognized him had they met without warning in the street.

"Who told you I was in New York, Leonard?" he asked suddenly.

"Give a guess," said the priest.

"One of the girls?"

"No."

"Mother?"

"No."

"St. John, then?"

Leonard's face hardened.

"I and St. John don't meet now. I haven't seen him for years, and I may say, I don't want to. No! I'll tell you. It was a priest in Brooklyn. We were on retreat last week and he asked me if I knew you were over here. He had a letter from a friend of yours. She"—he smiled knowingly at the word—"got your address somewhere—maybe from St. John?" The priest winked. "A young lady-friend of yours from near Fermoy."

Frankie felt himself blushing; he had not thought of Josephine since he landed, let alone written to her.

"A good friend of yours?" quizzed Leonard, delighted with the blush. "Is she your girl-friend?"

"She is a very good friend of mine."

"Is she your girl?"

"I never thought about it . . . much."

"As a matter of fact," insisted the priest, more serious in

tone, "you're no chicken now, you know. It must be about time you were thinking of getting married. Let me see, how old are you?"

Frankie looked his resistance to the authoritarian tone.

"I'm not thinking of getting married!"

"Huh!" A pause. "We-ell, perhaps we're not a marrying family. And perhaps it's just as well. But just for curiosity's sake, how old are you? Twenty-six?"

"Thirty-three."

"Holy smoke! Do you know my age?"

"Forty? No . . . I was nine the day you left for America. I'd forgotten. You were back, was it twice? I didn't see you."

"No, the last time was for the Emancipation Centenary, and you were out on the hills. You've suffered a lot for Ireland, Frankie."

Frankie laughed.

"How old are you really, Len? Mother marrying twice, I can never keep track of our ages."

"Pushing fifty, my boy."

They looked at each other, softened by this thought of the fall of time—so much life gone that would never now gather them close. They smiled and shook their heads.

"Ah, well!" they said simultaneously.

Leonard got up and got out the whisky bottle, and as he did the honours he said, in the brassy voice, and with that pertness which grows on men who are not contradicted often enough, and the heavy cheerfulness of the man who does not get enough opportunity to be hospitable to a variety of his fellow-men:

"Frankie, boy, I'm not probing. [Parenthetically] I keep thinking of you as a boy. [Paternally] And, of course, I am older than you, and I've seen more of the world. But I hear from my friend in Brooklyn that this Miss Hogan is a very nice young lady. He was actually under the impression that you were engaged to her."

"So is she," laughed Frankie, with a caddishness that made him blush for himself.

"Now, be serious," admonished Leonard, cold as from the pulpit, holding out his glass.

"I'm only joking," said Frankie, but he felt he had lost a point and was on the defensive.

"*Sláinthe!*" toasted the priest. "You know, you might break the spell that's on our family. Eight in one family and not one marriage! That's terrible."

"There's St. John!"

Again the face hardened and the eye chilled.

"I don't count St. John's marriage."

(Just then Frankie did not take this point; it came back to him, later, to puzzle him.)

"I've had no time to think about marriage," he defended.

"But you can't go on like this all your life?"

"Oh, some day. Some day."

"And then it might be this Miss Hogan?"

"It might"—grudgingly.

"You do like her, then?"

"Yes—yes."

Leonard leaned back.

"Then," he said, with finality, "you'll have to get a job."

"Now, look here. . . ."

"Now, look here, you. Now don't try to sidestep me, Frankie. I meant to talk to you about this when I found out you were here. After all I *am* pushing fifty. And I'm not trying to shove you into matrimony, but—no, let me talk!—there's the girls to be thought of. Natalie is young and a good-looker. She'll get married all right; though she's a bit of a stick, and if she isn't careful . . . however, that's her funeral. Eolie's doomed to be an old maid. It's too bad; she's a grand girl. Michael's too old. I don't know anything about Claude, he's such a kid. Now, Frankie, you just can't all go on living in that old barrack of a house in Cork that's like a home for celibates. It's not human! I don't like it. But that's not the only point. Whether you marry or not, it's time you pulled your weight. Mickey and myself—I don't do much, I can't—have been supporting the whole family for years. It's not natural."

Frankie got up, his jaw out.

"I didn't come here"—coldly—"to be preached at."

"I'm not preaching. But whenever I think of our home in Cork, I always think it hasn't gone the way it ought to go. Life always seems to have gone down a kind of blind alley with our family."

"Always?"

"Yeah! Always."

He was angry about it. Frankie sat on the arm of the chair and decided to probe.

"This is interesting, Len. I should have thought you, as a priest, would think it all very sweet and nice to have everybody living in that old home in Cork—a kind of perfect Christian community, a little happy Holy Family."

Leonard gave one quick look to see if his leg was being pulled. Then he said, briefly, "Rubbish!" and got up and took his pipe from the table. Holding it, and stabbing with it, he stood over his brother and, with intensity, in his hard voice, and with the American twang banging the cymbal of each individual word, he said:

"It's not *life*. We were all given certain gifts in this life to use and employ to the best of our individual talents. We must in duty bound use these gifts to the limit. If we do not do this we are not living as God intended us to live, fully, each man according to his talents. Look at the Irish over here. Answer me this question: do they or do they not set to work, and work darned hard, when they get the chance to do so?"

"They seem to."

"They *do*. I'm telling you, my boy, they *do*. That means that if they got the same chance over in Ireland they would do exactly the same. They climb to the top of the tree here. And why? Because they have the natural ability. And there is nothing in the Irish character that objects to work or that lacks ambition. But over there—what happens? They sit on their backsides and they pretend that they are leading a better life by doing nothing."

He sat down and he spoke more easily.

"I've no patience, Frankie, with that notion you have over there that life in Ireland in some mysterious way is better than it is here in America, or in England, or anywhere else on the globe. And when I say better"—waving the lighted match—"I mean better morally. It's easier, I admit. But it's easier because you take things easy—that's all—because you're plain, plumb lazy. Here we *can't* be lazy, and if we could we wouldn't."

Frankie, who had been listening open-mouthed, threw back his head and laughed.

"By God, Leonard, I've never heard a better capitalistic interpretation of the Gospels! Is that what America does to you?"

Angrily the priest jumped up and put his pipe almost into his brother's eye.

"No, sir! And you needn't laugh, for if you disagree with me you're in a false philosophical position. Because you imply that life, in its nature, is morally less good in one part of the world than another. It's not. Society may be. That's another matter. That's got nothing to do with a man using his god-given talents. When you say life is hard, if you do say it, you're talking about accidental things. It's hard *per accidens*, as a theologian would say. Work—hard work—weary bodies—sweat—long hours—competition—there's no harm in all that so long as it doesn't prevent a man from leading a decent normal life outside all that. These are accidental things. It is the same order of created life behind it all wherever you go, and man is given by God adequate grace to meet his problems no matter how difficult they may appear or be for these accidental reasons."

"Well, our problems are easier than yours, that's all."

"They—are—*not*. You meet the same problems on a better ground, *that's* all. And the easier, in that seeming way, your problems are, then the greater the incumbency is on you to do more, to make a better job of it. That's life, my boy. Whatever you have to do, you gotta make a good job of it. Well? Answer me this! Is it what you call making a good job of life to have a family like ours going literally to seed? Is it? And the same is true all over Ireland. The softer the job, the softer they try to make it."

Impressed, Frankie was silent. Leonard drove his point in deeper.

"Yeah! And then they start up a kind of fairy tale about good, and simple, and holy Ireland! To cover up their laziness. . . ."

Frankie attacked:

"Life gets warped and distorted! Take it here at the start, when they were pioneering, taming the great Wild West, laying the great railways across the continent. Our people did that—yes—and they had a fair chance to keep themselves intact. Yes, yes! All that—yes! But, my God, here in Queens, what chance has a man to do anything for himself? What the hell sort of a world is it where man is surrounded from dawn to dark with what you would call temptations? You know what I'm after—drink, women, money-lust, at every damned hand's turn. The whole blasted vulgarity of modern commercial life. They're not accidentals—they're *real*. . . ."

He was off the arm of his chair; in his excitement he did not care that he was attacking what only a few weeks ago had thrilled and delighted him.

"Poof!" scorned the priest. "It's life!"

"Poof away! It's not life. It's warped life. I don't care what you call it. You can't poof that away!"

"I can poof it away."

"You can't poof!"

"I can. And I do. Poof!"

They stopped suddenly, and fell on each other's shoulders, roaring with laughter. It was the old days in Cork, that, even as a kid, Frankie could remember, when as in all homes with large families, there was always loud argument. They sat down, and Leonard filled their glasses.

"Seriously, Frankie," resumed the priest, "you're on the wrong tack. All you say is true as far as it goes. After all I'm a priest. I ought to know about all that. But it goes only a short way. You're merely agreeing with me. Only, as far as I can see, or guess, you're on the Socialist, and, for all I know, the Communist platform. It's true life seems to be distorted over here, and I suppose it's the same in all great cities. We do shove the realities down, so's it's not easy to see them sometimes. But that's the whole point—life *everywhere* is one long fight for the realities, and the fight takes on different shapes. You talk of money-lust. Holy smoke, is there anybody more attached to money than your Irish farmer? Look at our match-making system in Ireland. I'm not against the system of marrying boys and girls off to those chosen for them by their parents, if it's done in reason, but it's not done in reason—or usedn't to be. Look at drink. We were once notorious for drink in Ireland—thank God that day is gone. But if it's not one thing it's another thing. And I tell you laziness is just as bad as greed." His voice fell a half-tone. "You spoke of women. How can you of all people talk of women in that way?"

Frankie stared at him, astonished; an antagonist again.

"What do you mean?"

"You know what I mean. You know our family as well as I do."

Leonard got up and walked away to the window. Frankie's eyes followed him. He felt a horrible contraction in his brain, as when a snail's feelers are touched. He knew enough about Michael to know that the priest might be talking of him; but that would be so unfair.

"These are rare exceptions," he said weakly, taking refuge on general ground.

Leonard turned.

"Oh, I suppose I have a complex about it. Forget it, boy. It slipped out of me. Only, somehow, whenever I think, in a weak moment, how nice it would be to be back in Ireland, as a priest, I go back over those days in Dublin when I had to decide what mission I'd choose. I could have gone to Maynooth in the beginning and been a priest on the home mission. I chose to go to All Hallows and take a foreign mission. Even then I could have gone to England instead of coming here. I chose the farthest-away place I could get."

Again he turned and looked out over the brass top of the matted half-screen at the wilted leaves on a tree in the yard. Frankie was silent, calculating how far back these memories were taking his brother. He started as he realized they could hardly apply to Michael, and he wanted to say, "Stop!" But Leonard had stopped.

Between them the memory of the little town-city of their youth drifted into the room, too warm now, silent. For him, a morning of drizzling rain over Cork, blanketing the sleeping and the awake, a rain so silent it would make no noise in the river, so light it seemed not to fall but to float down on the warm, southern air. And for young Leonard, that appeal of home on the one side, and all that he had to think of on the other; up there in Dublin, so rich and ruddy, so calm with the dignity of the century that made it.

"Yes," murmured Leonard, remembering. . . .

The windows of that Dublin seminary, on its light rise, give on the south, where the lava of roofs flows to the docks, the harbour, the sea, and the far Wicklow hills rolling against the sky—all best remembered when the sea was an inky line from one particular late afternoon in autumn, insistently dark, sucking storm from the sullen sky, and holding it in skin-tight blackness of horizon. The evening lights crept along the coast, past Kingstown, flashing there with two lighthouses, dimming and twinkling with seaside houses into the dusk of distance down the Wicklow coast. In those evening hours of autumn and winter every novice must, at some moment, feel the loneliness of the priestly life, and in his premonition of a life that will never again enjoy home, long deeply for it.

"I was weak," said the man at the window, "and damned angry. And lonely."

"Angry?" murmured Frankie. "Lonely? You used to tell Mother"—he smiled inconsequentially—"what a cosy room you had there in Dublin."

Leonard turned and looked at him. It was so long ago—a quarter of a century of time.

"Yes, so I had. The President once said I had great taste, the way I did it up. Do you remember the cigarette-cards they used to have that time—black, shiny, little, real photographs, all glossy? I stuck them on sheets of cardboard—pictures of places all around Cork. I had a strip of pink carpet I bought against the time I'd go away to be a priest. I bought it with pennies I saved up from pocket-money in that little side-street in Cork—what do you call it? Castle Street?"

Efforts to re-create home. He looked about him now.

"I used—God help me for a soft slob!—cry to be back at home. And then I didn't want to go home." His face blazed. "I hated going home!"

He faced Frankie in a fury. Frankie stared at the revelation of what lay behind those young, chilled eyes in the photograph he had kissed. . . .

"My step-father has a lot to answer for, God forgive him now!" cried the priest. "I hope God *has* forgiven him. For years I didn't. I don't know do I to this day!"

"My father?" asked Frankie.

"Yeah! Your father!" he rapped savagely.

Then he stopped suddenly, seeing the staring face before him. He went white to the forehead. He sank into a chair and looked into Frankie's eyes.

"God in heaven," he whispered. "Didn't you know?"

The two brothers looked at one another. The priest shivered visibly. Frankie thought of the old superstition—"as if somebody had walked over his grave."

"Know what?" asked Frankie in a low voice.

"Michael knows," said the priest, but it was less his voice that said it than his lips that shaped it. "Eolie knows." But still it was hardly voice. "Did my mother keep it from the rest of you?"—and Frankie had to lean forward to hear that, and he was afraid to ask what was it that he did not know. He managed to ask:

"What did my father do?"

Leonard ground his ravenous teeth together, and he said coldly, brutally, in his brassy voice:

"He whored. He drove my mother mad."

Slowly Frankie got up. He was shaking.

"He's my father. He's not yours. Do you know that to be true—what you've said to me?"

The priest downfaced him.

"She's *my* mother. It *is* true."

As they stood facing one another a telephone rang in the corridor outside.

"So many people liked my father," said Frankie, weakly.

"They always like that kind of man. Any fellow who is cheerful in a club, a good fellow, a mixer."

The telephone rang again.

"He can't have been so bad," protested Frankie.

The priest looked back at his brother, and opened the door.

"Your mother . . ." He stopped. "I'll be back."

Frankie put down the glass and went to the window. He was thirteen when his father died. He had died of a tumour on the brain. It was not what he could remember of him so much as what he could hold by way of feeling; what he remembered was trivial—the long moustaches that were so ticklesome to kiss, the bright sixpences given as rewards for running messages, a general softness, roundness, and warmth, the long fairy stories told him when he was sick from measles. He had come to love his father in his memory, which had in time become enriched by all the grand rollicking stories they told about "Phil Hannafey, the Broker" in North Cork; and by what he had read into that jovial, roguish face in the photographs on the wall at home. He now saw again the big, enlarged picture of his father as President of the Chamber of Commerce, and the other one showing him on horseback, a regular dandy. As he saw them, other lazarene memories came to him from that little provincial city, with its tight bourgeois life, its cosy wealth, its small club-life. There was the lounge in the Victoria Hotel where his father took him one evening for a glass of cherry wine—it was hot, sunny summer weather—and on the settees around were replicas of his father, smoking cigars. One man with a gold signet ring, just like his daddy's, in a tall hat and frock coat, kept turning compliments to the lovely lady behind the bar. "Aha!" his father said of that man, as they came out. "Old Carey-Condon is a gay dog." And Frankie had laughed because the gentleman had moustaches just like a dog. He had, Frankie also gathered, a yacht down at Queenstown and he spent his holidays in the South of France.

Then there was the time when his daddy had to go away to London on business, and when he came back, spick and span, jumping out of the covered car, calling up the stairs to his wife, loaded with rich presents for her and for them all. Frankie, the youngest but for Claude, had opened the boxes for his mother, and displayed the scarves and gloves and feather boas. . . . He could not now remember that his mother ever wore them.

The image grew in his mind of a hearty, florid man, and of a whole company of hearty, florid men, his father's friends, who were the little kings of that tidy provincial city, and who were probably even more royal during those visits to London and the "South of France," where they would be more able to spread themselves than they could at home. For in Cork they had no court (except the lounge of the "Vic") that was free of the constrictions and censorships of small-town society.

Another sudden flash-back, pointless but still giving a touch of precision, a funny little memory, recalled how his father, at home one evening after returning from London, said:

"D'you know, I was walking down Bond Street last week, and who should I meet but old Carey-Condon. Tall hat, frock coat, grey vest, stock; all as neat and complete as if he was walking down the Grand Parade here in Cork. D'you know, I was damned amused. I took out a cigar but my boyo ups and outs with his meerschaum. He lit it, and he stopped me, and held it up, and says he, 'Isn't it grand,' says he, 'to be able to enjoy a pipe in the open air? But, of course,' says he, puffing away, and looking around him at the Bond Street crowd, 'we couldn't do this sort of thing in *Cork!*'" His father had smacked his taut thigh, and laughed up at the ceiling.

"You can smoke a pipe in Bond Street in London, but not on the Grand Parade in Cork!"

The memory lit the edges of life back there in the 1900's, in Ireland.

The sirens began to scream all over Queens. Leonard came back, apologizing:

"A sick-call. I'm on duty. I must dash. I'm sorry I spoke out, Frankie, but you're old enough now to live it down. I was a mere kid when I found out about it all. How's Michael and the old lady these days?"

He was collecting his things, buttoning, locking up the whisky.

"Why did my father marry my mother?" asked Frankie, coldly.

"Why shouldn't he?"—anchored by his key-chain to the cupboard door.

"Well, she wasn't young. If he was a man about town couldn't he . . ."

"Couldn't he marry a young girl? God knows! You're not asking *me* why men do these things, are you? She was young enough, and handsome enough—what was she then? About thirty-five or -six? She was a mere girl when she married first. Your father was about forty-six? I reckon he wanted to settle down. Possibly it wasn't every girl who would marry him. But I suppose after all he was a big figure in Cork, handsome, gay, attractive—oh, I don't know! When it comes to marriage and what men and women marry for, leave me right out of it. I tell you this, Frankie"—they were in the hall now—"and I admit it with shame, and with the greatest shame—it's a sin against the spirit, against life itself, and I try to crush it down—would you believe it, I rarely, very rarely, perform any marriage ceremony with the slightest sense of pleasure? There's a confession for a priest of God to make. Heaven forgive me, I sometimes feel the sin of the Manichees inside in me."

Frankie's breath was tremulous. But he had to ask one or two more questions. They were walking side by side across the yard to the church, where the priest must collect the viaticum.

"Did my father drink?"

"When Claude was born your mother . . ."

The priest stopped. He turned an agonized face to his brother.

"Don't ask me, Frankie!"

Frankie held his arm, for the last question.

"Do you know St. John drinks?"

"I know nothing about St. John."

"What have you against St. John?"

"I've nothing against him, but his way of life isn't mine, that's all. He's a money-grubber. He cut himself off from his people over here immediately he landed. He's swallowed America holus-bolus. He turned his back on Ireland."

"Do you mean *St. John?*"

"Yeah. And I know what I'm talking about. Don't misunderstand me. I'm an American. I live for America. But no Irishman ever can be *of* America, though he's *in* it up to the hilt. Well, St. John threw away all he brought with him from Ireland, instead of using it. It's the old story all over again of the man burying his talents. I must go. Good-bye, Frankie; look me up again."

Hands clasped, they drew away. Frankie held on for a last second, to say:

"St. John is dying to get back to Ireland."

The priest threw up his head, shook hands, and as he dashed away:

"What will he take back? What'll he leave behind? Look me up soon again!"

Then he suddenly came back and laid a hand on his young brother's shoulder.

"Can I ask how your religion stands?"

Frankie squirmed; it was like being asked, "Are you saved?" But he supposed a priest has to be blunt and quick in places like Queens.

"I suppose I'm what you'd call a bad Catholic. But never mind—I'm all right."

"We're all bad Catholics in one sense. I'll offer up a mass for you next week, boy. Good-bye."

He dashed away into the church. To be called "boy"—a familiar Corkism—touched Frankie more than anything else in that evening. He made his way back as he had come. It was the great hour when every place is "entirely given up to foot-passengers and foot-standers, when the mass is densest, when the façades of the houses are alive with people, when the eyes gaze riveted, tens of thousands at a time . . ." —the evening hour after work. As he looked back again from Beekman Place, everything was just as before, except that the setting sun now bathed the entire vast sea of roofs, and chimneys, and houses. His brother, hastening to his sick-call, would be a speck in that desert, a man trying to keep a candle alive as he hurried through an endless wood.

III

He had intended to go that night to an Irish club downtown to open his drive for funds for the Party at home. He could not face it. He took down a play he had borrowed from the Public Library and began to read with wandering mind. It was an Irish play—*Exiles*, by Joyce—and for the most part he failed to understand it. But he could feel the dark surge of sexual passion coming up from the pages, and he was excited by the scene where the woman back from Italy is wooed by the Dublin journalist.

ROBERT

[*Puts his arm about her shoulder.*] Only the impulse towards youth and beauty does not die. [*He points towards the porch.*] Listen!

BERTHA

[*In alarm.*] What?

ROBERT

The rain falling. Summer rain on the earth. Night rain. The darkness and warmth and flood of passion. Tonight the earth is loved—loved and possessed. Her lover's arms around her; and she is silent. Speak, dearest!

BERTHA

[*Suddenly leans forward and listens intently.*] Hush!

ROBERT

[*Listening, smiles.*] Nothing. Nobody. We are alone.

[*A gust of wind blows in through the porch, with a sound of shaken leaves. The flame of the lamp leaps.*]

BERTHA

[*Pointing to the lamp.*] Look!

ROBERT

Only the wind. We have light enough from the other room.

[*He stretches his hand across the table and puts out the lamp. The light from the doorway of the bedroom crosses the place where they sit. The room is quite dark.*]

This he read in disturbance not only of mind but of body. He was hearing the whisper of the rains flashing across the Tipperary mountains; recalling one night when he and Josephine sat, arms about waists, for an hour in her cottage, hearing the *plink* of the raindrops from the eaves. The image mingled confusedly with the few images he had of this Dublin suburbia. There, once, during the curfew years of the prowling Tan patrols, he had walked by the wet tramlines, with his finger on the trigger, and the Ranelagh trees made a wet noise though the night was dry and hard. The thought of a dark, hot, subterranean life going on behind the discreet façades while he stole by on the alert taunted his blood, whispered into his ear, like the whispering wind and rain, of the secrecy of the heart, of its dim honeycombs where every separate cellular thought lurks from its fellow, of the multitudes of these dark secrecies, in every man, every house, every town, every city, every generation. . . .

He flung the book on the bed. He picked it up again. Why was the filthy thing called *Exiles?* Bertha spoke up from the page, talking to her husband, one of those hermit intellectuals whose life is the exploration of those smelly warrens of the heart where truth cowers.

> What I suffered then—when we lived in Rome! . . . I used to sit there, waiting. . . . I could see the roofs of the city and the river, the Tevere. What is its name? It was lovely . . . only I was so sad. I was alone. I felt my life was ended. And I used to look at the sky, so beautiful, without a cloud, and the city you said was so old; and then I used to think of Ireland and about ourselves.

His hand trembled as he laid down the book. From his window he saw the dusk fall down over Jersey City. He did not see the smokeshafts or hear the rattle and whistling of the great river, but his home in Cork, and the last rainfall was pattering on the roof of the prostitute's house behind his house. His brother Michael had a white emaciated face. He saw, too, this woman Bertha and felt her as the earth that the writer had thought of when it sucks in the rainfall. His whole body trembled. He ran to the book and savagely he tore it down the spine. Savagely he tore that half-book across, and the other half across. Then he was back, shaking, where he could hear the slow sirening of a barge, and the echo of a liner from its dock. A sullen drunken light, as before a thunderstorm, spread like a bruise over his innocence and incomprehension. He murmured one word, a groan of pain, or regret, or that disbelief that is both belief and confession, "*My* father!" Then the light in his brain contracted, and the words began to recede into smaller and smaller print—

like opticians' test-print vanishing with its meaning. The chimneys came into focus, then faded again, gave way to the old childhood scene. He knew that of all those he had always known he had never known anyone.

He could not remain caged in his hot room, so he went out to eat at a Childs—choosing, as usual, the noisiest and most crowded place he could find. He walked the most bright and crammed sidewalks. At last, tired out, he came back and deliberately set to write to Michael, a cheerful, chatty, flippant letter, full of descriptions of New York and quotations from Whitman. Three weeks later he got back a reply, and it was a single page with typed verses:

"Dear F.,

"Two brothers sailed from the harbour out in two vessels, fairest weather, sweetest noon, until from separate beaches, where there was room and room, they looked across two wrecked ships and the breathing sleep of a tide that never ebbs, at countless other islands, dotted from horizon to horizon underneath the moon. On each there sat a man, just like themselves, each facing another face, a mirror of his doom. So until the end, they sit looking, never touching, hearing only the gulls gull-crying at the night falling and the daylight rising, and the sea-wave sucking its silence from the sea. There they lie marooned. Dear brother, from the belly out, you and I have gathered life together, gone hither, thither, wearers of each other's clothes, sleepers of one room. We might be ships of one shipyard or stones of one building, but at the end we know each other not the little least bit better than if we never had been issue of one womb. 'Tis sad, but it might be worse. The fault's not mine, or yours. Adam's curse. Write soon.

"Michael."

When Frankie received this rhyming letter the mood which had evoked the reply was gone. He at once took down a postcard, a coloured one showing New York at night, and wrote a reply of which he was extremely proud:

> Dear Michael,
> This is all a melancholy whim.
> For if you can float, why not *swim?*
> Yours ever,
> Frankie.

(Some time later he showed both "poems" to Bee Hannafey. She read first the rhyming letter from Cork, put down the paper, and said, "I remember your brother well. He was an interesting man. I wish I'd seen more of him."

Then she read the second page, and went a hot red that drained the whole lower part of her face until, up to her cheekbones and all over her mouth, she went yellow as if she was going to faint. A little perspiration gathered on her upper lip.

"Did he ever acknowledge this?" she asked, twirling the card.

"No."

"Frankie," said Bee, "you are a great person in a hundred ways, I'm sure, but you can obviously be the most maddening creature." She looked sideways on the ground, ruminating, and then slowly lifted her big astonished eyes. "How he must hate you!"

"But," he protested, "I like him very much. I know, for example, a good deal about him that nobody else even suspects. Yet I like him in spite of himself."

"No. No."

"But I really do."

She rose and put a little hand across his mouth. "Tell me,"

she said, "about your adventures in the revolution. I like hearing you talk about them."

"But I don't understand you," he insisted.

"Darling," she said wearily, "it might have occurred to you that the poor devil cannot swim.")

Now, having written his chatty letter which was to produce the rhyming reply, he went to bed. The noise of the quays, which are never silent, mingled with his dreams. He dreamed of his father, and then of a blond foreign woman—a Dane—whom he called Martha, a warm, luxurious, enervating image that troubled him for days. It had the effect of hurling him into his work as if to forget all that his meeting with Leonard had set growing in his mind.

IV

For several nights after that he was fighting, not loving, the crowded streets, the shadowy blue canyons, the vista down Amsterdam from 116th Street before the sun was too high to dispel the haze, but hot enough to bring out the warm, lovely smell of beer and sauerkraut from the German delicatessen shops and breweries; or the eastward view from Morningside Drive on the rising of the mist; or the uprising pride of the arches of the Long Island railway bridge that reminded him of a Roman aqueduct; the French restaurant life across 52nd; the swarming, tawny Italian life on the upper East Side; all the medley of Poles sweeping the streets; big Jews in the cinemas and theatres; small Jews selling old clothes; Greeks in the soda-fountains; Irish all over the place, from trolley-cars to the City Hall; fat-breasted Polish prostitutes around Ninth and Twenty-First Street—said to be the best prostitutes in the world; Negroes and mulattoes on San Juan Hill. . . .

All that medley and rattle of drays on cobbles, elevateds, trolley-cars, buses sucking up the melting asphalt, the dirt and heat and sweat that he used to find so exciting, was being compressed *against* him now in the barrooms of little Irish clubs, where one section of it—his own race—gave him a close-up of what exactly was implied in human terms, whether in Manhattan, or Brooklyn, or New Jersey, by that boisterous, maggoty, swarming life, that racing tempo, that exciting vitality of his first experience of New York.

These meetings rattled him. One, on a Thursday night, a week after visiting Leonard, caught him in an angry mood, when he was determined to break down the resistance that he had now been meeting nightly for a week. He had shoved open the glass-panelled doorway at the end of the pinewood corridor (one panel was broken and patched with brown paper and glue) and halted to hear the skirl of bagpipes and see two boys and two girls hammering away on the floor at a jig to the rattle of the pipes. They wore the traditional costume of the dancer: tight black knee-breeches on the boys, white shirt, green sash-belt; for the girls, bright-green colleen shawls that danced as they danced, long black stockings, and short dresses showing the knees, and the legs, as with all dancers, muscular from overdevelopment. He leaned against the jamb and watched to see if they had the native skill to dance, as the saying goes, "with death in their eyes and the devil in their feet," the head so steady a plate could stand on it, and the legs flying. He saw a group watching them from a row of bent-wood chairs along the wall, boys and girls mixed: that at least America had done—reintegrated the sexes. At home the boys would be at one side of the room, and the girls on the other.

He suddenly recognized a familiar face—a man who had fought beside him in a flying column in Tipperary. He was at first surprised to see how urbanized the Tipperary man had become, and then, on the rebound of that impression, he considered how many years had passed since those days, and wondered if they had made any change in himself. The young fellow, in his sharply tailored suit, low white collar, hair clipped tight at the back of the head, might be anything from the manager of a chain-store to a rising stock-broker. Only the softness of his mouth, as he sat and joked with a girl across the laps of two others, marked the distance between his racial rural nature and the hard nature of the city. The girl he was teasing was as unurban as anyone living in, and dressed after the fashion of, a city could possibly be: she was as unaffected as a statue of Simplicity: she had a gentle dark beauty; she was like a lively cocker spaniel pup. He strode across to the Tipperary man and said:

"Hello, Shawn Kearney."

They all looked up curiously. The pipes and the battering feet went on behind him. Kearney stared. Frankie could see as plainly as a moving picture the old ghosts come flying back across the twelve years of exile, the hurting memories; the deliberate and unwilling forgetfulness slowly dissolving as the man rose up, recognition widening his eyes. Then he gripped Frankie's hand in his two big fists.

"Christ!" he moaned. "It's Frankie Hannafey."

There it all was, written on his face—the mountains, the hedges, the tramps across night moors, the bursting bud of love for land, the heart-thumping, triumphant belief, and over it all the comradeship of fighting beside your fellows, your friends, almost your loves. Everything was there that exile means to the exile—those images upon images upon images that haunt the heart like a lust, and which you satisfy, or better deceive, with the perversion—like a sexual perversion—of work, and more work, in order to be let live and forget.

"Frankie! You bloody ould scoundrel, yeh!"

They were laughing, maudlin, into one another's faces; they slapped each other's shoulders; the Tipperary giant was almost crying.

"Jasus, boy, I never expected to see you again."

"Then why didn't you come back?" challenged Frankie, shoving out his jaw. The bully in him protected his sensibility. "Why did you leave us in the lurch?"

"Shut up. Yerrah, shut up. Come away, boy."

He dragged Frankie across the floor into the bar, not even bothering to say an "Excuse me" to the girls.

"I did go back, you scut," he mocked, when he had his foot on the rail and the Paddy Flaherty—a Cork brand for old times' sake—warming their veins. "I went back, Frankie, but I couldn't stand it. I saw 'twas all over. 'Twas all done with. They're only all out there now to make money—cadging soft jobs from the government. You know it's true. And yet, look at me!"—standing back for another look. "God, you're at it still! Jasus, Frankie, you're a great bloody man, but you haven't a dog's chance. Not one in a thousand. It's all over, boy. It's all over."

He said it miserably—thrust it away from him, drank his disillusion again, said good-bye again to that dawn when it had been bliss to be alive—so blissful one could have died as a song dies on its top-note, in exhaustion of fullness.

"Yah!" sneered Frankie. "You're a greybeard. You're tired. It's not all over."

"Shut up. Tell me about everybody."

"There's nothing to tell."

"Shut up, boy. Nothing to tell? Listen, do you know who

I was dreaming about the other night? Mangy Murphy. Listen, Frankie"—breast to breast—"do you remember the night in '21 . . ."

Out it poured, over the brittle dams that the exile erects against his past. "Do you remember? . . ." In friendship Frankie remembered; but only for friendship's sake, because the more they remembered, the more it became like an unrolling of an old map that sends its dust into the throat. To remember gave too much value to time past. He was living in the present. He tired of it suddenly and rebelled.

"I didn't come here," he bullied, "to be wailing and weeping about what's dead and done with. To hell with all that. I'm still up to my neck in this fight, and I'm not quitting until I've made a job of it."

The other looked at him wistfully, plainly asking himself, "Could it be true? Could that old world be won again?" Other men had also begun to listen, some young immigrants, some Americans of the first generation, some old men who had been born in Ireland but left it as babies, some old men who had never even seen Ireland but who lived by it as absolutely as they lived by the Virgin Mary and Christ crucified. Frankie saw that they were listening; and he saw through their pretended indifference. He knew it was not that cold, snakelike indifference of the hardened city man; he could feel pulsing underneath it their own natural warmth, the racial passion that is never killed. They began to close in on him as he talked. To talk to them was like turning up the gas under a cold pot.

"Here's a guy," Kearney besought them, "still wanting us to go on fighting for the bloody Irish Republic."

"Well, let him!" said the nearest man and turned away, almost in contempt. Yet it was the same man, half an hour later, who became as excited as a child when Frankie told them that the first place he heard of their club was in Cork. ("In Cork? Boys, did ye hear that? They've heard of us in Cork!")

"But," insisted Kearney, "he *is* fighting for it. There's a price on his head this minute. He's Frank Hannafey. They want him for the shooting of General Blennerhasset. God Almighty, that guy has more English lead in him than any man alive!"

They looked more closely, still trying to pretend that they were not interested.

"That's all nonsense," protested Frankie. "And I'm not here to blow off about Ireland. Nor to do the old soldier stuff. I came here, frankly, to collect a few dollars, and if anybody has a dollar to spare I'm ready to take it. If you haven't got them, or don't want to hand them out, that's O.K. by me."

"For what?" said a youth.

Frankie looked at this youth. He had a chicken's complexion, fair hair, soft skin, albino eyes; he was about twenty-nine or thirty, slim as a greyhound, and with nothing in him but his chilly eyes to reveal his masculinity. Frankie glanced over him rapidly.

"How long are you over here?" he challenged.

"Five years and a bit," said the young man, coldly.

"Well, you must know what's going on at home. Were you in the Troubles?"

"I'm asking the questions," said the young man.

A truck-driver leaned along the counter.

"Ye-as, we're asking the questions. What's the money for?"

A great fat fellow—he might have been a policeman if his stomach had not such a sag on it—came around and stood beside Kearney. He proved to be Tim O'Leary, a well-known figure in Irish-Ireland circles in New York; he was a library assistant in one of the universities.

"It doesn't count," he said, "about us, whether we were here or there. If you're after dollars, let's hear you."

The bartender wiped the damp counter and leaned idly forward on his red elbows, and stared with red-rimmed eyes at Frankie. Other eyes came close. They hemmed him in. They were the slightly drooping tawny eyelids of the New World that suggest an Indian phlegm, or a Negroid passion, and they dulled even the windows of these Irish minds with an alien enmity. Somebody shut the door, and the piper and the dancing faded away. The eyes did not deflect. Their hostility was, as Frankie knew by now, merely the unsuavity of the peasant hard-driven by the city. He had met it everywhere he went. ("My God," he had said for every one of the past five nights, "I have to fight the bastards here just the same as I have to do in Ireland!") He felt at that second ready to fight the whole roomful.

"Mind you, young man," said the fat paunch, holding him back, "I'm not trying to crab you. I'm just asking you. Listen, what do we know about Ireland? We know what we're told and what we read. I've not been over to Ireland for ten years. I have the bog-oak shillelagh just the way I bought it in Killarney, green ribbon and all. That's about all I remember about Killarney, now, except for those bucking broncos they hire you out at the Gap of Dunloe for fifty cents apiece. Come on! You're not the first fellow to come here collecting dollars, and I suppose you won't be the last. What's your story?"

The others grunted approval of that speech.

"I'll tell you," said Frankie, and watched the eyes spread with interest as he spoke. "Some of you believed in what we were doing in Ireland in 1921, didn't you? We were fighting the English for freedom. Well, you're not fools. You know as well as I do that when we got our own Parliament that didn't set us free. No!" He suddenly pushed his way into the middle of them and put his back to the counter. "I'm not telling you an old story. I don't give a damn if you say it was the Republic, or something as good as a Republic—that thing we got in 1922. Call it anything you like. It was a damn good thing as far as it went. Look at it this way. Whatever it was, it ended something and it began something. Isn't that right so far?"

The albino-eyed young man agreed, with "I suppose so." The rest said nothing, just stared and waited.

"Now we signed a document in 1922. You're clever enough to know that to sign a bit of paper doesn't set you free. It merely gives you the right to do certain things in your own way. Just as when you buy a car you sign a paper, but you gotta drive that car before it's any use to you. Well, you all know something about Ireland, and you know we've got hundreds of years of slavery behind us. It's in our very blood—fears of every kind—all the habits of the slave-mind. If we signed five hundred documents it wouldn't free us from those things, would it? Listen . . ."

He tried to think how to illustrate this in a way they would understand, thinking quickly before that glaze of awakening memory would leave those staring eyes.

"Look here. I'll give you an example. If you went walking in the country, to this day, or in many parts of it, and were well dressed or in an automobile, the people would still tip their hats to you the way they always did to the landlords. A people who do that aren't a free people. The memory of the whip is in their hearts. *Are* people like that *free?*"

"We're asking you," said the truck-driver.

"Great God, I'm telling you! Do you take your hat off to your boss when you meet him in the street?"

The truck-driver laughed scornfully.

"It isn't only that," went on Frankie. "That's only one thing—the relics of slavery. The whole country is being run on the old lines. We are under the thumbs of the big bankers, who are under the thumb of London. Half our business firms are owned by Jews. Do you realize that the Irish government is still paying rent for Irish land to English landowners? Our money system is buckled tight to English gold. The whole commercial community is falling in the shadow of Manchester and Birmingham and Liverpool. The whole idea of the new bourgeois class is to make a quick turn-over and squeeze what they can out of the worker and the farmer. It's not Irish. The whole blasted thing isn't Irish. It's no more free than you fellows are free of Wall Street."

The bartender swished the cloth unnecessarily and turned away as with final decision.

"He's Red," he pronounced and began to polish the glasses.

"He's not!" cried Kearney. "He's absolutely right. I've been back and I've seen it. The country is going rotten."

An old man whose skin was drawn as a mummy's over his pointed cheekbones, whose teeth were brown with age and tobacco-juice, shoved in his tortoise head. He might have laid the first sleeper and bolted the first ties of the Union Pacific Railroad. He was of the generation of the shanty Irish, whose fathers fled from the Famine to lay the U.P. trail in blood and sweat, hammering their great hate of England and their foiled love of Ireland into the Middle Western deserts.

"Are you for de Valera?" he asked.

"Are you for the Irish Republic?" asked a man who looked like a cross between an estate agent and a prizefighter. He must have been a fine animal in his day. He was now a cocktail-shaker at the Astor; he had travelled the world; he boasted after that he could sell anything from ink to gum if it was in a bottle.

"I'm not a label!" said Frankie.

They put him through a third degree. They pressed him back, shoulder to shoulder, their drinks held up for safety out of the crush, their smoke blueing the room.

"You must be for something."

"I stand for the freedom of the Irish mind."

"You *gotta* have a programme!"

"Give him a chance."

"We don't want windy talk. He must have a platform. Is there a party behind you?"

"There is."

"How many? Have we heard of 'em?"

"The whole country is waiting to follow us. Yes, we have an organization. Let me talk, blast ye–get back."

The air grew red-hot: it smelled of sweat and tobacco and spilt liquor. It had been like this in every club, only never so aggressive as tonight. The chicken-coloured young man shouted:

"First of all, what about the priests?"

"They're dead against us," admitted Frankie.

"They don't matter a damn," said the old mummy. "They were against the Fenians."

"Yeah," agreed the boy, "and Parnell. And Sinn Fein."

"Buggur the priests," said Kearney. "Go on, Frankie."

The bartender shot forward a hairy arm.

"None of that talk here!" he shouted.

"You go to hell, Bottles," said Kearney. "You were never nearer Ireland than Yonkers pier."

"Oh, is that so?" and he knelt up on the counter, but the fat librarian shoved his face in and yelled:

"Shut up, you!"

"Shut up, all of you!" roared Frankie, and he dragged the two nearest men by the lapels. "Here's the facts. Choice of government is choice of agent, do you agree? Well, agents for whom? For the people or for the fellows who always exploit the people? Is there any alternative? No. Very well. Who are the people in Ireland? They're farmers, farm-labourers, mill-workers, busmen, domestic servants, transport workers, builders' labourers, builders' tradesmen. About a million working men and women. And a million out of work. There's two million adults with their families. They are run by about one hundred and fifty thousand cuff-and-collar blokes. Civil servants, commercials, priests, financiers, government hangers-on of every kind from policemen to major-generals. There's no denying it. I'm giving you facts and figures."

"Go on."

He shoved them back, and looked about at them. He took the offensive. He began to mock them.

"Have ye any brains? Can't you use them? Well? Well? One million adults out of work. Farmers going bankrupt. Plenty of money in the towns and cities. Rows and rows of automobiles in every bloody little one-horse city in the country. Is that what we worked and fought for? Is that what you gave your dollars for? Were they well invested in that kind of Ireland? The backbone, the masses, can't get on top now any more than they did a hundred years ago, and the curs who have them down are . . ."

"How do we know this is true?"

Frankie turned to Kearney.

"You've been back. *Is* it true?"

"A lot of it."

The room was stifling now and crowded. Others kept coming in. Some left. More took their places.

"It's all true," insisted Frankie. "Why should any form of imperial tribute go from Ireland to England? Yet there is—land annuities to English landlords. The British hold our ports. Directly and indirectly money is going out of the country into English investments."

"It comes back again as interest," said the librarian.

"It doesn't give employment. The banks are investing abroad—giving employment outside the country. Not only land but fishery and mineral rights are held by absentee landowners. All that is the old machinery of imperial control—not by guns now but by financial influence."

"What's your programme to end this?"

He no longer, after that, took stock of the questioners; he just answered the questions. Sweat was sticking his shirt to his back, shining on his face.

"Co-operative ownership by the people."

"That's communism."

"It isn't. State monopolies."

"That's fascism."

"He's a Red"—from the barman.

"It's not. I am not. Co-operative distribution. We don't want any dictatorship of the proletariat. We want state direction. Internal conditions must be regulated by the co-operatives."

"Is he talking about co-operative creameries?"

"Break the connexion with imperial England."

A roar met that. They understood that. They responded passionately to it. God, how their eyes spread at that!

"Ireland for the Irish. People like us—like you and me. The common people of Ireland who never got a chance. The workers. The people who had to emigrate. Your people back home. God damn it, you see that, don't you?"

"Aye, we see that."

"Who's this fellow?"

"What's he after?"

Somebody shouted gaily: "Up the Republic!" Frankie was hammering his fist into his palm.

"What we've really got to do is to free the people from the mental domination of the damned compact majority."

The phrase from *An Enemy of the People* pleased him.

"The damned compact majority is always there. The vested interests. Whether it's the Church or the politicians."

The bartender shouted above the clatter of the glasses, "The fellow is nothing but a radical! He don't belong here."

"There's always a vested interest," Frankie pleaded, and he wiped his eyes with his palm. "Power corrupts. You free Ireland from one set of agents and you install another. But nothing changes if the spirit doesn't change. We want a social revolution."

"He's a radical"—from the bartender.

"Shut up, Bottles."

"Let me see this fellow."

"I'm interested in this guy."

It was happening as it had happened all through the work; they shouldered and lumped him without ceremony from one to another. They took him up and dropped him. Fat hands dismissed him flabbily with flips of contempt. Others bade him come again another night. One man gave him a bit of paper with an address on it and humbly asked him to come there. Another man wrote down his name and address. They could catch certain parts of his ideas but never the whole, never get a picture out of it. They had no political education and they understood only the phrases that chance, or somebody else before him, had dinned into them by repetition. Whenever he talked of the "Irish mind," for instance, he could see the glaze of dream give way to the glaze of incomprehension. It went on for an hour and a half.

Then he shouted he had enough and shoved them away, and he had to crush his way out of the bar. It was getting late and they were getting rowdy and somebody in a corner started an Irish song.

Outside in the hall it was cooler. He collapsed on a bench and mopped his neck and forehead. The dancers were gone, but up on a little stage some boys and girls were rehearsing an Irish play. He had not collected a single dollar. He saw the dark girl among the players: she seemed to be directing them. The singer's voice vibrated behind the varnished rabbeted wall. A sliding-hatch let the voice out clearly:

"How did Lord Edward die?
Like a man without a sigh.
But he left his handiwork on Major Swann,
But Sirr, with steel-clad breast,
And coward heart at best,
Left us cause to mourn Lord Edward, who is gone, boys, gone. . . .
Here's the memory of the friends who are gone. . . ."

"Blast them!" he cursed under his panting breath. "The sentimentalists," and he almost went back to tear the guts out of the lot of them. But he was dead-beat. A girl passed beside him and rapped at the hatch.

"Pipe down in there," she ordered, with good humour. "We can't rehearse our play with that singing."

The song sank, and slackened speed as it quieted. The hatch was jammed tight. The lines muffled into incoherence. "*September 1803 closed this cruel history, when Emmet's blood the scaffold . . .*"

"Hello," said the girl, and he looked up. It was the dark girl. "You're a great talker when you get going."

"What do you know about it?" he said brusquely.

"The men in there"—she winked slyly at the hatch—"think they can say what they like. They might as well be making their confessions to us—we hear more than they think."

He laughed sourly.

"I didn't get much change out of them."

"Nor won't—not easily. Ireland isn't the great thing she used to be."

"What play are ye doing over there?"—looking across the shadows at the group behind the electric footlights.

"For a competition."

Kearney came out with a glass of iced beer.

"Hello, Eily. You did fine, Frankie. They lapped it up."

"They seemed to me just to want to blather. And where's the dollars I came to collect?"

Kearney laughed with his wide Irish mouth.

"You won't get money that way. Get them into a hall and give a lecture about Ireland. My God, you *argued* with them."

"I told them the facts."

"I could show you how to get money," said the girl.

"Yes, she runs lots of shows for us. She'll run you a concert and you can have a talk in the middle with lantern slides —a cinematograph would be better."

"Slides? Of what?"

"Blarney Castle. The Lakes of Killarney. The Rock of Cashel. Everything."

"Christ!"—with contempt.

The girl laughed.

"He's too high-hat, Shawn."

Frankie looked at them, and then sagged back on the bench.

"I want to explain to them," he said wearily.

Kearney chuckled and slapped his shoulder and sat beside him.

"People have been explaining to us until we're constipated with explanations. We know more than you think. Besides, which do you want? Recruits or dollars? No, we'll work, we'll help, but we won't listen to explanations. I'll be seeing you again, Frankie"—as he stood up. "I'm going on somewhere to a poker school."

They shook hands.

"Come over to the play," invited the dark girl, Eily. "Tell us if it's all right for Irish life. I'm supposed to be the authority, but, gee, I'm forgetting Ireland myself."

They went across the dusty floor and listened. It was a peasant comedy, and, as he listened, it seemed to Frankie that he was looking down the wrong end of a telescope. It was Ireland in miniature, with all the background left out. The undercurrents, the passionate fumbling, the defeats, the little tell-tale revealing flaws of character, the errors of self-deception, the irony, were all gone. It meant nothing to him.

"Yes, it's the thing, all right," he said to them and they were happy and pleased.

"Poor devils," he thought. "They want their Ireland pretty. Like all sentimentalists, they want what we want without the labour of working for it." And he remembered that the priest, his brother, had said that it was the Irish at home who bury their talents and make up a fairy-tale Ireland to hide from themselves the work they should really be doing. Life, Leonard had said, is the same in America as in Ireland. . . . He thought of his brother St. John and his brother Michael.

In anger he suddenly sat up and pulled Eileen's arm. Its softness touched him like the softness of these good-natured, soft-hearted folk who were seeing in this comedy their ideal image of life—like a child's image of God the Father, all blue sky and golden stars.

"Look here"—he pointed—"that's not the scenery you're going to use? That farmhouse kitchen?"

"Yes," she whispered.

"But not that settee, and not those gold-framed pictures."

"Yes."

"But they should have a wooden settle. Straw-bottomed chairs. No pictures at all. It should be untidy, even a little dirty."

"Oh, they wouldn't stand for that. They say that's stage Irish—Paddy with the pig. I told them the cottage should be whitewashed, for instance, but they said they're tired of whitewashed cabins. They're sick of people asking them, 'Don't the Irish ever have proper houses to live in?' "

He said, "What the hell do they care? A farm is a farm," and got up and walked around the hall, looking at the framed photographs of Killarney, Slievenaman—the romantic face of life—and he murmured the lines from Yeats's poem:

> "Romantic Ireland's dead and gone;
> 'Tis with O'Leary in the grave . . ."

and grunted, "I wish it were."

"Does all the world fly from simple reality," he wondered; "always need to turn reality into a myth before it can adore it?" Then he thought, "What is the most real thing in Ireland to me?" and it was the whitewashed cottages and the rain; the rain sucking into the land like a million croaking frogs of a late March evening—that soft rain that fills the sky with the scent of the countryside, hissing and then whispering into silence, until the air is shining and pure, and it is as if somebody had thrown a handful of colours into the sky and they stay there slowly melting. So it would be from the door of Josephine's cabin, with the *plink* of the raindrops on the sill, and the lovely sweet smell of the dungheap outside in the haggard. He came back and sat down, but the rehearsal was now over; disconsolate, cross-tempered young man.

"You look green," said Eily.

"It's the heat. Come out and we'll get a breeze and an ice-cream."

Her name was Eily Mallon; she was a masseuse in a hospital; she was free every Monday and Thursday night. They had peach sundaes at a Greek soda-fountain; after it the night heat from the sidewalks came up like a hot breath. Brooklyn Bridge was a gallows and dull thunder. They were imprisoned between the red sky and the dark earth with its steady lights.

"And you don't ever want to go back?" he asked.

"Oh"—the formula of every exile—"I wouldn't like to die in America."

The two went in among walls of packing-cases and found the oil-smooth river below them.

"I suppose you'll be going back to your old politics?" the girl said, and Hannafey grinned.

"My old politics? You'd think it was my 'old dog'!" They smoked. "I'm beginning to think my 'old politics' are the same here as there." He explained in reply to the questioning upturn of her pale face. "I'm not clear on it yet, but . . . I have a brother, his name is St. John Hannafey—that's my name—he makes H. H. Shoes—he comes over to Ireland and begins blathering about what a grand country it is and how he'd be happy living in Kilfinnane, lying in the fields, doing nothing."

"He'd die of the lonesomeness in a month."

He held her soft bare arm excitedly there among the arc-lit packing-cases, with the great bridge rumbling, and the red sky over it, and the river dark below it.

"You're right not to go back." (The softness of a woman who had the strength to fight a pitiless city.) "Nobody can, once they leave it for good. Ireland is too dead. There's no struggle there, and that's what my brother wants—somewhere to die in peace like an old worn-out jackass. That's it. To live and die in peace. No!—in sloth."

He let her arm go, and drew his cigarette into a red glow. He laughed into her face, pleased with her and with himself.

"You're a queer fellow."

"No, you've the right end of the stick, Eily."

"Have I?"—in rising key of disbelief and puzzlement. She sent out a light vibration of amusement, teasing and stirring. She leaned across and began to straighten his tie, which he had dragged all askew in the club bar. He permitted her to do it, looking into her gold-specked eyes that glowed over her cigarette.

"You know what I mean! Anybody with a bit of life in them would! In Ireland you sit all day long and talk and mope about. Or go to point-to-points, follow the harriers. But there's damn all to *do*, really. There's no challenge." He pushed down her hands. "They go dead as mutton—take to drink!" His eye followed a shadow on the river, lit by pricks of green and red and a few portholes of yellow. She said, "Where's that boat going to?" He said, "I've another brother who's like that—drink and women—the poor sot."

The sound of a stringed instrument came up from the deck and was lost in the general rumble of the city, and of an elevated train across the great suspended gallows.

"You shouldn't talk about your brother like that. I must be going back—I have late leave but it's time I went."

They got up.

"You get bottled up," the young man went on. Preoccupied with himself, he was paying no heed to her. "Like St. John."

"Bottled?" she trilled.

"Christ!" He turned on her. "That's us Irish all out. Can't you be serious? Listen, I got a good idea tonight. I must think it out. But I know this much now, our people are never going to get free until they get something to fight. That's what makes a man of a man."

"Haven't we had enough fighting? Who is there to fight?"

She caught his rapscallion wink, full of youth, freshness, eagerness, pride of himself. There was something so childishly naïve about it she took his arm as if she were his mother.

"Who?"

"I'm not telling you."

"Yerrah, why not?"

He laughed, triumphantly, flung his cigarette away, and began to hum a few bars of a jazz-song, "It Ain't Nobody's Business What I Do."

"I think you're goofy."

He squeezed her waist in a contemptuous friendliness.

"You wouldn't understand. It doesn't concern women anyway. But I tell you this, Eily, somewhere in the Bible there's a story about somebody wrestling with an angel. 'Twasn't Tobias, was it? No, he caught a fish. But that's the idea. You gotta wrestle with something. Our people fought the landowners. They fought the British. They fought even the priests. Well, I once slept in a priest's house one time I was on the run from the Black and Tans and he had a phrase he was always using. 'Every neurosis sets up a psychosis.' "

"What in the name of God," she profaned, furious with him, "*are* you talking about?"

He squeezed her again in good fellowship. A line of trucks rumbled by—machinery from the great depots on Canal Street.

"It means," he scorned, and delighted, "that if you kiss a girl you fall in love with her. Every time you hit a man you hate him. See?"

"If you squash me any more what's going to happen to us?" she said, catching his idea at once.

He burst out laughing in admiration at her quickness. There on the sidewalk he made her dance a few steps with him. Then he held her out at arm's length. The coloured artificial sky hung over all. Anybody would have said these two were a pair of lovers, they leaned so close together now. The talk had stopped.

A train came rushing along the tracks but the two did not stir; the young man's grip was tight on her arm, and he led her down to the empty end of the platform. She was looking at him curiously, tentatively, wondering if he was as much disturbed as she was.

"You'll have me climbing in the window," she murmured.

"Will I see you again?" he said.

"Maybe," she teased. "If you want to? You know what my free nights are."

"I'll see you home?"

She smiled invitingly. He laughed uncomfortably, unsure of what she meant, knowing he desired her. Her arm was warm. He slipped his other arm about her waist. She let him press her to him.

"I don't know your name," she whispered up to him.

"Frankie."

She searched his face from eye to eye. Her eyebrows were twitching. He could feel her leaning closer. Then, suddenly, as he heard another train on the opposite side, he released her;

and when it was gone another came roaring in on their side. He put her aboard and said, "Good night, Eily." Astonished, she waved her white arm, and said, blankly, "Good night," and then the young man walked away, down the stairs, and across to the Hudson side, and past all the piers to his room, walking so fast he was soon in a sweat. He was fallen like a stone through the air out of his elated mood, and when he got to his room, and undressed, and lay naked on his bed because of the gummy heat, he could not sleep.

He put on shirt and pants and padded down the corridor, where, on his way in, he had seen his neighbour through an open door, a Pole whose real name he did not know—he had changed it to Smith—typing on a noiseless typewriter.

He was in his B.V.D.'s at his table, with a green celluloid shade over his eyes. Frankie knew that he was a lawyer, just starting off his career, and that he was organizing the Poles in his ward; he had political ambitions.

"Hello!" said the Pole, glancing up.

"Smith," said the Irishman, "I've been trying to knock some sense into some of the Irish here. They don't seem to bite. Do you find your people just as tough going?" It was the first question that came into his head.

The Pole, a fat-jowled man of about thirty-one or -two, was very solemn and as ponderous as a Teuton. Within five minutes Frankie was sorry he had asked the question; for the Pole slewed around and said, "Well, it is this way . . ." and began a recital that started with the Slavic tribes, waded to the Mongol invasions, the Jewish refugees, the Swedish confederation, Sobieski, Kosciuszko, the partitions of the eighteenth century. . . . It would have been interesting if, simply, Frankie had been interested; but his eyes kept wandering to the green-shaded lamp; he was not seeing, listening, or understanding; his "I see" every two minutes was the voice of a sleepwalker. Finishing the conversation, he went back and undressed again and lay smoking on the bed.

When she had waved good-night to him with her white arm she had looked at him as if he had suddenly snatched her bag—astonished, disillusioned. He had robbed her, even though it was only in his thoughts; and then he had not, and it was a worse robbery. Her shadowed gold-speckled eyes were familiar to him, with their submerged crags. The pin-sharp eyes of his aunts and uncles back in North Cork stood out of the same kind of dim, milk-clouded pool where from time to time attention drowned itself. It was that softness in her that called him, to drown with her, and he half gave up his will to that dark entry, and then raced away from it again. His body squirmed, between fury and desire—anger at the vortex; the wish to be lost. And then he saw the hard, tawny-lidded eyes of the men in the club swoon out of their focus of application—the effect of endless labour—into the dream he had prepared for them, and he sat straight up in the bed in horror at the comparison between his lust and their love.

The telephone rang. Surprised, he looked at the watch on his wrist. It was half-past midnight. He was leaning on his side to keep the cigarette-ash from falling on the hair on his chest, and as he took the receiver he heard from the river the swish of a propeller and a plunging turbine; the sky was rosy with labour. It was the mournful, drunken voice of his brother St. John.

"Hello, Frankie? Lishen to me, boy. No, be quiet. I'm up-town at a night-club. Why the hell didn't you come to see me? I've been back for weeks and weeks. Been to a show with Bee—she arrived this morning. I wanna tell you someth'n'. I'm going back. I'm going back t'Ireland soon as ever I've nuff money. I gotta go back. And you, you whippershnapper, let *me* tell you thish . . ."

Over the drunken, whining voice Frankie could hear the faint strains of a jazz-band. The ash fell on his bare thigh and he cursed.

"Shurrup. I love Ireland. She's my own country—she bore me—she's my mother. I can't do without her. She's rich and rare land. I love my country. Hear that? I—hup—never fought for Ireland but I've given her what I had—money."

"Well," interrupted the naked man, "will you give *me* money?"

"What for?"

"Ireland."

"Give money to no f—g radicals. But I give it to Ireland. 'Cos I love her. I need her. I want her." He was sobbing it. "Most beautiful country. Pure and innocent country."

"Go to hell. I'm ringing off."

"No, wait. Wait. Wait. You can't ring off. Not when it's about Ireland. What I wanna say, boy, is thish . . ."

Frankie rang off. He thought of Bee, frail, with her blued hair, her big eyes, her trembling mouth, the way he saw her that night in Cove. What a life she must have with that sot! The bell rang again.

"Hello. You can't do thish to me, boy. Don't you dare ring me off. I have to tell you somethin'. I'm going back t'Ireland next month. When my children come home from Europe I'm going back to Ireland. Lishen. I want to tell you something about Ireland—something you don't know—nobody knows—I dishcovered it. Know what it is? There'sh a meaning to life in Ireland. Only country in the whole world. There'sh meaning to life. I discovered that."

"Go to blazes. I want to sleep."

"Just one minute."

Frankie rang off, and lay back. The sky was still red; the

turbines tumbling. His skin was sticky with the heat. The bell rang again and he ignored it. It kept on ringing and then somebody hammered furiously at the wall. He sat up on the edge of the bed and took the receiver.

"Go away, you drunken sot!" he yelled. "Go away."

"*Am* a drunken sot. I know it. Tha'sh neither here nor there. Lishen to me. I'm a drunken bowsy but I'm your brother. We were born same town, same country—Ireland. She'sh your mother. She'sh my mother. I love my mother. Frankie, will you come back with me?"

"Will you please go away? I want to sleep."

Somebody hammered at the wall again. Unless he held the receiver all night the whole house would wake up.

"For God's sake ring off—you're waking the whole house."

Again the man next door hammered, madly, like a machine-gun. Hannafey gripped his hair in rage. He put his lips down into the mouthpiece and hissed.

"F—— you, go away!"

"Lishen! I jush want you to know what I've done. 'Ve done a fine bit of work. For Ireland. I've got this band here 'way in Thirty-Ninth Street, lowdown, lousy, Wop club, full of blond floozies, to play for Ireland. Cosht me ten bucks. But do more'n that for Ireland. They're beginning. Lishen."

Hannafey could see the drunken old man, in his tuxedo, opening the door of the telephone-booth, straining the mouthpiece to the door. From his bed he could clearly hear the whine and scrape of the band—the saxophones, ukes, piccolos, horns—at the old emigrant's song of farewell. A nasal voice crooned the words:

"Come back to Erin,
Mavourneen, mavourneen,
Come back to Erin the land of thy birth . . ."

"Hear't Frankie," wept the drunk. "Christ, 's grand. Beautiful."

Then the drunken voice broke into maudlin song.

"Come with shpringtime, mavourneen, mavourneen . . . Oh, I can't help it. I have to cry. I love my counthry." His voice broke. "I love Ireland," and he roared it again, "I tell you—I LOVE IRELAND!"

Suddenly everything stopped. The band was shut out. A new voice came in—a woman's voice. It was Bee Hannafey.

"Who is that?"

"Frankie Hannafey."

"Oh, I am so sorry. St. John's been on the tiles tonight. Welcoming me home. You want to sleep now. Good night. Come to lunch tomorrow, will you?"

"Yes."

"Good night, Frankie."

"Good night, Bee."

He lay back. Her voice had been hysterical—trying to be normal. In her evening dress she would be taking St. John home. Everybody sniggering. Her first night in New York. Naked as he was, his body was cling-damp with perspiration. The turbines plunged and tumbled. The refrain wriggled in his brain like a worm. Still he couldn't sleep. His thoughts transferred themselves to Bee.

V

In the morning she telephoned that she would send her chauffeur to collect him at his lodgings at half-past twelve. She apologized again for St. John, said he was very shamefaced, and added, "We must all be very nice to him. It was for my sake he did it, poor man."

He spent until twelve making a fruitless call on a garage-owner who was supposed to be friendly to all Irish nationalist movements. (From this on he made a collection of "friendly" names.) The man was certainly friendly, but evasive. He was, it came out afterwards, running for some municipal job and had in the past fought with one of those local political groups into which the general pro-Irish movement split in bitter feud, in America as at home, on the founding of the Free State; now he found it necessary to make up his old quarrels and was shy of anything controversial. For an hour he talked about Irish politics, in New York and Ireland, hedging and meandering in a manner in no way peculiar to Irish politicians, but all with an air of frank good humour that nobody but an Irishman could have made appear so completely unaffected and casual. Frankie Hannafey, well accustomed to this art of ambiguity, agreed with everything the man said, believed none of it, and went away angry that he had not told the fellow what he really thought of him. The cream-pale limousine with its Negro driver was waiting at his door. To assert his emancipation he got in beside the driver and bade him go ahead.

They picked up Bee Hannafey at a flower-shop. Their meeting was, for him, an impact. He had remembered her as a woman several years older than himself; he was astonished to find himself speaking to her as if she were far younger. It was partly her figure, so light and so tiny, like that of a girl of twenty; partly her vivacity, but mainly it was her wide-eyed eagerness.

She wore a sophisticated little black hat, like a small drum, tilted to her nose, with two little horns out of the crown. It kept trembling in little shivers as if her heels were on springs. Her costume was in red and blue like an English postman's, with vast cloth buttons in red; and red piping outlined the collarless neck. It was a parody on a military uniform. Yet, in that luxurious florist's on Fifth Avenue, in her comic-opera dress, she reminded him suddenly of a line in Wordsworth —"surprised by joy, impatient as the wind." She was, once again, less a woman than an aerial creature that had alighted on earth and stood quivering to be off again.

"We must wait for my mother. Oh!" She whirled and seemed as if she would fly from the floor, out of doors, and over the great skyscrapers. . . . She whirled back, with her finger-tips (she was wearing red net gloves) to her lips and her eyes almost bursting with a farcical dismay. "She's coming to lunch! I forgot to tell you. *Do* you mind? I had to have her. St. John and I are going to the country for the week-end."

"I'd like to meet your mother."

"She's rather a person," whispered Bee, and gave a malicious look to explain "a person." "Don't you like my gloves? They're made of cord. The Austrian peasants make them." Then she apologized, murmuringly, for St. John.

He towered over her, but he felt no internal disproportion of size. He felt like saying, foolishly (for she knew it as well as he did), that the last place he met her was in Cove. It was merely a way of saying that it was the last place in which he had met any woman who really interested him. It was a way of thanking her for being herself. So that while she was murmuring her regrets for St. John's behaviour last night, he was feeling only that a hiatus had been bridged: and it was, to him, a hiatus of something much more than time. A gush of gratitude flowed from him, met something flowing from her, and clashed like sunlit waves. That lovely sensation of release, of sudden freedom, all the joy that he had got in his first ecstatic days in New York, but which had since been dwindling under the pressure of familiarity, sprang up again. He hushed her apologies, and loved to see the swift change to gaiety—she leaped from mood to mood like an antelope —and he was just about to say, "Look here, can't we dodge your mother? Let's lunch alone," when a tall lady in grey veils rose up between them like a gauzy ectoplasm from the floor. She drooped her veils over her daughter—such a tall mother for so tiny a daughter—and kissed her.

"Bee! Darling! It's so grand to have you back again." She had a rich, if theatrical voice, throaty, a fine contralto. It had only the merest trace of American nasalization, firmly held down in the cavern of the mouth. "But, you are wearing no stockings!"

"Oh, Mamma. The first time you see me in nearly three months! Nobody but you would have noticed it! Or said it! Do you notice everything? It's so *hot!* This is Frankie Hannafey—St. John's young brother. Or is it step-brother? Frankie, this is my mother, Mrs. Bland. Now don't make that old joke about Bee Bland!"

The tall old lady threw back her veils, right and left; so a woman combing her long hair throws back her plaits; she surveyed Frankie's face with insolent thoroughness. Always polite to old people, he smiled pleasantly; under her gaze the smile gradually turned sour; as his eyes moved towards Bee they had become like those of a child who has bitten a chocolate and discovered that it is a pill.

"Why have I not heard of you before?" Mrs. Bland asked in her throaty voice. Then, on the spur of some thought, she gyrated towards Bee. "*Where* did you say you met this young man?" But, on the spur of another thought, she looked back at Frankie, who was by now in a furious temper, and floating all her pink and grey wings about her she swooped towards the door, saying, "We cannot keep your husband waiting, my dear Bee." Bee's gloved palm pressed Frankie's wrist. She almost laughed at the consternation and sulkiness in his face, she was so delighted to find that he liked meeting her. A quick warning, appealing look was all she could give him, but her affection lightened it, her hopes gave it implication and undertone. It contained a promise and a pact. Nobody but a practised woman can do that sort of thing, convey in a side-glance, a bit lip, a pressure of the fingers, an appeal and an offering—all without compromising herself in the slightest way.

With frowning brows they hurried after the old lady, and Frankie felt like a telegraph operator who has taken in a hundred messages in double-quick time, and knows the words without grasping the meaning. For obstinacy, he sat sulkily with the Negro driver. He felt exactly like a child deprived of a great happiness briefly dangled before his eyes. The car edged into the sunlit traffic.

"Bee," asked her mother, as they shot forward in their line of cars, "does your young man always sit beside the chauffeur?"

Coming up from her warm dream, Bee gasped:

"I don't know, Mother. It's the first time I've sat in an automobile with him."

She conceded to herself that this was not a fact—that morning by Cove harbour, with the gulls afterwards squawking over the steely lochs.

"What does he *do?*"—from her mother.

"He . . ." Bee paused, considering her words, trying to calm the still simmering excitement of her heart.

"Yes?"

"Why, I don't believe I know. He's an Irish . . . I don't know how to describe it. A political . . . Well, St. John says that 'secret agent' covers a lot."

"Secret agent? I knew a man from Albania once like that.

He had black finger-nails! What does he agent for? What does he *want* in America?"

Her mother's voice had dropped conspiratorially.

"Oh, he's not an agent, really. I mean he's just . . . he's a kind of patriot. I suppose he's an agitator, really."

"I see." Then suddenly, as one who insisted on not being fobbed off with inadequate information, her mother said, "What does he agitate *for?* Tell me *all* about it."

Bee smiled, a bare, bored ripple of a smile. She glanced at the fair head before her, the firm wiry hair, the ears with pointed tips like those of some kind of wild animal, the strong shoulders. Then she looked out at the shafts of sun that poured on the avenue from the left, dizzying ladders of light from the tops of the office buildings. She looked the other way and saw a flock of pigeons rising into the sun from before the Plaza, sorry that in the noise of the traffic she could not hear their wings. She caught her mother's eye, fixed on her.

"Oh!" She started. "I really don't know. For Ireland. He's Left. Communist, I suppose."

She heard her mother say, in her throaty, accusing voice, "Why did you never mention this young man to me before, Bee?"

Bee tossed her head a little, and smiled.

"Forgot. It wasn't important."

"Hm!" pronounced the old lady.

The traffic had thinned; the avenue was almost quiet here, and the shops had become more intimate and luxurious and irrelevant. Up here Bee felt the happy touch of home. There was "her" *coiffeur*. A young woman in riding habit came out from the park through "her" gate just as they passed the little Zoo and got the faint stale whiff of animals across the asphalt, itself so rubbery odorous in the great heat that the car tires "pulled" at its softness. Now the shops were left behind. Everything shone so brightly it might have been an avenue leading to the Arc de Triomphe instead of to Harlem. The mother in the corner of the car said, with a timorous archness—arch because nervous, nervous because insistent:

"Is this chapter twenty-five, Bee?"

Bee looked crossly at her. The mood of slight memory and happy foretaste was broken. The heart's ease arising from the sight of the familiar place vanished. She said nothing.

"Or," smiled her mother, arch still, nervous still, but just as insistent, "shall we have to call it volume ten?"

"You don't know what you're talking about, Mamma!"

At that second the car turned off the avenue into their street, and drew up by the apartment door, and at once Bee clapped her red-netted hands and began to sway on her seat and hum a little song. It was a gesture of defiance to the present and of trust in the future.

"I'm home. I'm home. Isn't it grand to be home, Mamma?"

"It *is*, Bee," and the words reproved, and with them she decanted herself out of the auto and rose up in a pillar of veiled dignity on the sidewalk, her very stance a reproach to Bee for her evasion.

Frankie gave the old lady one look of awe-struck distaste. The doorman received her with his hat in his hand as if she were a duke's dowager. Then all four were crushed into the tiny elevator, smiling conventionally when their glances met. Bee buried her nose in her lilacs and Frankie noticed that there was a brief cross line between her eyebrows, even when she smiled at him, or her mother, or assured the doorman that it really *was* nice to be home again.

By the apartment door St. John stood awkwardly greeting the three of them, and, enviously, Frankie saw the elevator operator vanish downward into the lower regions. Mrs. Bland was conducted by the maid into the bedrooms. St. John attacked a cocktail-shaker and wrung its neck. Frankie sank into an armchair and took a gloomy stock of the room. Bee became busy with her flowers. Nobody said anything for those few moments.

In that hiatus of silence, as she moulded the pink snow of the lilacs in her palms, Bee looked across the flowers at the cream and grey of her apartment. Nothing there held out its hands to her. She had seen it in its goosey nakedness last evening, when she came from the boat—the first opening of the door giving her, as always, that shock of disappointment that comes when a room turns a cold shoulder. As she walked about, it surrendered its space to her, then took it back again, untouched. Yet, and she remembered it now, when she wandered again from room to room this morning, savouring the comfort of being "back," and the sun outside in the park made everything inside pearly bright, and at the same time, because it left the building in shadow, cool and dim, her home had still held back from her. The frost of two months' desuetude was still unthawed. Now she glanced about wondering what was the best place for the lilacs. Every one of her possessions seemed to need them. The room was like a table without its cloth. The Chippendale chairs bought at New Haven, the Delacroix in New York at some exhibition, the Irish-Huguenot tapestry fought for and won at Boston, all so long dallied over and considered, so filled with her thoughts that she had had to buy them for her thoughts' sake, were nothing but themselves. It was as if all their associations had become meaningless. She broke the silence with, "I must have more flowers!"

She spoke to the man who happened to be nearest to her—Frankie—and petulantly grabbed the telephone. "I don't like this table any more. Or, do I? . . . Hello! Philippe? *Ecoutez . . .*"

"This sounds more like Paris than New York," murmured Frankie sourly to St. John as he accepted a cocktail.

"Yeah. I often wonder why go to Paris?"

"Oh, just to hear American voices," said Frankie.

Wincing at the stale joke, Bee ordered more lilacs.

"Pat!" Frankie looked up. "This is all for you. You like lilacs?"

"Uh-huh!" Indifferently. She hung up.

"Do you like my apartment?" she asked Frankie.

"It's very nice." He spoke so unconvincingly that she frowned about her once more.

"You know it's like a photograph of some place I used to . . ." She stopped. She decided to rearrange the furniture some day, gave out a mighty sigh, and smiled vaguely at St. John.

"Ah, well!" she said, meaning, "I must get on with my job."

"Well?" asked St. John cheerfully, and examined the bottom of his glass. "Who'll have some cocktails?" as if nobody yet had taken any. He filled himself another. Mrs. Bland came in, her white hair brushed up from her forehead as smooth as a wig. She took a glass of sherry, sat down, smiled lovingly at Bee—though with a touch of the kidnapper surveying a victim. At that moment anybody could have told that the lunch was doomed. It was like a theatre on a first night of a bad play. The second after the rising of the curtain one senses the chill of failure.

"Well!" she throated contentedly. "Here we are all together again," and then shot a glance at Frankie which excluded him peremptorily from that "we." He replied by leaning over the side of his chair and peering down rudely at Bee's books. As he did so Bee, who had noticed the incident, came over with her glass and stood by him.

"Do you see something interesting there?" she asked.

"You've lots of volumes of plays," he said, with such a boyish seriousness that she smiled.

He must be at least thirty, but he sometimes seemed barely out of his teens.

"That's because she's so very interested in the theatre," explained St. John. "You ought to see her Little Theatre down on the East Side."

"You've got a Little Theatre!" said Frankie.

"No," she laughed, "I help a Little Theatre Group. It works in connexion with a settlement."

Everything she said conveyed more than the words. Irrationally he smiled back to her.

"Oh, and what's a settlement?"

"What's a settlement, St. John?" chuckled Bee.

St. John coughed, and choked, and shook himself red in the face and then smiled childishly at his mother-in-law.

"What's a settlement, Mother?"

Mrs. Bland held up her cigarette in its silver clasp. "Settlements, my dear boy," she throated down to Frankie, "are the consciences of the idle rich."

He looked at the three of them, one after the other, while Bee Hannafey assured him that a settlement is a very useful thing.

"I didn't mean to make fun of it," she said. "It's just"—a wave of her hand and an apologetic smile—"that we have to do so much with settlement work that to say, 'What is it?' is like saying, 'Who's Abraham Lincoln?' " Becoming quite serious, she composed herself for a definition and gave it out.

(Without her uniform-coat she was tiny. Her blued hair, brushed up softly over her lifted left eyebrow, clung in fixed curls to her right temple, snuggled into the nape of her neck. She was as graceful as a girl. He could not have known what art produced the captivating effect of maturity mingled with girlhood.)

"A settlement is an institution, usually a residential community, founded for the purpose of filling up educational gaps in a given geographical area." She pronounced her lesson solemnly. "It's always a poor neighbourhood. It is voluntary and is supported by free contributions. It has a social slant, so that if people come together but do not learn a great deal, well, it still does good work—has a good influence, and so on. Have you no such thing in Ireland?"

He considered.

"No."

She looked at his heavy but clear-cut face and was touched by the wavering sensitiveness in his cross, knotted-up eyes. Suddenly he looked up at her and said, not having heard much of it, "Would you mind repeating that definition? I think I have it right, but . . ."

Graciously she repeated it—slowly this time.

"That seems to be a good idea," he commented. "Yes—it does. I'd like to see a settlement."

A little gasp from Mrs. Bland made them look at her. She said, as if she had received a challenge, "I will show you a settlement."

"Oh, no!" protested Bee. "Settlements are my job."

"Or St. John, your brother," insisted the old woman, "will show you a settlement."

"Why, to be sure," agreed St. John heartily, and Mrs. Bland nodded approvingly and relaxed. Bee gave one look at her mother's placid, satisfied face, and then she threw her eyes right and her eyes left, shrugged ominously, and raised her eyebrows. She said to Frankie with a sweet smile, "I'll give you a ring some day about it. Why are you interested in my plays?"

"I'm very interested in the theatre. I've been seeing a lot of plays since I came. Reading them, too."

"What was the last play you read?"

"As a matter of fact it was an Irish play. *Exiles.*"

"Joyce?"—with shining pleasure.

"Yes."

Before he could say he hated the thing, she cried:

"I want to show you something very special. Look."

She led him to a heavily-carved Venetian chest in black oak, opened it, and took out a portfolio in green morocco, bound with purple strings. As she did so she suddenly felt the chest stir and come to life again.

"There is one of my most precious treasures," she said proudly. "I had to sell one of my ponies to buy it. It's gone down in value since, but I don't mind. I don't show this to everyone!"

He opened it and saw the fine handwriting. It was the original manuscript of the play. She picked out one or two of the more interesting emendations. They sat side by side, their heads close together, to examine the pages. She felt, in that instant, that half of the room becoming warm again.

The other two were obliged to make talk with one another. Only once she spoke to them, and that was when she raised her head to blow cigarette smoke swiftly to one side; her eye fell on a Jacobean armchair, and peering briefly at it she said to her mother, "I think we should get rid of that thing. It's phony," and returned to the manuscript. A few minutes later she lifted her head again and smiled perfunctorily at St. John, who was moving between the windows and his mother-in-law. Indicating the Jacobean chair, "Why don't you sit down, you restless creature?" He sat in the brown chair, and picked up a picture magazine. Mrs. Bland began to polish her nails and glance restlessly at the pair head-bowed over the manuscript.

They sat so, in a happy murmuring silence that any other man but St. John would have resented as much as the old lady—and she patently resented it—until a maid in cream-and-grey uniform opened the wide glass doors of the dining-alcove and stood to attention beside them.

"We'll leave our *Exiles* there," Bee smiled over her shoulder as she led the way. "Besides"—as they sat, putting Frankie on her left—"we're all exiles here. Even Mary."

The sun poured into the alcove. She felt the lunch was going to be a great success. Through an open window, up from the avenue far below, came the whizzing of the automobiles, smooth and powerful. Frankie looked at the girl, as they flipped their serviettes open.

"Are you from Ireland?" he asked her with a man-to-man smile. The girl, too well trained not to know her place, nodded distantly.

"Of course she is," said St. John cheerfully, and Bee smiled at her sweetly, and so did Mrs. Bland. Suddenly the general sweetness was too much for Frankie. The momentary intimacy with the manuscript was gone; only the formality of a white lunch-table remained: he refused to play that game.

"Then she's the only genuine exile here," he said. "The rest of us can go where we want to. *We're* not marooned."

The grapefruit saved them from replying.

"Anyway," he persisted to Bee, "if you could go wherever you choose, where would you choose to go?"

"I'm afraid," she said, "that I have no roots."

"I know," said Mrs. Bland, "where I would go. Straight back to Louisville." And she settled herself for that little discussion to develop entertainingly.

"Mamma, you old fraud!" scoffed Bee. "You know you'd do nothing of the sort. Everybody you know there is dead. You'd be bored to tears. Not," she mumbled to Frankie, "that they weren't all born dead down there!"

Frankie looked at the girl again.

"How long are you out of Ireland?" he asked.

The girl looked uncomfortably at Bee, who encouraged her with a smile.

"Three years, sir."

"Have you been back, since?"–digging at his grapefruit.

"Yes, sir."

Frankie looked sardonically at his brother.

"You waited thirty years to go back, wasn't it?" St. John flung him a sullen, defensive look. "All this exile business," commented Frankie, "is buncombe."

Bee's eyebrows leaped. Nobody said anything. With heightened colour Bee said, as lightly as she could:

"I hope you're not one of those awful, realistic young men who won't give anyone any leeway."

"Leeway?"

"I mean, leeway to kid themselves. Don't you suppose we're all kidding ourselves in one way or another?"

Mrs. Bland pushed aside her grapefruit and said, sweetly:

"Well, Mr. Hannafey, I'm glad you're going back. I take it you *are?*"

"I am," pronounced Frankie, a blush rising in his face. He saw that Bee was smiling. Suddenly St. John leaned forward, blowing out his gills. Glaring at his brother he said, angrily: "If I hadn't my business here and my family, I'd be back home for keeps in one month."

"Well, there isn't any real reason, after all, is there, why you shouldn't wind up your business?" asked Frankie coldly.

"My dear . . ." began Mrs. Bland.

"My wife," St. John explained irritably, still leaning over the table, "lives here. My boy is an American. My daughter is an American." He jabbed the table with his forefinger at each sentence, while his mother-in-law looked at him in pain and made little deprecatory movements with her hands. "You Irish sometimes give me the jitters. You take our money. You take our subscriptions. If you have any kind of political dog-fight over in Ireland, you come howling to us for help. But you really know as much about this country as an Eskimo. About the Irish over here. About anything!"

"My dear St. John!" implored his mother-in-law.

"And yet, you're always criticizing us," finished St. John, with a snort. "Gah!"

"What other plays have you been seeing?" Mrs. Bland, to the young Irishman, interposing swiftly.

For a moment he seemed about to ignore her. He and St. John were glaring at one another. With difficulty he pulled his mind to her question.

"You *are* finished with your grapefruit, St. John?" helped Bee on her side.

"Yeah!" He shoved it away, half eaten.

"Ibsen," said Frankie, shortly.

"Oh?" from Bee. "Which one?"

"*A Doll's House.*"

"That must sound a bit old-fashioned nowadays?" she said.

"I'm not sure. I never knew any women like Nora, except my mother—maybe."

"How extraordinary!" throated Mrs. Bland. "Did your mother dance—what is it?—no, she couldn't have danced the tarantella? I *am* stupid!" she laughed heartily. "Tell me about your mother," she encouraged resolutely.

"She had romantic notions. She used to get into a state of

mind whenever she was in debt. With the tradesmen, I mean."

"Yes," said Bee sympathetically. "The poor soul! That *was* the generation, wasn't it?"—a general question to the table.

"The country people used to call my mother 'Grandy,'" smiled Frankie. "That was because of her notions."

"Have you heard from her?" asked St. John in a more gentle voice.

"No," said his brother. "I haven't been writing home."

The two looked at each other apologetically, accusingly.

"My mother is a grand woman, the grand type of Irishwoman," soliloquized St. John. "I admire her immensely. Brought us all up. A great woman. I haven't looked after her the way I should."

"Never mind, my dear," patted Mrs. Bland. "You were a long way from home. Wouldn't you like to pass me the salad, Bee?"

St. John played with the cold meats. The maid offered white wine and German beer.

"Still!" St. John accused himself. "Of course if I actually were at home!" He looked fiercely under one eyebrow at his brother.

"*You* live at home?" asked Mrs. Bland, unwisely, of Frankie.

"Not much."

"I don't quite understand?"

"I'm mostly on the run."

"On the run? What is that? Curious expression! Tell me all about it!"

He explained. The old lady murmured, "From the police!" and looked at him as if he were a liar. "Darling! Can I have some more salad? It's *so* delicate!"

"Time you gave up all that sort of thing," said St. John. "Oh, it's all right"—he waved his fork, hastily, in apology—"forget that I said that. It's none of my business. I take that back."

"What did you actually think of the *Doll's House?*" begged Bee.

"It *is* none of your business," said Frankie coldly, refusing the question.

"All right! All right!" St. John kept his head down and his eyes fixed on his plate. He heard Bee sighing and turned to her gently. "I'm sorry, Bee." But then he immediately burst out, again red-faced, "But if I *was* at home, I think I'd make a hell of a sight better job of . . ."

Bee, from the head of the table, patiently but firmly, "St. John!"

He dammed himself up, swelled, and gushed out his exhaust. He fiddled and jerked with his knife and fork. He took up his plate and put it down. He blew out a vast breath, and growled:

"All right. I'm through. Sorry."

"Will you not take anything to drink, Frankie?" asked Bee quietly, indicating the waiting girl.

"Beer," said Frankie, looking up at the girl.

"Now," chided Bee, "you know how touchy St. John is about Ireland, Frankie. Let's not mention it again. Do tell us about the *Doll's House*."

"Tell me, St. John," on the other side, said Mrs. Bland, "all about your holiday at home."

There was talk of the play and talk of Kilfinnane. Bee was saying at one moment, "That's an interesting observation," and Mrs. Bland, at the same moment, "Isn't that cute? Turf, you said?" It all exasperated and bored Frankie. Presently, as

Ibsen and Kilfinnane exhausted themselves, the mother-in-law said, brightly:

"Of course, I never do—I'm very lowbrow, I'm sure—think of the theatre as a place to see plays. I mean that kind of play. While you were away, Bee, St. John took me to a theatre. It was a—I believe they called it a spectacle. Now, I enjoyed that."

"Yeah," said St. John. "It was a good show."

"Not too shocking, I hope, for Mamma?"—from Bee.

"Well, you know," began her mother, welcoming the ice with a smile, "I didn't mind. An old woman like me—these things *are* just a spectacle for me. But that silhouette scene! I really did wonder about that."

St. John refused an ice and lit a cigar. He leaned back, fed, pleased, in good humour once more.

"Was it very risqué?" asked Bee idly of St. John.

"The usual thing. But a bit more so. I don't see, myself, how it got past the police."

"A change from Kilfinnane," remarked Frankie, so guilelessly that Bee could not think he really meant to stab.

His brother, however, banged the table with his fingers. Then, seeing that the remark was not meant to wound, he looked around like a lazy old bull in an arena. His face was suffused with well-being and food, his eyes a trifle bloodshot from last night's drink, the beer, the heat. He looked at the window.

"That window, I mean," he said, and they all looked at it, in relief. "Do we have to have it open? The noise."

Bee rose and closed it swiftly, and the hissing swirl from the avenue died away.

"The songs weren't much," rushed on St. John, now eager himself to do his part in keeping the table friendly. "But," laughing too heartily, "I'm old-fashioned, I reckon. I like the old songs, 'An Old-Fashioned Street in an Old-Fashioned Town' and 'Just a Girl That Men Forget.' And 'There's a Long, Long Trail.' Aye, or"—waving his cigar generously—"even some of the old Irish songs."

Afterwards Frankie assured Bee he did not really mean to say it. It slipped from him even as he knew it was such a wrong and cruel thing to say. He had looked up and said:

"Like 'Come Back to Erin'?"

Bee at once leaped into the talk. She raced on and on. Only Mrs. Bland did not realize what had happened and she was gazing, curious, interested, at her daughter. Then she noticed that St. John was sagging down and down into his chair and that beads of sweat stood on his forehead and he was green-bilious to his white hair. Interrupting his wife he said, heavily:

"Can we have the window open?"

It was Frankie who opened it. Again the hiss and swirl of the avenue came in. Then Frankie came around the table and said:

"Would you have a whisky, St. John?"

"If you will excuse *me*," murmured St. John and got up heavily, and went out. "I'm lying down."

"How peculiar!" said Mrs. Bland. "Isn't he well?"

Bee resumed her chatter.

"You're always so light-hearted, daughter," appraised her mother. "I am enjoying my lunch."

Bee's talk went on. It might have been a lunch like any ordinary lunch: an outsider might even have decided that, after all, it had been fairly successful. He would, like the others, have been too entertained by Bee, as she talked with vivacity about her amusing adventures in Paris, to have time to think about that last little incident with St. John. As for

Frankie, he felt, as he sat listening to her and watching her that Paris must be one of the most exciting cities in the world; he wished he lived there; he took the fire of desire for such experiences as hers from envy of her fortune in having had them, and his admiration grew for her as a woman who had travelled widely and met many interesting people.

No further word was said about St. John until he got up to go. As she graciously loaned him her precious manuscript she said, and it was not, again, merely the words but the way she said them that affected him:

"Do come again. Or come and stay with us in the country some week-end. I want to know what you think of these anarchists. Besides, you and St. John must get together. I can see you don't know each other in the least. And he's really a pet."

He promised to come; he apologized for the remark about the song; she said she understood, and once more the words conveyed ten times what they connoted. He went away, feeling pleased with himself. Had a friend been by to ask him about it he would have said, with warmth:

"A damn intelligent woman."

That is, if he had been honest. He might as easily have said, "It was a bloody bore!" One hides the heart from itself when it is hesitating on the edge of an abyss.

VI

The telephone woke him in the morning at half-past nine —he had been out late with a lawyer over in New Jersey and written a dozen political begging letters when he came back. It was Bee asking him urgently to come and talk to her as early as he could before lunch. She did not say what she wanted to talk about—merely that it was a personal matter and that she needed his help. He was therefore puzzled for a moment to find a letter from her in the morning's mail, until he realized that it had been posted the afternoon before. It ran:

"Dear Frankie,

"It was sweet of you to come to lunch today. I enjoyed your being there, although at times you were like a beautiful, large cat that shows his claws once in a while, just so you know of what he may be capable. I don't know for certain to whom you *were* showing them—was it to me, or to poor St. John? You mustn't do it. Not to St. John. He has such an admiration for you. And why to me, when I like you? I promise you that there is no need of elaborate defence: first because I certainly don't want ever to hurt you, and, second, because I couldn't hurt you anyway. Nothing outside yourself can torture you as you can. Forgive me for writing like this, but I am so adept at recognizing the symptoms. I think it all comes of being Irish, and Catholic, not to mention Revolutionary. What a masochistic race the Irish are, shaving and whittling off bits of themselves to toss to the dogs!

> They that have power to hurt and will do none,
> That do not do the thing they most do show,
> Who, moving others, are themselves as stone,
> Unmoved, cold, and to temptation slow.

I am full of quotations. We talked of drama. We must talk of poetry.

> Even to one I dare not tell,
> Where lies my heaven, where lies my Hell.
> But to the world I can confide,
> What's hid from all the world beside.

That should be the epitaph of every Irish Roman Catholic.

"What rubbish I write. I really meant only to say two

things. To ask you to be kind to St. John. For my sake and for his sake. And to tell you that I'm planning a Grand Settlement Revue for the opening of the fall season. We are writing it now, and as most of the people are Irish you could give us a good deal of help.

"I am going to the country in the morning. It is too hot here. If you would care to spend a week-end with us in our country cottage do come next week-end—and help me to provide the Irish colour for my revue, which I will be trying to get in order.

"(I could so easily be quite cross with you.)

"Bee Hannafey."

He read this extraordinary letter several times. It gave him the unpleasant sensation of having been seen through; although he could not, for a line of it, recognize himself. The reference to his "elaborate defence" was especially puzzling. He felt, as he read it for the third time, as acutely uncomfortable as if he had eaten something that was now fermenting inside him. He shoved it into his pocket, saying, "Queer little woman!" deciding, too, that he was certainly not going to visit her in the country. Not that there could be any "country" within a hundred miles of New York. He thought of the Ballyhouras all stratified one way as if the wind had blown them, black and slanting, into wavelike ridges. She probably meant some place in Long Island!

There was also a letter from Josephine. He read it on the way to Bee.

He was at her apartment by a quarter after eleven. There were dark rings under her eyes; later in the conversation she confessed that she had been sitting up most of the night. She thanked him for coming and explained at once why she asked him to come.

"It's St. John. I won't have you upsetting him this way. It's not good enough, and I won't have it."

The sharp attack took him by surprise. She was talking to him almost crossly, as if he were an insensitive boy who must be made to see things as an adult. Still under the influence of her insinuating letter and her charm of the day before, he was so taken aback that he did not bridle up as he would have done at any other time. It only gradually came to him that this was the obverse of the public Bee.

"Frankie, you can't do this to St. John. It must stop!"

"What must stop?"

"You've upset him cruelly. It's not fair either to him or to me. All this Irish business has thrown him off balance, and it reacts on me. Now you must simply put him back on his balance again. The Lord knows he's always been difficult. I can bear that. I can bear his going blind drunk whenever he thinks of Ireland or of religion. But when it comes to talking about giving up everything and going back there for keeps —well, it's not good enough. How *could* you do it to me, Frankie?"

She was on edge. His conscience deflated him more and more, and correspondingly he began to bluster.

"But what have I to do with all this? I don't see at all!"

"Don't you see what it means to him to have you taunt him? As he says, 'You belong somewhere.' He says your life 'means something.' He really has a kind of intense admiration for you that makes him—or so I read it—feel small when you're around. For you to mock him is most unfair. It's cruel."

"I don't understand you!"

Patiently she explained:

"At lunch yesterday you stabbed and stabbed him, Frankie! I've watched St. John year in and year out. As I've watched you Irish in a dozen places—in settlements, in his clubs, at Saint Patrick's Night dinners, with the friends he brings here occasionally. I know them through and through—as even you couldn't possibly know them. Listen! When St. John was a young man . . ."

Her voice softened. She was the image of Patient Griselda.

". . . he worked like a nigger. And as long as he had to work he was happy—it satisfied him—it was everything to him to succeed. Every week for the first two or three years we were married—believe me, this is a fact—he used to say, 'I'll show the world what an Irishman can do!' As if he was Ireland! It was *so* silly."

She laughed. He laughed, but it did not seem so silly to him.

"But now—now, he's got on. He's raised his family. They're grown up. He's *done* it." She groaned and threw her head sidewards and her hands—after those years. "He's won so many rounds he doesn't care if the ship sinks. I'm mixing my metaphors." A bitter laugh. "You see, he has no defence against you, and no defence against this crazy nostalgia in him to get back—to go home. . . . Do you follow?"

"Well! Why not let him go home? If that's what he wants?"

"Be reasonable! He can't go home!"

"Can't he?"

Bee got up and walked in a circle around her chair. She was like a dog circling in his form. She sat again.

"I'm going to tell you something. It's a kind of parable. I once met an Irishman who is a judge, in India . . . or was. His name was Fitzpatrick. You'll find him in *Who's Who.* He's been knighted. He's got a dozen letters after his name. I believe he's considered one of the best administrators the British have in India. To look at him—he's straight, grey, stern, elegant, handsome, smooth as toothpaste—you'd simply take him for the typical Anglo-Indian. Oh, you Irish are all alike! You fit in better than any other people in the world. You're like rubber. But that's one of my old jokes—that you can fit a square peg in a round hole if the peg is made of rubber. This man was just like all the others. He's done everything to the Indians the British did to the Irish at home. One night he got to talking to me—so far from his base I suppose he felt he could talk frankly. He told me that every Saint Patrick's Night he goes deliberately blind raving drunk—absolutely insane. His servants lock up his guns, and fly out of the house. For one week that goes on, and then they find him somewhere—he said it himself—they are his own words—'a filthy mess.' The resident British call it 'Fitzpatrick's Fury.' Then for the rest of the year he's the perfect British administrator all over again. Now can you understand *that?*"

He did not look at her. He was trying to believe that there was such a man as Fitzpatrick; that this was not a parable about somebody else.

"Yes—I suppose it's natural. Yes. A form of compensation."

"Exactly! That man will go back to Europe—possibly he's gone now—when he retires. But not to Ireland—to London. I asked him, 'Will you fit in there all right?' He is an intelligent man. He has no delusions. He said, cheerfully, 'Yes, Bee, I'll fit in. There'll be lots like me. I'll get on with them all right. We'll all spend our days in clubs condemning British rule in India. I'll probably write a book about it. Like a converted prostitute.' Then he said, 'But, of course, what I'd honestly like to do—only it's a joke, it's too late—is to become a country curate in the west of Ireland.' "

The little American woman shrugged and looked her appeal at the young man. He smiled slowly, as she added, "I think he'd been reading some of the funny novels by George Birmingham."

"St. John isn't thinking of becoming a C.C. in Kilfinnane?"

She blushed; went pale all over the lower part of her face. Then she groaned comically.

"You *are* cruel. But he's entirely capable of it! I've heard him talk about forming some kind of society—to discourage emigration, I think. I gather that every Irishman, at some time of his life, starts some kind of society?"

They paused. There was a knock, and the maid, Mary, came in with coffee.

"Good morning," Frankie greeted her. The girl inclined her head in a formal bow and went out quietly.

"There's no use in your trying to corrupt my maids," smiled Bee. "They're too well trained. Smoke?"

Some dark anger scrawled his nerves. For one thing, his vanity had been hurt. Then there was the smoothness of this formal life encasing so much private unhappiness; smooth as the swishing of expensive cars along the avenue. Her story was like a cold, wet, dead something drawn across his face.

"I can't do anything for St. John," he savaged.

"Frankie!"

The more than appeal in the word, the fear in it, halted him. She said:

"I see I must tell you everything. St. John's been drinking hard ever since lunch yesterday. One of his bad bouts. I don't know where he is now."

He stared at her. She answered the questions racing across his eyes.

"He came in at two o'clock last night. I bolted my door and sat up until morning came. I hid the liquor. That was a mistake. He went out at eight for more. I tell you I have no idea where he is at this moment."

He sank his head into his hand and the ruffling of his hair told of the force of his emotions. He jerked up his head.

"You want me to find him for you?"

"No." They looked at each other. "But when we do find him, and he comes to his senses, you *will* help? It's always worst then."

She got up and suddenly, as if she could stand no more of it, turned the talk away from herself. They talked of his affairs for a while. Then she got up and took his hand.

"While you are here, Frankie, you must let us take care of you."

He held her hand as long as she held his. She released him with an assuring and at the same time appealing smile, as she added:

"You're becoming indispensable to me. And you will help?"

He left her, stirred, confused, almost panicking to find himself so emotionally involved in her happiness and unhappiness.

Another note from her came after supper. He called her on the telephone. St. John had been brought home unconscious, and she had sent him off at once to her country house with a male nurse. Would he be a good friend and come with her there tonight?

They drove out of the city, by Park Avenue and the Grand Concourse. They could see at the upper intersections the sunset over the Palisades. Then the hot trees were wilting overhead in Van Cortlandt Park. Yonkers sent the city behind them. So far nothing had moved silently towards the night but the clouds. He liked that. Something primitive in him responded to this untidy exit from the city. The crudity of the physical surroundings and the unconventionality of the occasion were of a piece; the ragged lots, the wooden houses, the screaming advertisement boards, the railroad tangles, the speed of the car, the nervous suppression of speech, the oddness of the situation, the oncoming night, the unnecessary blaring lights. A rough animal magnetism began to develop in the car. She felt that same vibration she had felt the first time they met. Some stir in her blood and his nerves infected each other. She said, "Not going too fast?" just to hear the taurine voice; he only shook his head. She was aware of his *hombría*, as the Spaniards call dynamic man-force. As they left the pseudo-elegant suburbs, with their plaster décor, and the solid concrete highway spun beneath them into Connecticut, she felt the graph of his emotions take a downward turn. He was thawing, becoming calm with the cooling wind across Long Island Sound, the fading maple shadows, the munching cattle, the sloping green fields.

"Cows!" he said, delighted.

She chuckled and snuggled deeper behind the wheel. She was wearing a grey astrakhan coat and a tartan scarf about her chin. He got with every movement of her body a gush of soft scent. She teased:

"What do you suppose you have with your cereal every morning?"

He laughed and their smiles met and mingled. He looked back. He expected to see the pencilled prodding line of the city they had left behind. He almost thought he could still hear its rumble, and smell its smoke-smell and its petrol. He saw nothing but the magnificent maples, and a beech wood right and left of the road—a fine dark spot for an ambush. Chastened and pleased by the sight of the lovely greenery and the traditional pasture, he asked:

"How far out is your place, Bee?"

"About sixty miles. Not far beyond Westport."

"Westport? That's a town in County Mayo."

"Mayó? Is that how you say it? It's a ducky name."

"Mayó," he agreed.

"Mayó"—tasting it.

"Mayó!"—approving.

"You know the place?" she asked. He fell silent again.

The map of Ireland, recording all the indentations of the Atlantic, made the Connaught coast a laced and wormy land, its lakes and lochs, and rock-pools, and veining rivers fraying it into a transparency. It was a sodden-edged manuscript, half its story fallen into decay. There was a song called "County Mayo," by the Gaelic poet Raftery, who sang to blind eyes and empty pockets, with his ragged back to a wall.

"There's a song called 'County Mayo,' " he remembered.

"Mary, my maid, comes from the west of Ireland. I do believe it *is* Mayo. I'm almost certain. I've heard her singing in the kitchen. I must ask her does she know it."

"It's in Irish. Does she sing in Irish?"

"I don't know, really. I only recognize one song she had—'I'm Sitting on the Stile, Mary.' I reckon it's 'cos her name is Mary. I asked Pat about it and he said it's called 'The Emigrant's Return,' and he sang it for me. Do you know it?"

He hummed it for her:

> "I'm sitting on the stile, Mary,
> Where we sat side by side,
> On a bright May morning, long ago,
> When first you were my bride.
> The corn was springing fresh and fair,
> The lark sang loud and high,
> The red was on your lip, Mary,
> The love-light in your eye.
>
> I'm bidding you a long farewell,
> My Mary kind and true,
> But I'll not forget you, darling,

In the land I'm going to.
They say there's bread and work for all,
The sun shines always there.
But I'd not forget old Ireland
Were it fifty times as fair.

There's more. I forget it."

She sensed his new emotion and made no comment. They passed through the neat streets of a town. In Ireland it would call itself a city, but unlike Irish cities—Galway, or Limerick, no bigger in size than this—it had never been the centre of any movement of thought, never stood in the path of history, never received the vestiges of march, counter-march, resistance, defeat, settlement: those marks of the endless strife in the heart of man. He was silent for a while and then he broke out:

"How big is this place, Stamford?"

"About thirty or forty thousand."

"Thousand *what?*"

She glanced at his cold profile, with the wiry hair blown down on his forehead, and the flat nose accentuating his suddenly savage mood. A traffic-light was holding them up before the neat grass triangle of the town hall. Civil War cannon pointed away from them. Yellow to green—the slipping in of the clutch was vibrant with annoyance.

"Do you always," she asked, "have to fritter away things like that? Must you have a cliché? What's that come from? Irish—or R.C.—or Communist? Eh?"

"I'm not Communist. I'm a collectivist, if I'm anything. I'm just asking what did this town ever do?"

She flew through the outer edge of the town and took the high road at a hurling fifty-five.

"It lived a decent life. It gave people a chance to be decent to one another." She glanced sidewards at him.

"Watch the road," he ordered.

"It just lived. Bred its children. Brought them up. Gave them a way of living. Let them live their minds in peace. What the hell do you *want?*"

"Had it any history?"—coldly.

"It had, and has, the history of its own people. What *do* you want? What would a history, as you call it, give it, except that people were killed? Things burnt and broken. Damn you Irish! The only thing you ever talk about is the one thing: what a grand place Ireland is and what a rotten place every other country is. And history—history—history. St. John shoved the history of Ireland down my throat for twenty years, and amn't I just sick of it? Fighting and rebelling and rebelling and fighting, it's all you ever did."

"It's something to have the guts to rebel."

"I suppose it is. But the trouble with you Irish is that you rebel against everything."

"And why not?"

"Against everything?"

"Everything."

She drove for a bit in silence and then she chuckled bitterly, her cheeks drawn in, her lips pursed out.

"Perhaps you're right. That's your métier. To rebel. Only, sometimes I wish you'd rebel against Ireland."

He had no retort for that. She drove on at a mad, angry speed, cutting out to pass car after car. She said once in a low voice, calmly and coldly:

"You Irish hate life."

"We love life. We enjoy life. We hate the things that spoil and ruin life."

"Life?" She shrugged and said, "I wonder what you'll make of it when you meet it. God, how young you talk!"

He retorted furiously, out of the side of his mouth:

"May we always be young, then!"

After a few more miles the speed slackened gradually to a quiet forty-five, and she said in a gentle, humble voice:

"I'm sorry. But you anger me when you talk like St. John. He talks that way whenever his dividends are nice and high. Always then. Conscience money."

"I have no dividends," he said quietly.

"I'm sorry. I'll say that again if you like. I shouldn't have blazed out. I don't want to quarrel with you, Frankie. But, after all, you were living in a country that as far as I can see has had nothing but history, history, history. You like it here, don't you? And we haven't got that sort of history. Or *do* you like it here?"

"I do."

"Then for God's sake take what the gods send you."

They were both silent at that. A side-glance showed that he was still angry—probably at being "put in the wrong!" She shrugged. She hated him. She liked him. They drove on without talking, turned off at a fork, and traversed several side-roads. These might have been in Ireland. Then they came to a small colonial house, all in white, flowers in window-boxes, a brief lawn, close-cropped. They turned into the little drive and she halted, jumped out, and gave him her hand.

"I'm sorry, Frankie."

"Sorry," he admitted.

"Forgiven?"—laughing, pleading, whimsically penitent.

He laughed back and dismissed it, in good humour again.

"Some day we'll thrash it out, though."

"Do we have to?" she pleaded.

"Well . . ."

"If we must! I'm no good at arguments, I warn you. Come in."

A manservant—her Negro chauffeur who had probably

driven down with the "body," his teeth and the whites of his eyes showing up in the now-fallen dark—came and took their bags. She ran ahead into the lighted hall, and her little figure was lost up the cream-and-blue stairs—cream panelling, blue carpet. The drawing-room was cool as a mushroom. On the walls were coloured prints of the eighteenth-century South. There was Jefferson's lovely house at Charlottesville, houses in Richmond, Charleston, Lexington; there were two old photographs of a tall, calm Palladian front, with ladies under daisy parasols sitting in a landau, and a Negro standing by the horses' heads. And then he came on Bartlett's faintly dramatic little prints of Irish scenes—Cork Harbour, Cove, Blackrock Castle, the Grand Parade in Cork, mellow, musk-brown, hand-tinted in blue and pink. In the dining-room was a magnificent set of Maltons; he had never seen these before and he was engrossed by their dignity and the dignity of Dublin that they revealed to him, until he realized that these prints were St. John's. He thought of the poor wretch upstairs; he wished he had not come. When Bee came down she found him gazing at Bartlett's miniature of Cove. She said, simply, but he was touched by the undertones in her voice, "We met there," and then, beckoning, led him to St. John's door, where, with a nod of encouragement, she left him. He opened the door.

In his bed, propped up, unshaven, shivering, was his stepbrother. When he got to know St. John's history better he found that he could become the merest candle-end of a man, like this, after one night, and take a whole week to be fit again. Or was "fit" the word for a man with such pouched bags under his eyes and a dog's bark for everybody? A tumbler of whisky stood by the bed and the edge of the glass was wet from a recent gulp.

"Hello, Frankie boy. Come in. Shut that door. This is a

goddamn lousy trick Bee's played on me. Send me down here when I'm under the weather and let me wake up without a hair of the dog that bit me! God in heaven, I pay for this house, all these blasted servants, and yet I can't get a glass of liquor to wet my lips when I wake up!"

His trembling hand steered the glass carefully to his lips; the gulp was fevered but not a drop was spilled.

"Well!" laughed Frankie. (Was this the best way to take him?) "You've been going the pace all right!"

"Hell! Can't a man celebrate his wife's home-coming? Sit down." Then, smiling cunningly, leaning to whisper, with an assumption of indifference, "Have a drink. Bee will send up the bottle."

"Not just yet. I don't feel like it."

"Well, maybe you're right." St. John sank back. His white hair stuck up behind his poll on the pillow. "Keep off it, boy. I would, only I gotta have something to keep going."

There was a dull silence. A hen cackled outside.

"You've got electric light here!" said Frankie, in surprise, and disappointment—the country to him meant simple ways. He looked at the silver lampstand beside the bed; next to it, under the pink glow of the light, lay a bundle of papers. They were copies of the Cork *Weekly Examiner.*

"Light? Yeah. Why not?"—lifting a bloodshot eye to the pink shade. Then seeing the papers. "I see old Pellier is dead, at last."

"Who's he?"

"One of the biggest stock-brokers in Cork. Do you mean to say you don't know him?"

"No."

"I thought everybody in Cork knew him."

"Did you meet him out here?"

"I never met him. I never knew him. But I thought he was

well known in Cork. Your father probably knew him."

Another dull silence. Suddenly a vast smile spread over the old ravaged face.

"Did you see they had a bit about me in it? I got it there in the drawer. They put it in after I left. Eolie sent it on. Get it—it's there beside you."

Frankie opened the drawer. The cutting peeped out from under a bunch of papers, apparently contracts or printed stock. There was also a rosary-beads.

"That's it! Read it. It's fine."

"'Among those who sailed in the *Carinthia* from Cove last evening was Mr. St. John Hogan-Hannafey, the New York boot-and-shoe manufacturer. He had been spending a holiday in Ireland visiting his relatives.'"

St. John nodded triumphantly and smiled at his brother and took another drink.

"That's me." Then, with sudden collapse, "Holy Jesus! I feel lousy."

"You're looking grand, St. John."

"I'm not. I'm cracking up. What the hell am I doing down here in Connecticut at this time of the year? All the winter stock going out. I got dozens of things to do. I should be at the factory speeding things up. Why the hell isn't Randall home?"

He took another drink—a smaller one. He was trying to make the drink last; his collation for the night. After the drink he fell back with a groan.

"I've gone on a skite at every time of the year, boy, except in July and August. I've never done it before. I know what's wrong, all right—I'm cracking up, I tell you. I can't keep going." His voice had been weak and complaining: it turned into a sudden bitter anger. "But why should I keep going? What's there for me to live for? Frankie, I'm cashing in. I got everything I want and they don't mean a thing to me. I'm going back to Ireland. No—don't try to bulldoze me. I know Bee brought you down here to talk sense to me, but I know better. I always said I would go back, and I'm going back." He leaned up on his elbow and grabbed his brother's lapel. "I know Bee's tricks. I know every bloody trick in her bag. It's no good. A wife's a wife, but blood tells. You're my brother! Don't rat on me, for Christ's sake. Amn't I right?"

He searched Frankie's heavy face. The scum of the drink was in his eyes. One of them closed. He sank back again and his jaw stuck out and he looked the full voltage of his hate. His voice fell to a whisper.

"The hell with you. You're just another one of her young men. Coming down here and . . . Blast you! Get out! Get out of here—it's my house." His voice rose to a scream and he clutched the bedclothes. "Get out!"

He tumbled over to get the whisky and finished it in a swig. Some of it dribbled on the bedclothes and stained the pale-green coverlet. Frankie saw that the hairs on his chest were metal-grey.

"Shut up, St. John!" he commanded.

"I won't." St. John glared up at him from his elbow. "Get out. Do you want me to say it ten times?"

"I'm going to talk to you," Frankie insisted, leaning over him, browbeating him, low-voiced. He shoved him back on his pillow. "If you want to go to Ireland, I'm not stopping you. Why don't you go? And when you were there, why the hell didn't you stay there? Do you know what you are? You're a sentimentalist. You want to have your loaf and eat it."

"That's not fair," whined St. John. "It's not true. I've worked as none of you ever worked. . . ."

"I'm not talking about whether you worked or not. Listen

to me. What way have you been treating your wife for the last five years?"

"Has she been talking to you?"

"Not a word. But I'm not a fool."

"You're thinking things!"

"I've been thinking a good deal."

"I've given her everything she wants."

"Have you been fooling with other women?"

St. John went red. "What do you take me for? But you ask *her!*"

"Did you ever hit her?"

St. John cowered.

"Go away. Go away. What are you up to?"

"Did you ever hit her?"

"I'm not going to be third-degreed by you. Go away!"

"Did—you—ever—hit—her?"

The wretch began to sob. He tousled his greying hair.

"I don't know," he mumbled and stuttered. "How the hell do I know? Go away! She's no right to be talking about me."

"She hasn't."

"I've worked and slaved! I suppose I did hit her. Blast you! What's it to you?"

Frankie took his brother's arm and pleaded with him. "St. John, I don't know what's wrong with you. There *is* something wrong. That's all I know. You've got to stick by her. You can't run away and leave her in the lurch. She can't go with you and live in Ireland. She'll have nothing left. Do you want the woman to be walking around the streets at night?"

St. John stared at him.

"What are you talking about?"

"You know the way my mother went. You know why she went that way."

"I don't." He stared again and then he began to laugh. "Bee walking around the streets at night! Bee! Jesus, this is rich! What *are* you talking about? You're a soft simp, Frankie boy. Oh, for God's sake go away!" He sat up and dragged up his knees and bowed his head in his arms over them. "You're talking bull." He looked up, then. "What do you mean, my mother going 'that way'?"

"I know about my father. He drank and he went with women. He was a grand man, in many ways. But he couldn't stand Cork. He cracked up on it. He died in the D.T.'s, I honestly believe. My mother went off her head before that."

The young man's voice shook as he revealed it.

"How'd you find this out?"

"Leonard."

"You've been seeing him?"

There was a note of scorn in the light emphasis on the word "him."

The two brothers looked at each other, long and questioningly, each trying to find out something from the other.

"Frankie, you're crazy." Then he looked again. "What've you been talking to that fellow Leonard about?"

"About our family."

"I never got on with that tyke. He was only a kid back in Cork. When he came out here I was years older'n him. He was raw as a carrot. He started lecturing me, if you please. I told him where to get off." There was a pause, a question, a dismissal of the question, and a return to his first thought. "We never spoke after I got married."

"Why?"

St. John shot him a glance.

"Bee is an Episcopalian."

Frankie leaned back in his chair. Leonard had never mentioned that to him; and he groaned internally at these Irish reticences. His brain began to race.

"Listen, St. John. Is it true that you and Bee haven't been getting on together? Have I got that much right?"

"Oh! That's right, all right"—bitterly.

Frankie wanted to ask if he had married Bee in a Catholic church. If not, there was yet another suppression boiling up in him, clamped down for years.

"Anyway," shot St. John, "it's got nothing to do with me. I mean"—with a sullen look—"he wasn't *my* father."

"I wasn't suggesting . . . anything like that."

They were silent.

"I can see," said St. John, maudlin, "why Clara went into a convent. And Leonard into the Church. Poor old Mickey! Stuck there at home. Frankie, get me another drink, for God's sake. Go down and tell Bee I've got to have a drink. Go on, be a sport."

Frankie went down to the mushroom-cool drawing-room. Bee was reading a fashion-paper.

"He wants another drink. You'd better give it to him."

She hesitated, and then went to the sideboard in the dining-room and filled a large glass of rye.

"Were you married in a Catholic church?" he asked.

Again she looked at him and hesitated.

"No."

He took the glass from her hand and, ignoring her troubled look, went to the door; he stopped there and came back a few steps.

"What religion is Randall? And . . . what is your daughter's name?"

"Beulah. Randall was sent to a Catholic school, and then to Fordham. I don't know what his religion is now. Is this all coming up again?" she ended passionately.

"And Beulah?"

She shrugged, sullenly, and gave her odd sideward look at the ground–right, left–dissociating herself from the whole of life and all its ways.

"She was brought up Episcopalian. My father insisted on it."

"Couldn't you–I don't mean exactly defy him, but . . ."

"We couldn't afford to."

He nodded and said, "Thanks," and went back upstairs. St. John had married money. (Later he thought, "Just as my mother married money . . . Grandy!") He was back in the bedroom, so restfully shaded and yet so bright, so full of little cosy creature comforts. He gave the glass to his brother, and then stood by the window, and saw far away a few pinpricks of window-light, and through the open valves heard the faint moaning of the waves. A car passing beyond the fields, picked out a line of low stone walls that could have been in County Cork instead of the state of Connecticut. Behind him his brother was savouring the pleasure and the relief of his drink. Over his shoulder Frankie said:

"I think it's a mistake not to see Leonard. I think you'd find him much improved."

He saw Leonard. He shuddered at his own hypocrisy. That brassy mouth and voice; those hard eyes; the loss of everything that Leonard must have had in soft abundance when he used to go, daily, from his seminary, in a crocodile across Dublin to the university; the sweetness, the youthful idealism, the benevolent trust. However, he might seem "improved" to St. John's eyes. And, anyway, what St. John needed was a priest, not Ireland.

"When did you see him?"

"Last month."

That moan of the sea was heart-breakingly like the heavy falling seas along the coast of Cork.

He waited, rigid. If St. John said it now, they might be able to help him: bring back to him the inner world that he had crushed as some animal's hoof crushes a fly. There was a world to which he must return. St. John did not say anything.

"Yes, Cursor?" he encouraged, over his shoulder, and looked back and saw the tousled grey pate shake itself savagely. "What's wrong? Cursor!" He saw the hands scratch the head over and under; heard him moaning from the bed: "I *want* to get back to Ireland!"

Just like a child crying that somebody has stolen its toy.

"It might be a good thing to do," appeased Frankie, and sat on the kerb of the bed. There a new thought struck him, and he had to say it, because there could be no dishonesty in a thing like this, "Unless your duty is here?"

There were the children. Randall marrying a girl who had probably no faith at all. Beulah? And Frankie, who thought very little about religion, had been to mass only once since he came to New York, whose whole political life had shoved him in rebellion against bishops and priests until, like the old Fenians, he despised and hated them for their politic dodging, sighed to think that his brother was caught in a net from which there was no escape. It was a hopeless business. For if St. John turned the back of his hand to the one thing, he must do it to the other: he could not have Ireland until he had paid her the last penny of her price. He patted the back of the bowed toper.

"You ought to see Leonard, Cursor. He's a good fellow."

"Maybe!"

"He's really a good fellow. He really is."

"I might ask him down here some time."

"I'll come up and see you again"—rising.

"Do, boy."

He went out and down the soft stairs. Underneath the landing-window a light from some room below shone on the still bushes. Far away the Atlantic sighed, faintly, but without cease.

After supper, it was so hot he and Bee drove down to the sea to swim. Through the dark, phosphorescent on the curl of the waves, he could see her cream bathing-dress diving and turning in the water. She swam magnificently—a slim dolphin—revelling in this, as in everything she did. They returned, chatted a little, and excusing himself he went, early, to his room. She encouraged him to go, saying he must be tired. He could not sleep for hours.

In the hot Sunday morning they again drove across to the shore for a swim after breakfast. When they had bathed, and were lying in the sun, a sea-fog came up to blot out the horizon. They agreed, as they looked across into that haze, that this same Atlantic was beating on the coast of Ireland. At first they did not talk much, content with the sun and the warmth. In her cream bathing-dress, she was slim and shapely as a cigarette—an Egyptian cigarette; she was so suntanned. He had not seen her before in so fresh and gay a mood; it was hard to believe this woman was the mother of grown children. She had brought morning coffee, iced, in a thermos, some fruit, and a couple of books. As they sipped the coffee, she merely fondled the books, too lazy to open them, mesmerized by the purring of the waves that sounded as tired as an old house-cat. The figures of other bathers flecked the low tide far out, their smallness at that distance making them insignificant against the desert of the shore and the sea. The vastness gave them isolation. The knowledge of the city, so far away as to be part of a foreign world, and only recalled vaguely now and again by the sight of a few bungalows among the scrub, gave them privilege, difference, individuality. The occasional murmur of an automobile was for the same reason restful. He enjoyed it all, deliberately postponing his worries. She smiled at him, rolled on her back, and shoved a dark-blue book through the sand to his side.

"I thought it was *The Faerie Queene*."

He read the spine—*History of Juvenile Delinquency*.

"Are you really interested in these things?" he asked, surprised as always by her serious side.

"Try to be." She crossed her legs and stretched her arms backward so that her small breasts rounded her bathing-dress. "Oh, this is my reward for bringing St. John down. How blue that sky is! Listen. I'll tell you something you don't know, Mister Frightfully Wiseman. Yesterday morning when I was sitting up in my apartment, at four o'clock, that sky was the most astonishing blue the eye of man has ever seen. A great, still sapphire. I hung out of my window and I looked down the avenue. And the city of New York was a perfectly black silhouette—without detail, just cut out of the sky. Do you know, Mister Stern R.C."—she sat up and looked at him—"that it frightened me, it was so beautiful. For a few breathless seconds I almost believed in the majesty of God."

"The God of Wall Street?" he teased. She sank back, and recrossed her legs. "Your legs are brown," he remarked, admiring them.

"Sunbathing on the ship. I suddenly fell asleep in the middle of that bright, early morning sunshine. It was just like being pushed into a cool, dark hole. Then at eight o'clock, O ye groves and streams of all my dreams, I woke up and jumped out of bed in a whirl. I'd heard the door bang and the lift going down. I do wish somebody would write a tract on 'How to Be Happy Though Marr—Though Hurried.' " She hastily dragged a book towards her to hide the slip and, turning over, ruffled the pages. "Do you read French?"

"I learned it for my Matric. Then I had to have some language for my B.Sc., so I did a small bit more."

She looked at him in surprise.

"B.Sc.? Science. Have you a college degree?"

"I never finished," he laughed. "The Troubles interfered."

She found a poem and murmured through it. He leaned over, beside her, trying to follow. She murmured gently:

> *"La mer brille au dessus de la haie,*
> *La mer brille comme une coquille,*
> *On a envie de la pêcher.*
> *Le ciel est gai. C'est joli Mai."*

"*Coquille?*"

"A shell."

"Who wrote it?"

Slowly she fondled the words:

> *"C'est doux, la mer, au dessus de la haie,*
> *C'est doux, comme une main d'enfant,*
> *On a envie de la caresser.*
> *Le ciel est gai. C'est joli Mai."*

She lifted her eyes and saw the mere of sea. Beyond it was a part of her life. That year when she had put out her hand and grabbed one last morsel of content that dribbled away from her as this sand in her fingers sifting to the sand. Paris. Late nights. Walking in the Luxembourg . . . Who was he? What was his funny name?

In the crisp, dry American heat, which made the body drowsy but did not enervate the mind, they lay, each in a separate world of thought. Paris was a sucked orange now. It had long since become a fading dream, a memory belonging to a time whose skin was sloughed, and she had not known it. Now it was finished for ever, all those so lovely times, all golden summer afternoons they had seemed—golden wines, little lights in little restaurants, hands touching, smiles speaking, life the body's slave. By a stirring of her body on the sand she hid a groan of regret and an acknowledgment that it was done. A wave breathed and sank with a hiss, and was devoured into the gentle mouth of the following wave that sighed as it died, in its turn, on the shore.

The stirring of her blood and the course of her thought moved her head about like some lovely cobra lifting from a doze. She touched his bare arm. He turned his heavy, blunt face.

"Frankie?"

"Yes?"

"What I told you about the other day at lunch. The anarchists in Paris with their bombs. Do you remember?"

"Yes."

"What *good* is it?"

"I don't know. I'm not a Frenchman."

"But don't you believe in bombs?"

"Sometimes"—cautiously.

She leaned up on an elbow. Earnestly she asked, "Why?"

Half closing his eyes, frowning in the sun, he said, "Force is sometimes necessary to make people wake up. People"—he went on seeing she did not follow him—"are selfish. And cowardly. They let life brutalize them. They become indifferent. To themselves and to others. Drugged."

"And when you do wake them up? Are you so certain that what you offer them is . . . any better?"

He leaned up and took his packet of cigarettes, frowning, and lit one. Indifferently he said:

"It can't be worse. And we *mean* better."

She shrugged as she lay, a slight movement of one round browned shoulder.

"You're all mad," she said.

She leaned over again, and took her book and read, while he turned to listen:

> "*La mer présente sur la haie*
> *Ses frivoles papillonnées,*
> *Petits navires vont naviguer.*
> *Le ciel est gai. C'est joli Mai.*
>
> *La haie, c'est les profondeurs*
> *Avec des scarabées en or . . .*"

She looked up at him who was looking at her, not listening.

"Only the French can write such a trifle, and then come in suddenly with such a grand sound, '*C'est les profondeurs avec des scarabées en or.*'" She read again, conscious of his eyes:

> "*Si doux que larme sur la joue . . .*"

Suddenly they observed two nuns walking along towards them from her left, one with her coif wrapped close about her, the other letting it blow out any way in the light breeze of her own motion as she walked. They looked solemn and splendid on that level place, two bits of the antique world erect against the haze of the sea—the fogged and vacant cosmos. The blowing one looked the more cheerful, as if it was she who had suggested the walk, while the other had agreed for mere obedience' sake. Bee smiled a swift smile at the merry one, who beamed back, with splendid strong teeth and cheerful eyes. The other nun kept her eyes averted, and her fingers kept nibbling at the stout wooden rosary-beads hanging from her girdle. When they had passed on, Bee made a *moue* after the severe one. Frankie was looking after them with the surprise of a man who sees a familiar face unexpectedly. They had woken him up from this idle dalliance.

"How simple it is!" said Bee, turning back on her stomach and displaying two small sandy behinds. "I mean for Pagans and Christians to meet on pagan ground. She smiled at me here. If we met in a church it would be messy and joyless and overlaid with man-made stuff masquerading as God's, or something."

"Do you believe in nothing?" asked Frankie, sitting up and probing. He was now thinking of his brother Leonard, the priest, and feeling through him the little currents that came from all the threads that linked him with every point on the widest arc of his life.

She said, half chaffing, half serious, but gradually becoming quite serious:

"I believe in lots of things, Frankie. *Le ciel est gai. C'est joli Juillet.* I believe I'm lying at this minute on the breast of God. Though I think it's rather odd to find sand-fleas on the breast of God?" She half squirmed about to look at the sea behind her, and put on her smoked glasses with their white rims, to be able to stay looking at it where it sparkled in the sun. "The hazy sea! *Avec des scarabées en or.* Lovely. And real. And quite unreal. Isn't it? The unreal things are the loveliest things. Sometimes, down here, at night, when it's too hot to sleep, I go out walking in the fields. I did that last night when you went to bed. I got possessed of an angel. There was a heavy dew and my feet got wetter and wetter. I had only sandals on. I saw things I never see in the normal light of the day."

They heard and did not hear the tears of the falling waves; she kept looking at them through her smoked glasses.

"Of course it never lasts. I go out like that on some really pouring wet days at Easter, and when I come back there's a tradesman to see, or somebody in for tea. . . ." She looked at him. "My mother, when we fight, says I'm an angry, restless person. Am I, Frankie?"

"I don't know"—hastily. "I don't know."

"Ha!" She laughed. "Silly talk." She took his hand. "Actually I suspect you know a great deal. I didn't ask you to come down, Frankie, only for St. John's sake. Two people listen and think better than one—don't you think—like positive and negative current meeting and making light?"

"I wonder."

She withdrew her hand. He took back her hand, awkward but still holding onto it.

"Bee! Take off your glasses." She did. "You're a serious sort of woman."

"God forbid!"

"You are. Listen. I must talk about St. John. If you don't want any religion for yourself, you can respect it. It means everything to St. John. Has he ever talked with you about religion?"

"Has he not!"

"You must play the game with him. He gave up everything he ever believed in to marry you. He can't take it any longer. He should have married an Irish girl."

"Frankie"—pleadingly—"this lovely morning?"

"Well, you brought me down for this, didn't you?"

"Partly!" She mocked him. "I thought it would be good for you, too."

"You do know that according to his religion he's not married at all?"

As slowly as time the sand ran through the fingers of her free hand. She said:

"We've had separate rooms for fifteen years."

The sea breathed out and in several times before he said any more. Then:

"The children? Hasn't he ever wanted them to be brought up Catholics?"

"I sent Randall to a Catholic school, and a Catholic university. Beulah belongs to me." That last was said firmly.

"Aren't . . . weren't you a bit hard on him, Bee?"

She looked sullenly at the sifting sand.

"For one thing, my father insisted on it; and after he died, my mother. My income comes from her. She's been very good to us. You have no idea about that. If it weren't for her, we might never have got through the depression. St. John, I may tell you, is a born gambler. Besides, Beulah is my child."

Once more, many times the sea gave out its double note of hissing fall and soft withdrawal before he spoke again. Had he come on something that he could never probe deeper? A hint so slight he dared not take it, something too faint to be thought of, so weak that had it been a touch on the most tender part of his body—the eyelid, the back of the hand, the inside thigh—he might already be wondering if he had been touched at all. He felt himself involved, puzzled, at once given entry and held outside. He remained all his life in doubt about the significance of that last remark. Had she said "*my* child," or just "*my child*"? . . .

She was slowly turning the wrist of the hand he held, waiting for his eyes to be caught by the shifting light. He looked. There was something almost apocalyptic about the slow movement of that tiny bone. He saw a two-inch, yellow-pink, puckered-up line on the outside of the wrist.

"Feel that small bone there. The one with the dimple behind it. It's called the radius. They operated on it at two in the morning. It was crushed in the jamb of the door. I was carrying Beulah. He had a gun, that night."

The nuns had come back along the beach. The red-cheeked, happier one was still a balloon of black. She smiled at Bee again and Bee smiled home to her. They passed on and were soon two flecks on the shore. His expulsion of breath was as loud as the sea on its sighing fall.

"You see, Frankie? But don't worry about it, *too* much. It has nothing to do with you."

"Why do you live with him?" he cried furiously. He was not pleasant to look at in his anger.

"Why, what would you have me do? Only you mustn't talk to *me* about religion. Here, I don't want to see you upset." She held up her wrist and smiled. "Kiss it and make it well."

He took the proffered wrist and examined the cicatrix with interest. Not raising his head he looked at her, under his eyebrows, and then back at the old wound whose line he rubbed with his thumb. His thumb was gentle. He did not kiss the wound. She tore her hand away and cried:

"It's time we went home. I know it's all hours!" She paused on her knees over the red French book, and read:

> "*Un gars est tombé dans le port?*
> *Mort dans la mer. C'est joli mort . . .*

What bathos!" She took up the book and hurled it as far as she could throw it. "How did I ever like such nonsense?" She knelt up by him; he was sitting up, gloomily and slowly, gathering the remains of the food. "I feel very happy,

Frankie. Please don't think I'm not. I *am* a restless, angry woman. Besides, it has nothing at all to do with you. I am sorry—I shouldn't have told you."

"Can't I do anything?"

"Help me to work him back from his bout. It's all anybody can do now. It takes days and days. It gets longer every time. I can't stand it any more. Arguing with him, encouraging him, fooling him with watered whisky. I just have to have somebody to help me or he must go away to a nursing home."

"You've tried cures?"

"The man has more morphine in his system. . . . He must have a tremendous constitution."

In their wraps (he was wearing St. John's) they shuffled off to the car. The fog was thickening over the sea. As they made their way through the wood he put his arm around her. She had the waist of a boy. His blood stirred for her, again. She did not look up, or smile, or give any sign that she felt his arm, but she began to hum a song.

"So, you see," she said all of a sudden, looking up, "I don't think you'll convert me."

"You never know," he laughed. She caught the tremble in his voice.

In the hot miasmic air, as they drove back, the wavering country took on a greater depth, and as the eye sees through the slit of memory as well as between its own lashes, he found in this hot Connecticut afternoon a food he had never found anywhere but in the summer Irish fields—desire giving authority to imagination. It was fairy-food. A clearer day would break the illusion of this foreign heat-haze. He felt the power he had so often felt on the Tipperary hills; well-being, pride, self-possession. He squeezed her waist, and he began to sing, blatantly rejoicing in himself, showing off—

Frankie Hannafey, the die-hard, out on a holiday, soon to be back among his old friends, having a good time, solidly based on the solid earth. She gave a little scream and said she could not drive if he pinched her; then she said she was cold and told him to lean against her. So they drove, and, pleasantly refreshed after the swim, halted in the drawing-room before lunch, to have a drink. In the pale room; dairy-fresh, with its peaches-and-cream curtains, pale-yellow panelling, and the clever maroon and pale-green carpet to give vibrancy, she was alluringly out of place—her long, browned legs stretched out, the tightly roped wrap defining her figure. He suddenly felt the blood rushing to his head. Then the blare of a motor-horn outside freed him from her—for the moment. Leaving her to her visitors he, in every sense of the word, escaped.

He went into St. John's room. The day was on the floor in dazzling squares; the reflected brightness showed up St. John's years to the latest hour. His growth of beard was white. A small collation of whisky in a Waterford decanter stood beside him; he answered Frankie's glance. His voice was still muzzy and his hands shaking.

"What'd you do this morning?" he growled.

"Went for a swim." He suppressed mention of Bee, somewhat to his own surprise.

St. John shivered. Then:

"Since I came to America I never once swam in the sea. I wouldn't swim in American water." He sighed. "Ah, to be young again and swimming in the old River Lee! Listen, I've been pondering here. Nothing else to do but have the willies. And I've made up my mind."

"Going back to Ireland?" asked Frankie.

"That's it. How well you guessed! But there's something else to do first. I'm going to see a priest. And a good priest, the best I can get, probably a Jesuit. I want to know what about my responsibility for my children: and I want to know how I get a separation from my wife, *a mensa et a thoro*—that's the way they say it."

"Well, there's Leonard," suggested Frankie idly.

"No, he's not clever enough. Do you think he's clever enough?"

"I don't see that there is anything much to be clever about. If it's a theological problem they all have the same answers."

"That's where you're wrong. There's various schools of theology. I bet you never read up anything about that, but I did. I'm very well informed, as a matter of fact, because I've been going into it for years. And I've had it out with a great number of priests. For example, did you ever hear of Probabilism? I'll tell you about it. Long ago in the Church—oh, the Catholic Church is a grand institution!—there was a school of theologians who held that if you believed in your conscience that something was probably right, well, so long as there was ever any doubt about it, and so long as you had some authority to fall back on, even though all the rest differed from him—of course he had to be a big shot!—you were entitled to go by your own conscience." He took a long breath after the intense effort to get his point clear. He leaned over and painfully filled himself a modest finger of liquor. Looking over it at Frankie, he went on more easily. "But there were other men who didn't hold with that. They said you should always take the safe position at any cost. Now do you get my point? I don't want to fall into the hands of one of these chaps. I've got to choose my man very carefully."

Frankie nodded. He had never before seen a man dodging about in the whorls of his own mind like this. The sight of it astonished and pained him.

"Now," said St. John, sipping, and talking as if to himself, "the Jesuits were the great Probabilists. That is—long ago. My trouble is I've not been keeping up with them in recent times. I don't know how they've gone. If I fell in with a priest who was one of those stern, unbending . . ." His mind failed. He gripped himself. "What did they call them? I've got it. Tutiorists. You see, I keep up with my religion, boy, and you gotta in this country or you can't defend yourself against all these damned atheists you meet. Bee, now . . . I can wind rings around Bee when we get to arguing." He shook his head sadly. "But she never will argue—she's too clever to give me the chance to show her up. . . ." His mind failed again. "What was I saying? Oh, yes—Tutiorists. Well, if I fell in with one of them, where would I be? I made a great mistake didn't go into it all with Father Tom in Kilfinnane. A great man. I'd have been safe as houses with him. Frankie, there's nothing on God's earth to come up to the Irish soggarth aroon. They give a fellow leeway. . . ."

Frankie was barely following him. He had suddenly remembered Bee's slim wrist with the healed scar.

"Well, there's the kernel of it. I'm going to go into this matter of a separation, see about the children, go to Ireland"—he sipped and his eyes spread with contentment—"and never come back."

Frankie woke up to find St. John staring angrily at him.

"It sounds a good idea," he said hurriedly.

"It is a good idea," smiled his brother, relaxing.

"If I may ask a question, why do you decide this now?"

"I don't know. It had to come some time. When a man gets to a certain age, you know. Stock-taking and all that. I reckon I've been dodging it all these years—that's maybe why I didn't go back to Ireland. I don't know"—looking blandly at Frankie. "There is a tide in the affairs of men . . ." He considered the remainder of the sentence. Perhaps he was thinking that his tide was at the ebb.

"Well, think it over carefully before you do anything," said Frankie and he got up. "I'll drop in again."

He left the pensive figure in the bed. Downstairs he could hear the piano lightly, tentatively, finger its way through a melody, going back and starting again, on the soft pedal, without a bass line. The afternoon heat covered the fields and the far scrub with a heat-haze. The sea mourned dully. There was no other sound in or out. He felt that a spring was being wound up somewhere in this house, tighter and tighter.

He went for a long walk after lunch. When he came back it was time for tea: the maid had already left it in the drawing-room and the two visitors sat expectantly by it, clearly ready to go; there was no sign of Bee. Running upstairs for a moment he heard her voice raised in St. John's room and as he was passing the door it half opened as if she were about to come out. She saw him and called him in. She was distraught.

"St. John says"—when he was inside—"he wants to separate from me."

"You run along, Frankie"—from the bed—the old man was in a state of excitement.

"What does it *mean*, Frankie?" she insisted. "I've heard all this before from him. Three times in the last three years I've had it." Passionately she threw her hands out to St. John. "What does separation mean?" She whirled to Frankie. "This wretched man has been doing nothing for years but run from priest to priest and bring me back their dirty little tales. *What does it mean?*"

St. John sank back. "Tell her, Frankie." She sank on the far end of the bed and looked up at Frankie.

"I take it to be a legal formula," he said.

She dashed her fists together. "It's so contemptible. So

meaningless. My God, we're separated three-quarters of our married lives. It's just a rotten kind of breast-beating to save his little drink-sodden shell of a husk of soul."

Frankie groaned. The passion and the pain of the woman cut through him. He closed the door tightly lest the others hear.

"It's not contemptible!" from St. John. "I have to put myself right with my son. It's wrong to have ever given him the bad example of our marriage. I must admit to Randall that it's wrong. I must break it up and show him I honestly and truly believe it's wrong. How else can I prevent him from marrying that girl?"

She jumped up and stood between them.

"How lousy it is! God, how lousy! I told him years ago he could divorce me if he wanted to, but he wouldn't do it. And why wouldn't you do it? Because you wanted my father's money." Turning—"Ten years ago when I ran away to Paris I wanted to divorce you and you wouldn't let me do it."

St. John moaned, "I don't hold with divorce."

She appealed to his brother, "He'll be all right with his God by saying to his son that we've lived in sin for all these years. As if I were a kept woman! His son will respect him for saying so! But if I did what he deserved and divorced him when I wanted to, what kind of picture would his son have of him?" Whirling back—"If I did it now? Look at him. Is there a court that wouldn't grant me a decree in five minutes?"

She jumped up, and went to the window.

"Bee"—from St. John—"you're not going to be vindictive! I'm only thinking of the boy's soul."

She spat at him, "You religious people make me *sick!* Oh, blast you!" and, hysterical, she ran from the room. The tea-bell from the hall rang its little graceful chime. St. John sank his head on his palms.

"She won't understand, Frankie. I know I'm not a good specimen of anything, but, Christ Almighty, what am I going to do? What's going to become of me? Oh, what's going to become of me?"

Frankie stole away and left him slobbering, and went down to the cheerful drawing-room. In two minutes she came in, as merry-faced as if nothing had happened, talking gaily of the revue, of this and that, but when they had waved the last wave to the departing automobile, lost in its country dust, she said to him on the porch:

"Thank God that's over. I'm going for a walk. Come?"

He demurred, so she went alone down the road, and along a path in the birchwoods, out of sight.

He spent the time before supper writing to Leonard, guardedly; getting his lists of "friendly Irish" into order; and writing letters to a few of them. (His correspondence was by this time growing rapidly.) At supper she was subdued, talked little of what had happened, and after it, restless, again said she was going out. He went with her, down the same birchwood path until, from a hill-clearing, they stood under the immensity of the pure night, riddled with its bright worlds, and saw and heard the far drum of the sea. She held his hand and he hers and her unhappiness entered into him like a sword. They saw, low over the fields, the scrap of the moon. Had it been a kid or a calf it would be long-legged and wet, hardly born. That pale arc, so gentle and so sweet, and the blackness about them, and the air salted by the sea, and the width and space—they could have fed on it all if their hearts had only been at peace. To the right, away over the invisible land, a few cosy lights gave their candles to the dark. Airy travellers went across the exposed parts of their bodies, hands, necks, faces. He felt her body shuddering and knew she was crying to herself. He put an arm, tenderly, about her shoulder.

"Frankie"—it was a whisper—"kiss me."

He kissed her. She clung to him for protection. He held her, all his desire roused by her touch.

"I feel I've lived a dozen lives—all wrong." She held onto him as if he were a rock. "You are a darling."

Then while he hesitated, in tumult, said nothing, and did nothing, she said, "Do you think you can find your way back? I think I want to be alone, now." She walked rapidly away.

He went back, shaken to his roots. He sat on the steps until she came. For that whole hour of waiting he could not command himself: he had no measuring rod from his active life to test this. He was like a sailor dreaming that his ship is sinking, in a sleep from which he cannot drag himself awake. Then she came up the brief avenue, in her blue cowled cloak. He rose to meet her, hardly knowing what to say, knowing only what he felt in his body. She said, in a matter-of-fact voice, "I must see my dentist tomorrow," and went in and brought out the whisky. The moon was now established as a boy-moon. She told him funny stories about her dentist, while he looked at her as if he were mesmerized. Once only she said what he could understand: "Frankie, I'm frightfully fond of you. Are you in the least bit fond of me?" Still dazed he said, "I'm *very* fond of you, Bee!" She put her hand on his knee and pressed it. With difficulty he held himself back from her. They talked a little more and then, at last, they went indoors. When he said he was again going up she held his hand, and pressed it, her finger in his firm palm, and looked at him long.

He knew quite well what that look meant but when he

closed his door he locked it as if to lock out some enemy. He undressed, and in his pyjamas sat in the window nook and looked over the fields and heard the whispering sea. Presently he sat by the table and took his pad and wrote a letter, with shaking hands. It said:

"My sweetheart,

"I'm here for a week-end and have a chance to write. Thanks for your grand letter about Fermoy and the railway clerk and the music you're hearing on his gramophone and all you are thinking and planning. I'm dying to get back home. I cannot stand this place much longer. I know nobody and nobody knows me. St. John is going to bits. I came down here to his country house to help him to get well, but I'm afraid he's done for. I am lonely here. I hope you are lonely too. Are you, my dear dark head?

"When you get this the hay will be cutting. Then you'll see the corn green in the stubble. Your last letter said you were going up the Barnane Walk for a stroll 'all by yourself.' I wish I were with you.

"My dearest Jo, I never missed you so much. Now for the first time I know what it means to be in exile. Everything reminds me of home. Today the smell of the seaweed on the beach—it's a place called Westport—made me remember one day you and I went to Crosshaven. I see the little stone walls here, and I'm back in the Ballyhouras. I can't shut these homey things out of my head. An old gate in Cork where they stored the steamrollers under a railway arch, keeps haunting me. I never noticed it. I don't know why I remember it. There it is. If anybody asked me what I'd miss I'd have said the view from your cottage over the County Cork, or the rain falling softly outside your window when your fire is lit, and your lamp shining. I never once thought of them. Only silly things like that gate. Sometimes I stop dead in the street and I swear I hear my mother's voice calling me. It sounds sloppy. But I really do hear it. Or in the morning, in bed, I hear the bell of Saint Augustine's banging away. I sit up and listen. I still hear it though I know I can't really be hearing it.

"My sweetheart, I need you so badly. When are we going to meet again? Do you think you could ever come out for a spell? Even for two weeks? To see you would mean so much to me; to hold your hand and kiss it. I see your eyes with the funny brown shadows all around them, your jet-black hair with the white 'street' down the centre of it. Do you smoke as many cigarettes as ever? I met a girl in an Irish club here the other night. She was a nurse, too, and reminded me of you. It's a bad disorder, Jo.

"I'm very interested in the books you're reading. I'm reading a lot, too. I know nothing about music. I enjoy plays. (It sounds like a matrimonial advertisement.) Why haven't we ever talked about things like that?

"Think about coming over. It's a dangerous thing for two people to be separated for too long. Do you feel that danger? I think I'll have to go back and risk being jugged. Though God knows why they want to arrest me. Judging from the Irish papers things are dead as a doornail. Dear Jo—write at once. You know how much I want and love you. . . ."

In her room Bee undressed, palpitating, and lay waiting in bed. The hours went by and he did not come—she began to hate him. And yet she wondered foolish things such as if he were warm enough, or if she had upset him, or if his room was quiet in the mornings. She started at every night-sound. The only definite sound she heard was the dull drumming of the sea. She wished with passion that she were young and beautiful enough to torment, command him. But she could see near at hand the oncoming years when she could never hope to be loved by any man.

She knew he was attracted by her. When he did not come she knew that it was she who would have to court him. For though he was not a young boy, his life had been spent in activity, and he was full of the most boyish shynesses, and hidden panics, and he lived by all sorts of ideals that she associated only with the very young.

By her bed she saw, among other books, one of those erotic Persian manuals on love, bound in delicate green moiré silk. Its glinting edge ridiculed her as one of those people to whom only the "beautiful" is true. She was beyond caring. She would give him a child if he wanted it. Besides, that was not the sort of thing she had to give. She understood him—his whole life—she could explain all his problems to him. The dear, dumb hick! The most enraging creature she had ever met; the most selfishly absorbed. He would take all she had to give and give no thanks back. The warning meant nothing to her. She would gladly give him everything she had and go away content if he only were happy.

The hours went to the slow ticking of that sea-drum. She could not give up hope that even yet the white door-handle might turn. Not until the dawn coldly took from her the last penny of her gamble with desire did she fall asleep, exhausted by her despairs.

VII

Frankie Hannafey decided to leave for town on Monday morning to collect his mail and keep an appointment. (Or that is why he thought, and said, that he was leaving. In his heart he knew that there was another reason.) He promised

Bee that he would either return that evening or telephone that night. In his manner towards her she could not detect whether he was lying or not: in fact nothing to please her but a reserved approval—very like a small boy saying, "Thanks for the holiday," and meaning it. She drove him to the train. As they waited for it he made her laugh with stories about provincial Irish trains that start and stop at the whim of the engine-driver or the guard. She cried as she drove home.

He met his man—an Englishman in the armaments business who happened to be in New York: he exported guns and ammunition to South America and the East. Over lunch Hannafey learned the terms and technique. What he wanted to know was whether any large quantity of Mills bomb-cases could be purchased in London. Then after lunch Frankie collected his letters—another had come from Josephine—and rang up Father Leonard. Finding him in, he went across to Queens. The journey over the river hurt just as much as when he stood, two weeks ago, looking across it for the first time from Beekman Place. The contrast that his mind then formed between the riches of Manhattan and the discomforts of Queens was accented this time by his visit to Connecticut: the heat and the smells here against the quiet fields, the sea, and the idleness of St. John's small but luxurious country house with its gardens, its pictures, its two cars, and three servants.

Leonard, his coat off, in black stock and blue aertex shirt, was finishing some papers. Bidding Frankie be at his ease for a minute, he pushed them together, making little piles of the small ones and deftly clipping rubber bands about them.

"A raffle for the Boys' Club," he explained. "We're not encouraged to have 'em in this country but the Church is as broad-minded about that as it was about Prohibition. How's life?"—rapidly working.

Frankie hesitated and then said, as if it was for this he had come:

"I've been down to St. John in Connecticut."

"Oh?"—coldly.

"Len, you've got to do something for him."

"I can't help him"—still coldly.

Frankie glanced at the neat piles of stubs, the ledgers and letters.

"If you're broad-minded about one thing, why not be broad-minded about another?"

Leonard glanced up but dropped his eyes swiftly.

"It's not a question of being broad-minded. Let's talk about something else."

"No. I came to talk about this. St. John'll crack up if you don't give him a hand."

"Drink?"—with a laconic glance up.

"Marriage."

At once the working fingers halted. Alert but cautious Leonard said:

"What do you mean?"

"You see him, if he agrees to see you, and talk it over with him. He's unhappy about it. He wants to smash it all up. And you mustn't let that happen."

Leonard smiled without pity, but with understanding.

"So his sins are coming home to roost at last?"

"It's not a question of sin! It's a human question, damn it. It just doesn't work, that's all."

"There's no such thing as a purely human problem," said the priest firmly, and even angrily. "Everything involves morality. You're not suggesting men are chemical compounds?"

Frankie shrank back from the arid, theological mind of his brother. In his heart he wished he had not come. He realized the chasm between them, bridged over occasionally, but never permanently closed. He was going to get no help here.

"I don't want to discuss that aspect of it," he fended off sullenly. Then, tentatively, "When a man is mentally and physically sick, don't you want to help him?"

The priest gave a "Hm," and returned to his work.

"There was once a philosopher," he said, "I think it was Novalis, who said that to be sick in the body is to be mad in the mind. He meant the two are one, and they are. That's the sum total of all I ever preach as a priest to anyone. It's my brother's soul that's sick."

"Damn it," shouted Frankie, "are you or are you not prepared to help a man? . . ."

The priest raised a hand, and said quietly:

"Keep your hair on. I'm prepared to help him. But I'm a priest. Every man to his own job. I'm not a wet nurse. I see you've found out his story. How?"

"You're a cold brute," said Frankie, and then he added, "He had to tell somebody, poor devil." He had the satisfaction of seeing Leonard wince. "Look here," he challenged, half smiling to assuage the charge he was about to make. "You wouldn't really fall out with a man because he broke what you considered a serious moral law?"

The priest finished his last bunch of stubs, and slipping on a grey alpaca coat, said:

"No. I wouldn't do that to any man. What St. John did, in point of fact, was to break a disciplinary law in the first place. He was married all right, even though the Church doesn't recognize such a marriage as a sacrament. No. What counted with me was what happened afterwards. Had he lived by his own lights, or rather the lights he inherited from a good mother and a good father—for he deserved no credit for what he believed when he first came here—if he lived by his own lights, I'd have said nothing. I'd have been sorry. I'd have said, 'He can correct that two-dollar rubber-stamp marriage any time.' No!" The latent passion in the man broke out here. "I turned my back on St. John when he turned his back on everything I respect—yes, and you too. He despised Ireland, for example. All through the Irish Troubles I don't believe he gave *that* to the cause." He picked up a nickel from the heap of coins on the table and flicked it down again. "He thought the Irish were beneath him. With his highfalutin double-barrelled name!" Leonard spat. "From the day he left it he never went back to Ireland until this year. He never sent a dime to his mother. He let his daughter be brought up outside the Church. . . ."

"Hold on, hold on," pleaded Frankie. "He didn't turn his back on everything. I know he goes to mass. He brought up Randall a Catholic. He seems to have kept in touch with . . ."

"Oh, yes," sneered the priest. "That sort never cuts the painter. They keep a leg in both worlds. And that makes it worse in my opinion, for if he'd honestly said and believed, 'This stuff is no bono with me, I'm through,' you could respect him. But, no! No! No! He knew perfectly well where his reason pointed. Where his whole nature pointed. But he just wouldn't follow his nose. For thirty years he's been neither his own man, nor God's man, not anybody's man. He's been a double-shuffler, and the last time I saw him he was a damned pompous, hypocritical, mush-minded, sentimental double-shuffler, and my attitude to that kind of man, if a priest dare say such a thing, is 'To hell with him!' I know the type! This city's full of them."

"You're a very stern moralist, Len. Any one of us might get confused from time to time."

"Put your hat on, we're going down to the Boys' Club

with these things. It hasn't done me good talking about St. John."

Carrying the material for the raffle, they went down across the baking cement yard, talking of indifferent subjects, hugging the shaded sides of the street as they made their way to a dead-looking district and a strange oasis in it that, in another city, less compressed, might have petered out in rank grass and rubbish-dumps. There was no room for dead-ends here: where one thing ended another began. A rhomboid where five blocks met was an ideal spot for rank grass. It was carefully railed off; would be built on when land pressure gave it the last fillip in values to make it worth the gamble.

"Is this the end of your parish?" asked Frankie.

"No. It's the end of the ward."

"The end of the world?"

"Looks like it. A tough district, all right," laughed the priest. "Here's the club."

It was a roomy building, well built and so well fitted as to surprise Frankie, who was not accustomed to any such elaborate form of church activity. His spontaneous praise of the gymnasium, and the little theatre, and the pool-room warmed them together again. The club had been almost wholly Len's work and his chief hobby for years. As he locked away the stuff and talked about the raffle and what they would do with the money, Frankie felt drawn to him again, and in a burst of friendly, brotherly defiance, he sat up on the long bench of the pool-room, and cried:

"Len, you're a Moses with the Tables of the Law. If I did what St. John did I bet you'd turn me down like that"—snapping his fingers.

Leonard slowly closed the door of the cupboard, and

locked it slowly, and then straightening he leaned against the table, tilted his straw hat from his grey-green head, and put his hands in his trousers pocket. His blue shirt surrounded his stock.

"Just what are you getting at?"

"Well, I haven't been to mass, confession, or communion, since I came here. That's not right, I did go once, but only once. And very little for a year before I came here."

"Why not?" asked his brother, with an abstracted professional air. Frankie rushed on at full speed.

"Because I'm fed up finding God all the time on the side of the big battalions. The finer the thing you fight for in this world, the less chance you have of getting it. Even your Holy Mother the Church, as we found out in Ireland, to our cost, is on the side of the big battalions. You know the Irish bishops excommunicated us for fighting for the Republic? Look at the world today. Look at Abyssinia, Italy, China, Spain. It's force that wins every time. No matter how evil it is. . . ."

The priest's eyebrows had kept rising and rising. Now he took one hand out of his pocket, and obviously sure of himself, hard, unsympathetic, he said:

"I've heard all this before. Those reasons that you're giving me—you don't believe one of them. I'll prove it to you. I'll just ask you one question. I suppose you realize that if a man throws in his hand for that sort of idea he isn't just stalling off one brand of religion? He's saying good-bye to all religion."

Frankie wilted. Leonard was right. He had not said what he wanted to say. In coming to see Leonard again he had wanted only to dig down around, to lift out like a bad tooth all the considerations that had tormented him the night before as he sat waiting on the step for Bee to return from her walk in the woods. At the thought that he had not been able to do it, and would never be able to do it, with Leonard, or with anyone, he was appalled by his own isolation, as well as by the chasm that once more gaped between himself and the man in whom he wanted to confide.

"You see," hammered Leonard, "what you're trying to say in your highfalutin way is, 'This is a bum world and I hate the guy that made it.' Isn't that so?" Frankie did not reply. Leonard pressed on sarcastically. "Don't answer if it hurts. I expect you haven't thought it out, anyway. You might think again, now that you see what lies ahead of you?"

"You said a second ago that you'd have respected St. John more if he'd followed his own nose?" retorted Frankie. "A man can't run away from his own experiences!"

The priest considered him for a moment. Then he looked sadly about him at the stuffy room lit by the cloudy skylight, through which sun slanted on the baize. Then, as if a game were on, and the place was full of boys, and the lamps lit, he sat up beside Frankie and lit his pipe.

"I could easily refute that," he said, with an almost bored air, blowing out the smoke. "I could say, 'Follow your nose into a pit?' But I'll play ball with you." He turned and laid a hand on his brother's knee. "You're an idealist. And like all Irish idealists you've gone off the rails. They go like bulls against the dirty, material things in life, and before they know where they are they're going against life itself. It's all right, my boy, to have fine values. Take care they're not values that have no earthly relation at all to the world as it is made. You fought for fine things in Ireland. Don't get so sour as to go the other way just because somebody stole your bun. Which was probably a bun that never was on sea or land! Frankie!"

In spite of the hard, ravenous mouth, and the hard voice and chilly eyes, his face somehow or other began to glow as with a fire that had turned all those externals to baked stone.

"I'm a priest. I must talk like a priest. You've had some hard experiences, I gather. Where'd you get them? Yes—it's a straight question and a fundamental question. I'll tell you where you suffered those experiences. In your belly. In your senses. The world as you've felt it put its mark *on* you, and *in* you, and it went through you and through you until there's a kind of phantom world inside your guts and brain. It's not my idea, it's Aristotle's—every man lives the world. Do you get me?"

"I think so."

"Very well. Since man was man he's drawn conclusions of every possible kind about those experiences. We get a kind of empiric, rough and ready rule of life out of them. Not to eat too much, not to drink too much, and so on up to 'Love thy neighbour as thyself.' It's a kind of technique of living. In some countries it's finer than in others. Sometimes one wise man can impress the truth of his own experiences on a whole people! You agree?"

"I suppose so"—considering.

"Now, you're a reasonable kind of fellow. You acknowledge that you extract these different ideas and hold them in your head. More, that they exist and in life? As you might say, in the air, as more or less permanent ideas of one kind or another?"

Frankie sighed. In spite of himself he was impressed by Leonard's earnest manner.

"I'm afraid my ideas are all very simple ideas, about poverty and injustice and so on."

"That's all right. All I'm concerned with is that you aren't a materialist. You admit those ideas exist permanently. Let's call them Truth. But, mark you, this Truth would exist just the same without you. Because though you are a part of an immense movement of life, Frankie, you're only a part, as the humblest and greatest of God's creatures is. Do you deny that?"

"No"—slowly, this time, wondering where the catch was.

"You can't! Truth is eternal and immutable. It was before you were and it will be after you're a smell. There you are! Truth eternal on the one hand, and our little conclusions from our little experiences . . . possibly on the other, possibly part of that eternal fact. All that matters is that the worth of our behaviour here—in short, our life—depends on whether our conclusions agree with the origin and end of life or do not. If you say life begins as an itch and ends as a stink, say so. I don't care. You're the arbiter of your own fate. You're absolutely free. But don't go talking to me as if your experiences, as you call them, are absolute things to which you can give any interpretation you like." With a most solemn hush in his voice—"Know that it's you against the nature of the world."

"But," cried Frankie, "what the hell else have I to go on?"

"Your natural instinct, bent, body and soul, towards the end for which you were made."

"But if I don't know that end?"—jaw out.

"You do!" bullied the priest, his jaw out, too. "Don't you try to kid yourself. If you didn't know it, you'd be a gangster or a big businessman. Haven't you been fighting all your life against the idea that this is just a place to make money and be comfortable? Isn't that so? *Isn't that so?* All your ideals . . ."

"But they don't work!" cried Frankie.

"For whom?"—like a bullet.

"Lots of people. They get on without these ideals."

"They don't. And what we're talking about"—the priest gripped his brother by the stomach, and shook him—"is God Almighty!"

"People"—almost in a shout—"get on without God Almighty!"

"They do not! Take this rotten city. There's more people to the square inch in this city than in any other part of the world who act as if they believed life was a place full of booze, and dough, and women. Yet, give me one of them alone in this room for half an hour and I guarantee I'll have him sobbing on my chest and handing out a wad of dollars for some tomfool cause that neither he nor I ever before heard of."

"Then is it all a confidence trick?" raged Frankie.

The priest jumped down and faced him.

"Look at the way they poured into the Great War twenty years ago. Look at the way they build churches in California bigger'n Roxy's when a she-priest gets wringing their lights and livers with a shovel of slush a baby wouldn't spit at. This country has its tongue out a mile for heavenly ideals. Why? Because they know there's *something* there—call it God, or call it X, call it Christ Scientist, call it Mumbo Jumbo—there's something there, but"—and he lifted his fist hovering over the green baize, and his eyes burned in his head—"they won't live up to it because it's hard, and they're soft, and that's *all!*" And down crashed his fist on the hard slab.

Frankie stared at him. Leonard came nearer. He said, gently—gently for all that nasal brassiness of his voice:

"Frankie boy, don't be rough with that thing inside you. Don't be a blasted intellectual. Just because the Faith is handed out to you in some little whitewashed chapel by a country curate with a brogue, and in words of one syllable for simple people . . ."

At last Frankie said it, with sullen passion. "It's no good! It doesn't work for me! The Faith always going with dirt and poverty and misery, and the down-and-out believing in a happy life ever after!" (He thought, as he spoke, of his mother, and of Aunt Maggie and her Honesht Tam, and his other aunt with her cancered throat, and the resignation with which they all submitted to misery and misfortune.) "I can't believe it! It's a fairy-tale. I want more from life than that."

Coldly the priest asked:

"Then what do you believe in?"

"I don't know. I must follow my nose."

"If that means follow your nature, I trust you."

Frankie shook his head wearily and clambered down from the bench.

"I don't know. Ten years ago I'd have said I was certain about it all. We all did in Ireland. We laid down our lives for our certainty."

There was a pause. He added:

"I used to be a daily communicant." He burst into a sudden rage. "It was the bishops first made me think about things. The way they told us we were heretics because we fought for Ireland. The way they turned on the poor. They simply grabbed God and sold him to the British Empire."

"Oh! Irish bishops!" said the priest irritably. He rolled a red ball after a white. As they cannoned he said, "They're like that–ivory from the neck up."

Frankie did not know now whether he wanted to go on talking or stop talking. He did not know whether he wanted to talk about Ireland, or talk about Bee, or talk about himself. Wearied and troubled, Leonard led the way down the room to the door. It was then Frankie saw the picture. Bee's familiar, fawn-large eyes looked down at him, gentle and young and proud and beseeching.

"Who is that?" he said.

"St. John's wife," said the priest, looking up at it. "This is called the Bland Room because she donated it. That painting was done, let me see, in 1915—twenty-one years ago. I was just two years out then. It's funny—St. John met her here."

There can be few things so affecting as an early portrait of a beautiful woman now beginning to say good-night to her beauty. Bee Hannafey, aged twenty—Beatrice Bland—her hair as glossy as the ace of spades, her skin rosy, her mouth soft, all the heart-breaking assurance of inexperience in her grey eyes. He stared at it and in that instant he either won or was lost. For such minds as his, the imagination is more powerful than the fact. That picture, seen in the excited moment of revolt, stirred him as no touch of her hand or mouth could have done. For no man reared as he was easily confesses personal desire, and when desire comes to him it comes always as a dark wave where he swims at night; no object not cast about with imaginings and dreams can attract him any more than the naked woman who revolted Saint Anthony. Which was what Bee, not being a romantic of his order, could not have known since those days when she was very young and romantic herself—days and emotions long forgotten: it may have been the reason for her failure with her husband, by nature a dreamer, and a man of affairs only by practice; the whole secret of whose life was that, though defeated time and again, he had never acknowledged it.

Almost against his will, yet received with joy when it emerged from the haze of his imagination, there entered into Frankie's heart a picture, at first dim, then breath-takingly clear, like to this picture, of her present positive face and form, an ideal, lovely, desirable Bee. He almost suffered a disjunction of brain and limbs. With difficulty he spoke, trying to be calm:

"What do you think of her?"

The priest was still looking at the portrait.

"I haven't seen her for nearly twenty years. She was a nice girl, then. Warm-hearted. Very impulsive. Spoiled, like all American society women. Full of self-confidence. A bit of a snob like so many of these spare-time social workers. Yes! It was the self-confidence struck me most. She thought she could do everything. Oh, she was full of herself, all right! I believe she came from a good family, the Kentucky Blands. Lumber."

Frankie hated the way he spoke of her in the past tense. As if she were dead.

"Strange she couldn't hold him," went on the priest. "But I suppose desire drives out desire. She was very beautiful. She, maybe, seemed everything he wanted. Then the old, deeper thing comes back. Perhaps. Who knows?"

Frankie, hating the idea in the words "hold him," said:

"He used to beat her. One night he had a gun. She was going to have her second baby. She showed me the scar on her wrist."

He did not see the shrewd eyes of the priest veer around to him and peer at him through half-closed lids. He heard the reply, in a gently ominous voice.

"Perhaps she deserved it?"

"What do you mean?" cried Frankie, sharply, looking at him.

"I just wondered."

Frankie could not keep the glare from his eyes even though he knew he was glaring. The priest looked mildly at him and opened the door and as they went out, said, casually:

"A man doesn't beat a woman for nothing, you know."

They were out in the stagnant pool of the back-street, with its odd quietness and smelly heat. As they walked back, Leonard said suddenly:

"Well, all I can say to you is, keep in low gear. Or this —it was Spinoza said it—'The nobility of the soul follows the disposition of the body.' In other words, the senses make honey."

They strolled on.

"I always keep to the body when I get preaching about the soul," he laughed.

They left the oasis behind them and were surrounded by the roar of Queens.

"People talk too much about the soul as if it were a kind of ghost. Body and soul are one. Our object isn't merely some magic dream. It's this world about us." He waved his hand. "We're not angels! Nature has to come and be incorporated in us, through our bellies and brains, our senses. And Nature doesn't mean daffodils!"

"Yes," said Frankie, too eagerly. "I see that."

The priest shot him a sardonic glance and finished quietly:

"But the senses, as you might say, have to inform themselves. . . . Does St. John really want to see me?"

So they returned to their first subject and to the presbytery gate, where Leonard offered supper. Frankie excused himself. The momentary bridge was down. Each seemed to wish to say something more. Either he could not find the words, or the propitious moment was passed. They parted.

He went on, free at last to hold closely that lovely image that had visited him, and that so filled him that he felt suffused with it from head to toe. He did not know where he was going, preoccupied with his thoughts of her. He saw a cheap lunch-counter and went in for supper. He hardly ate and he did not hear the clanging and banging of the trays, the shouts of the waiters, the babble of voices. He took his Irish stew and coffee to a corner of a marble table, crushed by a couple of truck-drivers and their girls, and began to wonder when he would see her next. What a life she had lived! And he began to consider the tragedy of that life as it had been suddenly revealed to him in the contrast between her young and innocent pride, and her later defeat. Her loneliness, his own benevolence, all her woman's allure, his sympathy, his need for friendship, physical desire so long repressed, to all these his senses became so subject that he could hardly breathe. Just then, in searching for his pocket-book, he came on Jo's letter of that morning. He had not yet read it, and opened it casually. Its contents shocked him. The old cancered woman, his aunt, was dead.

". . . Happy the grave the rain falls on. It was a terribly wet day when we took her into Kilavullen. It was all just as they arranged it that night. Jim Barry went under the coffin, and three others—no relatives. It was a great funeral. People came from miles around. I'm sending you the cutting from the Cork *Examiner*. There were four priests at the graveside. She was bright to the end. She had great spirit. She asked after you several times. She used to say, 'That fellow is a wild limb of the divil but his heart is in the right place.' God rest her . . ."

There was a little more; local gossip; a word about herself. He paid his bill and left the clanging place, and for hours he walked and walked the streets. His mind was as clear as daylight, but between it and the object of his thought (whatever it was) there was a cloud of emotion. Now and again if he cut through it he came on another cloud, a smoke of desire. He suddenly saw where he was, under the Brooklyn

Bridge, and he remembered the night he had talked there with the girl, the masseuse, Mallon. He remembered the things he had said to her, his light-hearted mood, his assurance, and he felt so shamed that he blushed. From this side more lights stabbed the river than from where they had stood then, across on South Street. He thought of ringing up her hospital, of going to see her. But he could imagine the kind of home she had, an apartment in an old Brooklyn brownstone; as antique as Abraham Lincoln; there would probably be a young man from the Gaelic League; he would be introduced to a girl from Kerry; they would talk Ireland and politics, and then they would have a gramophone and play on it "The Stone outside Dan Murphy's Door," or "There Goes Muldoon, He's a Solid Man." It would be grand, and homely, and everything in its place, not a conjecture in a corner of it —one solid taunt to him and his alien, inimical desires.

He crossed the bridge and took a subway from City Hall to the Grand Central Terminal. There he still hesitated, until he saw, again, her liquid eyes, her ever-parted lips, her tiny hands, and with decision he put through a long-distance call and spoke to her. Yes, there was a train leaving town at eleven. He would be very welcome.

At the little station a lamp fell across her face and it was as childlike and pure as that twenty-year-old portrait. It packed the blood up under his eyes. She, who had been wondering and hoping ever since he called her, immediately understood everything, and, understanding, the look of youth passed from her face. She took his hand, and felt his tremor as she led the way to the car on the dark road. For a moment she held herself in poise, until she could be assured. Then, suddenly, she flung every coin on the table. She looked up at him and said:

"Darling, why did you come?"

Unwilling to reveal the force of his desire, he said:

"I saw your portrait in the Boys' Club."

"What portrait? Oh, *that* one!" and she tried to see it.

He took her by the waist. The train was rolling out. In his arms she kept looking at him.

"Bee, what a hell of a life you've had!"

Her eyes sank, and her head. He could only see the top of her furry cowl. He heard her say, calmly:

"Yes? I suppose I have had a rather unhappy life."

He felt her body go rigid and resistant.

"Bee!"

"I don't . . ." She hesitated, and then, firmly, undeceivingly, of herself or him, she said, "I don't want pity."

She withdrew from his arms. Terrified of that house, that empty room, she said, postponing misery:

"It's very late. Would you hate it if we had one look at the sea before? . . ."

"If you want to," he agreed, overcome by disappointment.

"Please?"

They got into the car; she switched on the lights; she drove past the scrubby woods that looked frighteningly dark, past a sleeping house, and came at last to the hissing void. The headlights streamed ineffectually across the pit. Her brown wrist switched off the ignition. They sat looking and listening to the rumble and fall and the backwash hiss that faded into a little moan.

"Let's get out," she said. "Switch off the lights."

As he did so, he saw by the pale-green clock-light that it was half-past midnight. The exhaust-pipe crinkled as it contracted in the cool air. He remembered that night he drove to Cove—the early morning avant-light, the grey expanse of harbour, the silence before the great double sun came up.

This was a like solitary hour. A lone window-light repeated the mystery of the window in Cove, eavesdropping on the morning. When he met her there, he had felt the same sense of suspended life.

As she lit a cigarette from his she shivered, and bade him get her the rug. He draped it over her shoulders. She said, "Come down to the sea," and they walked on to the foreshore. The tide was out. They felt the damp spray.

"I was just twenty when that portrait was painted. I married the year after."

"Were you very much in love?"

"I thought I was. But"—bitterly—"one soon finds out. You Irish don't fall in love. Or so I think. Oh, you're passionate enough. It isn't that. You're all . . . I'm tired and can't find the right word so don't be offended . . . you're all half savage, violent in love, but full of . . . Oh, I don't know!"

"What?"

"Fear, I think."

"Fear?"

"I'm talking about the only kind of love I know, romantic love. I understand that. I don't understand the other kind. Domestic love that centres on the family. It's good. I envy it. I've envied it all my life. Comradeship, kindness, forbearance." She took his arm as if she asked these things of him. "The kind that comes from your match-making marriages in Ireland. You understand that, all right."

The waves turned gleams of fish-white; they moaned all the time at the two solitary figures walking beside them.

"I only know," she went on, "the Paolo and Francesca love. Tristan, Dido, Paris. All the old . . ." Her free hand moved in the dark to form her thought into a physical shape. "You remember, in the *Inferno*, 'The lily in the mouth of hell.'

They walk for ever and ever in the *aer perso*, wailing like flutes in the wind."

She knew she was fantasticating. What had she ever had, or ever would have, but mere passing affairs? She held out her hand with the cigarette glowing to the sea. She laughed a little bitter, choking laugh.

"It wails like the winds of hell."

She paused and looked up at the face of the man beside her. He was looking out into the dark, as though he were seeing a ship with lights far out to sea. Her words might have called up for him a picture of a ship of souls. The fair hair on his brow barely lifted. She felt herself surrendering. She knew it was a folly, but she could not face that empty room. His cigarette in his mouth lit the brief "beetle" of his nose.

"You see! I'm not your kind of woman."

All but imperceptibly his head shook a *No*. Her heart jumped. To what was he saying, "No"? Was he agreeing or denying? He threw away his cigarette and turned and looked down at her, so frail under her hood and rug that she might have been an Irish girl in a shawl. She was about to say, "Romantic love is a folly," when he clipped her to him. He kissed her in a way he had never kissed a woman before. She sank into his arms and burst into tears.

"Bee! Poor Bee!" he comforted.

For the first time in his life he knew bodily love, its loveliness whose hunger, once satisfied, can haunt men until they die, and all its shame that was to remain with him as a residue of disgust. For her the old sirens sang, a joy so intense that when he left her she almost cried again to remember it, both because he had been so briefly and so imperfectly hers, and because she had no certainty that he might ever be hers more fully or ever hers again. The fierceness of his love had frightened her. It had been like dropping a match into a little furze bush and finding a whole moor on fire. It implied a love so great that she could not recognize herself as its source and was filled with doubts and jealousies as to its true nature. When he left the next day for New York she drove him to the station. There he was so gentle and so regretful that she was convinced he loved her. Yet, she said good-bye in a little voice, like somebody timorously unsure of what she is saying, or not quite knowing to whom it is she really speaks.

VIII

As August came near, New York consumed itself in a frenzy of heat. The sparkling bay mocked the city. In the slum districts kids in bathing-slips crawled in the gutters where kindly firemen turned on the hydrants, and the passers-by watched with envy. Outside air-cooled cinemas in the Forties, pasteboard icicles buckled and faded white. Once he went to Coney Island in a lunatic wish for the sea—thinking of those days he had spent basking at Westport with Bee. It was as if somebody had upset a mighty can of black beetles on the shore. The edge of the sea was invisible; nothing there but the striped awnings of the hired chairs and the ungainly, half-dressed bodies of thousands of people. In the heat the air was one babble of sound. He almost got a physical vomit at the sight—it was so utterly at a pole from the original feeling of freedom and remoteness that he got from New York.

In his oven of a room, dressed only in his trunks, his arm dampening the paper with its sweat, he sat and slaved. He ate nothing but iced tea and cold apple pie with the ice-cream melting on it. That became his routine for the next three weeks—cold cafeterias, the lime-kiln streets, a baking room. In this crackle of heat he counted his money. He had in the world ninety-two dollars and a few cents. He stopped going to plays and cinemas—even to museums, unless they were free. He did his own laundry. He cut his cigarettes down to five a day. He ruined his digestion eating at low-down lunch-counters.

To be hard-driven on the Irish hills was nothing to this. There you might sleep on three chairs in a kitchen, or have to borrow a shirt in one cabin and a pair of socks in the next. It did not matter. The body was only a vehicle. It carried no desires other than the simplest. You slept the thing when it said it was tired. You fed it when it said, "I'm hungry." Black tea and dry bread in a miserable mountain-cabin were as satisfactory a meal as any. You were as natural as a stream, a rock, an animal—and as sexless. Emotions were few. Fear was the most powerful; and then you ran to earth, sweated it out of yourself like a hunted beast, and forgot all about it or retained only so much in instinct as instinct required for self-safety. Here—you were made self-conscious. That was the difference. It made for endless, gnawing, wearing pressure. He was aware every day of the day's challenge and the world's resistance.

Had he been able to fight back he would not have minded; instead he merely felt the compression of the bridle. He squirmed with dissatisfaction ten times a day when he realized that he had not enough capital to make any really big move to collect money. An accumulation of trifles wore him down and the slightest thing could sting him. If he chose badly from a lunch menu and found his meal down and his belly still hungry; if a policeman looked suspiciously at him; if a group of workmen looked at him with a contemptuous, gum-chewing inquisitiveness—each time he felt the bit across his jaw.

He met Bee, a week after that visit to Connecticut, and

had tea with her in her cool, pearly-bright apartment. (She chose that meal because the maids were still down the country.) She found him tempestuous; she could not know what explosiveness had been generated in him by a week's compression of his will, a thousand doubts.

"I know"—he banged the arm of his chair as she arranged the dainty fingers of cinnamon-toast and untied her baby-apron, "why those Frenchmen you talked about sent bombs through the post. Christ! I'd love to send bombs all over this cursed city!"

"Oh, tell me why?" she begged, clasping her small hands, and sitting opposite him to hear. She loved his fury and fire. She was wearing a wet-slate-blue frock with tiny white lace frills around the edge of the skirt and edging the baby sleeves.

"Why not?" he stormed. "It's the whole effect of this kind of life. It makes you want to destroy things. It's all right here so long as you're cock of the walk, the Big Noise, the Boss. But if you're not, then it becomes a prison."

He was not seeing her. His wiry, fair hair was down on his forehead like a Hermes' or a bull's curls. His collar was sticking out at the points. His tie was fallen loose. His great frame was hulked into the chair, and his hands were goading his arguments fiercely out from him as if they were cattle that wanted to stampede.

"I understand how he felt, all right! Nothing counts in the end but the man with the one idea. The fellow who puts across a fresh idea on people who've been living by dead ideas all their lives!"

"But, my sweet Frankie, people have been destroying all their lives long. As long as I remember I've met people dissatisfied with things, wanting to tear them to pieces! Can't we ever just live, and let live? After all, if you had a family . . . If you and I, my dear wild one, were to live together here, or anywhere . . . If we had children . . ."

"I'd become just like the rest of them. I know it! I know it! Not through my own fault, though. Only because I'd be steamrolled out of myself, like St. John and like Leonard. What I like about a great city like New York is the way it makes men be themselves. What I hate about it is the way it kills men's selves." He boasted, "That's why I've devoted all my life to the smashing of the system of the British Empire!"

"Have some cinnamon-toast, darling," offered Bee.

"I understand those anarchists"—taking the toast. "I'd like to meet some of those chaps!"

Bee sat back. "I wonder," she considered, "are there some people whose vocation is to destroy. Have you ever read Turgenev's *Fathers and Sons?* It was the book that invented the word Nihilist." He shook his head, and while she went to her books to find him a copy, he continued to argue violently, now describing the city in terms of hate, now in terms of love; so that as she looked from the shelves to him and from him to the shelves, she began to realize how close love and hate are in such people, and she felt that if she had been a young girl she would either have thrown herself on him in complete abandonment of her will, or else fled from the dark thing that kept surging up in him like smoke through flames. Even as it was, when they loved that afternoon she felt her former terror at his savage force, and then was moved almost to weeping when she found herself mothering him, his tousled head, out of sudden, weak, inexplicable tears of his own.

He drove August before him, responding in savagery to the heat of the city. He wrote and wrote his begging letters to his "friendly Irish." He tried to encourage himself by thinking of men like James Stephens the Fenian, plotting year in and year out; Mazzini in London; Garibaldi in New

York; Wolfe Tone in Paris with nothing but his flute for company; even little Arthur Griffith conspiring over his bottle of stout in the Bailey pub, day after day, for years, in Dublin. None of them, he told himself, had ever had any more hope of success.

He worked his way slowly through long lists of names—subscribers to a Catholic periodical, members of an Irish-American Insurance Society, subscribers to some Irish memorial hospital. Sitting half naked at his table, his routine was—work until noon; then a thirty-five-cent lunch; work again until three; then he was free until the evening—he could not work in the hot afternoon. In the evening he was working again, meeting a few of these people now in their homes, now in clubs or saloons. For this was not like the old days of the revolution when an Irish rebel had a dozen societies behind him, lived in fine hotels, was fêted constantly, could address large meetings, got endless hospitality. He had to meet whom he could, where he could, collect what he could, from a dime up.

He saw the insides of all sorts of New York houses: rich apartments; the old brownstones; three- and four-decker tenements; workers' flats that somehow he remembered later—when all these experiences had merged into a blur—as made of cast-iron. He saw the kind of houses that get more and more miserable as you climb; he saw the kind that get more and more elegant the higher the elevator flies. He discussed Ireland with an old man in a boiler-basement. He talked of her while prowling with a night-watchman about a closed department store. Always the talk was on the same two topics, local Irish politics and family history—where the Mahoneys (pronounced Ma-ho-neys) lived, or what the Egans (pronounced Aygans) had done in Irish history.

At first he was oppressed by the majority of those he met.

He felt that they were all stuck in the nineteenth century. Their minds had not moved a step since the days of the Famine, the Land Leaguers, "poor ould Oireland," the Parnellites and anti-Parnellites. Even when they talked of de Valera it was party politics they talked. They seemed to him to have vanity without pride. Their thought of Ireland was not so much a political belief as a religious cult. They did no brain-work, had no general ideas, read nothing and studied nothing. This endless pawing over the pages of history was part of that—it was so sentimental. He could never, for example, understand what they wanted with family coats-of-arms. Patiently he would explain that Irish life does not concern itself with the inventions of the English Heralds' College, or the Ulster King at Arms; that these feudal bearings allotted to Irish families were marks of their servitude, the signs of their defeat because the sign of their exit from the Irish system into the English system. It made no matter: after that little speech some Whelan, or Quinlan, or Keogh would just say:

"It may be so. Still I'd very much like to know what the arms of my family are. Can you get them for me?"

So off he would go to the Public Library and dig them out of Hart's *Pedigrees*, and draw them in coloured crayon and post them off. He became accustomed in the end to this pathetic desire to find the non-existent glorious past. He began to see the joke of it that he, more or less a Communist, a man who believed in an Ireland beginning *now* to build itself out of nothing ("In that sense," he said to himself, "I *am* a Nihilist"), should be so often asked by the people he was trying to evangelize for armorial bearings they did not own and a glory that could only give them a pride wholly foreign to themselves.

Then the joke went sour. A woman wrote to him, "Is it

true the Irish only live in small cabins? Have our people at home no big houses with many servants, and so on?" In a fury, wiping the sweat off his lids, he wrote back, thinking of the ragged army that had fought for six years for the Republic, "You are a snob. We lived in mud cabins for hundreds of years. In wattle huts before that. The Normans, the English, and the Anglo-Irish had big castles and big houses where your people slaved for a pittance until they rose up and butchered their masters, just as they did in the French Revolution. I thought you Americans believed in 'From log-cabin to White House'! For God's sake, woman, have some pride in *yourself!*"

He was bitterly ashamed of that letter afterwards. He told himself it was only half true. He remembered the Catholic gentry who helped Daniel O'Connell, the big Leinster merchants who stood behind him, the Northerners who helped Wolfe Tone, the Grattan-Bellews, the O'Neill-Daunts, the ffrenches, the Earls of Fingall, the Catholic Latouches, the O'Connells themselves who won title and fame in the French and Austrian armies; not to mention the hundreds of thousands of Irishmen he could not respect, who had found no scope in that downtrodden Ireland and served the British Empire so well that the Irish are often said to have made it. He ruffled his hair in genuine exasperation and comical confusion, and then, just as he was feeling sorry for having upbraided a woman who had merely wanted to be proud of her race, he leaned back and laughed and laughed. Here he was, by these people, being weaned from his own conception of life that makes itself out desperately and magnificently of the Now and the Nakedness. So that when he opened the next letter, still chuckling, and found a Murphy asking for the armorial bearings of his clan, he all but tore the paper with the fury of his pen. "The arms of the Murphys are a spade and shovel on a ground of blood, sweat argent, and prison-barred! God damn you for a . . ." He tore up his wild reply. He threw aside his work. What he wanted was a punch-ball; something to pommel and kick and tear. He went to the Y.M.C.A. on Twenty-Third Street and got the punch-ball, and, dripping with perspiration, rushed through the shower, and hurled himself steaming into the cold pool.

Back in his room he found an Irish letter waiting for him. It was Josephine. She had answered by return the passionate letter he had sent her the Sunday night of his first visit to Connecticut. It was dated July 26. It began, "My dearest sweetheart. This is the first really nice letter I got from you since you went away. . . ."

She was now in rooms in Fermoy with a railway clerk and his newly wedded wife, and their one baby. It was the clerk who had the gramophone, and liked serious music. She wrote of the "1812 Overture." "We have it every night, now. It's grand to hear the guns going off, and the horses galloping, and to see Moscow burning. It took us out of ourselves! His wife, who is a knitty woman, says he's daft. So he is—but she doesn't know it. . . ."

Then there was a bit about the countryside. He saw it in the great July heat at the top of growth, all Ireland one great bursting pod, a land of greenery and dust. The mountains would be dim in the heat-haze. A bloom of heat would soften the nearest fields. He saw Jo, with the queer brown dye about her two eyes that gave them such a stage-tragic look, walking about Fermoy in her nurse's uniform, all in dark blue, with a blue hat; very slim; a greyhound figure; tall as a reed. There would be a tang of turf-smoke in the air. The reedy river would be low tide. He searched in his wallet and found her photograph. It brought her so near to him that he had to put it away at once. He went back to her letter. There was a cross to indicate love. The kiss was like a mark over a grave. He thrust away her letter and gathered in one of his lists. He rose and stripped to his trunks. He sat down and took up his pen to write some of his begging appeals.

He did not write. He had no strength left to ask those poor, hard-working, yearning, trustful Irish of New York—so many replicas of the little group in the club—to give him money to go home to Ireland and refashion life. The ambition was an impertinence. It had, indeed, ceased to exist. He looked at the calendar. He was in New York, now, since May 27. Bee had landed on the Friday afternoon of the second week in July. In three days from that date he had taken the cluster of lights he held before his face and flung them away. He could hear them crunch under people's feet like so many glass prisms where they fell.

How much, really, to begin with, did he love Bee? He saw her wide eyes, her brown cheeks, her line of jaw, her convex curve of shoulder, amber-smooth, mushroom-soft—and it became impossible to tell. It is said that if a man asks, "Do I love her?" he does not love her. In truth it is not a question: love has no answer but love. The wise question is, "Could I forget her?" The rebuttal of love is not hate but the death of the heart. Frankie Hannafey did not ask himself that question, but had he asked it he would have had to say that he would never forget her, not to his dying day. The saying of Balzac cannot be wholly true (life has constantly rebutted it), that it is only the last love of a woman that satisfies the first love of a man. But it is true that the last love of a woman, like the last harvest of a tree, is the most abundant, a rain laden with the pollen of all the richest flowers of her lifetime seeping down to the roots of a young man's heart. To it his fresh heart opens as wide as his arms. From the memory of that rain of love there is no mortal escape.

"Desire drives out desire?" Her love and the love he had given to the impalpable, unfleshly loveliness of his land, were two kinds of deep desire. But Ireland has loved many men and her love is never the last love and it always kills. That small brown face, with the white eyes, and the high cheekbones, and the parted lips all meant life, and the desire for life, that drives the nails into the palms, and catches the breath. That is the other side of the love of a mature woman for a young man. Only youth finds and draws out from the last love of a woman all her zest for life. A young girl, the most gentle and sweet, a slip of a shoot of a tree, could never have roused him as this woman in whom he found all the age and experience of the world. Those lit grey eyes, that deer-like lift of head, offered him not merely a cup of love, but everything that love had won, in victory and defeat, flowing over. . . .

He sank his face into his arms to think of her. Sleep came to him there, but in its maternal arms he dreamed of Ireland. Nobody who has not suffered ache of exile, more gnawing than ache of passion, can know the happiness of such dreams; more intense by far in their illusion of joy than any sexual dream. He heard nothing now of the rumble of New York. He sank down and down into a feather-bed, and grassy mountain hills soothed him like the paps by which so many of them are named. He felt the haze of rain falling diaphanously over his little city—its mist seeming to hang suspended in the vacuum of Sunday silence. He re-dreamed his thoughts in Cove that morning in May.

The shop-windows were brown-blinded; there was no sound except when the newsboys cried the Sunday papers. Kitchen-tables littered with the relics of breakfast spoke of the same rush for church in every house. He could distinguish two separate, familiar bells, whirling him to two separate corners of the city: a rapid tolling, a little bell—Saint Augustine's; and from beyond it a slow clacking of a larger bell—Saint Francis's. Had a recording angel wished to start there, with those two bells heard in mixed misery and happiness by the sleeper, he could have found between any one stroke and the arrival of its sound on the air the whole story of a childhood, a boyhood, and a first manhood—a life's growth, ambition, content, discontent. And found, when the sleeper stirred with a little groan, and came alive slowly to the growling of New York, and the heat of the room, and the damp of his body, his present despair. Awake, Frankie still heard those two bells. He felt not only all they meant to him, but to the hearts of the thousands who had heard them with him, in lane and street, garret and parlour. His eye fell on the familiar handwriting of Josephine; then on the lists; and, with the urge of his body reminding him of Bee Hannafey, he returned to them now. The telephone rang. Even before he took it up he knew who it was and what he would say to her.

"Hello. Bee? Tonight? Dinner? Now? Very well. But it must be a Childs. I have no money. Of course. You *are* my sweet one. . . . Good-bye, my darling."

He gathered up his lists and papers and Jo's letter and pushed them all aside. He felt he was postponing a decision and in that conscious or half-conscious acknowledgment he half acknowledged, also, that from now on postponement was about to become part of his technique of living. He had a cold bath, dressed, and went across town to her place on Fifth Avenue. She wore an evening frock of off-white; her shoulders emerged from the soft material like a nut from the white pericarp. He told her so, and she asked the meaning of the word, and he was glad to smoothen the awkwardness of their meeting by explaining from the residual memory of his college botany—stroking the bare scapula with his fingers, gently exploring the delicate hollow of the collarbone with his thumb.

"A brown nut," he said and she shook her head part sadly, part comprehendingly.

Then he drew back and surveyed her.

"But you are all dressed up? I said a Childs!"

"Frankie, I've just got a cable from Randall and Mary Garland. Mary is his fiancée—you saw her for a minute at Cove. They're landing from Europe tomorrow. Randall will be here from now on. It's our last free night. Let's celebrate."

He looked down at her, knowing what she portended, foreseeing that in tonight there might be a last decision he could not revoke.

"Let's have a real bust," she pleaded.

"But I'm not dressed for it." He looked down at his grey tweeds.

"I thought of that. There's a tuxedo of Randall's here."

He yielded and she showed him into Randall's room. Everything was ready. But when he began to change he found that the shirt and jacket were too small. He called to her. She clapped her hands with delight.

"You look so domestic! Of course it won't fit. You're too broad in the shoulders." She was happy examining and fitting. "I know. You must try one of St. John's," and she ran off and came back with another shirt and another suit. This one was a bit too large; the jacket was flappy about the stomach, and the safety-pins, laughingly inserted by her tiny hands, lapped the trousers across. He looked fine, she assured him, when he came out, all brushed and smooth, his blob of fair hair neatly curled over his right eye.

She had sherry ready. It stimulated him. After these weeks of frugality it was good to have one easeful night again.

"Now, where do we go?" she asked, and produced a *New Yorker*. "Sit here and decide with me. We must go to a show after dinner."

They sat side by side, their heads close together.

"Look!"—he pointed. "There's Paintings and Drawings by Seventy-Five Relief Work Artists. Oh, too bad"—the Artists' Union shut at six.

"What a shame!" she pouted. "Are you sure you wouldn't like something soothing, such as ceramics or ancient bronzes?"

He loved the wicked tilt of her nose. Seriously he cried, his eye catching the title:

"Look, a Strindberg. *There Are Crimes and Crimes.* Where's that?"

She took his strong fingers and twisted until he squealed. Then she made her head rollick threateningly and shot at him out of the side of her mouth:

"Have you forgotten that my household, compared with Strindberg, is a Children's Hour?" She nicked with a purple thumb-nail a Gilbert and Sullivan at the Adelphi.

"What's wrong with you, young man, is that you don't know how to live."

"Do you?" he asked, not without intent to stab.

"Yes. Now read out that dinner and dancing list while I phone for seats and a taxi."

She went to the telephone while he read the names. "Coq Rouge, Pierre Roof, Plaza Persian Room, Versailles, St. Moritz, Larue . . ."

"We *are* in America?" he teased.

"Yeah," she snapped, between genuine cheerfulness and genuine nervousness; for she was aware of the under-motif of resistance in this light sparring between them. As long as he kept teasing her she must tease back. "And I'm having no arguments with you, tonight, my child. Read on."

"Waldorf-Astoria Starlight Roof."

"That's fine. Just what we need." She turned to her phoning.

He hastily read the details, wondering how much it would cost. "Guy Lombardo and his orchestra alternating with Xavier Cugat's tango band. Dances by Georges and Jalna. Dress." She finished telephoning and sat by him again, and began to remember all the singers she had heard in *The Yeomen of the Guard*, back to her childhood when they did it in a barn at school, and when they did it again in Bryn Mawr. The first time she saw it in New York was when her mother came up from Louisville and took a house for the coming out of her daughters. They had all gone for the first time to Europe that summer.

"You have sisters?" he asked, astonished.

"My sweet, it's so nice to think you thought me unique!"

The sparring went on. Every lover will recognize the pathetic, fond technique. Touch by touch the moment has to be approached, or the gods will refuse their blessing. The end is not inevitable. It may vanish like a frightened deer. She dared only to lay her fingers quietly on his, and as she touched him she held her breath. Just then the buzzer sounded. She gathered up her wrap and they finished their drinks and went down to the car. By their gentleness with each other, each knew that they had already come very close to their fate.

She guided him first to a café on Fifty-First Street, where they had a cocktail each. The drink thawed them a little more; they so enjoyed the intimacy of the little compartment where they sat that they dallied long and had to hurry to the hotel. The increased tempo was propitious. In the taxi she frayed at his big hand and rubbed her face to his shoulder, and said:

"My Frankie! What would I do without you?" And his answering smile led them another step forward.

In the elevator they grinned at each other. He thought, "It might be one of the buildings I saw my first night in this city." The great cool roof-room had the loftiness of an airship hung motionless in the sky; from their table they could lean and look, through the plate-glass, over the roofs of New York. Shading his eyes from the brilliance of the room, he looked down on the glittering city and saw one single tower with a few late windows stuck in its flank. It was like the mother-of-pearl "Memento from Lourdes" they had at home; its few windows iridescent in the cloudy coloured searchlights that smoked about its tower-face. It had all the old thrilling remoteness and isolation and independence of his first image of the city. The sentimental tango played about them caressingly. The boatload of diners, in white ties, low bronzed backs, black tuxedos, all seemed to be conspiring happily over the white tables, the delicate flowers, the wine in the glasses. It was all detached, floating, aerial. In his excitement he grinned and pressed her toe under the table. She moued at him a wide-lipped, soundless, "My sweet." Then, sighing with content, she dived behind the great menu.

"Shall I order for you?" she peeped over the menu-card.

"No," he said obstinately, and began to explore line by line from the telephone number, Eldorado 5-3000, down to the colophon. Seeing *Seagulls' Eggs à la Russe*, he looked up frowningly and found her peeping laughingly at him. He laughed back. She said:

"Darling, why not let Alphonso choose for us?"

"Is that his name?"—looking up at him.

"They're all Alphonso"; she bowed nicely to him and the waiter bowed to her and hovered paternally. He suggested and they (or rather she) accepted his brief menu, thereby giving him a great deal of pleasure. He believed, he told them, in putting only a few choice dishes before clients. He wrote it down:

Melon Cantaloup
Consommé gelé
Truite froide au court bouillon. Sauce verte
Salade St. James

The sweet he left to them, and Bee, who feared that this light dinner might not satisfy so big a man as Frankie, suggested crêpes Suzette to follow.

It was perfect. The trout came in a little silver boat, cased in ice, with paddles shaped in ice and a flag of coloured ice at bow and stern. With enthusiasm Alphonso described its cooking—the white wine, the pepper, the tiny, tiny drop of vinegar, the careful slow method of cooling. The salad was hearts of lettuce, tomato, French beans, and Bee persuaded Frankie to notice how the beans had absorbed the flavour of the tomatoes, and the tomatoes had been flavoured by the touch of the beans. The wine was a good, sharp Pouilly Fuissé. She chose that, too.

Their table was pleasantly far from the music. There were just enough people to create an adequate atmosphere of friendliness without preventing intimacy. As their heads and hands drew closer over the meal, their spirits too became aware more and more sensitively of each other, and content mingled with affection, and affection was heightened and tautened by the challenge of a secret growing anticipation of final love.

"Frankie," she said, with infinite gentleness and pleading, "I'd hate anything to hurt you. I'd rather my head were cut off, I'd rather be cut up into a thousand little pieces, than be the cause of hurting you."

"You couldn't."

"You mean I am not able to hurt you?"

"Perhaps you could as part of something else. Not you of your own wish and will. I know you wouldn't want to. That's all I mean."

She again moued a silent word of affection. She said at another time:

"I feel I've been searching for you all my life."

He said, "I haven't been searching. But I feel I have found something I couldn't find anywhere else. It's like the way I thought I found—maybe I did find—here, there"—looking out at the silhouette pricked with light and the reddish sky —"something I always wanted." He shaded his eyes and peered out, and she did the same. "It's a great city."

She shook her head fondly down at it. "It brought you to me." She threw it a kiss.

Then came the sad flaw in the evening. It was when the waiter and his little *marmiton* of an assistant were going through the rite of the pancakes. Frankie was watching with interest the burning blue flames of the brandy in the silver dish, the skilful fingers of the old man folding the batter. His eye suddenly caught sight of the eyes of the boy intent as a neophyte at a religious ceremony. He did not interrupt his talk with Bee. It was one of those scarcely conscious moments that can alter the whole tone of an evening. A juice released inside the viscera might do it as quietly; a drop of blood passing over the brain. Bee caught the motion of his head—she was not forty for nothing—and looked at him hard. The look called him back to her, but he brought back something cold and critical that vanished in a smile. He looked down at the blue flame again.

She tipped his finger with her finger and he looked up.

"Yes?" she murmured.

"What?"

"You were thinking?" (All but jealously.)

Leaning over the trailing sweetpea on the white linen he covered his whisper of, "That boy's face." She looked sidewards, pushed the salt to him, and smiled.

"Isn't he cute?" she murmured. "A Donatello."

The little Italian boy slewed his lovely face around, and looked at them with parted lips and wide brown eyes. He was beautiful, but of more than face. From the cleft of his chin to the little tail of crisp hair down in a V on his forehead, repeating the wings of his eyebrows that swept converging in another V above his nose, every feature was as soft as childhood. They prophesied rather than defined. In that face no muscle had as yet responded to the secret hardening within, or constricted lip or eye, or line of cheek. As, in obedience to the old man's sign, he wheeled away the dumbwaiter, Frankie stared after him. Just as he went, the gamin put his finger archly to his lips behind the old man's back. It was a perfect image of "Joy—its finger ever at its lips . . ."

Under her eyebrows Bee watched her consort. Then, slowly, she took up her knife and fork, with a sigh.

"What's the deep sigh for?" he asked, startled.

"Nothing; enjoy your pancakes."

"I'm going to," he smiled.

She ate a few mouthfuls and said, "Ooh, they're good," got no reply, put down her fork, leaned forward, and said:

"Frankie, why aren't we like that?" Her gestures explained, hands clasped, fingers dovetailing. "Instead of that?" Tips of fingers buffering, tapping hopelessly. Her voice filled with misery. "Frankie, my sweet, do you never enjoy things as they come?"

"But I always do!"

"No!"—sadly. "All the time I've known you, there's been something at the back of your head interfering . . . interfering. You looked up just now with a face like a Christian virgin taken out of the catacombs to a Tiberian orgy."

"Rubbish!"

She shook her head; lifted her fork; sighed. Then she shrugged and laughed and said, "Never mind. These crêpes are perfect. I must live up to my motto. Enjoy them."

He leaned his jaw on his fist and glared down the room.

"It's all commercial," he said solemnly.

"Darling," she gurgled. "I love you when you're disapproving and sweet."

"But it's a racket!"

"Don't be a *bore*, darling. Forget it."

She smiled her snowy smile, and leaned over and laid her hand on his, to calm and soothe him.

"I warn you, Frankie, you're just going to fly off the handle in two minutes if you aren't careful." And again she held her breath and watched lest he should, he was suddenly so overwrought. As she watched she saw him become so rigid that he swayed in his chair. She could hear his fingers in his fist creak along the skin of the palm. She could not have known that he was suddenly made conscious of himself by that boy—breaking across that delicate hyper-awareness of one another on which they had been mounting to a peak of oneness. He was aware that he was sitting there in her husband's clothes, reefed about by safety-pins, petted, all but made into a gigolo. . . . He did hold himself in. His very breathing was stopped. She could see an emotional storm coming, like the one earlier in the day in the theatre.

"Frankie!" she begged, and he glared at her wide-eyed. She whispered, "This is our night out. This is our celebration." Her lips trembled. "Our last night that . . . we . . ." Then, happily, she had to laugh. As she laughed she broke into a little despairing apologetic sob. "Darling, I can't help it. I suddenly felt it was like . . . it was like watching Randall when he was a little boy in church, to see if he were going to sneeze!"

It saved the moment. He laughed, too, and relaxed. He had fortunately seen, too, the tension in her, and felt they were both at an equal level. He folded his arms and looked close to the glass to see the speckled roofs and towers.

"Oh," he groaned, "I don't know what's wrong with me. The way I look at myself is this. . . ." (She felt like saying, "For God's sake *don't* look at yourself!" He was so solemn she did not dare to.) "I thought I knew exactly the sort of life I believe in, and the kind of world I believe in, and I don't think I know any longer."

"Darling, you do know. You do know. That's what I like in you. The same way that St. John likes it in you. You're a kind of stubborn, rocky person. Like those pictures of dignified Red Indians with their arms folded across their chests. It makes you sometimes a bit obstinate, and obtuse, and maddening. But it's you, just the same. Why on *earth* do you say you don't know?"

"I shouldn't have said it like that. I do know, for myself. But I don't know for others. Take Ireland. Supposing I could go back to Ireland tomorrow?" He paused. "I wouldn't fit in."

She shook her head.

"You had ceased to fit in before you left it, Frankie. If you ever did."

"No, no!" Rejecting it with a disbelieving shake of the head. "I fitted in during the revolution, all right."

"People like you always fit in 'during the revolution.' My sweet, it's what I've wanted to say to you ever since we met. Your world is your own world. You are a big and great person, Frankie, too big to 'fit in' as you call it. Do you remember how I told you my joke about Irishmen? That they are the only square pegs that fit into round holes—because they're made of rubber? But you aren't. You fit in here all right because here nobody fits in. They're all out on their own. Frankie, stay here! You would be happy in America."

Because she had articulated his secret thought he fled from it instinctively. She saw that flutter of flight in his eyes, and the stubborn return in the jut of his chin. He shaded his eyes again and pressed his forehead to the glass. The irregular silhouette, blazing with darkness and brightness, moved towards him like an army and stood at attention, and just like an army, and just as he had so often seen it before, it was merciless and magnificent. Then his eyes returned to the room—the chattering diners, the fat men, the handsome women, bald men, young men, their wives, lovers, friends. Then he looked at her. She looked back, all poised to fly with his slightest thought; she was an edged rapier of a woman; she was also a soft flower whose edges were just turning a gentle brown.

"No," he said; lightly, because quite positively. "I'll go back to Ireland . . . some time."

She looked sad and said simply:

"I shall die."

Their hands held.

"I shouldn't fit in here any more than—much less than—in Ireland. I admire Americans in lots of ways. There's no fluff on them. There's something clean-cut about them. But"—he shrugged—"God knows what they live by—or live for. When all is said and done, there's something warm and soft about Ireland. Like the rain on a Sunday morning."

Suddenly she gave in. She was weeping. It had reminded

her of a Sunday afternoon sitting with the little French wife talking about the Midi; the same pull of home. The sense of the tap-root; of enveloping friendship and common love; all that she had missed in life.

"Our celebration," she sobbed, and her face became red and absurdly comical. "It's such a damn silly way to spend an evening!" The painted mouth was lowered at the corners, and tears were streaming down her face so that he wanted to laugh, and at the same time he was cut to the very skin of his heart. "Why the hell," she choked, "do you have to start your moralizing . . . on a . . . night we wanted to be so happy in?" She searched, blinded, for her handkerchief. "You great fathead, I love you so much! But you've got as much sense as . . . as a goldfish!"

He could see, out of the corner of his eye, that Alphonso was watching, and he was angry with her for that. But he wanted, too, to take her into his arms, and comfort her: to take her on his lap and joke her out of her fit.

"I'm sorry, Bee. I'm a bloody fool."

She was already powdering rapidly, peering at angles into her compact-mirror. She allowed herself one furious spurt.

"What the hell you get out of your blasted country? What you've got better to offer than . . ." She looked around the brilliant room. "Look at all these dumb hicks enjoying themselves, and we two . . . Oh, Frankie!" She put her compact down with a rap. "You've got such a grand aura. Why don't you *live* by it, and forget everything but?"

"I dunno. Maybe it's being a Communist—or whatever I am."

"You sweet, sweet, sweet sap! You're as much a Communist as Nicholas Murray Butler." She shook it all off, then, on the instant, the fruit of a long life of practised, learned, and hard-earned buoyancy. "Eat up, Frankie. Those crêpes. Look at them. They've gone cold."

She beckoned to Alphonso. He came, full of troubled solicitude.

"Madame? The crêpes are not right?"

"Alphonso, we've been having a set-to. I'm so sorry. They were lovely. But we've let them go cold. Get us something else. An ice or something?"

Miserable at the ruin of his crêpes, and full of eagerness to help her—never once looking at the young man who had presumably been the cause of it all—he recommended *ananas glacé sibérienne*, the specialty of the evening. It restored her to complete joy; she was like a child over it; for it was a small pineapple with something like a bridal veil over it, and with a base of transparent ice fashioned to represent a snake among leaves. Inside the pineapple was an ice. She clapped her hands and the old man was charmed. To Frankie that innocent excess of joy was something he never forgot—so spontaneous, so irrelevant, so much part of her nature. His last glance over the city was a glance of wonder that it should hold and create such simple happiness—much as if a butterfly alighted on some enormous lethal machine.

"Frankie?"

This time his eyes were as if somebody had opened a mollusc and disclosed the tender visceral fleshiness beneath the scale. They tipped fingers. Her weakness had broken right through to his heart. He felt as if he had suddenly fallen in love with her, and that the more he knew of her the more would he go on falling in love with her until . . . There he paused, in excitement; even in fear.

They finished with a brandy. They shared the bill—eighteen dollars and seventy-five cents. He tipped lavishly. Late for the show, they fled helter-skelter. They took another taxi and in it they kissed as if a doom hung over them—some destiny whose sentence they could not read.

They drew closer to one another as they found their places —she with an infantile giggling at the shushes of the audience —and slipped into their enjoyment of the prettily delicate, smoothly gelatinous production. Once in a pause she whispered, snuggling across the arm-rest to his shoulder:

"Oh, goody, goody! I want this to go on for ever and ever. Never to stop. Never. It's heaven on earth." And in an interval, "Frankie, I'm going to burst into tears when the curtain falls at the end. I warn you. I'll howl like an Alsatian wolfhound right here in the stalls." Seeing he really half believed she might, she laughed with joy. When, at last, it was all over, and the pale-green trees and the brilliant limes and the pretty dresses and the bright illusion were all folded up and the men were holding up the white furs and golden wraps for their womenfolk, and she and he oozed out into the hot neon night she moved as if in a dream with glazed eyes.

"I believe," he teased, "you'll dream of it tonight, just like a child after her first pantomime."

"I don't want to dream," she whispered, tremblingly.

In the taxi she swooned in his arms, and then, as if in fear, or as if to postpone the final moment's final danger, she said:

"We'll look in at the Crystal? Do you mind? It's near. Just one dance?"

As if he, too, wished for respite, he nodded.

The contrast between the brilliance of the mid-avenues and the dark raucousness of the streets across under the elevated railways was day and night. Flares along Fifty-Third Street lit the night-work on the new subway. The night-club was on the edge of the water, a blob of light in darkness. Inside, the orchestra was playing a waltz. They floated into it as they might float into a pool. Then they had an iced whisky apiece, and he saw a flicker of lights below which steadied into the blue and green of a passing boat.

"What is the river?" he asked.

"The East River. Welfare Island over there. Queens on the other side."

He said, merely, "Oh?" and looked at her. A kind of backward tentacle of the mind pushed Queens away. A slow one-step drew them on the floor again, but in the middle of it he said, "Let's go." As they came along the gaseous mirage-smooth asphalt of lighted Fifth Avenue, and the dark bulk of the Metropolitan Museum hove in sight, she said, as if in a daze, "I wonder are the children asleep?" As she said it a lamp fell across her face, and it was, as that night when he came down to Connecticut on the midnight train, childlike and pure. Then she woke up and became forty again. "I'm dreaming," she said. He waited until they were alone in her room to ask what had she been dreaming.

"It was the music. And the waltz after it. The last time I heard that music and that waltz was at the end of the war. I was twenty-three. I was not much more than married. It reminded me."

In his heart he knew that she was reliving her youth. At the same moment he saw again her portrait in the Boys' Club. He suffered thereby an inexpressibly delicate conflict of emotions between the cry of that lovely vanished youth and his jealousy that she had shared it with others. She read the conflict and trembled. Her hands were partly raised. Her head was faintly poised. With a touch she would dissolve. And yet if there must be always in such a relation this sharp regret—and in regret she, too, must have known it—that late love is not virgin love, there is in that loss a gain of feeling that all the heart's sentimental flutterings and trepidations, as of a moth about a lamp, are much more than a mere current of the blood. The pity and tragedy of life's declining graph makes it part of the pulse of nature itself as it moves, and flows, and falls towards that lip of rock below which is the valley and the sea. These are not mere phrases. Marriage is nothing if it is not a refuge and shelter, a wild desire to shield, and hide, and soothe. As he saw her there hovering, looking to him with her great dissolving eyes, he recalled her saying that night on the beach at Westport that she had known only romantic love. With a little, sardonic, pitying, loving gasp at such weakness in such strength he touched her.

IX

St. John returned to town, cured, that first week of August, and Frankie and Bee escaped to Connecticut from the continuing heat-wave. They spent two magnificent weeks there, and then, just as the first barely perceptible crispness began to rarefy the air, and a gentle melancholy tone overcast the skies at early dusk, they came back to the city. There Bee found that St. John had gone to stay for a week with his brother Leonard in the Queens presbytery; later to take rooms in a modest hotel on that side of the river. When Frankie heard this it made him feel more than anything else could the click of the knife on a period. Two more warm letters from Josephine consolidated the sense of the passing summer. A hard note in the second, or what he felt as a hard note, scrawled him lightly. She said:

"No more news of the search after you. I think the whole thing is dying down. A seven days' wonder. Maybe soon you may be able to return. Do you want to?

"I find it difficult to write. Since you put 3000 miles between us—you can't deny you DID—it seems hardly worth while writing. By the time you get this I'll be so completely different to what I am now—I'll have forgotten what I am saying now. But if you didn't go to the New World, maybe you'd be in the Next World!

"I may as well write, though. I talk to everyone here. Being a nurse I can—not human, you see. Nurses have no sex-appeal. I'm always making plans. I've just now made one which is going to ruin my classic beauty but which is going to keep down my adipose. Which loss would you dislike most? Here is my plan. Get up at seven sharp every morning and not go to bed until twelve at the earliest. In this way I'll have time to read and think. It will at any rate make me feel freer than those other female women who slave like niggers to keep their bits of faces and preserve their market value. I object to such tyrannies. When I said that to Mrs. Jimmy (the landlady) she nearly ate me. 'It's easy for you,' she said, 'with a natural wave and a straight nose.' I regret to say I was flattered like anything. But this regime will cure that. I'll get thin and withered and have a stooped back and thin scraggy legs and a pair of hollow eyes, but it will be a blessing when that stage comes. There will be no further need for vanity and dress. Cheerio. Three times three. I'm off for a spin on the bike up the river. Jo.

"P.S. Would you mind? P.P.S. I've been reading light books, all too foolish to finish. I've finished one on Sicily and Italy, the South of Gold and Blue. I wish I could be like you, out of this sodden, bitter country. From which you may guess that the sun is gone in and it's raining."

Across the top of the envelope outside was written, "Sun out again. This is a *lovely* country."

During those weeks he saw Bee every day. Every night she wrote him *petits-mots*, and she rang him the first thing every morning. He worked less and less as August moved on to September, and his days came to exist only for her. Knowing how little money he had, she would sometimes send him small gifts—books, potted fruit, tickets for the theatres. These last she would ask him to share with her, and they went before or after the play to some (as she thought, but not he) inexpensive foreign restaurant that one of her "boys" had told her about. They were mostly private houses where French, Austrian, or Italian immigrants gave their own kind of food to those who could pay a little extra for it.

These homes gave him another glimpse of American city life, the foreign middle-class *quartier* life of Europe wedged into little out-of-the-way cubbyholes in a city that did not have more of them only because it was not organized that way. Yet it liked these intruders to intrude, and was amused, and touched by the fussy draperies, the heavy food, the *mère de famille* who cooked, the daughters who served at table. People were more kind and forbearing to these places than they would have been at chromium-and-glass restaurants in the centre of town. Lovers liked their atmosphere of homeliness and cosiness. Tables for two were the most common.

Sometimes she would send little verses with her gifts, as when, with a packet of *tilleul* (offered after he said he was finding it hard to sleep), she wrote:

Frankie,
Here's the Lime T,
And T stands for Trial It,
If wakeful you be.
It is on my guarantee,
Full of flowers sweet as violet,
So please find my tea
Lying under my triolet. Bee.

Or, in the first week of September, asking him to take her to a film, she mentioned her Settlement Revue again:

These rehearsals, will they never cease?
I long to walk through grasses lush,
From burning youth I seek release.

This Irish lightning will not give me peace!
Its thunder will it never hush?
Its music, will it never cease?

Day by day my woes increase.
These flames within I cannot crush.
From burning youth is no release.

Oh, this revue, why did I sign its lease?
I crave a tramp through bog and bush.
This music will it never cease?

My life is broken. Piece by piece
I watch it fall, its life-blood gush.
From burning youth is no release.

My sword I will with thy heart grease
If thou from me to Ireland rush.
(I said "release" not that surcease!)

How much I love thee, let me please,
O love long sought mid sound and hush,
Tell thee at *The Man on the Flying Trapeze*

For which two tickets, O Golden Fleece,
Let's go before the evening rush.
Dear music may thou *never* cease!

They went to this film, as she had suggested, in the afternoon; and then he went on to meet one of his Irish friends. Afterwards if it was not too late he was to come to her.

At this time there had hardly been a night that they had not seen one another, even if it were only for as long as it took to drink a glass of sherry and smoke a cigarette, though their real meeting-time was the usual hour for all such as they—when the rest of the world is still busy; just as the day begins to turn towards evening and there is some slight touch or promise in the air of the night they cannot have. He knew what she meant by "if it is not too late"—Randall and Mary were in her mind, as in another week there would also be Beulah, finished with Europe. So, when he found that it was after eleven o'clock as he stood in the avenue, he did not, for this night, dare to go in. Instead he rang from the nearest call-box. To his astonishment she said, sharply, "All right, thank you," and hung up. He decided she had company, shrugged uncomfortably at this unpleasant note of subterfuge that had entered into their relationship, and went home.

In the morning she rang to explain and, if he were hurt, to soothe him. She had had company—St. John. He had come to demand a legal separation on terms. He claimed Beulah, who was still a minor. He could not control Randall, who was turned twenty-one, and anyway Randall was a Catholic so it did not matter. Bee refused, offered a divorce, which he would not consider, and that argument had been going on when Frankie, walking along the park side of Fifth Avenue, saw her lofty windows lighted. An hour before he had telephoned her, St. John had begged to be allowed to bring in Father Leonard to talk to her, and at once produced the patient man from his car in the street below.

"So that I had two of them battering at me, until I felt like Joan of Arc before Cauchon and was looking around for the instruments of torture."

Just before eleven Father Hannafey had given it up and gone home, but St. John kept getting up and sitting down, and getting up and sitting down, until she was exhausted and almost in tears. He was still arguing at midnight. Then, suddenly, he became violent. Then he began to cry. Then, seeing that they were both crying, she had to laugh and he went off in a fury.

"The poor wretch"—all this over the telephone—"hasn't been doing a thing at his business. As far as I can make out he does nothing but read books on theology. . . . Ireland? Oh, that seems to have faded out of the picture altogether. He only mentioned it a few times. . . . Yes, he's drinking again, too."

That afternoon at the rehearsal she was haggard; she looked every one of her forty-one years. Listening to her, Frankie felt like going around and beating up his step-brother. He felt it that night, again. As he was setting out to meet an old Fenian, who was taking him to a dinner (to the Incorporated Society of Plumbers and Gasfitters) in an upper Broadway hotel, she rang him up to say that St. John had just telephoned. He was coming around again. Frankie at once telephoned Leonard, who was unsympathetic.

"Frankie boy, you keep out of this. I understand what's wrong with poor old St. John. I want to help him to reform his life and save his soul."

"But you would have nothing to do with him when we talked about him in July!"

"That's right. But I didn't explain why. And I can't now. All I can tell you is that his marriage is wrong, and always was wrong. I also want you to know that I have studied psychiatry for years. I'm in constant touch with a very able priest who hopes to run a clinic in connexion with the church for just this sort of case. I . . ."

"I don't give a damn about your clinics. The man is pestering Bee."

"You've got him wrong. You see, he's got a peculiar complex. It's really a form of overscrupulosity arising from years of suppressed fear. It's the swing of the pendulum. He's been for years and years crushing down his conscience. All these years it's been boiling and boiling inside in the poor old chap, and now, well—he's simply burst his boiler. In other words the Holy Ghost has spoken to him. Now what we've got to do is to calm him down, and to tell him just what the Holy Spirit really requires of him. I think . . ."

Frankie seized the mouthpiece as if it were a gun.

"Is St. John there?" he roared.

"Yes."

"Well, tell the bastard that if he goes near that woman tonight I'll beat him to pulp!"

He rang off, trembling with fury.

It ruined his dinner. He sat among the gasfitters and plumbers with his white beefsteak bib around his neck and the white paper chef's hat on his head and hardly touched the sandwiches. The beer he drank freely, glaring at the man who sat opposite him, thinking that at that very moment St. John was, maybe, bullying Bee, even being violent with her. He was about to get up and go to her when the chairman spoke of him directly.

"Brothers, we have here tonight a man who fought for Ireland on Irish soil. . . ."

And he proceeded to give Frankie a great "build-up" as an Irish patriot. While he was speaking the old brown-jawed Fenian kept rubbing his hands with satisfaction. (He had the peculiar habit of tucking his whiskers inside his bib, and his paper hat was only prevented by his steel spectacles from slipping down his nose.)

"Good stuff this, my lad," he kept whispering. "The right kind of speech from you now and you'll pick up fifty dollars here tonight. Oh, great stuff! And all my doing, I may tell you."

"Speak?" said Frankie in dismay. "You didn't warn me of this. To hell with it!"

And in the middle of the speech he flung down his napkin and raced out. The foyer outside the dining-hall was crowded. In the booth he heard the tremulous voice of Bee.

"Darling, I'm glad you rang. I'm in fear and terror."

"St. John? Has he come? Is he there? Let me talk to him."

"He hasn't come. He's just been on the phone again and I know by his voice he's been drinking. Oh, it reminds me of the time . . . Frankie, can you get away? The servants are all out. I can't stay here alone."

"I'll be around at once."

Her shaking voice had released the flood of his feelings for her. He rang off, and dialled the presbytery. Outside in the foyer people were sitting waiting for their friends, reading, chatting; across the foyer as somebody came out through the double doors of the dining-room he could hear for a second the sudden distant burst of applause. The buzz-buzz at the other end went on.

In the next booth an Amazonian black-visaged Jewess, in a black toque with great feathers like a Roman helmet, was talking furiously to somebody; he heard her say, "This is the second time you let me down, you lousy double-crosser." He dialled again, heard the buzz-buzz, and then somebody lifted the receiver at the other end. It was Leonard.

"This is Frankie. What's happening with St. John? Hurry up." He suddenly saw his own reflection in the glass partition —the ridiculous paper cap and bib.

"Now, Frankie boy, I didn't like the way you talked to me a while ago. . . ."

"Hurry up. I want to know where he is."

"Look, this is an exceedingly difficult problem. He promised me faithfully he'd keep off the liquor. . . ."

"Where *is* he?"

"Well, that's the trouble. I don't know. He gave me the slip again a half-hour ago, and I can't imagine . . ."

Frankie hung up. The Jewess was making sulky faces. She was evidently being mollified with difficulty. Tearing off the hat and bib, he ran into the street, hailed a Checker taxi, yelled the address to the Negro driver, and told him to drive like hell. It was eight-forty. They took ten to twelve minutes to cross town and reach her apartment.

The elevator-operator said, yes, Mr. Hannafey had gone up, and agreed—with a grin—that he was "a bit off, all right." They sailed up gently in the golden lift and there, while the quizzical eyes of the elevatorman floated below floor-level, he held his finger on the buzzer of the apartment.

Nobody came to the door. He heard a crash inside, and grunts of exhaustion. He turned to the service door and buzzed there. He tried the handle: it opened. As he rushed through the hall, kitchen, pantry, servant's room, and connecting corridor, he heard another bang as if somebody had hammered hard on the wall. He dashed to the living-room door and flung it open.

There was St. John, his tie askew, his grey hair down on his forehead in one streak. He was methodically smashing everything in the place to bits. Already with that horrible shrewdness of the man who has lived for years with the same person, and seen far deeper into her heart than even he himself has ever realized, he had begun with her little collection of French poetry. In sheaves of tawny paper and yellow covers, the books lay in tatters on the carpet. Her pictures, mostly French, hung battered and torn on the walls. He saw a reproduction of Monet's *Notre-Dame* dripping its blue and yellow Paris *brume* down the wall. He was now standing up in the middle of the upturned Jacobean table, leaning his rump against one leg, and levering the opposite one out of its sockets. Grey foam outlined his mouth. He stared up, stupidly, at Frankie in the doorway.

"Where's Bee?" yelled Frankie.

St. John swayed.

"Dunno. You tell me. She ought to be here. I told her to be here."

The table-leg parted with a crack.

"I'm shmashing 't all up. It's my home, but it's all wrong. My life, but it's all wrong. Every bloody thing in this house is wrong. I'm wiping it out."

"These books aren't yours. The pictures. You bowsy! You dirty, drunken bowsy!" He looked at the torn books and his veins gorged with hate.

"All part of it! Wipe it out! Wipe it all out! Wipe her out!"

In sudden terror the young man turned and fled through all the rooms, one by one. There was not a sign of life in any of them. St. John, when he returned, was looking about him for the next thing to smash.

"Get out, Cursor. Go on. You're driving the woman mad. Just like my father and my mother. Get out!"

He took his arm. St. John threw him off.

"She's a bitch! She ruined me! The whore!"

"Get out or I'll throw you out!"

"You? Me?"

He saw a great blue Aztec jar, with delicate whorls of flowers, like marguerites gone faded, on its smooth side. He embraced it in his hands, raised it, hurled it into a corner, where it fell in dusty pieces of pottery. Visiting cards, old letters, fell out of it on the floor. He turned triumphantly and shook his mane.

One blow on the absurdly triumphant chin was enough. His sodden body fell on the floor. He lay shivering—lay there for a second; then he leaned up on his elbow. In his eyes there was pain, but not the pain of the blow.

"Frankie?" he chided. It was the squeak of a child, or it could have been the voice of an old woman: it was so weak, so heart-broken, so palpitating. "Frankie?" That was not much more than a frail insect-cry. "*You* hit me?" He gave out a tiny sigh—as if this were more than he could bear—and got on his knees, and from that to his feet, and then, whimpering, staggered across the room and put his arms about his brother. "I ain't got anything against *you*, Frankie boy."

Frankie took him in his arms. He had to or the old man would have fallen.

"Oh!" It was all he could sob. "You bowsy!"

St. John surveyed the wreck over his brother's shoulder.

"Look at it. My home. A life's work. Gone."

His coughing racked him, and easily Frankie laid him back in an armchair, where he lay, gasping. This time Leonard seemed to be waiting at the end of the wire.

"That you, Frankie? I've been ringing the police but they'll do nothing for me. Where on earth can he be? Where are you speaking from?"

"St. John's apartment. He's here."

"Oh, thank God. I've just asked a man I know on the detective division to go around there. I rang twice but got no answer. How long has he been there?"

"He's been smashing up the place in the best Munster Fusilier style. He couldn't hear you."

"Where's Mrs. Hannafey?"

"I don't know. I'm going out to look for her." The buzzer went. "One second. There's somebody at the door."

It was Father Leonard's friend, a hearty, big Irish policeman in plain clothes.

"Well, well," he said, with expansive cheeriness. "And what's all the throuble about now?"

"Take the telephone. Father Hannafey's on the phone. He'll tell you."

He waited only to hear, "Hello, Father, is that yerself?" and went out and down. He had no idea where he could expect to find Bee. He began to walk distractedly around and around the block, looking into the eyes of every lone woman who even slightly suggested the small, weeping figure he was so anxious to see. All these hours he realized and confessed to himself how tightly he was bound to her, how lost without her. He went up and down Fifth Avenue and Madison Avenue. He crossed to the park and went about the lake, looked at the people on the benches, down to the pond, back again along the avenues and the transverse streets near her home.

Never had the great crowded houses, the cold geometry of the streets, the lights of the towers seemed so impersonal. Even the rosy glow overhead, as of vast flowers opening their petals in the sky, seemed evil, almost carnivorous. The dull summer air, so heavily indifferent, cut to the heart's loneliness. He felt himself cold-shouldered by the shut faces of the apartments, the closed shops, the wealthy automobiles hissing past him. Nothing cheered him. The lights failed to illuminate. The houses did no more for those inside than shelter them. A railway waiting-room would have done as much. The whole edifice of the city weighted down the night, obliterative, dead, absorbent. All that Bee Hannafey had suffered that night in Paris he suffered in those hours.

At last he came on her. She was strolling along in her cowled cloak and her red heels, and, as he had foreseen, crying softly to herself. A lost child. She was indifferent to everything—the late hour, the stares of passers-by—and even as Frankie approached her a man and a woman paused, looked back, and went by with a joke between themselves. She did not feel his touch until he held her arm firmly and spoke her name. All he said to her was "My love," and embraced her, and she only said, "Darling," and gave him her lips, weakly; then clinging to his arm she let him lead her home.

The maid and housekeeper were before them, with the elevator operator, gazing at the wrecked room. By the smell he knew the man was smoking her cigarettes. The housekeeper was holding two fragments of a broken statuette, trying to piece it together. The three looked at Bee as a street-crowd looks at a woman who has been in an accident, wondering if she is very much in pain and whether she may die. She bade them go to bed—which they did unwillingly, anxious to help, especially the old cook, whose good-hearted fussiness was difficult to silence. When they were gone Bee sat in the debris of her life, and after a drink she revived a little. She gazed blankly at the torn books, the starred glass and tattered paper of the reproductions, the slashed canvas of her beloved pictures. With twitching eyebrows she picked up a leaf, torn in two, horizontally, and read, "*O mon Dieu, ne sera-t-il jamais possible . . .*" She let the page leaf fall to the floor, saying, "*Que je connaisse cette douce femme . . .*" She buried her face in her hands. Then she said, "Will you drive me to Connecticut, Frankie? I must get away from here."

He knelt by her. She smiled sadly and gave him the key of the car and garage, and told him where the garage was. When he drew up beside the apartment door she was standing in the corner of the bright hallway, holding a small travelling bag. The doorman, outside on the step, watched the flight with curiosity but without any sign of emotion.

He drove, taking the same route as when she drove him down that first night, gradually sending behind them the flesh-eating sky, entering at last the clean, cool dark. Presently the tang of salt blew across from the Sound. The night had the echoing hollowness of incipient autumn. All the way she clung to him. Once in a town, stopping by the lights, he looked down at her and her eyes were wide and dark, as if drugged, but when she looked at him they blazed. Even when they reached her house, all empty and dark, and were walking the few steps to the door she clung to him.

Before they fell asleep it was dawn, green over the tossing Atlantic. During the night she had said, once, "My love, you must never leave me," and he had said, "Never." Just before she sank into a sleep, sudden when it came as a stone dropping down through a pool, she had said:

"Frankie, we *are* married?"

And he had said:

"We are married."

She slept like a child.

PART THREE

Ireland

I

MICHAEL HANNAFEY left the pocket of the city and walked over the steep southern hill to the little Lough of Cork. There he sat on a bench in the dusk, and smoked his pipe, and watched the coots flitting in and out of the darkening reeds. Their squeaks had a piercing clarity over the water. The murmur of the city far below, the cries of children playing on the other side of the loch, did not so much interrupt the silence as measure it. Those faint sounds were like a clock in a sleeping house. In his pocket he had a small Balzac, a translation of *Mémoires de Deux Jeunes Mariées*. He did not take it out. Besides, he had read it too often before. He was content with his pipe; the quiet, akin to loneliness of his retired nook on the edge of the city; the tinned daylight. He felt hungry but did not stir. Later he would have a drink and a sandwich somewhere. He would walk to induce a good night's sleep.

He had spent the day in the middle of people; the sorters in the post office, the rolling wagons, the general untidy come-and-go—with its endless "Mick, have you seen . . ." and "Michael, would you attend to . . ." and "Hannafey, what about . . ."

After an hour or so of peace he became aware of a murmuring hullabaloo across the loch. At first it made him only the more aware of the quiet on his side of the water. Then, as his attention became directed on the distant cluster of people, he gathered that an accident had occurred, and presently he learned from a man passing his way that a child had fallen in and been drowned.

"A poor woman from the lanes is the mother," said the man. "And they say it's her only child. God help us!"

Deeply moved, he got up and walked away back down into

the city. To soothe himself he tried to make an elegy for the child. Weaving words, he passed through the streets, preoccupied, sidling. When he came, on the northern edge of the city, to the hill that streaks up out of it in a sudden red rubble, a gradient too steep for any car, he climbed painfully step by step. On the plateau at its peak he heard a piano playing in one house. Its window lit the barred railings before the tiny terrace. He leaned on the wall and looked far and wide over Cork. He was a gargoyle against the web of smoke.

Josephine Hogan came panting up the last steps over the edge of the summit. In the terrace a piano was playing softly. Down below the wall on which he leaned children ran and shouted under the gas-lamps. She laid her basket on the rubbled wall and greeted him. They made no surprise of the chance meeting, though she did explain, for the sake of conversation more than anything else, that she had missed the nine o'clock bus and must now wait for the eleven.

"What have you in the basket?" he asked.

"A pup."

She lifted the lid and took out the soft ball of furry brown hair.

"He's a thoroughbred. I got him from a man on the quays. I want to rear him."

"Isn't he lovely!" He fondled the morsel with pleasure. "And what time will you get home, now, Josephine?"—in his flaccid voice.

"Five past twelve. Fermoy will be like a graveyard."

She glanced at the low fleck of moon. When she landed in Fermoy it would be gone. There would be a fog over the river. She said to herself that when she next wrote to Frankie she would say that Michael had looked biblical—mourning over Jerusalem. Really, the poor man was a pity; and all he needed was a more active life, and a few nice friends. It was not easy to talk to him.

"I came to have a look at the view. Is it to see the view you came, Mr. Hannafey?"

He played the game back to her, bowing starchily. "It was to see the view I came, Miss Hogan."

"Isn't it interesting, Mr. Hannafey!"

Again the buckram obeisance, one finger to the first button of his vest, one finger pointing tentatively to the city, eyebrows raised for:

"Would you like me to show you the chief items of this noble *Blick?*"

"*Blick?*"

"*Das ist der deutsche für* 'view.' " She would not know whether his German were wrong or right.

He pointed out a few church-spires, and the glint of river where the country fields licked the town, and the rim of the highest hills to the south. It was old and lovely and gentle in that amber September dusk, little lights flickering everywhere. He dropped the game of guide when he mentioned the Lough, and told her how a child had been drowned there about an hour ago. The pup stumbled and toddled between them on the top of the wall. Now it was he who patted it; now she let it bite her finger.

"You're a great walker, Michael?"

"The way it is, Jo, I don't sleep too well. I often get up in the middle of the night and walk around the streets. I wouldn't meet a soul. Except a Civic Guard."

She recommended mild drugs such as luminol. He shook his head.

"I've tried everything. If I took them I'd jump awake at three in the morning as if the bed were on fire. The French call it the *coup de trois heures*. For a while, after I wake, I lie in a kind of manacle. Then I get up and walk about. To get cold I stand by the window. It often takes me fully five minutes to wake up properly, walking around the room. There's no noise at that hour, you see, and things don't seem real. Not even the light in the room! Or that I'm real myself! Did you ever feel like that? 'Tis a kind of awful paralysis."

She got frightened. The road was so empty. It was good to hear that piano and to see the lights on the railings. She rushed into a spate of talk, about this and that, mainly her life in Fermoy. They were looking north, and she was thinking of the way the bus would soon be swaying over those hills, yellow-lit and hot and musty, full of people whom it would gradually drop along the way.

"I got a letter from America, the other day," he said.

"From Frankie? Really?"

"From St. John."

A disappointed, "Oh? What did he want?"

"Yes," he admitted, taking her point—that nobody would want to write to him merely for friendship's sake. "It's funny the way he writes to me. I saw so little of him here. And he hadn't written for years before that. He's been having a tough time since he went back. First the business, then everything. He's separating from his wife."

She recalled the little American wife, her two visits to Quit Rent, the foolish business of the water-closet.

"What a pity!" she cried. "She was a nice little woman. Only a bit flighty. I am sorry for her."

"Of course," warned Michael, "it's St. John is asking for the separation. He says she never suited him. You know these American women. I mean that's what St. John says." He washed his hands of it hastily. "Of course I know nothing about it. I'm only saying what St. John says."

Her spate of talk had come to an end. Something rose at the back of her mind that she wanted to think about. She stuck down a little flag "to mark the place." From the half-ruined barracks around the corner, burned down in the Troubles, they heard a bugle-call. It was the Lights Out. He was talking about Balzac and ruffling the pages of his volume. He said it was a profound story and he made her so interested in it that she insisted on taking it with her. She said what she wanted now was travel-books. He mentioned a few–Loti, Stephen Graham, C. N. and A. M. Williamson, Hudson–and said he would lend her a few. The titles dated him. His reading, like that of all provincials, was bought not borrowed, and therefore only what lasted long enough to go into cheap editions–semi-classics. He read the kind of books that always leave his kind of reader years out of touch with their own times. Schoolgirls in such places probably still read *Infelice* and *The Garden of Allah*. By the time they discover later writers they too will have ceased to be modern. He took a note of her address in order to send her some books. They put the yapping puppy in the basket and went down the long flight of steps into the city.

It was half-past ten when he left her, reverting shyly to the guide-game, bowing low. She was grateful. She knew when the pubs close and knew that he had sacrificed himself to her. She went for a glass of hot milk and biscuits to a little dairy in Old George's Street–they had changed the name since the Troubles to Oliver Plunket Street, but her memory was tied to the "good old days before the revolution." The pup, released again from his basket, was given a saucer of milk on the floor and the customers and the shopwoman delighted in his tumbling antics, even when he wet the linoleum. She then got into the dim-lit bus, with her basket by her side, and while she sat there waiting for the start she read over again the loving letter Frankie had sent her in July. Since then he had not written again. July . . . September.

". . . I am lonely here. I hope you are lonely too. Are you, my dear dark head? . . . My dearest Jo, I never missed you so much. Now for the first time I know what it means to be in exile. . . . My sweetheart, I need you so badly. When are we going to meet again? Do you think you could ever come out for a spell? Even for two weeks? To see you would mean so much to me; to hold your hand and kiss it. I see your eyes with the funny brown shadows all around them, your jet-black hair with the white 'street' down the centre of it. Do you smoke as many cigarettes as ever? I met a girl in an Irish club here the other night. She was a nurse, too, and reminded me of you. It's a bad disorder, Jo. . . ."

A woman sat beside her and the bus started, so she put away the letter. The lights dimmed for a second and then went on full. She looked around her. Although the bus was so crowded that men were standing in the passage she recognized only two people. All but these two would be getting off at little villages along the way. Watergrasshill, Rathcormac, a cross-roads here and a branch-road there, from which they would walk home with their parcels through the dark, into the fields, hearing the murmuring trees, to somebody waiting for them by a dying fire.

Whatever else she did she would not go to America. It would only put her into a false position. Her pride revolted at what the people in Fermoy would say—that she was "chasing" him—and she grew angry at his obtuseness and at the same time her heart grew soft for him. His cry had been like this little barking cry that came now and again from the basket at her side. She tried to think in what letter she had said that he had put three thousand miles between them and grew hot lest he should think she was hinting at something. Then came the thought—July . . . September?

They were out of the city now, and driving beside the Lee across which a factory hammered, clangingly, its iron-bound windows shining down into the full tide. Suddenly rain fell heavily. The bus became a fog of tobacco-smoke, its windows speckled with rain outside, and covered inside with a film of steam. At Glanmire the woman beside her got out and she took up her letter again.

". . . To see you would mean so much to me; to hold your hand and kiss it. . . ."

Each time she came to that line the blood mounted to her face. It was so intimate—as if somebody had seen her through her window peeling off a stocking at night; or in the morning, washing in her straps with her hair pinned up. "To hold your hand . . ." Many and many a night they had sat by her fire, and she had placed her hand in his and felt his arm tight about her waist. Now and again they had kissed. She had a photograph in her bag. She took it out surreptitiously, as if the sight of it would make the idea of his kiss less troubling. How far away it took him to think that she had him there before her in the flesh, and yet that it was nothing but a pitiful scrap of paper! She had never been the kind of girl who kisses photographs; she would have squirmed at the idea; even if she had been she would not have kissed this picture in her hand. He was becoming remote.

Again her eye caught that bold sentence—"To hold your hand and kiss it . . ." This time a wave of anger saved her from the intemperance of her emotions. He had had many an hour to hold and kiss her, and he had only neglected her; talked at her; pushed her aside as he did the very last time he was with her: that was the night the Americans came to Cove.

She had cried all that night. After that he had not written for nearly two months. . . . Finally, and firmly, she shoved letter and photograph away and stared at the dribbling rain on the glass. The bus travelled on, climbing the hills. Her mind revolved on its keel, moving but keeping to the same spot. Why had he not written since July?

At blank spaces all along the road people got out. They must have recognized their stopping-places by intuition in that rainy dark. As the bus went farther and farther on it grew more empty. Gradually it took on that last-bus feeling of being out on its own. It would have seemed natural if the driver stopped suddenly and said he didn't think it worth while to go on for the sake of three people. Life was out of its routine. A few miles or so from Fermoy the two people she knew got up, and said "Good night, nurse," and went out. She was left alone with the driver and conductor.

The conductor came strolling along the passage to see if anybody had left anything behind.

"Bad night," he said, lightly, picking up a discarded evening paper.

"Isn't it?" she agreed, with a smile, hoping he would talk.

"Yerrah," he merely growled, "it's a rotten bloody climate."

He did not want to talk to her. He slid back the glass by the driver and stuck his head out and talked to him.

She stared at the rain. It swept pitilessly over the plateau. It would pour the whole night long, ceaselessly, hissingly, all over the great limestone tableland; it would fall on the towns and villages at its edges, dripping down through its demesne woods, into its rivers; swelling the Blackwater and the Funcheon, the Awbeg and the Araglen; arrowing down from the mountains to the north.

She dared what she had never before dared, to think where they would live if they married. A little house somewhere like Fermoy? If he could get a job there? She did not ask much, God knows; a few books, a few records of music, a run into Cork on a Saturday to a play, a few friends. Or would it be better if he got a job in Dublin? It would be hard, for everybody was looking for jobs these days, and he was trained for nothing. She tried to be wise, to remember that after New York he would find a small town lonely. She did not care where they lived so long as they had a home. Then she thought, "Would we have children?"

Her hand let its idle finger down into the basket and the puppy licked it softly with his wet-dry file of tongue. She shivered all over at its touch. She was a nurse, and no fool, and she knew her own nature. That tradition about people with her illness was not an old wives' tale. She couldn't help having children. Her whole nature would always be wanting bodily love. So her thoughts turned and turned, and she was held back from decision only by the fact that he had never asked her to marry him.

The bus was hissing down the asphalt street between the sleeping houses. It stopped in the square. Protecting her basket under her coat, she raced for her lodgings. She pulled the string, and let herself in, shaking the rain from her coat. Late as it was Jimmy had the gramophone still playing in the back-kitchen. She stole forward, opened the basket in order to let the puppy in through the slit of the door, and peeped in gaily to watch the surprise. The young clerk was standing beside his young wife. Her blouse was open. He was fondling her creamy breast and kissing her wildly on the lips. The sight ran a sword through the girl. Grasping the fat belly of the puppy, she drew the door to, stumbled back into the narrow hallway, back to the hall-door, and went out again. She leaned there, in the dark, with the rain beating hard on her face, and the tiny animal in her hands scrambling helplessly against her bosom, away from the storm. She heard the swirl of the river across the road. She heard the faint music inside —a Russian hymn.

At last she knocked loudly at the door, pulled the string, and went into the hall shouting, "See what *I've* got!" Then to give them a few moments, she doffed her coat, wiped her face, and ran in to them, laughing, holding out the brown wet lump of fur in her two hands. As they stooped over the puppy on the floor they did not need to hide their flushed faces.

"What'll we call him?" said Jimmy, tumbling the puppy on his back. Laughing and laughing she said:

"We'll call him Frankie!"

For a long time after they had said "Good night," she stayed up by the bars of the kitchen fire. They had left her so hastily—hardly bothering to conceal their eagerness to be gone—that she knew they were love-making upstairs. To distract her mind she took Michael Hannafey's faded green Balzac, with the chipped gold lettering on its spine, and forced herself to read. There were two stories. The first story was *Une Fille d'Eve.*

For a while she was held by the description of the two sisters, the two Maries, so innocent of nature, so repressed at home by their mother ("Her eyes seemed to read the very words on their lips"), so ingenuous, so inexperienced, two poor lambs for the slaughter, that they must either sink into imbecility or hope for the release of an early marriage; to whom made no difference, only that it must come quickly. "*The ball-dresses of the poor little things were models of decorum—high-necked muslin frocks with an extraordinary number of fluffy frills and long sleeves. . . . The girls were pitied, and hated it. . . . For where is the woman who would not rather excite envy than compassion?*" Jo read with sympathy as she sat with the puppy in her lap, asleep, the rain beating outside. When she came to the elderly man who married the highly strung Marie Angélique then as dewy as a spring morning, she sighed with relief that he was so kind and patient, leading her gently into the great world of fashion and guiding her through all its snares and plots as if she were his daughter rather than his wife. At that point (it may have been sentimentality or her own inexperience, a thing she would have hotly denied) she began, unconsciously, to see in the description of this elderly man the face and figure of the elderly man she had been talking to in Cork. Or perhaps it was because she had to visualize somebody in whom there was a great fund of kindness, that virtue secretly prized by all women above every other, since, though less satisfying than love, it lasts longer and serves a deep need. The book slipped from her hand. She kept lighting one cigarette from another. Only occasionally was she aware of the steady downpour, hearing it only when its gusts startled her into attention.

But to try to penetrate to the thoughts of such a girl at such a time is impossible. Her thought was her living self—her mortal body; so slim you might well think to catch her waist in a fistful; her eyes made darker by her thoughts, and by the brown that surrounds them like a dye, softened and made velvet by the rappel with her skin that is itself not marble-white but faintly brown; the sensuous lip, receding below ("the kind of lip from which a kiss would slip"); the long, almost but not quite bony hands and bitten nails; all speaking of a nature as intense as it is gentle, not well to rouse for her own sake or the sake of others. Her thoughts are her involuntary movements; her bosom that rises and falls in sudden sighs; the shiver that takes her twice as if she must at any moment jump and call for a horse; and when she sinks back each time, and her eyes cloud over, it is almost as if her impulse was so slight that the little sleeping dog can check it. All that is clear is her unrest; and for the meaning and origin of that one would have to search her whole life. She reminds one of a boat tugging at a chain when the wind is calling all the other boats to sea.

II

After much rain, and a cutting, drying wind to follow, a deep September warmth began to float over Ireland; ideal harvest weather. Josephine first noted this change on the fifteenth of the month as she was coming back from Benediction in the convent chapel. It was the evening of the Feast of the Seven Dolours, the end of a novena she had begun for her own private intention. That night, her window, sealed by the rains, had to be flung wide. The river, high and placid, held the serene sky among its grasses; the weir was muted by its own fullness; there were stars shivering under the far bank. As she raised her eyes from these wavering lights to the far lights crowning the opposite side of the town they did not dance there like frost but wavered as on a summer night. For days Ireland steamed in bonus days of almost too hot sun.

Made restless by this moody weather, which had the drawback of early night (sundown was around seven) too warm for indoors and too dark for anything but walking—and even for that the phenomenal air was too lazy and idle—she found herself wishing for the variety of some other sort of life. (Her novena, she said to herself, was evidently not going to bring her the peace she had hoped for.)

Over her breakfast one such morning she scanned the paper for advertisements that might offer her an escape:

> Wanted experienced nursemaid for eight children, two school-going, baby seven months.

> Must be clean, healthy, and honest. Good home and wages to suitable applicant. Apply with references to Mrs. Henry McCarthy, the Green, Youghal.

> Wanted an experienced young lady to take charge of hair-dressing saloon . . .

> Wanted for country-town hotel, strong cook; general wages, £30 . . .

Over her teacup she regarded Mrs. Jimmy bathing her baby by the kitchen-fire.

"Did you ever feel you wanted to get out of this place, Mrs. Jimmy?" she asked suddenly.

Mrs. Jimmy upended the baby and seized the talc.

"Out of Fermoy?"–considering and powdering while the baby chortled. "Of course I did. Often! Before I was married. I was terrible restless. But I'd be lonely now, if I went away. Sure I know everybody here." She held the pink baby up in the air, and the wide sun of his face made her face burn like a moon. "No! We're here for life now. Aren't we? Hoops-a-babby! Aren't we?"

As Jo lit her first cigarette of the day her eyes wandering back to the paper saw that same sense of contentment consolidate itself in the routine life of the country. The game-preservation notices; somebody selling a cabin-boat with engine; farmers offering sows and bonhams, one a litter of thirteen; other farms selling bawn hay; their wives offering day-old chicks, or tomato plants; a Mr. Martin of the South Mall, in Cork city, would remove superfluous hair painlessly by the latest methods: "100 permanently removed for 5*s*." There was only one note of restless desire:

> Lonely young farmer, counted good-looker, nice manners, with substantial fortune, would

> like to meet young lady with business or land with a view to matrimony. Apply 259 this office.

Otherwise the soft, grey sheet of paper, hot in the sun hot at her back, was a blanket of warm, cosy life. Even the war news from China was balanced by news, equally important, of a big society wedding in Dublin. It all repeated this contentment of a baby being dressed; of the sun warming his boy-blue garments, shimmering on the soapy bath-water, edging the white arm of the mother. She gave a little groan.

"Wisha," cried Mrs. Jimmy all of a sudden, "sure, 'tis all out of an eggshell! Wherever you are, you want to be somewhere else!"

Jo regarded her bitterly and went about her work. All day she did it without zest, and then, following a sudden impulse in the afternoon, she drove in the bus to Cork. She went to the post office with two travel books Michael had sent her and asked for him at the counter. The man she spoke to said he would get him in a jiffy, and she noted with amusement how he winked at his colleagues when he left: they would joke poor Michael pitilessly for this visit when she was gone. (Later he told her that they had said, "Mickey, there's an old lady outside asking for you"—their innocent idea of a joke.) Seeing her he immediately grew uncomfortable, and tried with his palm to hide his blushing face from his fellows. She was both amused and annoyed. He ought to have had this sort of thing knocked out of him long ago.

"I was in town, Michael," she explained, "and thought I might as well hand in the books. I suppose I'm doing the post office out of a job by not posting them!"

After she had said that, a panic rushed over her. She thought that he would say, "Thanks," and she would have to go, and there would be the empty hours before her with nothing to do that she could not have done as well in her home town. For in small cities like Cork there is nothing for the stranger. Its sights are soon exhausted, its hospitality meagre, nothing left but its cold commercial purpose whose closure for the night closes everything indigenous in city life. Her panic made her face go red, and this in turn embarrassed Michael all the more. Aware of the joker down the counter who was murmuring something facetious to a friend her blush deepened with anger. She threw back her head, spiritedly and haughtily, not wholly unaware how fine she looked when she did that and plunged ahead:

"Michael, I'm not doing anything else until the bus goes . . ."

She stopped. He would be shocked. He would become afraid of her. She scurried about for some cover for what she had said. Lying manfully, she cried:

"I mean I thought of buying a few French books. I want to learn French. Could you tell me of a good one?"

He was immediately relieved of his embarrassment. "To be sure!" He looked at the clock. "I'm not really through until six but I could slip away at a quarter to. I hope you don't mind waiting until then?"

"No, I have some shopping to do," she fibbed.

"Are you sure, now? I might manage it if you . . ."

She was delighted with his courtly manners. He was just as courtly as that count in the Balzac story, and, as she had guessed, just as kind, and—using a characteristic Cork word of approval—he was "such a *quiet* man."

"In the meanwhile," he considered, "have a look around. I used to know a little book by Henri Bué. But that's idioms, and you want to begin, don't you? There's Hachette. Heath is the standard school-text. I think I have one at home. What you really want is a book with lessons and text combined."

He took a telegraph-form and wrote a few titles and explained to her what to look for.

"You're very kind, Michael."

"Yerrah, not at all, Jo. I'm only too glad to help you."

He leaned over the counter to talk about the books she was returning. He was now entirely at his ease. Indeed, when a man wished to pass in through the little drawbridge of the counter, and begged Jo's pardon, and looked admiringly at her, and then inquiringly at Hannafey, Michael nodded an easy hello with an almost smug pride in her good looks. That was not all. When she was leaving she dropped her glove at the door, and in stooping for it caught the jocose clerk winking archly at Michael, and there was Michael winking back at him. She went off chuckling.

They met at a quarter to six. Now he was not at all embarrassed: he was just as courtly. They kept the bookshop open after its due hour, examining texts, and he bought himself a two-shilling Chateaubriand (*Mémoires d'Outre-Tombe*). It was easy for her, then, to inveigle him into asking her to tea. She would have preferred him to take her to the new big cinema restaurant, all bright and mirrored and variegated. Instead he led her to a restaurant over a now-closed chandler's shop, a small place that catered for lunch more than teas and was now empty and silent. On the stairs were brass tips which gave back every footstep. In the room were blue rep curtains, the original Victorian mantelpiece (Cork's good days were in the nineteenth century), commercial cards on the walls, panels with distempered desert scenes. But he talked here as he might not in a crowded place—these compressed souls have a neurosis about the susceptibilities of others—and when this thought occurred to her it gave her a pang like the pang a mother feels when a child tugs inside her. For it was just what Frankie might have done. With him you thought you had a big, tough, hardy fellow, protected by a shell like a tortoise: suddenly you found a shyness in him like a kid and you wanted to hug him tight as a barrel-hoop.

Under her eyes she beheld a different Michael. He was like one of those trick paper flowers that unfold magically when a chemical is dropped on the knotted bud. She could not have described how it happened. It was a concert of the slightest notes; a solicitous gesture with the cakes, a self-consciously self-satisfied gesture, or perhaps it was merely the unusual joy of having somebody to be solicitous about. It was all summed up in the elaborately reticent way he folded away the bill; something too crude for her eyes to see.

He talked chiefly of the one thing: he had been in Paris that summer for one week. As he talked, his lined face—he had two sharp crevasses down each cheek, so that when he shaved he must have had to pull the skin apart to get at the hollows—and his distant eyes, became so mobile with emotion that the crevasses smiled all the time, and the eyes kept softening and dimming; his pleasure in his holiday surviving its own elegy.

Once she came sharply against the thorn of another Hanafey characteristic when she said, just a shade too eagerly:

"I'm *glad* you enjoyed it so much, Michael!"

She could have smacked him when he drew in his horns, resentfully, and said in the most lofty voice:

"Oh, I naturally enjoyed it. Why wouldn't I?"

Well trained by Frankie, she retrieved her position of obedient listener by saying without interest, brushing a crumb aside:

"I suppose there was nothing in particular you liked best of all?"

No! Nothing was better than anything else! Unless walking the quays by the bookstalls? Or sitting in the gardens? Feeling a grand, cultured civilization all about you? Once he had seen a workman in a bus reading Maupassant. Really, in a way, that was the high point of the whole thing! To see a common workman reading Maupassant! And then, of course, the cafés, on the open pavement, with people drinking and talking for hours. And there he looked out miserably into Cork at the line of closed shops, inhospitable as a wall.

"Are you never down our way?" she asked, to restore his good humour.

"As a matter of fact I ought to be," he smiled. He began to search among a wad of papers he drew from his pocket. "I told you St. John was writing to me? Two months ago I got a draft for two hundred dollars from him to go down to your place and see about getting running water laid in to your aunt's house. But . . . I never did anything about it. And she's dead now! Only yesterday I got a reminder from him."

He smoothed a wrinkled page. Taking it idly, she told him she knew all about it, and in recounting the days when Bee Hannafey wanted to put a W.C. into the old farmhouse they forgot the letter in their amusement.

"Do come down!" She pressed him. "Manus will give you a bed for the night. Come this week-end."

"I ought to, you know. Especially with the winter coming on. Of course," he grumbled, "I hate going into the country. I am the real metropolitan, I'm afraid," he simpered.

"Well," she offered, hesitant, "you could stay in Fermoy? There's a good hotel. Manus has an old crock of a car now. And anyway the plumber would drive you out. Michael, why don't you?"

He seized on the offer and she drew him back to Paris. He promised to lend her Lucas's *A Wanderer in Paris*. As he did; all thumb-marked and blue-pencilled over and over. Leaving him in a scurry to catch the nine o'clock bus, she ventured to say jocosely:

"When you go again I suppose it'll be . . ."

"It'll be years," he said.

"You can go on the honeymoon," she teased. "I bet there's somebody in the background."

He raised his palm in shocked denial, but he was delighted. When he walked away she thought he was a straight figure of a man. She liked the free way he swung his arm. Her thought again was, "He's very quiet!"

It was only the following morning that she read St. John's letter. She read it idly over her breakfast cigarette—until she came to:

". . . I was terribly sorry to hear the old lady had died. I gave Father Leonard—he's a grand chap, oh, a fine fellow, I don't know why I missed him all these years—ten dollars for masses, and I was at the mass myself and I prayed for you all. God help me, I didn't go to the altar. How can I? I'm cut off from God. It's cruel. But it's all my own fault. I'm paying for my sins. You know the truth now, old Mickey, that I married out of the Church, and I don't know what to do about it. Bee was never any good to me. She was no wife for an Irishman. She broke my heart. God knows I wasn't much good to her, either. I've made a mess of my life and hers too. But she's never gave me a fair deal. Oh, God, what is going to happen to me? I'm half mad thinking and thinking about it. My business is gone to hell. I haven't done a stroke of work for weeks and weeks, only thinking, thinking all the time. Oh, Mickey, you're happy. Stay happy. She's fooling about now with Frankie. Imagine it. My own step-brother. I hate his guts. Did you know he knocked me down? In my own house. I was drunk. I admit it. But it was my own house and he knocked me down. He's fooling about with her all the time. I have a detective watching them. I have enough evidence to get her any time. I don't want to harm anybody. I'm half loony over it all."

Her eyes read on but her heart was thumping and she hardly absorbed the words:

"Do get the running water laid in. How is my mother and everybody? I am going to go over in the fall and see you all again. They were the happiest, happiest days of my life, there in Cork, and in Kilfinnane. I should have done it long ago. Get a white, good big white sink with chromeam taps and make it swell, it's nothing at all I wish I could do anything for them there the grandest people on God's earth. Did I send enough money? Write to me and tell me how you all are. Now don't write a short letter, but give me all the news, what you are doing and what all are doing. I'm going over sure and certain in the fall. . . ."

Her eyes saw no more. She was staring before her. She suddenly heard Mrs. Jimmy saying:

"Bad news?"

She said, casually:

"Ah, no! No." Then she saw the look in Mrs. Jimmy's face and realized that it must be a reflection of the look in her own. " 'Tis somebody not connected with me at all," she said hastily. "Somebody I used to know."

She got up and folded away the letter, and said she was going for a walk, at which Mrs. Jimmy looked her astonishment, for she knew that a dozen people would be expecting "the nurse" after nine o'clock. Josephine visited nobody that morning. She walked out of town into the country, aimlessly, like a mad woman. She came nearer and nearer to a flag that she had stuck in her memory, and it was a fort she knew she should have assaulted long ago. At last she stood in full view of it: the American woman . . . this lie (if it was) about Frankie . . . and yet he had not written since July. These were its three sides and it had no door. It had nothing but the hostility of pointing guns.

Suddenly everything exploded. Her mind became a roaring crater of hate. She saw as clearly as in a cinematograph, in towering close-up, Frankie holding Bee Hannafey in his arms. She saw his mouth that he had wanted to press to her hand clung to the painted gums of a silly, wriggling, scented, ogling little American bitch, with her kiddy mannerisms and her stupid prattle! Christ! The thing was old enough to be his mother. She had grey hair. Her legs were gone hard. She was dried and withered. The disgust of that picture bled her white. It outraged her nature, her pride, her love. It fouled her dreams. Not until a cart came into view around the corner of the road did she come back to herself. She found herself muttering aloud the most horrible words. Terrified, she ran to a gap in the hedge and fell sobbing on the wet grass.

She lay there, soaking in the dew and the hoar-frost that still swamped the ground under the overhanging thorns, until despair stirred the last residue of endurance. She started up then, and from the rising ground—the road climbs there along the Kilworths—she looked over the mapped plain of the Blackwater, over its million fields, its haze of exhaling moisture. It was all so rich and soft and friendly, a rock of the familiar, that she cried, "It's not true!" as if this friendliness must make that hostility impossible. Then, in her hard sanity, she said, "It is true," and turned the knife against him, and fleshed it, and tore at herself, and hated them both again not only because they had robbed her but because they were reducing her to the state of an animal woman. Flinging herself back on the sodden grass again, just like an animal, she exhausted herself in an excess of that very anger she hated, and would have despised in another woman.

She found herself out on the road, again, walking on and on, now, in wild hope, refusing the picture, now, in her wisdom, accepting it. But, slowly she began to see how it could have happened, and became touched with pity for all of them—even though she was sure that there was something unfair about the way it had happened—unfair to her and unfair to poor Frankie. She began to see then how easily it might have happened to anybody; even she herself might have . . . but she could not think that was possible. And then she thought, again, that perhaps it was all exaggerated; and really not true at all in the way she saw it—until again, seeing the American woman, so bright and smart in all her ways, so flattering, so irresponsible, practised, rather pretty, probably stopping at nothing, she would admit that her hopes were a foolishness and acknowledge the fact. So all the time she went around and around that hostile fort, without rest, all the time walking on and on, until she was exhausted and hungry.

In the afternoon she found herself on the far side of Mitchelstown, on the foothills of the Galtees, with another and even more vast plain stretching to the east below her in a sea of land, until, perhaps twenty miles away, across thousands of intersecting black hedgerows, diminishing in size, it swept up to a low line of hills. The sun had dispelled the morning's exhalation. The cornfields shone white. Near at hand she could hear a threshing-engine chugging busily. She bought a bottle of stout in a roadside pub and ate bread and butter with it, sitting under the low window, looking at hens pecking in a haggard.

She was no longer the victim of mere anger and disgust.

She had set against them the fund of the purity of her love for Frankie. She even said, in her heart, now and again, "Poor Frankie!" Leaving the pub she turned towards the distant blur of Fermoy. The sun on its downward course behind it held the greyness of its hearth-smoke.

She did not enter the town until the night was far on and everybody asleep. She had spent hours along the way, looking over the plain, halting every couple of miles to rest and think, taking in from the land as it took in from the sun the soothing milk of nature's endlessness and persistence. In making her, so tiny a morsel of that morsel of the whole, aware of her own smallness, that ocean of land helped to diminish the force of her pain. The very exhaustion of her body reduced the impact of it by reducing her resistance. When at last she straggled into the dark and sleeping town she was at once beaten and victorious; for she was calm and yet she was afraid of what might come with sleeplessness. She stole to her room and drugged herself to sleep. Even then, though wearied in body and mind, she fought the drug to keep awake, and when she did sleep she kept moaning like somebody who is being cut open under an anæsthetic.

III

When Michael came down that Saturday morning his first question was about the letter. She said she had not taken it from him in the restaurant, and that he must have put it back into his pocket with the rest of his papers. He said he had gone back to the restaurant, but they had not found it.

"You're sure you didn't take it?" he questioned her. "You might have put it into your bag without noticing."

Carefully and ostentatiously she opened her bag in the station-yard and went through it before his eyes.

"No! Are you *sure* you haven't got it, Michael? Was it very important?"

"No. It was about the sink. It was a private letter between St. John and myself. All talk about his marriage. I didn't mean to bring it out at all. It was the old letter I wanted to show you—the one with the draft I got months ago."

"Maybe you didn't have it at all that night?"

He shook his head weakly.

"Maybe I didn't. Oh, it doesn't matter! Only it was a wandering kind of letter full of nonsense. . . . Have you any news about him at all? From Frankie?"

"I didn't hear from Frankie since July. Except for a short note about politics."

"Aren't you and Frankie . . ." He paused in his step.

"What?"—surprised.

"I mean . . . I thought ye were great friends. To tell you the truth, I thought ye were . . . well . . . more or less engaged."

She laughed.

"Frankie and me? We're great *friends*, but that's all. I think in all I got three letters from him since he went away. What on earth," she cried, astonished, "made you think we were anything else?"

"Och, I just had the notion." He halted her, full of concern, in the hilly street. "I'm sorry if you think I'm probing, or being inquisitive. Please don't think that."

She raised her eyebrows, shrugged it away ever so casually.

"Not at all, Michael. For God's sake, why *should* I mind? Sure, people are always saying things like that."

He walked on beside her, relieved. She explained to him about Manus and the car, which was late in arriving, and how it would come to the digs, and would he have dinner with her there after seeing the plumber? Pleased, he said yes, and they went on down into the square, at this hour full of people in for the market. There were creel-carts, with the upper parts in mat orange and the wheels a bright chalky blue; motors of every age, filling up with parcels; there were farming folk, and Big House people, the farmers' wives wearing every kind of fashionable hat and the others without any hats at all. The main Dublin–Cork road runs through Fermoy, so that passing traffic made a constant hooting through the sluggish motion of the square. High over it all at one end, above the town clock and the houses shouldering one another up the hill, was the quiet face of the convent; and looking back, the way they had come down the wide street, beyond the bridge, they could see the sky through the empty windows of the burned barracks. The Blackwater tinkled over its weir. It shone moodily above and below it between the fading foliage of the trees on its banks.

Michael said little. He was preoccupied, watching everything. And when he stood still, halted unconsciously by his interest, she stood patiently beside him, taking pleasure from his pleasure. When he said suddenly, "Isn't it grand!" she nodded; her world at its best; so loved, so hated, where she would now live for ever.

They wandered around, and she acted as guide, telling him anything she knew of the history of the town and its people: how a Scotsman named Anderson had made the town out of nothing at all in the eighteenth century, built a few houses and a hotel, manœuvred to get the military barracks, built them, introduced mail-cars before even Bianconi, made his fortune; how the Abercrombies got it after him; later on the kind of life there was in the town when she first came there to the convent school; with the red-coats dotting the streets, and then, during the war, khaki soldiers filling the pubs every Friday night with noise and singing as their officers filled the two hotels. Then there were bands playing, troops marching off to the station for the war in Europe. Then came the Black and Tans and the Auxiliaries tearing about in their Lancias, the nights full of noise and terror, the final marching away of the English, the coming of the Republicans, the burning of the barracks, the decay of the town on the departure of its best customers.

"The place was dreadful-looking for years. Down at heel. The shopkeepers weren't even painting the shops! But, thank God, 'tis picking up now again."

As they leaned over the river-wall on Artillery Quay she seemed to sigh a little for those old days, and as she gossiped on about the town it appeared that she saw it as an image of the ambiguous, confused, far from romantic repossession of Ireland by herself that the old Messhouse Lanes, and Barrack Streets, and King Streets and Prince Albert Streets had become changed to Gaelic names that meant nothing to anybody; or that the great man of the town, a local solicitor named Carroll, a hard, bitter, self-made man who began life as a barefooted urchin, had in the heel of it all taken his cheque book one day and "bought the whole damned place lock, stock, and barrel," for he had promptly sued half the tenants of Fermoy for gale-day arrears which the Abercrombies had forgotten about or been too easy-going to collect. The fallen leaves on the water beneath their eyes, curled inward by the tide, held by the slack water under the wall, delicately tinted by the oncoming autumn, had something of the slight melancholy of her voice and mood, and induced in both of them a regret that the mutations of life so rarely equal the memories they replace—until in time they themselves become softened and sweetened to a recollection.

"Let's see your plumber," she said, suddenly, and led him away.

The plumber was an old man with hair of that yellowish-white that suggests the remnants of a henna dye. He was between merry and melancholy, like a man who has had a good time in life but knows just how much it cost. He had a tired, patient expression that was articulated in his heavy greeting:

"Well, sir and lady, and what is on your minds now? Some little trouble, I hope, that Cassidy can cure?"

He constantly referred to himself in the third person, as Cassidy. "Cassidy will do the job. For a small fee Cassidy may be trusted to do any job. *Leave* it to Cassidy!" And so on.

"Running water in a farmhouse up in Quit Rent? Glory be to God, isn't that in the mountains?" he cried, when Michael explained, gently and precisely, what they wanted. "Sure the whole damn place is nothin' but running water! In the name of God what's coming over the country? 'Tis baths they'll be wanting next."

"We were thinking," said Jo, impishly, "of installing a flush-lavatory there."

He looked at her shrewdly, a joker who was not going to be taken in by another joker. She gurgled inwardly at what she could see in that look: a whole medley of improper jokes racing across his mind, and he dared not utter one of them.

"Madam," he said, at last, "the Ballyhouras *are* a flush-lavatory! What is it you wanted exactly, sir?" he asked Michael, annoyed at having his leg pulled and not being able to retort. His dignity was so stiff that it crackled.

Michael explained once again, just as precisely:

"A sink, which must be white and have chromium taps, two taps, with running water, fixed in the kitchen of Miss Mary Jane Hogan of Quit Rent."

"Why two taps? Is there a boiler in the kitchen?"

"I don't know," said Michael, and looked questioningly at Jo.

"No!" She shook her head. "It's just an open fireplace, like any farmhouse kitchen."

"Then," said Cassidy, "we only want one tap."

"No," insisted Michael. "There must be two taps."

The old plumber looked shrewdly at the pair. Then he philosophically hunched his shoulders and said:

"Two taps. Very well! Do you want water to come out of the two of them?"

"Not necessarily," said Michael. "Water need only come from one of them. How much will that cost?"

"We'll have to see the place," said Cassidy. "We can't say without seeing the place, can we?"–hands appealingly stretched to Michael, patience with the folly of all humanity in his eyes, almost boredom. "How much may Cassidy expect you to pay him for all this?"

"Not more than forty pounds," said Michael firmly.

Cassidy gave a groan. He turned and looked sadly at his stock–the sinks, the lavatory bowls, the lead coils of piping. He stroked his chin and ran his palm over his yellowy-white hair and down across his face, looked again at Michael, and let out a vast belly-sigh.

"Ah!" he grumbled. "Human nature! Human nature! Sir," he almost shouted, "Cassidy could install a bath fit for a Roman emperor for forty pounds! A sink? A common kitchen sink. . . ."

"With chromium taps!" warned Michael innocently.

"With silver taps!" groaned Cassidy. "Sir, for forty pounds Cassidy could install such a sink . . ."

His eyes became gooseberries as he contemplated his masterpiece. Suddenly he rushed to a little cubbyhole which he probably called his office and produced catalogues. From his face they could see that Paradise had opened before him.

"For years," he cried, "I've wanted to do a job like this! All my life . . ." He became suspicious for a second. "This isn't a joke?" he demanded, but Jo explained hastily where the money had come from. He was satisfied immediately he heard the word "American." He showed them an aluminum sink, the latest model, used only in big hotels and hospitals, the sort from the bottom of which crockery bounces rather than breaks, defying rust, light as air, nothing to chip, easy to clean, with drain-boards to match, flexible taps with rose attachment. "Sir! Madam! People will go on pilgrimages to this sink! When can we go and see if there's any spring-water within a hundred miles of this bloody backofbeyond?"

"At one o'clock," said Jo. "My brother has a car. We'll call for you. You won't fail us?"

"Madam, if every lavatory in Fermoy should burst, Cassidy will not fail you!"

And he showed them out like a prince and princess, all but fawning before them as they went. This odd old character, the bright day, the crowded streets, the prospect of a drive into the hills, the holiday feeling, all contributed to draw the two into a happy mood that was renewed as they sat waiting for dinner in the front parlour of Jo's lodgings, among Mrs. Jimmy's little household gods—so modest, so few, so new, so poor—with the market noises outside and the autumn giving richness to the very air. In the tiny room he felt himself enclosed in a segment of the most intimate life of the county, while she, once again reinformed by his awareness, began to look with affection on what had so recently seemed without colour or attraction, so wearisome, so dead, so stale as not to be borne.

So they sat opposite one another, creaking at one another

in the two frail basket-chairs—the "Jimmys" had not yet been able to afford the Chesterfield suite which every such household covets. They were content in this cosy coop of a room so long as the sun was caught in the lace curtains and the sounds of the market-day still echoed in the square to tell them that the day was young. She got him to talk to her again about his visit to Paris, and she got down one of his travel books and opened the maps of the city, and he traced with his bony finger the great streets, boulevards, monuments, buildings, museums, quays. . . . He became almost painfully emotional as he talked. His ravaged face so lit up that she put her palm flat on the map and said, impulsively:

"Michael, why don't you go there *every* year?"

He had his fountain-pen in his hand—he had just been tracing the outer circle of boulevards on the Left Bank; with it he began to scratch little lines on the margin, at first defensively, then querulously, then viciously. In dismay she saw his face knotting tighter and tighter. At last he burst out with:

"Christ! How *can* I?"

"Michael!" she murmured, and he subsided, and he returned to the map.

"Why don't *you* go abroad?" he asked her after a while.

"I don't know. Other things always came in. There were the Troubles. I wasn't well for years. My brothers. I couldn't leave Manus. I had no money."

His eyebrows flickered at her as much as to say, "Then why ask *me?*" At last, still drawing his niggling scratches on the paper, he said, "I support the whole of my family. Or most of it. For all the years while Frankie was . . ." He stopped. He washed out the phrase with a weak wave of his hand. His head sank in his fist. Weakly he turned the pages of maps.

"Well, I'm glad you went there!" she said brightly.

"Yes," he said glumly. He gave her a long, poised look. He was about to burst out with something when she quickly pointed to a black outline on the map.

"What's that building?" she asked.

"That?" he said, while his eyes wandered all over the intricacies of the surrounding streets. "Oh! That's the Louvre." He turned back the page to the Champ de Mars, the Trocadéro, Passy, Auteuil. He turned back further until he was in the Bois and Longchamps, and by the Seine running northwards beyond St.-Cloud. Then, giving her another long and poised look, he patiently restrained himself from saying what he had been prevented from saying a moment before, closed the maps, cried "Yes!" and, leaning back with averted eyes, began to fill a pipe. As he fiddled with the tobacco in the pouch or packed the bowl with shaking fingers, she sensed that he still wanted to say that something to her. He lit a match, twirled the flame over the bowl, but still he did not put the stem near his mouth. He looked up again, impulsively. She said hastily, for she suddenly felt that whatever it was he wanted to say it would be better if he never did say it:

"Did it cost much?" She encouraged him with a smile as he opened his lips to speak.

He subsided once more.

"Oh, about twenty pounds."

"I suppose you went by Dover?"

"The cheapest way," he said, vaguely and impersonally, as if it were really about somebody else they were talking, or as if they were talking about some trip he would make some future day, "is Newhaven–Dieppe."

"And what's the journey like, then?"

The edge had gone from his voice. He had made her believe every word he said about Paris. Now he was as lifeless as a time-table.

"Well . . . you go through Rouen of course."

"There's a cathedral there. Did you get off?"

"No!" He almost snapped at her.

"Did you cross by night? That must be exciting!"

His voice complained a little:

"Well, you can cross by night, of course. If you want to."

"Did you?"

He looked at her all but in resentment. She could not understand this sudden reluctance to talk about his holiday. Her presentiment as to what he was bottling up inside him made her wish Mrs. Jimmy would come in with the dinner.

"I . . . you can . . . I prefer the day crossing. I . . . I left Dieppe about four in the afternoon. . . . I got to Paris about seven. The lights were springing up." He glared at her, suddenly, his eyes dilated with the longed-for image. He cried, almost shouted it:

"Josephine! This is all. . . ."

The door opened and Mrs. Jimmy came in with the tray. The two smiled at her. Jo, who suddenly understood the horrible confession he wanted to make, saw to it that from that until the end of the day they were never alone. She brought Mrs. Jimmy with them in the car to Quit Rent: it turned out to be a merry journey, they were so packed, the five of them —Manus and the old plumber and Michael and the two women —in the tiny car, and they all talked so much and Cassidy was full of such light-hearted nonsense. Even when they were at the station at the end of the day she brought Manus with her on the platform. As it happened there was no need. Michael was in high good humour. She saw that his day had been a varied adventure, and by the grace of God he had not spoiled it. His last word was that he would come back in two weeks when Cassidy had his marvellous aluminum sink (with *chromeam* taps—a joke about St. John's spelling) installed in the farmhouse. "We'll have a formal opening!" he called as thc train drew out. "Of the sluices!" she yelled after him. He waved his bowler hat. She sighed with pleasure in his happiness.

He felt that the city, at Blackpool, was welcoming. In the dim September evening light and with the wind-dropped smoke shrouding the old crapulous roofs, it looked benevolent and kind. All its natural voracity—that cold power that is in every provincial city to nip and gnaw, to mine and scuttle—was asleep. The long wide Mall was lovely, its ruby buildings full of the dignity of their age, its fading trees in quiet accord. The island was floating in a full tide that hulked a steamer high against the irregular slum-roofs to the west and far down by the grain-docks lifted a great five-master until its spars prodded the dusk creeping over the harbour. As he sat to his supper in the kitchen, with Eolie now attending to him, now smoking by the fire as she read the evening paper, he contemplated his day in the country.

At every turn the dark virginal face of Josephine smiled at him. He was relieved that he did not confess about Paris, for he had felt her interest in him, and he was warmed by it, and he wanted to retain it until their next meeting. Not that he allowed himself any illusions—it was his secret boast that he was a man without illusions. He knew that he and she would never be nearer than they were today. But when he thought of his squalid life, with a shudder of despair and a sigh of self-pity for his diseased body and the brutality of his desires, she shone for him like a star on the forehead of a Madonna.

He was gentle with Eolie that night. They walked out together, and he told her all about the kitchen sink, and they discussed their own affairs, the household troubles and their sick mother, money matters, Natalie, Claude's future, in a way they had not done for several years. Even Eolie could not help saying, "You ought to go into the country more often." He said he intended to. And when he awoke the next morning after a refreshing sleep, with Cork wrapped in its Sunday morning calm and before him a quiet day that—unusual experience for Sunday mornings—he found he was in a state of mind and body to enjoy, he repeated that vow to himself, marking on his diary under the tenth of October: "See Josephine at Fermoy."

For all his studious realism, however, he found himself, as the week wore on, thinking of her more and more in terms of intimate affection—in shy dreams made up of admiration for her sweetness and purity, and her quietly unostentatious vitality, mingled with fantasies that revealed in her a secret admiration of his knowledge of the world and of books—a travelled and well-bred man who could not, indeed, offer her youth or comfort but who had what youth or wealth could never buy. From these fantasies he would wake up in the middle of the hurry and scurry of the post office; or find himself cold from too long sitting by the Lough; or at home by a dying fire over an unread book.

Then, as if on an impulse, one afternoon he suddenly begged leave from his superior to pay a call in the city. It cannot have been wholly an impulse, or else it was one that came at the end of many previous efforts to thrust his will in that direction, for when he came to the doctors' quarter, on Patrick's Hill, without hesitation he climbed to a particular door and rang.

Nothing in that quiet corner of the city, no passer-by, no stir in the curtained windows, no whisper of some recording angel's wing, marked that little adventure of will and desire; only a door that opened and closed, and that opened and closed again, on a humiliated heart. Unnoticed, he sidled through the streets back to the post office. There only one or two of his colleagues may have noted, in that cipher among their fellow-workers, the drawn and haggard face, and, without the faintest notion as to the reason, guessed from his trembling hand the palpitation inside. That night he drank heavily. He drank for several nights after. Eolie used to hear him come in at two in the morning.

IV

When he got out of the train in Fermoy, exactly nine days later, Josephine was aghast at his appearance. For a while she said nothing: then, as they walked downhill to the market-square she took his arm and said firmly:

"Michael, you must go on sick-leave. You're not well."

He smiled weakly at her, and weakly rubbed the knuckles of his hand, and said, so quietly she could hardly hear him:

"I haven't been too well, Jo."

"You look it! You're like something the cat brought in. Now"—brisk and businesslike—"what you're going to do, Michael, is to go out to Manus and spend a week there. No arguments! I have a week's holiday coming to me, and I've been wanting a spell out of this place. I'm going to go out there with you and keep an eye on you. You're to see a doctor with me this very morning, get a certificate, and when we go out to see Cassidy's marvel, you're going to stay there! I'll be out there as early in the week as I can manage it."

He protested, volubly. He had brought no clothes—not even a razor. Eolie would be terrified. He would have to think about it. His work . . . She cut him short. On the bridge she halted him and as they leaned over the parapet to look at the weir she took his wrist. He hardly resisted.

"Be quiet," she ordered him. "You're like all men—you don't know when you're really sick. Let me feel your pulse."

The touch of her fingers seemed to quiet him. As her hand closed on his bone he bowed his head over the water and closed his eyes. When she held the artery and watched the second-hand of the watch on her own wrist she shook her head. Not only his wrist but his whole arm was shaking like a rickety machine.

"You foolish man!" she said as she released him. "You ought to be in bed. And, Michael"—he looked humbly and obediently at her—"you're going off the liquor."

He did not protest. He just muttered:

"I'm a wash-out, Jo. I'm a wash-out! I feel I could drown myself."

"You're a pity, Michael. All your life you've paid no attention to your health. I could *shake* those sisters of yours!" she scolded. "What on earth have they been doing that they didn't attend to you?"

"Och!" he sighed. "Poor old Eolie! She has enough to contend with. My mother. The house." With a sudden chuck of his head he summed up a life of devotion.

"There's Natalie!" she grumbled. He only shrugged. "Come on!" she ordered. "Manus is at the digs. We're not bringing Cassidy with us today. I'm driving you out, and Manus must go to Cork for your things."

He let himself be guided by her, and she brought him alone in the tiny parlour of her lodgings, to rest, and went out to the front garden to give Manus his instructions; there was a bus at twenty-five to one, and a bus back to Kildorrery at six in the afternoon; she gave him a list of books; the rest she left to Eolie. Then she found the doctor and went back with him to Mrs. Jimmy's. Michael was in the basket-chair by the window, dozing. In sleep his face was like Death. They did not awaken him. One look was enough: a glance between Josephine and the doctor said as much. In the hall he wrote a certificate which she handed on to Manus. Then all three went out. The change outside from whispers to normal speech was so ominous that even she began to get frightened.

She woke him for dinner, and after it they drove off in the old rattling car towards the mountains. The food and the brisk autumn air seemed to wake him up. He was apparently aware of every feature of the lively, stony country, its little glittering rivers, its odd ruins, its bare muscular trees, its quiet villages. There was no doubt about his interest as they climbed the first foothills. He drank in the grand view of the roll to the north and west and the lofty peaks to the north-east, talked about them, asked their names, bade her see how the sun brought out the deep colours of the bog, the heather and the furze and the slab black of the cut turf and the rich brown of the ricks piled dry against the winter. Then he grew silent. Presently he touched her arm and said:

"You're an angel out of heaven. You are, Jo! Truly you are!"

"Am I?" she laughed, throwing up her chin in her old dashing way, and looking at him mockingly out of her brown-ringed eyes. "That's all *you* know!" And she tried to distract him, for she knew that if she let him go on, he would soon become abject and effusive like all poor devils fighting their demons. She cried, throwing out a hand to the hills sinking down to meet them, "Look at the white of that cottage! I love the houses in the autumn when they are all new white-wash and the hay and the turf is all piled in the yard like that.

The thatch new after the harvest! Look at the way it shines, Mickey! Look! And look at that one!"

He looked, and nodded, and they were both looking then far and wide over the plains of Cork vanishing off and off into Kerry, off where the faint blues of the farthest mountains were kissed by the clouds. He took such a deep breath of the mountain air that she laughed at him again.

"St. John used to do that!" she said.

"Why!" he cried. "I got a cable from him. He's on his way home!"

"Is he? But, of course, he said he was coming in the fall!"

For a second she was terrified. He would guess she had read his lost letter. Fortunately, he was too dull-minded and weak to see the implication of what she had said. He was fumbling, too, for the cablegram. With half an eye on the road she read the printed message spread fluttering on the steering-wheel:

ON MY WAY BACK TO THE OLD LAND SS GEORGIC TOUCHING COVE THURSDAY. GOODBYE AMERICA. GOD BLESS ALL.

CURSOR.

"When did he send that?" she asked sharply.

"Thursday."

For a minute she was distracted by a sheep-dog that rushed from a cottage-yard and ran beside them barking foolishly at the wheels. Then she asked:

"Is he alone?"

Michael held down the windy flimsy paper on his lap.

"Apparently."

"For how long?"

"You saw! 'Good-bye America'—he means for ever."

"I didn't see that." He held the cablegram again on the wheel, pointing to the words. She spoke them aloud. She did not speak again until they were almost at the high part of the road where the boreen turned to the left to Manus's cottage and a gap on the right opened on the wheel-tracks that led across the fields to Quit Rent. There she said:

"You haven't heard from Frankie?"

"Nothing. Not a word. Not for months. Only one card since he went away."

It made it seem ages, the way he said it, since he had gone away. It made his going appear, at last, final and irrevocable. She halted the car. The vast spread of land over which she could now look back gave her mind such a sense of what distance means that it made the distance between that and him dilate into infinity.

"And now," said Michael cheerfully, "for the marvel!"

She had to stare at him to know what he meant. Understanding, she led the way down over the bare saucer of mountainy land to the farmhouse under the shoulder of naked hill. Her four cousins were grouped at the door to meet them, two young women, one young man, a year or two older, and another young man a year or two younger than herself.

"Well?" she cried. " 'Tis running?"

" 'Tis running grand," said one of the girls.

"Are you satisfied with it?" she asked her eldest cousin, Jack.

He chucked up his chin with a motion of indifference that was almost contempt. They all moved in to look at it. There it was in the outbuilding at the back of the kitchen, eight feet of spotless aluminum, with the two blue-silvered taps. Cassidy had done the job well. He had lined the back wall two feet high with white tiles, topped by a green beading. A rose on a metal flexible tube dangled from one of the taps like an animal's snout. Jo turned a tap but nothing happened.

"That's the glugger," said Jack in contempt. "Nothin' comes out of that wan."

She turned the other and the cold spring-water sprayed out with a hiss and ran gurgling away.

"What's that yoke for?" asked her cousin Bill.

"It's a rose," said Josephine. "I don't know what it's for. Washing dishes?"

" 'Tis all bloody nonsense," he grumbled.

"Indeed," upbraided one of the girls, "what a thing to say! Ye didn't have to be carrying buckets of water from the well on dirty wet days. 'Tis lovely, Jo. Sure all the people around are coming to see it. As they say, you could eat off of it!"

The men walked away, still sullen. They obviously had a feeling that the whole idea was foolishness; that something very near to a joke had been played on them. Probably the neighbours had teased them endlessly about their "contraption." They had probably computed to a shilling what it cost, thinking of the many necessary things they could have bought with all that money. Secretly Jo shivered at the thought of what would have happened if St. John really had installed a flush-lavatory. She turned off the hissing spray. Then Michael turned it on and off a few times.

"Well," he said to them, "St. John will be out next week to see it."

He showed them the cablegram, thereby throwing the girls into a flurry at the thought of the preparations they must make for their benefactor. More than anything else, this made Jo realize how foolish the whole thing must be, seeing that St. John, their cousin, who should have walked in there like one of themselves, freely and easily, had only succeeded by his excessive generosity in putting a chasm between them and him. One of the girls covered the "contraption" with a blue-checked apron and they left it for the warmth of the kitchen-hearth. There they all sat while tea was prepared—nobody needing it, but all respecting the ritual—and then they sat chatting for another bout until they could part without unseemly haste.

It was by then only five o'clock, but Jo insisted on putting Michael to bed. She lit a little fire in the tiny bedroom (the teacher's cottage contained only three rooms in all, on a floor space of about twelve feet by twenty), put one or two books by the bed, and lit an oil-lamp on the wall. The sun had now set for this hilly place, though from her doorway the lower, open land on the plain still glowed with direct light. The air was cold and dry. From the valley the *croc-croc* of a homing cart came clear as whip-cracks. At half-past six she peeped into the room. He was asleep, tired out. She stole out, went down to the road, and set off in the motor to meet Manus. The bog was a mystery of dusk. The arched road by Bowenscourt was dark. The demesne trees were raucous with rooks. On its hill Kildorrery village showed its Saturday night window-lights. When she drew up by the chapel people were going in. The bus would not arrive until after eight, so she joined them.

Here where she had made her first confession, and her first communion, she always had the feeling of being stroked by some rough but kindly hand that in trying to soothe her hurt as much as soothed—memories brushed the wrong way. She prayed before the dim side altar, and as she prayed her lips began to tremble. She had felt in the sharp October air over the bog and along the road the touch of winter; now in her heart she felt another colder portent and a weakness that could not brook it. She made her confession: little sins of no account—forgotten prayers, bursts of temper, small white lies. But she was aware of the futility of that litany, which was not her life, and which had no real relation to any part of her life, so that at the end she could not help making an appeal (for what she hardly knew) to the priest.

"Father," she whispered through the latticed grille, "I feel arid. I don't feel I am making a real confession. I get no satisfaction out of it. Is there something wrong with me?"

"Have you told me all your sins, my child?" the old priest whispered back.

"Yes, Father. All I know."

"Are you deeply sorry for them, my child?"

She paused.

"They don't seem . . ." She was going to say *important.* "I don't know. I don't feel anything much, Father. I used to get such consolation. Now I just feel . . . I feel nothing."

"You must be sorry, my child, to have offended God?"

She said, "Yes," but she really felt that it was all meaningless, because she could hardly think that she had been offensive to anyone. All she really knew was that she was suffering in body and mind, and that the confession she had made was all spun out of her brain, or her prayer-book, or out of habit, and that there was no form of words that could get anywhere near the inmost truth of her life, or near the life of anyone at all—Frankie, Michael, herself. Somewhere, she began to feel, there must be a fault in her that she had never realized and so could not acknowledge. In some way she had sinned and was paying for it—how she did not know—and she realized that it was a folly to expect this old priest to know. He was whispering to her, now, so close to her eyes that she could smell the musky smell of the snuff he always brought into the confessional, to protect himself from the coughing and sneezing, from the smells of rain and bog-water and cow-dung that came in the coats and petticoats of his flock.

"My child, if you are sorry, you thereby give pleasure to God. And if you do that you should be happy and pleased."

"Yes?"

Then, sensing perhaps that his penitent was unable to feel

sufficient emotional recoil over such innocent faults, the priest suggested (a common and wise formula for such cases) that she should tell him a sin of her past life. She bowed her head and thought. Once she had permitted Frankie to fondle her breast. She had forced herself, once, to admit it as a fault. She said, again, now:

"A sin of immodesty, Father."

But as she said it she knew that she lied; that it was no sin; that her only sin was that she could not resign her heart to losing him. In that revolt she revolted against everything on earth. The old priest accepted her offering, spoke her penance, and as his hand rose to absolve her he might have been lifting her poor shrinking sacrifice to the eyes of God. He said "*Absolvo te* . . ." murmured through the cleansing incantation to the coda of "Pray for me, my child," and drew the slide.

She went out into the night. The land was wide and dark. She stood and looked. She desired life. And life withheld itself. She wanted love, marriage, children–she was quite simple and honest about it–and she was given none of them. She would have given anything–anything–to Frankie if she could have him. She knew that. She knew that because of that all the formality of her confession, and all the injunctions on which it was built, were nothing to her. She did not think then or ever that she had lost her faith. She did know that she kept it and would always keep it only because she had not been, and never would be, called on to test it finally. In that thought she was made humble, and downcast, and fell into a mood very near to despair.

She smoked in the car which she had now driven to a point on the hilly road down to Rockmills. From there she would be able to see the lights of the bus come leaping over the plateau from Glanworth. They came, jumping like kangaroos over the hills, before she had finished her cigarette. She returned to the stopping-place, and after a minute or two the bus came, and halted, and Manus alighted. He was carrying a suitcase. She saw that he had drink taken and she was glad of it because it meant that he would not notice her mood. In the car he handed her two letters—one from Eolie to herself, all about Michael's pet needs and fancies; one for Michael. He then handed her a cablegram which had come for Michael that afternoon, and which Eolie had opened. It read:

LOOK OUT FOR ST. JOHN SS GEORGIC TOUCHING COVE THURSDAY FAR FROM WELL. SERIOUS. EXPECT TO ARRIVE MYSELF FASTER BOAT SAME DAY.

GEORGE LUCEY.

During the Troubles every prominent Irish revolutionary had had a pseudonym. "George Lucey" was the pseudonym of Frankie Hannafey. She did not show the cable to Michael; she did not go back to Fermoy; she sent Manus there on Sunday morning to find somebody to take her place, and remained at Quit Rent.

V

The weather broke on the following Tuesday. Fog and mist came rolling down the shoulder of the hill in torrents of smoky damp, hung in the saucer of Quit Rent like mist in a web, and blotted out the great valley.

Michael had not got out of bed since he came, but she had now and again opened the door and talked to him as she went about her household work. This wet day, as he sipped his collation of whisky—she allowed him a glass every day—she talked about St. John. The subject came up when she promised Michael that she would meet him in Cove. Talk of St. John took them back over Michael's youth in Cork city, to his father and his step-father, to his mother's happy years with her first husband, and her second flood-tide that ended with the creeping rot of her mind. Michael did not say much about that. All he said was, "The fact was, Jo, my step-father thought more of himself than he did of anybody else." She had asked, "Did you get on with him?" He had replied, "I admired him . . . in lots of ways. But he rode roughshod over us all. A selfish man."

As he talked, Michael unconsciously revealed to her so much of his own character that she began to see the way his whole life had grown out of one rooted weakness. All along the line he saw himself as virtuous and long-suffering; she realized that he had not so much been sacrificed to others as surrendered weakly to them. When she realized that she ceased to hear him. In a bold flight of reasoning she began to wonder, instead, how many people make that same surrender of the will for the same reason. She even dared to wonder whether what such people as priests and nuns and soldiers hide under words like courage, and loyalty, and love, is not cowardice before themselves. Suddenly he fell asleep, in the middle of a self-pitying phrase about some people having to do all the work in this world. Gently closing the bedroom door, she began to mix and knead a soda-cake on the table by the little window, looking often with wide eyes out at the swirling mist.

One particular thing that he told her stuck in her mind. He had told her—it must have happened twenty-five years ago—how one morning his mother opened a letter plainly addressed to "Mr. Michael Hannafey" and discovered that he was corresponding with a young woman. "There was nothing much in it, Jo—just something about a dance we were going to. And we never did go to it in the end." Then he described the rage of his step-father, when he was told about the letter—not with him but with his mother; and how his mother had taken to her bed and wept the whole day. Finally, to comfort her, Michael tore up the letter before her eyes and burned it in the bedroom fire. "My step-father," he concluded, "didn't speak to either of us for a week! That was the sort of hot-tempered devil *he* was!"

Jo all but wept as she thought over this love-story that ended so pitiably with a letter falling in the fire in shreds under the eyes of a jealous mother. In fury she rolled the dough with her knuckles. Besides—three times in the last three days Michael had complained in one way or another that he had never married. Once he told the story of that letter. Another time, talking of St. John's marriage, he said, wistfully, "I suppose—do you think that was it?—he was the only one of us anybody would have!" And he had mentioned, for the first time this morning, a young girl in the Post Office whom he admired, saying, "Not, of course, Jo, that any handsome girl like her would ever look twice at an old badger like me." She had laughed at that and said, "You never know! Some day, Michael, you may shake the heart of some good-looking widow!" He had groaned, then smiled, and joined in the joke. Then, turning to the wall, he said he was going to sleep. She was sorry, now, for that teasing. She saw again those poor loving words, and those fluttering bits of paper falling ignominiously into the grate.

Perhaps, she thought, some early defeat like that had discouraged him. Her eyes sank. She dragged the stringy dough from her fingers. How could she tell? Her own life was a closed book to herself. All she felt—for she felt it rather than shaped it into a form that her mind could grasp—was that we all follow a light that is both in us and at the same time outside us, follow it as by a vow without words. She looked through the four-paned window at the fog creeping down the valley to meet the fall of dusk. What fogs and mists cover up every light! What a great number of jack-o'-lanterns crop up through the mist! What an easy voyage it all seems at the start, every rock marked, warnings from here and warnings from there . . . and not one of them is the least bit of help because no two voyages are ever alike. She heard a cart go by on the road below, its axle bumping hollowly. She could not see it. It came out of the fog, and gradually it took its cavern-echoing sounds back into the fog. Then there was nothing though she held up her head to hear, until from far away in the hills came the long, wavering bleat of a sheep, lost and afraid. Idly she dusted her hands with flour and idly rubbed them clean, still looking out of the window, or rather —for the kitchen inside was brighter now than the remnant day—looking at the little crossed windowpane. Her own ghost looked in at her. It shook its faint face at her. Its cavern eyes were wide and empty and black. In fright she strode to the back-wall lamp and turned up the wick. Crouching over the hearth she poked the turf into a flame. The racing devils of fire began to dance. Flying with them from her thoughts she rubbed the bottom of the bastable with butter, smartly brought across the cake, and slipped it in. As she arranged the glowing coals on the cover of the bastable, coaxing them into place with the delicate fingers of the tongs, she was murmuring to herself, "Poor Michael," drawn, as we all are, to the deepest pity for others by a sudden fear of self.

She finished her work briskly. When everything was done, the table cleaned, the utensils put away on the dresser—the milk-jug, the soda-tin, the water-mug, the flour-measure, the knife that carved the cross on the dough—and the hearth swept about the little oven, she hung up her apron and sat by the fire. She sat there for a silent hour, then rose and peeped into the bedroom. The little cell was dark. The light behind her threw a protective shadow of herself over the head of the bed. She could just see the face on the high pillow. Suddenly the eyes opened and he whispered:

"Jo! Is that you, Jo?" Then he cried out with the frightened voice of a child, "Jo! Is that you? Who's that? Who's that? Who's that?"

She ran in and stroked his damp forehead and held his clammy hand.

"Sssh! It's me, Michael. You're safe here with me."

Still caught in the manacle of sleep, he could not realize it. He whimpered again and again in his terror:

"I want Jo! I want Jo!"

His nightmare whimpering, just like a puppy-dog, began to wander off into a groan, sank into an audible breathing, at last became a profound sigh of relief. Then he said:

"I was dreaming."

"What were you dreaming, Michael?"

He paused to recapture the dream. When it came back to him in all the brilliance of its illusion he sobbed out, unable to repress it:

"I was dreaming I was living here."

She said nothing. She still stroked his forehead and held his hand.

"You'll soon be rid of me," he assured her.

For a while she said nothing, and then she said:

"You're welcome, Michael, to stay as long as you like."

He looked searchingly at her for a few moments. The lost sheep bleated on the mountainside. He lifted his grey head and appeared to listen to it. She patted his hand, and cried cheerfully:

"I've just made a soda-cake, Michael. You'll smell it baking in a minute. Manus will be in soon and we'll have a nice hot cup of tea, and we'll get him to play a tune on the fiddle."

She released his hand. "I'll get you the lamp and you might read."

"It's so peaceful," he said, with satisfaction, his head still cocked to the window.

"Yes, Michael."

"I wish," he went on, "I lived here all my life. I wish I never saw a city. In this little cottage, with its rick of turf and its stack of hay. . . ."

"It's the other way round," she laughed, "stack of turf and rick of hay."

The correction pricked the bubble of his dream. He was a city man. He must always be a city man. He lived in Cork, in the house on the island. He had sisters, brothers, a mother, a job in the Post Office. He would be back in the middle of it all next week.

"Yes," he said, shortly, accepting the fact in her correction, and with it all the facts of which it reminded him, "I think I will read for a while."

He read. It was a book about South America, the record of a farmer's life in Tierra del Fuego.

VI

The following morning she left him in charge of Manus and went into Cork to consult with Eolie—about him, about St. John, about Frankie. It was a clear and warm day after the rain of the night before. The southern air was washed and the sunlight a glare. The whole plain exhaled a hot, fuzzy, heathery smell. Even the city of Cork never had seemed so gay and pretty and foreign; and though this was a thing she had occasionally heard strangers say about Cork—that it has a Continental look—she had never until today understood why. Actually, if somebody had asked her,

"Where is this foreign look?" she could not have pointed to any particular thing. It was just the general cut of its jib, the blare of the ruthless sun, the shawled women, the multitude of spires, the obstinate age, and the malt smell of the laneways. It was in the lazy tempo, the sleepy air, the general odour of time fermenting like hay let lie into the autumn, when it dry-rots and gets dusty and musty and full of field-mice and flies. It was in the high peaked roofs of the older houses, the narrowness of the warehouses on the quays, their colours weatherbeaten like the sides of old ships, some of them slated and bellied in front—the colour of snails. It was in the browning trees along one stretch of the river, and the docks along the next; or in the bright tucked-away greenery of the residential houses up on the hills, with tumbledown slummery held fast between them and a last line of sedate houses in old brick footing the water's edge. That was the main thing—the close relation between all the minute and compact parts of the city, so that if she looked at one corner she saw every corner; if she looked at the sun-streaked masts of a ship she saw the whole city caught in the threads of its tackle. It was not Cork. It was an Irish Lilliput.

She came to the island. The tide brimming the deserted quays, the single rusty buoy, the solitary hand-winch crane, the peeling paint of the walls. . . . She got again that smell of liquorice she got on the spring night when she last saw Frankie. . . . She wondered had it really happened and did she dream that Michael once said to her, "Don't you think this bit of Cork looks like"—what did he say?—"Boulogne?" As she stood in the sun on the worn steps of the island house and looked at it all she thought, "Maybe it is a bit like Boulogne." Then, shaking herself so angrily that a passing shawled woman looked at her in surprise, she said to herself, "My God, I'm getting as bad as the rest of them! It's not a bit like Boulogne! Anyway, do I *know* about Boulogne? Or what does he know about Boulogne?" Then she saw a peeping piping of far-away green shining over the peaked houses, and smiled with pleasure. She was still smiling when Eolie opened the door.

"Isn't it lovely!" she said, waving a hand over the old quays.

Eolie, thin and wiry as ever, gave it one uninterested look and hauled her in and kissed her, and just as on that spring night six months ago they talked in the front parlour—but now with the window wide open and the October afternoon sun pouring in. There was not a scrap of change in Eolie, or in the room, except that the sun now sought out and disclosed every rubbed corner and frayed edge. She gave her news of Michael, pushed away Eolie's thanks, and then—their voices fell. They talked for a while in whispers.

"And the last time, too, you were here," said Eolie, "it was about Frankie you came. We were wondering then, too, would he be arrested."

"He won't be arrested," comforted Jo, but she caught Eolie's pale eyes wandering to the window. "You don't mean to say?" she began.

"Yes," sighed Eolie. "He's outside. Or he was this morning, Jo! It's the same old story all over again."

"Then they noticed the cable?"

Eolie just looked at her. She made no movement. She said no word, too tired to feel any further emotion. She had the resigned face of an old woman. Josephine jumped up.

"Where's that boat going to after Cove?"

"I don't know, *a gillie*. England, I suppose? Which boat?" She threw out her hands. "Jo, I can't make plans. I just can't. And I won't! If he's to be arrested, let him be arrested. I'm sick to God and the world of it all."

Jo grabbed her purse and her hat.

"Wait there until I come back, Eolie."

"Where are you going? What are you up to? You've only just come!"

"I'm going to the shipping office. Frankie mustn't land at Cove."

"And what about St. John?"

"I said I'd meet him, and I will!"

She said that from the door. She was thumping down the stairs. The next minute the door banged. She could see no sign of a spotter on the quiet quays, but she believed Eolie that he was, or had been, there. For the next half-hour she was cooped up in a telephone-booth—because it was the Wednesday half-holiday the shops were now shut—verifying the hours of arrival of the two liners, wiring them from the post office. Both ships touched Cherbourg after Cove, then going on to Southampton to dock. Frankie's was due at Cove that night at ten o'clock. St. John's was due on Thursday morning at four a.m. She engaged herself a single ticket to Cherbourg on Frankie's boat—it would take nearly all the money she had—not because she intended to go with him to Cherbourg but because she must go out on the tender, stop him from landing, and give it to him. Whether the police would also go out on the tender to meet him she did not know. There was a chance they would not; and the wires she had sent would increase that chance. (Each telegram had said: *Meet you on the quay at Cove, love, all is well. Josephine.*) She had hesitated long over that word *love* in her message to Frankie. She had thought of signing it in Eolie's name. She decided finally that it was more likely to mislead the police if she signed her own name and added the lying word. It was still in her throat as she stood at the post-office door and, trying to forget, asked herself, "What next?"

Excitement died away in her with the completion of her tasks. The sun was gone behind a pall of cloud. There was the closed row of shops? The empty street? The sombre tawny quality of the autumn light? The sudden October chill? The dusty pavements? The gaiety of Cork was departed with the sun and she became aware, only, of the languor and inertia and indifference of the place. As she stood and watched the faces of the few people who walked the unbusy street, she seemed to see only old men and old women, toddling along with eyes fixed on nothing, greyheaded, shabby, without edge or elasticity. Young people were rare —possibly they were all cleared out of the city for the half-day, sporting by the sea or in the fields. When Shandon began to play a tune, missing out all the notes above or below the octave of the bells, it sounded like a gaptoothed old man humming sleepily over the town. It was only three o'clock. At the thought that she had seven hours to wait her nerves began to leap in her like electric wires. She decided to fly from the city. She returned to Eolie, told her what she was doing, bade her also send a telegram to Frankie and St. John, promising to wait for them on the quay, had a swift cup of tea that merely had the effect of overstimulating her stomach, and rushed away for the five-twenty train.

It was dusk now, and in the station the lamps had been lit. The flying movements of the train, in even time with her own restlessness, helped to steady her. The estuary was smooth as milk. Across it the lights of Blackrock and the lights of Passage floated on the water like night-candles on oil. A flat anvil-clanging came on the sharp air from some tiny shipyard. Once or twice she got the smell of late autumn furze, rich as buttermilk. It was thick dark by the time they came to Cove. The cosy windows of the suburban houses at

Rushbrooke made her feel lonely. As the train drew in she heard the weird cries of seagulls. The scrawlings of boisterous travellers on the wooden partitions bade her farewell. One was obscene. Another said, *Come again.* A last one scrawled with a diamond on the window shouted, *Up de Valera.* As she entered the shipping office to verify the hours of arrival, the cathedral rang a sweet angelus over the harbour.

The shipping-office clerk was expecting her. She had spoken to him over the telephone in the afternoon when she booked her ticket to Cherbourg and asked about the arrival of the *Georgic.* The wire to St. John had been referred back to him; he held it in his hand now, and as she looked at it in puzzlement, and became aware of the solicitous look in his eyes, she received from him something of his own seriousness and intentness.

"Is everything all right?" she asked nervously, responding to the atmosphere of drama he was creating.

"You are Miss Josephine Hogan?" he asked.

"Yes?"

"Did you send this cablegram?"—handing it to her (*Meet you on the quay at Cove, love, all is well. Josephine*).

"Yes."

"To a passenger of the name of St. John Hogan-Hannafey?"

"Yes."

"Sailing from New York to Cove?"

"Yes!"

"Is he a relative of yours?"

"Yes!"

The man stroked his chin and dropped his voice another note or two.

"I see." He fumbled for words.

"Is there something wrong?" she cried, leaning across the counter.

"I'm afraid there is. Something very wrong, Miss Hogan. You must be prepared to hear some bad news. Please come inside."

He led her to the inner office. At the same moment another man appeared in the doorway. With relief the clerk beckoned to him. Jo caught a look and a nod as the manager came forward to her and led her inside the office-door. The clerk followed.

"This is very bad news," he began, but she cried:

"What? I haven't been told. What is it?"

"Mr. Hogan-Hannafey is not on the boat. He left New York all right, in good health and spirits. This evening we received a long cable from the captain reporting that he was missing."

"You mean he's . . . he's . . ."

"He was missed on Monday night. His cabin-steward reported that he had not slept in his cabin. The dining-room steward said he had not come down to breakfast or lunch on Tuesday. Of course, a passenger can occasionally—very, very rarely, I needn't tell you—get lost for a day, or even two. He could be hiding. He could . . ."

She cut sharply in on him.

"But that's nonsense. St. John wouldn't be hiding. Why should he?"

"Of course. Why should he? Nevertheless, I need hardly tell you the most careful search of the ship was made. Every corner of it. You know how tactful the captain of a big ship has to be. It wouldn't do, d'y'see, to report that a passenger was missing and then for him to turn up as fresh as a daisy."

The man pulled himself up. He had for a moment been seeing the ship, relishing the excitement of a report that a man was missing, entered into the whole thing as if he were the purser and the captain and the company. He altered his tone quickly.

"I'm afraid, Miss Hogan," he said, now seeing it all from her point of view, "that there can be no doubt about it. The captain has definitely reported that Mr. Hogan-Hannafey is missing."

Jo looked at him, and did not see him. She saw instead the wide Atlantic; the lighted ship moving steadily through the dark; the crowded saloons; the wide, empty deck; and St. John standing by the gunwale looking into the hissing darkness of the waves. She bowed her head. The man was sympathizing with her. She heard only that ominous dark hissing of water and the widespread rumble of the sea. The liner would come in and go away. There would be no tipsy old Irish-American this time. She got up, and excused herself briefly. She said, "I will come back again."

The yachts inshore swayed their riding-lights. A sharp breeze came in from the sea. She heard the half-hour strike from the great cathedral, and without thinking she climbed the steep hill, step by step, until she stood panting before its triple doors on the terrace over the bay. She remembered his telegram. *On my way back to the old land . . . touching Cove Thursday . . . Good-bye America. God bless all. Cursor.* He would never see the lovely aluminum sink at Quit Rent. His troubles with his wife were over. The nipping wind sent her into the great nave. Its single red eye over the tabernacle, and the brighter glow of a half-candelabrum in a side chapel, accentuated the echoing darkness. She prayed for his soul, cried softly for his poor lost body swaying down through the nave-deeps of the sea. She cried to think that he was not even buried in Irish soil. She stayed there, so overcome that she lost all count of time.

When she came out she climbed still higher out of the town and wandered into the black country behind it. There were things she should do—Eolie . . . the island house . . . there was still Frankie coming back, probably to be arrested . . . for nothing. She could not think or act. She sat under a hedge and smoked for a bit. She walked a bit more, and then took sudden fright as, from over the trees and fields, she heard a three-quarter chime on the wind. She walked back quickly. The tender would be leaving at half-past nine, maybe before it. She had heard that it often has to wait in the harbour for an hour for a liner, afraid lest it come before its time. The cathedral rang nine when she was dropping down into the streets. At the shipping office she once more verified the hour of Frankie's arrival. They were puzzled about the ticket for Cherbourg, for she had said she was meeting the *Georgic*, and that did not come into Cove until four a.m. Afraid that they might be in touch with the Guards, she blathered that she had made a mistake. But she would not have it rectified. They did not press her, though they were obviously mystified. They probably concluded that the bad news had upset her. They assured her she could settle about the ticket at any time. All they wanted was that some relative should be there to receive the captain's report. She wrote out a tactful telegram for Eolie and bade them send it off. She would have to come down now. There was a last train at eleven-fifteen, they told her. She said that would be all right and hurried off to the tender with the clerk. He asked her where her luggage was. When she said she had none he looked at her as at a mad woman. She did not care what anyone thought of her while her own thought was all of Frankie.

Once the tender moved off she left the clerk and wandered about the deck among the passengers and the customs officials, trying to see if any of them might be a detective. As this was not the season for Continental travel there were only a few people on board. All huddled in the lee of the tiny bridge, wrapped in rugs and greatcoats. In her haste to get away she had not brought anything to protect her against the night wind, which now cut through her like a knife. Excitement rose up in her like a physical vomit. She could hardly breathe. She kept getting up and walking about the deck, peering cautiously in the dim electric light at every man, checking them off one by one—crew, passengers, customs and postal officials, nondescripts, coming back several times to two men who might easily be police in plain clothes. And yet, she told herself, if they were what could she do about it? She peered out to sea. She hated this meeting with Frankie. She began to resolve what she would say when she saw him. She would say at once, "Frankie, you must go on to Cherbourg. Here is the ticket. There are spotters waiting for you. Don't argue. St. John is dead. He was drowned accidentally coming across. We can talk of other things later on." And then she would say, "Good-bye now, and God be with you," and run from him . . . for ever.

The engines stopped suddenly and there was a protesting hiss from the waves, which sank quickly into a heavy, sullen flapping. Everybody looked out to sea. There was nothing there but the blackness of a void. Away back across the wide harbour were the enviable lights of Cove. The tender began to roll and toss. People asked questions and received casual answers from the crew or the customs officers. The more experienced travellers went below deck. She remained, shivering now with the cold, unable to face the brighter lights below. She dragged her coat tight about her and walked up and down, resisting the dissolution of her stomach and the horrible drip of saliva that she feared to swallow. The void of a no-moon night and the cold and cruelty of the indifferent sea reduced her to the nakedness of her elemental self; she did not feel afraid; all she felt was anger that her body was such a weak miserable vessel, and a despairing and utterly impersonal determination to save Frankie.

Suddenly, as she held the damp rail and stared into the dark, she was aware of a man standing beside her. She looked at him. He was tall; he wore a felt hat; his greatcoat was belted; he was burly and powerful. She knew immediately what he was and her bowels turned over. He must have been down in the engine-room all the time. He said, without stirring, in a hard Cork voice, dry as metal:

"You're going out to meet Frankie Hannafey."

She said nothing. She might as well not have heard.

Towering over her, and yet not stirring, he said, looking sideways at her:

"I've just heard about the old man. I'm sorry about that."

Still she said nothing. There was nothing she could say, except to revile him. She saw a faint line of lights appear across the water. She could have cried with anger. He kept her in her misery for a minute; a typical Cork sadism. Then he said, with an equally typical Cork warmth of heart:

"Don't worry, girl. We don't want him. We're just interested to see where he goes. Good night."

When she looked around he was gone. She got sick. After vomiting she took a fit of racking coughing and that made her sick again. She heard the passengers come up on deck, and went aft. The engines started. Over the black tossing water she saw, clearly now, the lines of porthole lights, and became aware of the presence and size of the liner. Sinking on a pile of ropes she began to cry, glad to release all her pent weakness. The tender moved nearer. On the bright deck of the liner a band was playing "Come Back to Erin." She edged her way downstairs to the tiny ladies' room, combed her hair, powdered her face, pulled her jacket into shape, and perched her hat to her satisfaction. Then she begged a steward to get her a glass of brandy, telling him she had been sick and was all in. Fortified, she went on deck. The giant was above them. She could see faces on the cliff-top, where the old syrupy tune went on and on. Hearing it, she thought of St. John who would not hear it again. From their cockle-shell, which had hitherto seemed so safe and solid, the first-class and tourist passengers were being helped into the bowels of the liner; as she had a tourist-class ticket, she went along with them. Inside the belly of the liner she felt lost, and became overwhelmed by a series of fresh panics: perhaps the detective was deceiving her; perhaps she would miss Frankie; perhaps he was not aboard at all; after St. John's fate she was ready to believe anything possible. All that unintelligible delay, too, which attends landings and arrivals, and which upsets even experienced travellers, intimidated her and she suffered the usual groundless fear that the boat would carry her away, or the tender leave without her. She seized a steward and made him bring her to where departing travellers were waiting to be taken off. He assured her smilingly about the time of the tender's departure, telling her that mails and luggage, including two motor-cars, had to be taken off and mails and luggage brought aboard, so that they might well be there for an hour yet. They were, by this, up on the promenade deck, where passengers in greatcoats, and with wraps over dinner-jackets and evening frocks, were walking around and around, and where she was sickened by the smell of hot, stale cigar-smoke and heard dance music swaying up from below deck. At last she saw a group of passengers waiting by the rail, clutching hand-luggage and rugs, staring down over the sheer of the liner at the tender, at the squawking gulls, the flapping waves.

She could see no sign of Frankie and for a moment her panic returned. Then—there he was—the old, fine-looking, familiar figure, broad-shouldered, in a fleecy greatcoat and a soft American hat, as prosperous-looking as a stock-broker. She ran to him, called him, gripped his arm when he whirled on hearing his name, and cried, dragging him away from the gunwale:

"Frankie, quickly. Come over here. I must talk to you."

He resisted, and at the same moment her first impression fled. There was such a foreign look about him; he was so elegant. She did not know what exactly made her think that —it was the clothes, the hard look in his eyes, the vulgar cigar. He had said, when he saw her, "It's Josephine," and looked back over his shoulder. Now he was hesitating, flustered, considering, so that when she cried urgently, "Hurry, it's serious, quick!" he did not seem to hear her. Drawing her by her own impatient grip on his arm towards the crowded rail, he stretched out his free hand to tip the shoulder of a little woman in a blue cowled cloak. Just then she was laughing impishly up to an enormous American beside her. Jo saw the two wide and wondering eyes, the gash of white teeth in the tawny face, the great red parted lips—Mrs. Hannafey.

"Bee!" said Frankie. "I want you to meet Josephine Hogan."

She turned on her high heels and came forward, delighted.

"But, my darling!" she cried to Josephine. And to Frankie, "Of course I *know* Josephine. We've met."

"Oh, yes! Yes—of course," said Frankie dully, remembering the two or three occasions when Bee had talked half flatteringly, half in patronage, of Jo.

"Yes!" she insisted, wondering at him. And to Jo, "Haven't we, Josephine?"

The girl's ears drew back, tautening her skin. Her eyebrows extended. Her mouth receded with tightened lips. Her breath was held. She did not refuse Bee's hand, so much as fail to see it. Intent on her own affairs, she was not to be short-circuited by politeness.

"I must talk to Frankie," she said; indeed she ordered it.

"What about?" asked Bee, her face, too, swiftly closing up.

"The police," said Jo, dropping her voice.

Bee relaxed.

"My dear! That's all settled."

"Settled?"

"Of course. You don't suppose I'd let Frankie run into danger like that? Why, I just rang up a good friend of mine in the District Attorney's office and he did the trick in four hours. He cabled your government to ask if they wanted to extradite Frankie. Not that he'd have done it! Not on your life! They said they didn't want him. He cabled back then to ask if they wanted to know when he left the country. They said they'd like to know, but just the same they weren't much interested." She laughed with relief. "No, Josephine. That's *all* over!"

Jo looked at her. Then she looked at Frankie. In her jacket pocket she crumpled the ticket for Cherbourg. The same weakness that came over her on the tender, when the detective said he did not want Frankie, returned with an even greater effect of bodily dissolution, and all she could say was, "I see," and felt a fool, and at that a weak, self-deceiving, soft-hearted fool. All her worry and work had been for nothing. There he was, safe, large, comfortable, well-off. All the other clamorous thoughts she battened down. She could not even look at Bee, let alone think about her. Feeling that she must justify her presence in some way, she murmured:

"I thought, Frankie, you . . . maybe . . . should go on to Cherbourg."

And she produced the crumpled paper voucher and held

it out. The three of them looked at it where it lay on her shaking palm.

"But," said Frankie, "I got your cablegram! We expected to see you on the quay."

Josephine noted the word "we."

"That was to blind the police. One came out on the tender. He knows you're on board. He said they don't want you. I didn't trust him."

There was a silence between them, then. Jo tore up the ticket and let the scraps of paper flutter on the deck. She held out her hand.

"Well, that's all right. Good-bye, Frankie."

He gripped her arm.

"I want to talk to Jo," he said to Bee and Bee smiled and walked away. Jo looked coldly at Frankie.

"I must get back on the tender," she said, and she tried to move off, terrified that she would faint or get sick again.

"But we're going on the tender!" he cried. "We must wait in Cove for St. John. That's why we came."

She said nothing about that. She had had enough of worrying about his affairs. He would find out for himself about St. John. All she craved now was to get away, to lie down somewhere, maybe to sleep, to rest, to cry—anything but not to have to see him and talk to him. He started to bully her—very much the old Frankie. She stopped him sharply.

"You mustn't talk to me like that. Good-bye, Frankie."

"I'm not saying good-bye. Not after seeing you for two minutes. What do you think I came home for?"

Her last spurt of energy blazed in her—there on the lighted deck where anybody could see and hear.

"You didn't come back to see *me*. Why didn't you write since July? I don't want to talk to you. Go and talk to *her*."

At the whiplash of that last word he released her arm, and

she whirled and went off as she had come, down the wide promenade, through the circulating passengers, the stale cigar-smell, the odour of scent. She found a steward and demanded to be taken to the tender, so fiercely indifferent to his protestations that visitors could not yet return there that he shrugged and led her down through all the decks to the gangway. There somebody else stopped her, but she was again insistent that she must leave. Fortunately for her the shipping clerk was standing near by; he intervened, whispering rapidly, and at once the opposition dissolved and she moved off the ship among the procession of men carrying luggage and mail. Aboard the tender she went again to the tiny cabin, and flinging herself on a settee fell into a stupor that was partly a coma of her overburdened mind, partly a paralysis of her exhausted body. It was a nightmare ship in which she lay, and a giant chimera that towered outside above it and her. Winches ground overhead. Great weights fell on deck. Men's voices shouted. About her the dim prison of the cabin, empty, deserted, forgotten, musty, lit up madly from time to time as some bright light outside shot past the portholes. This was her hell, to be there; to have no escape; to know that Frankie was on that ship and that woman with him; that they would follow her and meet her again.

The waves licked the sides of the tender. God alone knew what hour it was, when they would get back to Cove, what she would do, having hardly any money—and would she have to go into all that matter of St. John's death—find Eolie on the quay . . . She surrendered at long last, like a wrecked voyager who gives up the ghost and slips from the raft to which he has clung for hours. She sobbed and sobbed like a child.

Suddenly she felt a hand on her shoulder and starting up saw him leaning over her. She had not the strength to say,

"Go away." She sank her head on her hands and continued to cry, hysterically. At last, through her tears, she managed, chokingly, to say it, "Go away, for God's sake, go away." He sat beside her and put his arm about her shoulder. Trickling tears through her very nose, knowing she looked hateful and absurd, she pulled herself up to look at him. She choked out:

"Why is she here?"

"St. John! I suppose. Damn it, the poor old sot ran out of New York in the D.T.'s. She couldn't leave him . . . I mean . . ."

"Frankie, are you in love with her?"

Ever so gently he said:

"I don't know, Jo."

She got up and walked across the cooped floor, blowing her nose and wiping her eyes. With her hands limp by her sides she turned and faced him where he sat looking miserably at her.

"You *must* know!" She walked away, stopped, looked at him again. "Oh, but it doesn't matter. If you can say that, it means, anyway, that you aren't in love with me."

He jumped up.

"Jo, I tell you I don't know what way I am. For months I've been trying to know. I'm very fond of Bee. I'm very fond of you. . . ."

She stamped her foot. She nearly screamed it—"Stop it!"

They looked at one another. The lights shot across the portholes. A thump hit the deck.

"Frankie, I don't care what you do . . . or where you go . . . only if you could only go away and I'd never hear of you again!"

"But, Jo, all this between me and Bee is impossible. She's married. She . . ."

"Frankie!"

The word was a command. He waited.

"She's not married. St. John is dead. Drowned. He fell or threw himself overboard on the *Georgic*. Now, you can marry her. If you want to!" She moved to the companionway, holding up her frail palm against him. "Don't follow me! If you do . . ."

He took a single step towards her where she all but cowered against the rail-head. He cried, wildly:

"I love *you*, Jo! I know it now that I see you. I told you to come out. I warned you. Being away from you was madness. I told you. But I *knew* all the time. I know now I want *you*."

The liner let out an ear-splitting, nerve-tearing blast from its siren. Feet pattered on the deck overhead.

"I don't believe you. You don't believe yourself. There's the siren. Go back. She'll be looking for you. And, Frankie, for God's sake don't land in Cove. There's nothing to land for. St. John is gone. I'll attend to that. I'd hate you to be around. I'll look after everything. Go on to Cherbourg. Good-bye now."

She dashed up the stairs. He called her, raced after her, caught up with her at the top of the companionway, where the liner hung its bulk and lights over them.

"Jo, I'm not going to bother you. Whether I land or don't land, I'll see you again. I'll write to you."

"All right, Frankie. Now go on! Go on!" And she pushed him away with her two hands, afraid that he might touch her.

He gave a look, devouring, despairing look at her. He said, "I'll see you again." He dashed away. She watched his figure slide along the deck, struggle up the gangway, crushing people right and left until the gaping maw received him. She moved away out of sight of the liner, and tried to pull herself together, hoping they would start soon for Cove, where she might get a hot cup of tea to revive her frozen body. But the tender did not stir for a long while after that. Men still kept coming and going. She saw a motor-car swaying in mid-air, amid the shouting of men and the pale glow of lights, and guessed that this was the last stage of the disembarkation of luggage. Aimlessly she moved to and fro. When she looked up at the rail next hardly anybody was looking down: it was after eleven o'clock and the passengers were probably retiring to their cabins. She heard only the voices of the men, and the flapping of waves, until, at last, the siren again tore the air and a trickle of people began to come aboard—the landing party.

She locked herself into the ladies' lavatory. She heard the engines start and the tender begin to vibrate; peering out through the slit of porthole she saw the white swirl spread and spread into view. Presently she saw across the dark sea a line of portholes that faded and vanished as either the tender or the liner swung its hull end on. She stayed there, sitting on the edge of the seat, until they grated against the quayside. She waited a long time after that, hearing the same bumping overhead again and the same tramping of feet.

When she came up all the passengers were gone ashore to the customs. She edged out, a miserable, bedraggled, lonely figure, without as much as a handbag. She stood at the door of the customs shed and examined the few remaining travellers. He was not there. She had to make humiliating explanations to be allowed to pass through, for she neither had a visitor's ticket nor a passenger's ticket, but her story of St. John had apparently got around, and they passed her out as one might pass out a drunken woman—between pity and embarrassment.

The town was dark and deserted—it was nearly a quarter

to midnight—and Eolie's train had come in and gone out, the last train down and up. She counted her money: exactly seven and fivepence. She chose a modest hotel and got some tea and some bread and butter, for she had eaten nothing since half-past four, when she drank a cup of tea with Eolie in the island house. The old man who acted as night porter took pity on her and led her to the kitchen to warm herself. In order not to be left alone she told him all about St. John, and by degrees, after many questions, it came back to him that St. John was the American who had been brought there, drunk, six months before. He described the wife, the young man who brought him in, the two young Americans, the Lincoln, the departure in the dawn of a May morning for Cork. He sighed over the drowned man, told her other similar stories, fell silent, staring at the kitchen-fire, and then went off to collect the boots of the family and the one or two lodgers. She dozed by the fire until three in the morning, dimly aware of his occasional presence, the rubbing of the brush on the leather, his sibilant comings and goings as he cleaned out the public rooms.

When he woke her it was pitch-dark outside. She went out onto the starry, windy front, met Eolie at the tender, and told her everything: but she had not the energy to go with her to receive the captain's report, borrowed a few shillings, and returned to the hotel, to take a room. A glass of rum-punch, a hot-water bottle, and the kindness of the old commiserating boots helped her to fall into a drugged sleep in the antiquated bedroom, with its creaky brass bed. Then sleep took the prints on the walls of antiquated men-o'-war, the mottled photographs of bygone Queenstown regattas, the flowery ewer and jug, until all of them and the dark furniture and the discoloured, worn carpet swirled and faded in her mind into a phantasm of tossing seas and drowning ships.

They in turn smoothened, mercifully, into an illusion of a May morning dawn, a sea and sky the colour of milk, and she and her lost lover were walking happily beside a glaze of water that hardly whispered on the shore.

When she woke, at the lunch-hour, she found Eolie sitting quiet as a breath by her window, gazing out at the rain that swept blowing over the harbour, hiding the far shores and the sea. They ate in a cheap café and took the train to Cork. All the way they sat side by side, without speaking, holding one another's hands, watching the mist sliding past through the steam of the engine.

VII

For weeks, almost without a break, the persistent southern rain kept sinking down all over the country, from the coast to the mountains, less a rain than a condensing moisture. From her lodging window Josephine could see it as damp on the street, and down one side of the tree-trunks by the river; feel its dew on her upturned face; but see it actually falling only where it floated down past dark objects, such as the eaves of the river-bank, or the flanks of the patient animals standing in the fields. It was as silent as snow, and like snow it darkened the day, so that when the letter came she had to lower it to catch the light from the window. It was signed, "F." It had been posted in Cork city.

"My Dear Jo,

"This is just to say that I am back in Ireland. I am not quite sure what I am going to do. I have no profession. No trade. I'm afraid that what a certain person said to me is true, that all I'm fit for is to be a rebel. It's about all Ireland gives us, damn her, to be able to fight. And half our time we don't know what we're fighting for. But we won't be happy until we get it. I thought of all sorts of things. Even of joining the French Foreign Legion. But what's the use? I'd run away from that too. Michael is trying to get me a job, as what you would never guess—a Warble Fly Inspector. Something to do with a disease in the hides of cattle. Or I might go back to America if I could get on the quota. Dig the roads, be a Sweepstake agent, a ganger, work in an office, in a chain-store. Well, there's thousands like me. And if I go I suppose I'll come back to Ireland when I can stay away no longer. Some day, couldn't we meet, in town here? That is if you would like to?

"Your friend, F."

Slowly her ivory fingers returned the letter to its creases. She looked out to where the hilly roofs of the town met the sky. Her finger and thumb caressed the rough folds. Then she half laid, half tossed it on the windowsill, pushed it away with her palm, edged it from her almost as if it were something human that did not want to go. There it lay for several weeks, hidden in the corner behind the geranium-pots, until, coming on it accidentally, she picked it up again, dusty now and damp, and bound by a web to a dangling petal overhead. She glanced through it, and was about to tear it across when her eye caught, through the window, a seagull being blown high and far before the October wind, whirled over the edge of the roofs of the town under the shaggy clouds. She watched it disappear, and when it was gone her heart felt a stab of pain.

On her next free afternoon, a day of lashing wind and rain, the residue of the equinoctial gales, she went by bus into Cork, and went along the wind-torn streets to the Hannafey house. As she went she saw one or two side-streets submerged by the flooded rivers. The winds tore and tore about in the cup of the valley of the town as if, having got in, they could not get out again. The age of the town, so well hidden normally under its rouge of paint ("Like a French seaport?" she smiled to herself), was shamelessly exposed in the rattling and shaking and shivering and banging of all its poor decrepit parts. The weather-slating on one or two houses on the island had suffered during the night, and the quay was strewn with chips of slates. Everywhere, as she ploughed her way with bent head, gutters were spilling, pavements rippled with their floodwater, hoardings were flapping, and it was impossible not to feel that nature had made the little city almost a part of the elements on which, as a port, it had thrived. Eolie met her at the door. She had to shake herself like a dog before she went in.

They were all at home, except Michael, who was at work. They sat about the kitchen-fire, the cosiest room in the house, Eolie, Natalie, Claude, and Frankie. The mother was resting in bed. They talked of the storm and the damage it was doing. Natalie said that the river was rising every minute and repeated some gossip about how the poor people, in one of the lower parts of the town, had to go shopping in a boat. Jo said that the road from Fermoy was full of broken slivers of trees, with twigs and branches flying everywhere. Then she noticed that the girls were dressed in black, and that even Frankie was wearing a black tie, and she asked:

"How did the mother take it?"

"We never told her," said Natalie, in her own prim way. "She doesn't know. We're dead from warning people, in shops and so on, not to mention it to her."

Frankie began to talk of his work—he had got the job as cow-inspector—and he was so amusing about it that when Michael came in for his tea it was not ready for him. He was in great form. He was full of more gossip about the storm —wires down; posts late; a dead sheep had been seen floating down the Lee from the flooded country upriver; one postman swore he had seen a piano in the river. But they derided that. "We hear that every year!" they mocked.

It was evident that the storm had excited him.

"You know," he cried to Jo, "it makes the town like a Dutch town! What you'd read about in Hans Andersen."

And when they were all seated about the table to tea, he suddenly lifted a finger, and said, "Listen! There's a ship coming up the river." And far away, as if the wind were against it, they heard, out of the warm kitchen, from ever so faint and far away, down the river between its mud-flat banks, or on its first lochs, the gentle hoot of a siren, a cock-crow of triumph for safe entry from the sea.

He winked at Jo, and shook his head boastfully.

"*Statio bene fida carinis*," he mouthed, quoting the motto to the arms of Cork, which record that endless adventure: a ship between two castles entering the faithful-to-ships.

After tea she had to go, and Frankie offered, timidly, to go with her, an offer which she neither accepted nor refused. So they went out together into the windy rain, shy and silent with one another. Presently she said, under her umbrella:

"Are you glad you didn't go back to America?"

After a few steps he said, with a dry laugh:

"I'll know that in ten years' time."

"Aye," she said, after considering it. "That's the way you know things." Then, "Is Michael more contented these days?"

"Ah, Michael takes life hard. He'll always be the same old three and fourpence. But he's on the top of the world these days. St. John left us a thousand pounds in his will—between the five of us—two hundred each. Michael is going to spend his Christmas holidays in Paris. His first visit."

(She made no comment: she had guessed the truth of that.)

"And what will you do with your two hundred?"

"Keep it. St. John said that the two hundred was to be a dowry for each one of us." He laughed. "The undying optimist."

"You are hard, Frankie."

He glanced at her: the first time she had used his Christian name that evening. At the sight of her profile his emotions surged into his gullet.

"Jo . . ." There was a long pause as they drove into the rain. Then, "You never answered my letter?"

"Well . . . I came myself?"

He was afraid to say any more. They had come to the waiting bus. She stood on the step, looking down at him. Her face and hair were damp from the rain. As in all consumptives her cheeks were of a lovely high colour, her eyes unusually large and bright, and when she smiled down at his pathetic, doglike look, her Indian summer shone. As casually as if he were talking to any man-friend he said:

"If I'm around Fermoy way some time, can I call in on you?"

"Do. If I'm there."

"Why wouldn't you be there?"

"Oh, I'll be there for a while, anyway."

He looked up at her unearthly smile, and seized her pale hand.

"Jo?" he cried.

The conductor banged the door with his ticket-holder. He winked cheerfully at Frankie.

"Good-bye," smiled Josephine. Frankie released her soft fingers. The conductor rang the bell. She waved, and slipped into the bus, which immediately moved off down the street, out of sight, lost in the rain.

At home Michael had the kitchen-table strewn with travel-folders. Eolie was knitting.

"See her off safely?" asked Michael.

Frankie made no reply.

"Poor girl," said Michael, drawing a folder towards him. He offered a paper packet to Frankie. "Try a French cigarette?" he offered. "I bought them today."

Frankie did not hear him. He was staring into the fire between the bars of the grate. Outside he could hear the wind moaning through the rain-washed town, and then another, far-away ship softly sirened her way into harbour, in from the sound and the surge of the sea, in to where the creaking and dripping of her moorings meant silence and utter peace. Eolie lifted her eyes from her knitting as the window rattled, and her glance, on its return to her needles, swept softly over him.

Presently he heard Michael murmur, "You know, I dunno will I go to Paris at all now." He saw him slew around on his chair and say to Eolie, his eyes lighting, "Why, sure, with two hundred pounds I could go to New York!" She nodded and smiled encouragingly, although there was hardly a city in the world that, during these past two weeks, he had not talked of visiting. "Would you ever come, Eolie?" Then, "Tell us, what are you going to do with your two hundred quid?" She laid down her knitting, willingly, and sat up to the table, and reached for one of his French cigarettes. There, with their elbows on the table, the two began to discuss in happy murmuring voices where they could go, and he, to evade his thoughts, joined them.

DATE DUE

JUN 26 1971

FEB 3 '75

GAYLORD

PRINTED IN U.S.A.